THE CUPBOARD

Rose Tremain's novels have been published in 27 countries and won many prizes, including the Orange Prize, the Whitbread Novel of the Year Award, the James Tait Black Memorial Prize, the Prix Fémina Etranger and the Sunday Express 'Book of the Year' Award. *Restoration* was shortlisted for the Booker Prize and was made into a film (1995) and a stage play (2009). Two of her novels, *The Colour* and *Music & Silence*, are currently in development as films, and the best-selling *The Road Home* is being adapted for television. Rose Tremain lives in Norfolk and North London with the biographer, Richard Holmes.

ROSE TREMAIN

The Cupboard

VINTAGE BOOKS
London

Published by Vintage 1999

11

Copyright © Rose Tremain 1981

Rose Tremain has asserted her right under the Copyright, Designs
and Patents Act 1988 to be identified as the author of this work

First published in Great Britain in 1989 by Hamish Hamilton

Vintage
Random House, 20 Vauxhall Bridge Road,
London SW1V 2SA

www.vintage-books.co.uk

Addresses for companies within The Random House Group Limited
can be found at: www.randomhouse.co.uk/offices.htm

The Random House Group Limited Reg. No. 954009

A CIP catalogue record for this book
is available from the British Library

ISBN 9780099284178

The Random House Group Limited supports The Forest Stewardship
Council (FSC®), the leading international forest certification organisation.
Our books carrying the FSC label are printed on FSC® certified paper.
FSC is the only forest certification scheme endorsed by the leading
environmental organisations, including Greenpeace. Our
paper procurement policy can be found at
www.randomhouse.co.uk/environment

Printed and bound in Great Britain by Clays Ltd, St Ives PLC

For Johnny, with love
and for Bo Dean, with high hopes

'We are all cupboards, with obvious outsides – which may be either beautiful or ugly, simple or elaborate, interesting or amusing – but with insides mysteriously the same – the abodes of darkness, terror and skeletons.'

–Lytton Strachey

At the age of eighty-seven, Erica March died in a cupboard. She wrapped her body in a chenille tablecloth, laid it out neatly under the few skirts and dresses that still hung on the clothes rail and put it to death very quietly, pill by pill.

She left a note, but the note made no mention of her suicide, nor of the cupboard in which she had chosen to commit it. In the room, she had seemed only to make ready for the night, turning down her bed, setting out her indigestion tablets, drawing the curtains and switching on her bedside light.

She had known, however, that it would be Ralph who would discover her body. She had left the door unlocked for him, certain that he would come in next afternoon to say goodbye as he had promised and that when he found her, he would do everything she had asked, exactly as she had asked it. And only after it was done as it had to be done, would he call up his editor at *Bulletin Worldwide* in New York and say, 'Okay, Walt. I'm coming home.'

'I don't know where you want me to start.'

The voice didn't sound particularly old. There was an almost childlike breathlessness in it.

'I don't know either,' said Ralph, 'but I hope you're not shy of talking.'

'Shy? I'm eighty-seven, you know.'

'Old people are sometimes shy . . .'

'Are they? They're deaf, those ones, I expect. I'm blind, without my glasses, but I'm not deaf.'

'You don't feel shy of me?'

'How old are you, dear?'

'Thirty-five.'

'Well. I'm eighty-seven.'

He looked up at her. He expected to find her stern, but she was smiling. She fingered her neck. Ralph noticed that her right hand was arthritic, bent hopelessly sideways, but that her left hand was quite straight. It was the bent hand that moved almost constantly.

Ralph smiled, the smile acknowledging his own nervousness.

'Where would you like to begin?' he asked gently.

'Is your machine on?'

'The recorder? Yes, it's on.'

'I don't know why they sent you.'

'*Bulletin Worldwide?* Oh they didn't send me really. I asked to come.'

'You see, lots of people have come, over the years. Even a lady from Finland. But I never thought an American would come. I didn't think I was important enough for one of you.'

Ralph laughed. She was dressed as a gypsy really. That was how he would photograph her, in the bright scarf she wore tied at the nape of her neck, but put on so badly, it hung over one eye. She caught him looking at the scarf.

'I'm almost bald, you know,' she said. 'That's why I wear it. My hair used to be thick – in big plaits – but now it's just like duck down.'

'Begin there!' he said suddenly. 'When you had the plaits.'

But she was silent. 'I had plaits for years,' she said at last.

'How many years?'

'I don't know. I think as soon as my hair was long enough to plait, they plaited it and I still had a plait going round and round my head when I was seventeen.'

'What colour was your hair?'

'Black. Yet both my parents were fair. My father used to call me his little witch.'

'When you were a child ?'

'Yes. And I was a child a long time. People were in those days. I think I was still a child after Gully had grown up and become a man and gone away.'

'Gully?'

'Gully was made out of the Norfolk clay – that's what I used to imagine! I used to dream that they dug down and down, making a

2

pond as they dug and then they found him, with his head stuck on sideways. And then they ran a mile when they saw him! Dropped their spades and scrambled off. Because he was odd with his twisted head and no one trusted him at first, except my father who found him, and me.

'He was scavenging, you see? Hiding and then taking our chicken scraps. My father chased him over two fields and my God, that boy could run! But my father knew better than him how to run on the plough, and he caught him and brought him home. But he wouldn't talk, wouldn't say a word till we fed him.

'In those days, you see, people could get lost. We didn't have a welfare state – oh no! And Gully was one of the lost. Even the institutions were badly lit. People escaped round corners, into shadows and then they ran helter-skelter and it was impossible to find them. And they could be lost for months, living off pond water and mushrooms like Poor Tom in *King Lear*. And Gully was one of these Poor Toms. Until we found him.

'My dad cleaned him up and took him to the orphanage, but Gully hadn't come from there. He wasn't registered. So he was brought home again and the questioning began:

"Who's your Ma, Gully?"

"What's your Pa do?"

But Gully wouldn't say. "My name's Gully" – that was all he'd tell us.

"Come on Gully, then. Tell us where your Ma lives, boy. She'll be missing you, I reckon."

Shook his head and shook his head.

"Got to get you home, Gully. Can't keep you here, with your poor Ma crying her eyes out and missing you and thinking you drowned."

'But we never found them, his Ma and Pa. So he stayed with us and I remember the first day I had to take him with me to school, I was ashamed of him. "He's not my brother," I wanted to say, "nothing proper like that. We just found him."

'And the children were mean and cruel:

"Reckon'e's batty," said John Tomkins. "What you doin' with a batty bor, Erica girl?"

"He's not my brother . . ."

"Bet 'e don't know no sums nor nothin' like that."

3

"He's not my brother. We just found him."

"Found him? Found 'im where, eh girl? Found 'im in a rat hole? Found 'im in a pig's arse, eh eh?"

'They all crowded round Gully and me. They were staring at us and laughing. And then I remembered what my father had said to me when he gave us our dinner bundles: "I'm counting on you, girl" he said, "because children can be mean mucks and yew don't forget it. So you make sure that bor don't take no harm."

'So I whispered something to Gully. I was punished afterwards for what I whispered and stuck in a corridor all afternoon waiting for the schoolmistress to beat my hands with a ruler. My hands got so cold and numb in that corridor, I couldn't feel the beating when it came. And anyway who cares about beatings?'

Ralph waited.

Erica March had shut her eyes. Her head had dropped and she seemed quite suddenly asleep. He watched her. The tape recorder hummed on the table between them. He was leaning forward to switch it off when he heard Erica chuckle.

'We had a lark that first morning at school! And after that, things were never so bad for Gully, even though they were bad enough. You see, I'd never liked big John Tomkins and his gang and I wanted them punished good and sound for their sneering. So I whispered to Gully: "Get your willy out and piss at them!" And he did it right away and splashed them all – John Tomkins and Charlotte Bunn and thin Sonny Aldous. And they went crying, telling the teacher, so I nudged Gully, "for heaven's sake get that put away 'fore Miss Miller sees it."

'Gully came to live in our house, just before that time. Our house was an old Suffolk farmhouse with half the farm animals wandering in and out. It was a farm of bad-tempered animals which kicked and pecked! Even the two cows were standoffish and when I tucked my head in to milk them they'd open up their bowels and the mess would flop onto my boots. I told my father, "I'll never be a farmer when I'm growed up!", but he took me onto his knee and held me and said "nothing to give you, girl, no money nor grand education, so yew take the farm when I'm gone an' be grateful." And I expect he cried, thinking of Ma and Ma's blue skirts in the forget-me-not field. And I snivelled round his collar, which was a straight-up band with no proper collar on it and always grimed as if he never washed his neck. But then he'd stop his crying and blow his nose and say "Where's Gully, Erica? Not lost again, is he? Not gone again?"

'Gully only ran away from us once. He ran to a clay pond that was almost dry and hid. And when I found him there, it was then that I thought, this is his real mother, this pond. This is Gully's flesh. He'd thrown his boots into the water and I knew this was a dreadful ungrateful thing, because my father often and often said, "Shoe leather's dear and you'd best take care of it. Boots is not stoons to be let lyin' or lost." So I yelled at Gully. "My dad's gone white with dreams of you drowning!"

I said, "He could die from being so white. So you come back, Gully bor before I turn you into a maggot!"

'He let me run on towards the farm and then I saw his lopsided shadow following me and after that he never ran away again to the pond. But nor did anyone come for him: no mother or father or person from the orphanage. So he became ours and we called him Gully March.

'And when I think about my child's lifetime, I see him always. Our Gully. He had black, tight curls and a man's eyebrows that met over his nose. The first sum I taught him was, "How many inches are between London and Newmarket?" But I don't remember the answer now. And the second sum I taught him was, "A rich nobleman in Spain owns twenty-five castles and in each of the twenty-five castles are twenty-five rooms and in each of the twenty-five rooms are two sacks and in each of the sacks are one hundred and forty guineas. How many shillings, then, does the rich nobleman possess?" And all of this we worked out on the kitchen table, with a big drawing of the nobleman and his castles to help us. But the answer came to so many shillings, we didn't believe it.

'But Gully did begin to learn a few things. He never understood anything which began "If a man throws a girdle of barleycorns round the earth . . ." because he had no real notion of what the earth was – not then. And he wrote his numbers so blackly, they looked like a pirate's hand. But when he came to us, he couldn't write at all and I think it was we who taught him most because Miss Miller was afraid of his big head (I suppose she thought he'd butt her in the stomach like a bull and knock her over!) and she put him in a corner of our classroom and forgot about him most of the time. And he often stayed away from school to help my father: at harvest time and with the sugar beet and even with the fencing and ditching, because he was strong. And I remember that when I was at school and I saw the sunlight outside, I longed to be in the cornfield or on the cowshed roof and put a curse on God for making me a girl.

'He had the room above mine in our house. He cried at night and we never found out why. I put wool in my ears and one of my dolls, Ratty May, over my head to blot him out. Perhaps he cried in his sleep like Bernard, I don't know, because he never told us. Perhaps he had dreams of being lost again with no boots. Perhaps his old lopsided head remembered a time when it pushed out of the clay like a mushroom. Who can say?

'He was ten when we found him. His hands were wide and red like butcher's meat and perhaps it was because of this – because of his hands – that when he left school he became a butcher's apprentice. He didn't know how to care for his things or say thank-you for anything my father bought. And one night, I walked with my father to the forget-me-not field and in the dark he said, "I reckon he's got to go, that Gully." But I'd grown fond of Gully by then. We had secrets, I think, one or two and I liked doing sums with him and I'd got tuppence or threepence saved for his Christmas present. So I said "No!" I said "If Ma was alive she'd keep him with us and see to him."

'But this was a terribly unkind thing to say. It turned my father to stone – absolutely to stone – and he couldn't move. He lay down on his face and the moon came up and shone on him and I beat his back with my fists and shouted at him. But he couldn't hear me. So I ran and ran to the house and snatched Gully by the hand and we tore back to where he lay and tugged him and lugged him over the field and up the lane and over the yard, till we had him lying down by the fire.

'Gully ran a mile for the doctor and the doctor came at midnight and gave him brandy. And after that, my father never again suggested that Gully should leave us. So Gully stayed and on his eleventh birthday I gave him an old map of the world so that he could throw a girdle of barleycorns round it.'

On this first day, Erica March had prepared wine and biscuits for her American visitor. It was about three in the afternoon. She watched him as he poured the pale pink wine, handed her the plate of sweet biscuits.

'Tomorrow, we'll have vodka, if you like,' she said, 'and caviar. What about that?'

Ralph shook his head. 'On my *last* day, we might have caviar and vodka.'

'When I was a child, we were told that all Americans were rich. I think I imagined everyone owning twenty-five castles full of precious things and gold pieces and bones of Indians. But now you're not rich, are you? Only some of you, with homes in Bel Air.'

'I'm not rich,' said Ralph. 'I have quite a bad apartment in Brooklyn. Walk-up. Repairmen won't walk up to repair it.'

'But you're paid well, aren't you,' and she looked round her little room, 'for this sort of assignment?'

'It depends.'

'On what?'

'On what I make of it.'

'Don't you *know* then, dear? Isn't it going to be something for your magazine?'

Ralph hesitated. 'I'd like to stay in London for quite a while,' he said. 'I'd like to come and see you every afternoon, and you can talk – about anything you like, about your work and about your life, anything you remember – and then I'll know what I've got.'

Erica looked at him sternly. 'They wrote a lot about me at one time. After *The Hospital Ship* became popular, they used to put me on panel games. But then they forgot me.'

'I know,' said Ralph.

'I suppose you're reviving me, dear, are you? Before I pop off? I think it's quite clever, because I can't go on much longer, can I? I might even die before you've finished.'

Ralph smiled, took a sip of the wine.

'I'm serious,' said Erica, 'I say goodbye to everything every night now, just in case. I say: "Goodbye square which is my room, goodbye London, goodbye pigeons on my ledge, goodbye Ratty May, goodbye books, goodbye noisy lavatory, goodbye lamp, goodbye cupboard . . ."'

'Do you?'

'Oh yes. Because at my age, death doesn't need to send an army, does it? It sends something rather quiet, I imagine, like a paper dart.'

'You seem very strong, really.'

'Do I? Well, I think I am most days. Not very strong when I wake,

7

so that now and again I think I'll have to ask Mrs Burford to stay the night and bring me something in the mornings. But this would be inconvenient for her and I've always hated the idea of servants. So I go on. By the afternoons, I usually feel all right.'

'Have I tired you today?'

'Oh lord no, dear! I've tired *you*, I expect, with all my chat. But it's a very long time since I talked about Gully. Or even thought about him. And yet for years – until he came to mistrust me – I treasured him. Do you understand what I mean? I wasn't in love with him or anything like that. Heavens no! But he was a wedge in my heart.'

Erica reached out with her left hand and turned on a Tiffany lamp. The light was the same colour as the wine. Behind her head, the sky at the window was deep blue.

Ralph got up. The camera held at his brown eye didn't belong to him. So that he would never be tempted to forget this fact it was labelled in red lettering *"Property of Bulletin Worldwide Inc."*, but he held it carefully and it brought him rewards which were his own. In front of the darkening window, half of Erica's face was lit by the lamp.

'Please turn towards the lamp, just a fraction,' Ralph asked.

The head moved. Behind the thick glasses, the eyes were grey, like polished stone. Ralph took the picture.

When the wine was gone Ralph prepared to leave, but Erica handed him a box of matches and said, 'It gets cold in here. Light the gas fire for me, will you dear, and then we won't feel it.'

It was a very old-fashioned kind of fire, made of light brittle tubes which eventually glowed red. Ralph knelt and held his hands out to it.

Erica sat in silence for a while and then she said: 'The cupboard I mentioned was my mother's. She used to keep her clothes in it – the long skirts women wore in those days and the embroidered blouses. She did all the embroidery herself. And you never caught her looking shabby. Blue was her colour and her hair was blonde. I think the cupboard had been her mother's before, because it was the only good piece of furniture we had. And she kept it polished. Not like the old kitchen table which we scrubbed with soap.

'I was eight years old when the cupboard came to be mine. My father took it almost to pieces to get it out of their room and rebuilt it in mine. He knew he couldn't part with it because it was in the family, but he didn't want anything left in his room to remind him of her. I told him, I didn't want the cupboard either. If you got in it, you could smell her, and the smell of her was both wonderful and unbearable. I spent nights in the cupboard holding her clothes over my face. I think I wanted to suffocate. Because, to be eight and to lose her was terrible. And not to know why, you see. Only to be told: "The bull kicked her. The bull was angry and kicked your Ma and she's dead." That was all: "the bull kicked her and she's dead." Because they couldn't *tell* me, you see, Ralph. I was eight years old and it was their grown-up secret. They did it each year for eight years and in all that time the calves born to their cows were strong and healthy and fetched good prices, and their love was the same, I suppose, strong and good and there for all to see.

'But some years later, I found out what they did, from Father's diaries. And if she hadn't died, then I would have laughed, because there was a wonderful madness in them. I can remember the kind of thing I read in those diaries. I can remember how he tried to describe it:

"Did the bull today," he'd put.
"Better than last year. Last year my Ellen dressed herself in red but this year all in blue and lay down as usual in the forget-me-not-field.
Haggard's bulls are fine. Of exceptional size. Bull not attracted at once by Ellen's waving blue skirts so she calls it. And it comes lolloping. It noses her and she laughs. She begins whispering our fertility rhyme. The bull is on top of her and she strokes it. Then she shouts to me and I open the gate to the cow's field. The bull almost runs and together we shut him in. As he mounts a cow, Ellen kisses me. She is hot and trembling."

'A game, you see! They played it each year for their land. The land was all they had and they gave it their own desire. Each year she'd played with the bull while he watched her and waited to open the gates as the bull came to the cows. And every year the calves born were strong, until the year of my eighth birthday, when the bull trampled her to death.

'So you see, by the time Gully came, she was gone. I was nine when we found Gully and he moved into the room in our attic.

'When Gully came, my father woke up from his mourning and saw that everything was neglected. He seemed to wake up all of a sudden and start mending things. He'd get up at five and work till dark. I was very thin because we didn't eat well. The vegetables weren't planted for one whole year and horseradish took over the patch. We had eggs of course and I expect the fresh eggs and the milk kept me alive. We had a rabbit or two and cheese sometimes, if he'd made any, and fruit in the summer. And fresh air. Often, when I remember those times, I think that we lived on the air.'

When Ralph returned to his hotel in Harrington Gardens, he walked down his corridor to a machine which dispensed miniature bottles of gin, whisky, brandy and vodka. He paid for a little bottle of whisky and walked quickly back to his room. He poured tap water into the whisky and sat down at the narrow teak desk which, apart from an extraordinary polished clothes-stand and an armchair, was the only extra piece of furniture the hotel provided for the price of the bed.

He rewound the first tape and switched it on.

'I don't know where you want me to start,' he heard Erica say. Ralph smiled because, once started, she had talked without stopping, her memory seldom letting her down. He switched off the machine. He had expected to find her frail, forgetful. He had had a bad time persuading Walt that she was worth company time.

'You see old people, Ralph. They're no good for this kind of thing. They're sentimental as hell. Especially women. And Erica March? Who cares? She was a name in the forties and fifties, but who needs her now?'

'It's worth it, Walt,' Ralph had insisted. 'No one else has done anything about her for years, and she's gotta die soon.'

Walt complained about the month Ralph asked for.

'Jesus! You got a girl in London, or what?'

'No, Walt. It'll take that long.'

'Okay, kid. But if the old lady's senile, you chuck it and come on back. You hear?'

Remembering Walt, Ralph took out a piece of hotel writing paper from the desk drawer and began: "Dear Walt . . ." But he got no further. He sat back and yawned, remembering that on his only other

10

assignment in London he had felt tired all the time, oddly undernourished despite the meals he had bought himself. It had been a depressing assignment, loosely titled 'Research into why Americans are universally disliked in Europe' and involving Ralph in a tour of Europe's capital cities in which he had tried to put the question 'Why are Americans universally disliked in Europe?' into idiomatic French, Dutch, German, Spanish, Italian, Portuguese, Serbo-Croatian and Greek.

It had been a Frenchman who had pointed out to Ralph that the word 'universally' was inappropriate to his question, indeed utterly misleading, and that when he moved on to his next questionee he would do better to leave it out. Yet while on his London stretch of his 'Why are Americans?' assignment, no one – not even Ralph himself – had noticed the redundancy of the word 'universally', and it had therefore travelled with him to France.

What London had done for Ralph, however, was to seem to confirm the hypothesis that there did exist a dislike of Americans, but that hardly anyone could say why it existed or when it had begun. A lot of people of course had said that Americans weren't disliked at all and where on earth had Ralph got his silly idea. They went on to stress that most Americans ("I mean, gosh, take Robert Redford as an example!") were courteous, hospitable, generous, articulate and quite often handsome, and that never, never should it be forgotten that they were the saviours of Europe twice in her blood-soaked history. But Ralph noted that when he encountered this kind of answer, he tended to disbelieve it and felt reluctant to write the answer down.

His final report to Walt on the 'Why are Americans' assignment had made isolationist reading. It had been filed discreetly in the *Bulletin Worldwide* basement and never used.

The possibility that the work Ralph intended to do with Erica March would end in a drawer marked 'English novelists. F. Biographical Data' depressed him. It won't happen, he told himself, just as long as she doesn't die.

'After my mother's death,' she said, 'I was obsessed by funerals. Hers was so terrible, so utterly solemn, that I didn't dare weep till the flowers flopped down on her but then I thought oh no! I wouldn't like that! Oh heavens, no! Not all those flopping bundles of wet flowers on top of me. And I *started to* scream and I suppose someone had to take me away.

'But then, if an animal died – a piglet or a gosling – I buried it with my trowel and cut things from the hedgerows like hips or blackthorn to put on the grave. And I said all kinds of dreadful prayers in rhyme like "Oh God this piglet take, though it will never wake." And one day, I took down the fly-paper from over the kitchen table and picked off all the sticky dead flies and put them into a box and I buried the box in the muck heap because I knew flies like manure and would feel at home there in their after-life. And for some months after this, I always had a flies' burial, and I stuck stones into the muck with the number of flies I had buried written on them, like "August 20th, 1901. Seventeen flies" and "September 30th, 1901. Twenty-two flies." It was very macabre, wasn't it, and strange? Especially when I had so hated my mother's funeral. I daresay I wanted everything dead to suffer what she had suffered – the terrible service with the white flowers and the mumbled prayers.

'But do you know something strange? When I met Emily, my friend who died in 1913, she told me that when she'd been a child she'd found death very satisfying and romantic and had once buried some flies.

'We laughed and laughed and I told Emily about the muck heap and all the other graves of dead things littered around the farm! But life is so odd, Ralph, don't you think, because the next funeral I went to was hers. And I expect you've seen pictures of this, haven't you? Of the carriages, and all of us in white with our sashes and our purple and orange flowers, and the great crowd. It was the most gilded funeral of its time.'

It was early afternoon in Erica's room. Next door, in the small bedroom, Mrs Burford was hoovering. A squat woman of fifty with unlined skin, Mrs Burford had given Ralph the scant greeting that was all she could ever find in her for strangers and warned him bluntly: 'She's tired today.'

Erica wasn't wearing the scarf, and without it, her serenity had gone. The head with its dusting of white down was at once repulsive and faintly comic. There was a scab on the crown of her head which her bent hand touched from time to time. Ralph sat down and waited. But she couldn't speak. Not today. Did you imagine, said

12

her limp gesture of dismissal, that we old people are the machines of history? Don't you understand that we very often forget?

He turned up the next day and she was refreshed. She wore a red silk turban.

'And what dreams, Ralph!' she said before he had closed her door, 'of a town that I've often seen somewhere in me and it was that town I tried to write about in *The Hospital Ship,* where the people come running because the scent of the air is so wonderful and they go helter-skelter down the white streets and they find camellia trees, taller than pines. And of course they want to bag all the vacant houses and put up notices saying "Private Property. Keep out." They want to possess the town and breed in it and put down their pale roots into the soil. And only after a while do they find that the roots keep pushing through the earth twisting and growing and burrowing through the foundation of the white houses till the houses begin to crack and splinter and the roots start coming up again through the floors, tiny white growths at first, like capillaries, then wider, fleshier, stronger, coiling round the furniture and round their feet . . . Oh yes! I often take myself to this town. When I'm tired, my mind spends whole nights there, being a silent girl with limbs that can climb the camellia trees, and from high up watching the struggle of the Rooters and rocked to sleep by the flowers.'

'I remember the Rooters,' said Ralph.

'Do you? They became very pale, didn't they, with their own struggles? The sun shone on them but their struggle to be normal was so great it made them white with pain. And the pallor of the Rooters, you know, was inspired by someone I knew, my Uncle Chadwick who was the palest man – the palest human being – I've ever seen. And I remember my father saying to Chadwick once: "With your money, Chadwick, I don't know why you don't go on a cruise!"'

Erica laughed and leant back in her chair. 'Chadwick was what people used to call a "card". He lived in a style we never dreamed of, with books in glass bookcases and meals at his club. He was quite well known in his day: Chadwick March. He was compared to Oscar Wilde and really in many ways he was very like Oscar Wilde except that he wasn't as witty, not by a long chalk, and he never went to prison, because he was a discreet man who never had love affairs with sons of Marquesses or anyone like that who might make trouble.

'His plays had ghastly titles like *The Fortunes of the Honourable Avis Brimstone* and *The Weathering of Lady Winchelsea,* and they were all about the aristocracy, of which he definitely wasn't one! He'd started out as a vicar, but I suppose he must have gone too far with the choirboys because the Church didn't keep him long, and I remember him arriving at our house the summer before my mother died and sobbing. And I thought, I can't imagine why he's crying (grown-ups didn't usually cry like that) unless he's hurt himself very badly, and I waited to see whether any of his blood would run out under the kitchen door, but it didn't.

'I grew very, very fond of Chadwick when I was older. I don't think he ever did go on a cruise, but he sometimes came down to our house for a kind of holiday, and I used to go for walks with him and he'd talk about London. He was very restless. Sometimes he'd announce after supper: "Think I'll just go and see what's to do in the village," and off he'd go, off into the night, full of excitement, as if he expected to find travelling players or young members of the Garrick. But of course he never did! All he found were the cottages in darkness and a few ducks on the pond and a signpost pointing three ways. But he never seemed to be put off. He went time and time again to the village, even on winter nights, and I suppose he just walked about in the silence till he felt tired, and then he'd come home and say: "Nothing much doing tonight. Bit quiet in the village!"

'He was a terribly quiet man. Gully was afraid of him at first because he looked so strange in his London get-up, as if he'd come out of another world from the one we knew. But then in time, he won Gully over. He told him made-up stories and tried to help him with his school work. The only time in my childhood that Chadwick was angry was when Gully told him that at Christmas the vicar came to our school with nuts for all the children, and he'd throw these nuts onto the floor of the schoolhouse and laugh as we children scrabbled about trying to pick them up. This made Chadwick very, very cross. He said that a man who didn't treat children with dignity deserved to be hanged. And he tried to make my father take us away from elementary school and employ a governess for us instead, but we knew this wouldn't happen. The money just wasn't there.

'I suppose I ought to describe Chadwick. He was my father's brother, but he was nothing like my father. They were Jacob and Esau: one hairy (my father) and one smooth (Chadwick).

14

'Not, of course, that there was any question of one of them trying to trick his way into some silly inheritance, because there was no inheritance, only the farm which had been left to my mother by her mother and then to my father when she died, and then to me. And Chadwick was rich. He got rich very quickly with his plays. He had a terribly slow walk, I remember. You had to keep pulling him along and this was irritating. But his hair was a wonder! It was parted in the middle and grew in ripples. His eyes were round and blue, and when I was older, I understood that his heart was rather like his eyes, always darting about in search of love.

'Gully once told Chadwick that when he grew up, he wanted to be a Red Indian. And instead of laughing, Chadwick said: "Well, better build a tepee, eh?" And they went for a walk along the boundary of the farm and cut sticks from the hedges and began to build their tepee on the grass outside the kitchen window. The structure was very good, very professional, but the skin was hopeless. They tried to sew together pages of the *Illustrated London News* (Chadwick always brought us back numbers of this when he came to stay), but in the night the wind came and scattered them and bits of the Death of Queen Victoria Souvenir Issue went flying up onto the haystack.

'I don't know where Gully got this idea about becoming an Indian. It was long before the time of the great Western films. Perhaps there was a drawing of a Red Indian in our geography book or in a children's atlas. Chadwick pretended to take it seriously, anyway: I remember him sitting in the ruined tepee, with a few shreds of the *Illustrated London News* flapping on the frame like vultures, and saying to Gully: "If you're going to be an Indian some day, you'll have to watch out for your white skin. Because the white man inside his white skin will come plundering, and give you worthless things for your land and try to talk you out of doing your rain dances. So you watch out for him, your white man enemy, and never let your arrow sleep." Gully was baffled, of course. But years later, he said to me: "I got that straight now, Erica – what your Uncle Chadwick was on about. He said there's more 'an one side to a person and yew never can tell what the one *side* might do to the other. And in 'imself he had two sides an' they were never at peace, not what you'd call peace. I'nt that right, girl ?"

'*Gully* was a butcher by that time!'

*

In his hotel room, Ralph had copies of Erica March's three novels: *The Two Wives of the King* (1921), *In the Blind Man's City* (1945) and *The Hospital Ship* (1954). He had read them all, but he planned to spend some of his spare time in London reading them again. But he hadn't begun yet. He had given his evenings to what he called his Summary; he wrote very little down, yet promised himself he would write more. He sat in silence in the half-empty dining room, where bland, uninteresting food was served by disdainful waitresses in heavy shoes.

He was bearded and rather pale. His hair was black and wiry. He was shorter than he might have been because of what his family referred to as 'The Tennessee Incident'. The Tennessee Incident had occurred when Ralph was fourteen. On holiday with his Grandma while his parents travelled in Europe, he had fallen in love with the only girl ever to come near the lonely ranch house where his grandmother lived in aged and defiant isolation – her coloured maid. She was called Pearl. Her father had been an errant English colonel. Her skin was amber. Ralph lay sleepless in his high, soft bed and dreamed his first dreams of a woman.

His grandmother noted exhaustion in his eyes at breakfast time: "Reverend Jones do have some things to say 'bout young boys of your age!" But Ralph shadowed Pearl, savouring the movement of her hips, the fire of her black eyes and above all, the smell of her, which made him want to weep.

The days of his vacation slipped away. On his last night at the ranch, he splashed cologne onto his jaw and crept like a burglar to Pearl's room. Outside her door, he stood limp and afraid. Where were the thousand-and-one nights of his lust? Where, in his imaginings, had her body gone?

He knocked and there was silence. Then he heard movement inside the room and Pearl tiptoed to her door and unlocked it. Blocking his entrance with her body, she stared at him in the darkness. He suddenly sensed the ridiculousness of his white flesh inside his striped pyjamas. He cursed himself for having made the longed-for journey to her door and then finding that he couldn't say a word. Gently, Pearl smiled at him and whispered: 'Got my man inside, see? Can't ask ya in for a cookie nor nothin'. Not tonight, Ralphie.' Then she reached out and touched his face, just where he had splashed on the cologne. Her hand felt heavy, very hot. Then she closed the door quietly.

Ralph ran out of the house. He had never felt rage and humiliation like this rage, which was a hard stone inside him, a stone he wanted to hurl with his shout and smash with his fists. Running didn't lessen the rage, so he let it climb, and the climb he made was the climb ever afterwards known as the Tennessee Incident and which marked him for life.

Dawn found him on the barn roof, astride the ridge like a saddle tramp. But as the sun got up, sleep at last took him and his grip on the roof weakened. He fell thirty feet to the ground and broke both his legs in several places. The pain, when his head woke and felt it, was far worse than the pain of loving Pearl and he lay on the hard white ground, screaming.

The Tennessee Incident probably stunted Ralph's growth by three or four inches. 'Other incidents,' he noted in his Summary, 'have stunted my mental and emotional growth and my progress towards the package (i.e. perspicacious appraisals, empathy with the condition of all men, the ability to engage in enlightened reasoning and generally to eschew bullshit and untruth) I understand loosely as wisdom. I've made hogshit of all my love affairs and the dentist says my teeth will crumble to pus before I'm forty.' Ralph then wrote: 'I suppose I start with myself,' and under this scribbled pessimistically 'Probable cost of having teeth fixed = a thousand dollars.'

'You know I only had one friend,' Erica said, 'before Gully came. She was an invisible friend and her name was Claustrophobia. I thought Claustrophobia was a wonderful name for a girl, ever since I heard my father say it. I suppose he said something like "there's claustrophobia in that ole cowshed," but I went straight away to look and see if I could find her and ask her if she'd be my friend.

'But I found no one. Of course I didn't! Only the cows and the milky smell of them and the carpeting of straw and muck. I called to her, I think. I know I could say her name perfectly – every syllable. Claustro-phob-ia. Claustro-phob-ia! But no one appeared. So I invented her there and then. She crept out of one of the cow-stalls and sat on the gate, looking at me. She was terribly pretty and fair, but a little smaller than me. And I remember that she couldn't run as fast as I could, and when we went running down the lanes for blackberries and elderberries, I'd have to keep on calling to her to hurry up.

'Claustrophobia appeared between the time of my mother's death and Gully's arrival. She stayed about a year and a half, I suppose, and then she went away. I put her in the cupboard to sleep, because the cupboard frightened me then, and if I imagined her in it, I wasn't so afraid. And of course I talked to her. She had no mother either, so she knew how horrible this was. At night, we often had very long conversations and I'd break off now and then and ask in a posh voice: "Are you sure you're quite comfortable in the cupboard, Claustrophobia?" And she'd reply, very politely: "Oh, quite comfortable, thank you very much. In fact I prefer a cupboard to a bed, Erica my dear."

'So this was very satisfactory, you see, because through her I conquered my fear of the cupboard and through her I learned about friendship, because she was very loyal and I was loyal to her, particularly on the question of her existence, in which my father refused to believe. He thought I was going mad, but Chadwick now, he quite liked Claustrophobia and once brought me two gingerbread men in a box from London – one for me and one for her. But then later, he stole her name – without even consulting me – for a character in one of his awful plays, and I was very cross about this. Very cross indeed.'

Erica pursed her lips, sat back in her chair. Ralph watched her, but she looked away from him.

'Oh, why did you come?' she said suddenly.

Ralph switched off the tape recorder and folded his hands round the notepad he kept open on his knee.

'I think . . .' he began hesitantly.

'Please tell me,' said Erica. 'I want to know why you came.'

'Well, I think I asked to come here because I didn't seem to be going anywhere much. I thought I was, ten years ago, but now everything seems quite bad . . . and I guess I thought that if I could listen to someone who's been so far . . . I'm not explaining this well, Erica . . .'

'Yes you are. Go on.'

'Well if I could talk to someone who's got near the end, then perhaps I'd begin to make better sense of it all.'

'It all? What's "it all", dear?'

'Well my life just follows the same idiotic pattern as an assignment I once went on called "Why are Americans disliked in Europe". I go on and on asking a question, getting different answers and then I find there is no real answer – just a list of possibilities which is too divergent to make sense of. So I try to find another question. But I keep getting stuck with the same one, like I got stuck with the "Why are Americans" question. It just wouldn't leave me. So I took it back to the States and I began asking it there – to people in restaurants and bus lines and to blacks and Poles and every goddamn ethnic group . . .'

'I wonder why you got stuck with that? It sounds rather a stupid question to me, Ralph dear.'

'I just don't know. I suppose I thought, if I could collect enough data on that question, then I could get on to other more advanced questions and that eventually I'd be asking questions to which there would be sound answers, I mean answers that I could believe in. But I never got further than the "Why are Americans" question because the answers I got back home were so pathetic! I mean one woman said to me: "Well I blame Clint Eastwood. That's entirely the wrong impression to give to the world – silence and gunshooting!" And a guy from the South said he blamed the Statue of Liberty. He said, "that statue gives everyone the idea that liberty is desirable and that in America every sonofabitch's second name is Liberty. But name the man who's free. Liberty's hogshit! No one's got it and what's more they don't *want* it!"'

Erica threw back her head and laughed. 'My poor Ralph,' she said after a while, 'you probably won't do any better with me. I don't have any answers. I never have. But I think it's very nice for *me* that you're here. I can feel you doing me good. Let's have some wine!'

Obediently, Ralph poured it. Wondering if the wine had become a ritual, one she couldn't really afford, he said: 'You don't have to give me wine every day, Erica . . .'

She sat up and took the glass he handed to her.

'No of course I don't,' she said, 'but it helps me. It oils my mind and my memory, and both are very rusty. Especially when I'm trying to remember that early time, when I was a girl in brown boots and pinafores. I love to dream of that time because there was a lot of innocence and wonder in it. I dream of Gully very often. He had a very large penis, you know, and over the years I dreamt a lot about Gully's penis, although you mustn't record that for your magazine, will you? But I think that's why Gully got on, after he became a young man and was apprenticed to Tom Haggard (cousin of the other Haggard, Eric, who kept the bulls) and learned the butchering trade. Because the girls liked him, you know, despite his head being on sideways and I think I was jealous for a while. I believe I thought Gully was mine. I was fifteen or sixteen, I suppose, when Gully went courting and he would have been about seventeen, and his hair was thick and wiry like a bull's hair and he had the smell of a man – or so it seemed to me.

'I remember that I lay awake, almost every night at one time, waiting for Gully to come home to his attic room, and often it was near sunrise when he came in and we'd have to be up at six to get the milking done before he went to work. So in the milking shed, with my face pressed into a cow, I once said: "Where d'yew go then, Gully March, that you be out all night?" But Gully didn't answer. He just milked a bit faster and swore at his cow.

'So a few nights later, I went up to his room when I heard him come in, and he was lying on top of his bed with all his clothes on, fast asleep. I shook him and said: "Gully! Tell me where you go at night." But he rolled over and wouldn't say a word. And I believe it was then I felt jealous. Not just jealous of what he did, but of his secret which he wouldn't share. So I began to tease him, even in front of my father.

' "Gully's courtin'!" I said. "Gully's after an old witch who lives on the pond!" On and on I teased and watched him blush, till one day my father shook his fist at me and said: "You leave Gully alone, girl, or you'll git shut up in the cupboard!"

'But I didn't leave him alone: "Gully thinks he's growed up, don't you, Gul? Planning to get married an' all, eh?" And rude things I said. Dreadful things a girl my age shouldn't have dared to say. But I wanted to punish Gully. Punish him good. But it was me who got the punishment in the end. My father shut me in the cupboard one suppertime, and I thought he would leave me there all night, so I kicked and screamed and I know they heard me down in the kitchen – Gully and my father witn their good supper of soup and bread and ham. But no one came to let me out, so I put my head on a blanket and tried to sleep, and the hours passed like this, thinking about my lost supper and trying to sleep on the prickly blanket.

'Then I heard someone come into my room, and it was Gully. He'd left my father asleep by the fire and he put his face very close

20

to the bottom of the cupboard door, where the door didn't quite fit, and he whispered: "Tell you what, girl, yew's the one is right! I bin courtin' an' all and with Dot works up at the Manor. An' maybe we ought to git married an' that, 'cos I had her now seventeen times."

'Seventeen times! I couldn't imagine seventeen times, not at fifteen and shut in a cupboard which still smelled of my mother's clothes. "You wicked bor!" I whispered. "You din' ought to have done that seventeen times. You'll pay for that in hell, I reckon."

'And then we both laughed, and Gully said: "That's not hell, girl! That's more like heaven!"

'But whenever I saw Dot – in church, or at one of our village festivals – my stomach would flutter at the thought of those seventeen times which, as the summer went on, no doubt became eighteen times and twenty-eight times . . . I thought, you see, that if Gully could do it twenty-eight times with Dot, then he could surely do it just once with me – to show me how it felt, so that later I wouldn't be afraid.

'But he never did and of course I never dared to ask for it. And soon afterwards he married Dot and Mr Haggard gave them rooms over the butcher's shop.'

2

Mrs Burford brought the satin eiderdown from the bedroom and covered Erica with it. She was cold. Mrs Burford lit the gas fire and left.

Erica dozed under the soft covering. Outside her window, rain fell silently on London, and in Erica's dream two young nannies, heavily shod, began to run with their prams through the crocuses in the park. The pert crocuses were bent and crushed, and the rain, elsewhere so silent, tapped like hail on the round brown hats of the two nannies. Dry inside their prams, the babies laughed with joy at their jolting ride, laughed and bounced until their bellies were full of wind and they belched a green sickness.

'Drat it, Nanny Purvis! My Rupert's gone and brought up his pudding,' said one nanny to the other, and Erica woke. The gas fire burned near her temples. Her turban was awry.

'Terrible . . . terrible . . .' she whispered.

'I've brought you a present,' said a voice.

Erica looked up. Ralph was sitting opposite the sofa where she lay. He was smiling. Erica didn't know how long he had been there. She sighed.

'My hands are dead,' she said flatly.

Ralph's heart began to race.

'I'm sorry . . .' he began, 'I won't stay today . . .' And he thought, with old people there is no warning: deterioration comes like a moth in the window. So he got up, leaving the freesias he had bought on the floor, where she might see them. But she didn't notice the flowers. Her eyes followed him urgently.

'I've never written it down, what I want . . .' she said.

Ralph stopped, his hand on the door.

'But I should have written it down . . .' Her voice was faint, like a voice used up. She took a breath and her left hand crept out from under the eiderdown, fumbled at the edge of the scarlet turban.

'You could do it, though, Ralph!' And her eyes stared and stared at him. 'You could tell them, there used to be the smell of her dresses in there and the odour of the forest, sometimes in the darkness, and I imagined the trees that made it. And afterwards, there was the smell of books, like a clean sanctuary, and never in there was there anything that hasn't been a part of me . . .'

She paused. 'Oh, you could tell them that,' she said, and closed her eyes.

Ralph hesitated by the door. He was dismayed at her. And dismayed at himself, at his presence which got in the way, at his failure to understand her.

'Shit!' he said under his breath, and crept out onto the landing, shutting the door quietly behind him.

But the following day she was as bright, as straight as a daffodil. She wore a yellow cardigan; her eyelids were shaded blue. In a thin glass vase were Ralph's freesias.

'Rain sickness,' she said as he sat down. 'Chadwick had it, too, sometimes, and would lie down in his silk dressing gown on the hearthrug. I think that was the first time I saw Chadwick's legs, when he had his rain sickness and couldn't get dressed, and honestly Ralph, they were the whitest legs I've ever encountered and the question of his going on a cruise would then enter my mind. And I'd imagine him sitting in a deckchair with those white, quite hairless legs of his hanging over the front of it and in his heart hoping to be recognized as a celebrity with his rippling hair and dying, of course, of internal combustion for the deckhands in their tropical rig! I forgave Chadwick, of course, for stealing Claustrophobia. I had to forgive him very soon after he'd done it because he brought me to London to stay with him in his rooms (he lived in a flat in fact just off Bryanston Square and it was a very spacious flat with four bedrooms, but he insisted on referring to it as "rooms" for a reason I've never really understood although perhaps he thought "flat" was plebeian). Yes, he brought me to London to see his play with the character Claustrophobia in it and I remember that the play was called *The Weathering of Lady Winchelsea* and it was full of people asking each other to dinner and leaving calling cards like they do in Jane Austen, so really the butler had a dreadfully busy time opening doors and handing round salvers and announcing people, so that the butler could easily have been the main part but he wasn't and the character Claustrophobia was a cloying friend of the Winchelsea family with five daughters to marry off. Very boring, as you can see, but extraordinarily successful at that time, heaven knows why, and Chadwick was enchanted by fame and the flat was full of flowers and messages of rapture.

'I honestly don't know why Chadwick had time for me. I think perhaps he saw that I was in a kind of bondage to my father and to the farm, so planted you see, in the monotony of the house and the animals, and my life would have gone on, unchanging in my father's need of me, and Chadwick snatched me away – only for a month, he said – but in the end I stayed in London for two years. Chadwick abhorred bondage of any kind, "And the farm!" he said, "you can die on that farm if you want to, Erica, but not until someone has let you live!" I was nineteen. Gully and Dot had a child by then, a little boy who was always known as Buckwheat. And my father? Well, Chadwick knew and I knew that he'd marry Eileen soon and then his need of me would cease. He complained of course, my father. I'd done the milking for him every morning for at least ten years – three thousand six hundred and fifty times I'd milked the cows! And for years I'd done the cheese making and all the cooking and lit the fires and swept and cleaned like Cinderella, and I was a woman by then, almost a woman. So he let me go.

'He did what he could about buying me new clothes, but when I came to live with Chadwick, well, the clothes, the *wonderful* clothes of the women in London!

'I couldn't believe the rustle of them and the beautiful sewing. Mine were like fustian in comparison. And the strangeness of London. It was full of bells, you know. Hardly a quarter hour passed without a bell chimed, yet nowadays you scarcely hear a single one. And horses and motor vehicles both cantered round the streets then and I thought of Gully in his butcher's shop and I said to myself, if he heard and saw all this, his head would fall off!

'I was ashamed of my Suffolk accent: that's something I remember. But what a snobbish thing! I wished I'd had a governess as Chadwick had suggested and been taught elocution.

'But I was a weak vessel then. Very ordinary. Very susceptible to things. I was amazed by my room in Chadwick's "rooms", with a bath next door and a Thomas Crapper for my use alone, with its comfy polished seat.

'I touched all the surfaces in my room and they were all beautiful in one way or another. I had a mahogany dressing table and mirror and a rosewood writing table, inlaid with other kinds of wood, and a velvet-covered armchair where I put Ratty May. Ratty May sat in that comfy chair for two years and watched me change. Poor thing! Luckily, her hair was yellow wool or she would have gone grey. Luckily, her body was bran.

'I've told you, haven't I, that Chadwick disapproved of bondage. Yet he was bound himself by the morality of the day and his own struggles made him very aware of all the dead old ships stuck in the tides of English life, and one of these was the attitude of men to the Woman Question.

'Of course Chadwick was too much of a drawing-room person by then to be an active Labour man like Keir Hardie, but he knew and liked Frederick Pethick Lawrence whom he'd met at the Reform Club, and little by little he'd come to sympathize with the aims of the militant suffragists, and although I don't think he spoke at meetings, he gave money to Mrs Pankhurst's Women's Social and Political Union, the WSPU.

"And so when I arrived, as soon as all the excitement over *The Weathering of Lady Wincbelsea* had died down and the bouquets began to droop a bit, he started to ask me, didn't I realize that for centuries women had been prisoners of the law and that now, at last, they were no longer twittering like sparrows but had begun to roar like lions? "Up there," (he always referred to our farm as "up there"), "you probably don't even realize what's going on. You don't hear any roaring and most of you are content with your miserable lot, but *here* . . ."

'Well, Chadwick was idiotic in a way, because this was 1912 and of course people in Suffolk knew about the Suffragettes, though he didn't believe me when I said we did. I suppose he thought that no one in Suffolk knew anything about anything except the ways of the fields and the weather and that we all imagined the world was flat.

'I'd never dreamed, though, that I would meet any of those women. They were like film stars in their way – especially Christabel with her extraordinary beauty – and it was difficult to believe they had skin. I'd only seen them in photographs. I never thought I could touch one of them.

'But it wasn't long after the first night of *Lady Winchelsea* that the Pethick Lawrences came to tea with Chadwick and there was a great deal of talk about Swan and Edgar's bankruptcy because this had been the time of the incredible window smashing in Oxford Street (Swan and Edgar's was a shop in Oxford Street, you see) and poor Fred Lawrence was being sued for damages and all his money was used up.

'I sat very quietly in Chadwick's drawing-room. Mrs Lawrence wore a wide hat with a veil, Chadwick had a finicky preference for herbal tea which tasted of daisies, and we all drank this although I thought it was absolutely disgusting. And then I suddenly heard Chadwick say: "Erica is a child of ignorance," and I thought, how dare he say such rot to strangers when he's never seen and smelled the birth of a calf, never got his fingernails green. And I wanted to stand up and say I was off home. But I didn't. I sat there, staring down at my daisy tea, and I expect the Lawrences smiled very kindly at me because they seemed very kindly people, and then they forgot about me and began discussing their house in Dorking which they'd lost or were just about to lose, I can't remember which.

'When they'd gone, Chadwick said to me: "They are very fine, Erica, because they've given everything they possess to the cause, and here you see how human nature can divest itself of all that is ordinary and petty and take on the nobility of a wild white stallion." Dear Chadwick! His use of imagery was often rather transparent and poor and I honestly think a white stallion must have stalked his erotic dreams because he so loved to compare things to it – everything from the nobility to the Pethick Lawrences to a cloud he saw one day above Fleet Street.

'But of course he was right in his way about the Lawrences. They were wonderfully brave and when I went to bed that night and thought about the house in Dorking and everything else they must have lost I knew that I really was a "child of ignorance", sheltered all my life by the boundaries of the village and the farm. I cried for all that I didn't know. I got Ratty May off her chair and took her back to bed with me and I said to her: "I'm not going home till I find out."

26

'My finding out was a bit postponed, however, because of Chadwick's crisis. Chadwick's crisis began the next day, the very day after the Pethick Lawrences had come to tea. It was terribly sad. The only good thing about it was that it enabled me to stay on in London after my month was up because poor Chadwick had become very ill by then and couldn't walk with his swollen-up legs, and it was I who nursed him, just as we nursed sick animals on the farm. He was a bit like an animal in his suffering: very mute. Except that he cried occasionally, and of course no animal does this, cries real tears.

'He got this letter from Venezuela. It arrived the day after the Lawrences came, and when I went into the dining-room for breakfast (he had two servants, Chadwick, which was why everything was so polished, and I'll tell you about these servants later on). Chadwick was sitting there reading it and he was quite petrified with sorrow. It was as if he couldn't breathe or move or make a sound and his face was burning red with a kind of fever. I said something to him and he didn't answer. Then he drew in a little stifled breath and I knew that he was in a state of shock. I ran to the sideboard and poured some brandy into a glass and I knelt by him and held the glass to his mouth and eventually he took a tiny sip. And then he pulled my head towards him and pressed it against his clean silk shirt and said, almost inaudibly, "Athelstone's gone to Venezuela.'"

A familiar sense of destitution haunted Ralph's return to his hotel. He felt lost. Like a US Marine, stuck for the night in a corner of death's backyard. He lay down on his bed and covered his eyes against the ugly, overhead light.

A week had passed and he had talked to no one except Erica. He had eaten the mediocre dinners they served in the hotel dining-room, listened to each day's recording, made notes and pondered idly how it would feel to make the film. THE FILM. But he knew he was nowhere near it. For without a sense of direction what, in the end, would the film be *about*? 'Nothing,' he decided. 'The film will be horse's ass.'

On the days when Erica had sent him away, he had walked a little. Untempted by the zoo, he had noticed the first chilly signs of spring in Regent's Park, the grey-green winter dusted here and there with colour. Pigeons had begun their distant, ruffling love-play. And Ralph had sauntered and watched, a stranger with his hands in his pockets ("and gosh, rather short for ar American!") his nationality camouflaged then perhaps, his identity hidden, but haunted by his Manhattan dreams of nullity and by Walt's voice:

'If you fuck this one, kid, I mean if you don't get something really good from the old lady, I think we're going to have to look quite hard at your job situation . . .'

The bleakest answer Ralph had ever got to his 'Why are Americans' question had come from a French professor of literature, member of the Academie Française, with whom he had hoped to spend a little time, imagined foolishly that the eminent man might defrost his grey, manicured exterior to reveal a warm Gallic heart offering statements of global importance over a glass of Ricard. But no. *'Quels Americains?'* the academician had snapped. *'Moi, j'ignore les Americains.'* And now, alone in London, with the threads of his career seeming to slip from his hands like leaves blown downstream he'd begun to inhabit an April of desolation.

He hated his hotel room. Lying under the ugly light he compared it to Erica's room where, in the glow of the Tiffany lamp, he had once caught a glimpse of his own shadow and Erica's, face to face on the wall and suddenly been appalled at the importance he was attaching to this assignment. He had wanted to shout out: 'Don't you see why I'm here? I'm halfway through my life and the first half's fucked. I need help.'

Her room was small and faded and cluttered. Sometimes she sat so still, she seemed only to be a part of the room, something set down carelessly, dusted by Mrs Burford three times a week. Ralph imagined Mrs Burford's hand flicking over the scarlet turban and thinking, peculiar thing! Don't know what anyone would want this for.

To think of her room was comforting. In it, Ralph didn't feel destitute. Yet as soon as he left it, fears brushed his heart like a conjurer's flowers. *'J'ignore* Ralph Pears,' said the downcast eyes of the English in their streets and parks. 'I don't know or care about his existence.'

Ralph got off the bed and sat down at the writing table. From the shallow drawer, he tugged at the paper headed 'Summary', He took up a pencil and wrote:

'The nearest I can get to an image for our two lives – Erica March, 87. Ralph Pears, 35 – is two basins of wheat. Her basin, which should be almost empty, is heavy and full. The wheat is spilling over and some grains have fallen. There is no mental nor spiritual famine here. But my basin, which should be full, is very light – about a quarter full only. I have almost no knowledge of how the grains got used up. But I know the grains left are too few. I'm not nourished . . .'

Ralph paused, took the last Marlboro out of the day's pack and lit it. He noticed that the familiarity of the design of the Marlboro pack was comforting. On his walks, he had sometimes taken the Marlboro pack out of his pocket and just stared at it. He inhaled, picked up the pencil again and continued:

'I think what I'm doing is putting my basin near to Erica's. I'm kinda hoping grains will fall from hers into mine, hundreds of grains, so that it begins to fill up and there is some RECOVERY.
This is simplistic and over-optimistic. I admit this. It is also stealing.'

Ralph let the pencil drop. He felt tired. Tired with himself and his own whining. In the magnificence of her Tennessee night, he suddenly heard his Grandma pronounce: 'I never saw in any-*wun* have what you' Ma do have, Ralphie, and that is leprosy of the soul. Now you must mind it ain't catchin!'

Mrs Burford was there. Ralph smiled at her as he walked past her stare into Erica's sitting-room. She looked away. She was married to a retired postman, Erica had told him. He'd had a Battersea round.
'I didn't sleep very well, Ralph,' said Erica. 'Sometimes I don't and that is very annoying. But never mind. I'm going to tell you about Chadwick's crisis today and then about some meetings I had while he was ill. But I didn't put out any wine this afternoon because I think it would send me to sleep and then your time would be wasted, wouldn't it? How much more time have you got, dear?'
'All the time we need,' Ralph lied.
'Till we get to the last day and we eat the caviar!' said Erica and laughed.
'Right!' said Ralph.

Before going to bed, Ralph had written to Walt, the first of his promised bulletins on his progress.

Walt had told him, 'Don't bother writing, kid. Just call me and tell me how you're doing. See if you got anything there we can sell to United Artists!' But Ralph hadn't wanted to talk to Walt and had written only a short report:

'Dear Walt,

Just a line to say the old lady's verbal and quite sharp. You'd never believe she's three off ninety. Nor is she stuck in a sentimental time-warp. Not so far. So it's looking good and I'm running out of tapes fast. It's also movie material.

Cold spring in London. Everyone still muffled up, including me. E.M. has no heating. Only an antique gas fire. I think she's very tough.

I'll be in touch again next week.

Say hello to the other office furniture for me.

Ralph'

'The thing about Chadwick,' said Erica, 'was that he was almost always in love. At the time of the crisis, he had been having an affair with a very beautiful but rather stupid young man called Athelstone Amis (no relation of Kingsley, I think, or he might have been a bit more sparky, but who can say?).

'But Chadwick could never really match his love affairs to his life. He fell for the wrong people and they deserted him. It was a bit like his play-writing in a way. I mean, there was Chadwick, a defrocked vicar, indelibly homosexual, diving off his pulpit into the world of drawing-rooms! The fact that he came to own a drawing-room himself very quickly really makes it no less extraordinary, because the people he put in his plays with such success really weren't the kind of people he cared about so that you always felt with Chadwick, the writer and the man are absolutely separate. And so it was with his lovers. He never, till the end of his life, loved anyone who loved him back, not really loved him, not with their hearts, and he died full of yearnings. This Athelstone was no exception. He had dallied with Chadwick for a year. Chadwick had spent a fortune on gold tie pins and silk foulards. He'd even discovered some extremely expensive hair elixir which he thought would make his ripples yet more

Raphaelite and thereby entrancing for Athelstone's fickle fingers. Oh, he'd done everything! But the minute *Lady W* was over Athelstone upped and offed to Caracas or somewhere in Venezuela in search of adventure and suntanned boys and Chadwick was ravaged by his departure, ravaged by it and began to decline.

'He was really very ill. His doctor came and looked at him and uncovered his white legs which could so easily have been on a boat with Athelstone Amis but which in fact had swollen up to terrible proportions with an absolutely unidentifiable malady and which gave him constant pain. There was talk of putting him into hospital so that tests could be performed on his legs, but he refused to go. I think he knew he would recover when his heart began to mend, and meanwhile I was there to nurse him, and he knew I would.

'The servants were a Mr and Mrs Hogan from County Cork in Ireland. They lived in the basement flat and we shared them with the ground floor tenant who was a widow called Mrs Garnett. Chadwick always thought of the Hogans as "his" and never admitted to anyone that we shared them. They were very loyal to Chadwick and though they came to disapprove of my antics when I joined the movement, they were loyal to me too and Mr Hogan once said to me: "Prisons, Miss? Tis outrageous entirely if they can do these things to a woman!" and he made me broth and porridge when my mouth was bruised. So Chadwick was lucky in a way, you see. He had the Hogans to cook for him and keep the rooms tidy and me to read to him and sit with him, and in time the crisis passed and his swellings went down.

'I think I told you, didn't I, he was terribly silent while he was ill? Perhaps his mind was tangled in a rain forest with Athelstone. I began to read him *Little Dorrit* and this was ironic because the time wasn't far off when I got to know prisons. Chadwick cried quite a lot during my *Little Dorrit* readings and he came to look a bit like a drowned man, wet and white and swollen. I wrote to my father and said "on no account can I abandon Uncle Chadwick who is took right poor with the heartbreak and yew must manage longer without me." I was still very Suffolk, you see. I was still a child of ignorance. But it was all beginning to go.

'Visitors came. And one day I answered the door and it was a woman of about forty with fair hair and dressed in dark green. She stood very, very still with her head slightly on one side, and then she smiled and said: "You must be Erica March."

31

'I was confused because I'd never seen her before and I couldn't imagine how she knew I was there or what my name was. I showed her into the sitting-room – or rather, the drawing-room, because Chadwick always called it that – and she sat down and took off her green gloves and said: "My name is Emily Davison."'

Erica closed her eyes. For a moment, she kept them closed as she talked. Her head was tilted back and she began to speak very fast, as if the images she held in her memory were fleeting and might suddenly elude her.

'Emily was the first of my meetings at that time, Ralph, and in a sense the last, although from that day on my life was full of meetings and I was caught up by an extraordinary tide which rocked me and pulled me and flung me down and then crept to me again and dragged me back and held me moving and moving until it was all over. I was weaned in that peculiar ocean. And once it had taken me in, that very morning when Emily arrived at Chadwick's flat, I became wild! I don't believe the wildness of those days has ever completely left me. Even now, when I'm far too old to be alive, I feel the hard stone in me and my hard stone has shaped me and been my rage and my understanding. And there could have been no understanding without my hard stone don't you see? Because to understand, is to see the world with an eye of steel and a belly of fire. And to people who believe that love and compassion are born of tears, I say no! They are born of fire!'

Erica opened her eyes and they were wet.

'Ralph dear,' she said quietly, 'will you ask Mrs Burford to put the kettle on and make us a cup of tea?'

'Sure,' said Ralph. He switched off the tape recorder and stood up. 'I can leave now, if you like,' he said, 'if you're tired.'

Erica smiled.

'You're very considerate,' she said. 'I think Americans are, aren't they, although in all my hundreds of years I've hardly met any. I don't know why I haven't. Just accident I suppose. I met an American airman once. He was considerate even though he was in pain. He'd landed in our greenhouse.'

Ralph laughed and went to the kitchen where he found Mrs Burford on her hands and knees scrubbing the floor. She looked up at him accusingly. He hesitated.

'Don't you have a sponge-mop for this job?' he asked.

'A what?'

'Well, a mop – so you don't have to kneel down . . .'

'There's 'alf of wot a person needs in this flat. But wot can you expect? She's old i'nt she, and she don't fink.'

'I could get you a mop, if you like . . .' Ralph began.

'You?' snapped Mrs Burford.

'Sure. Why not?'

'Journalist you said you was? Well I'll tellya somefing, love. Never trusted you lot no furtha 'n I'd trust a politician. Pack o' lies, you are.'

'Miss March trusts me,' said Ralph.

'Yeah? Well she don't know no better. Old folk don't 'ave no choice.'

'Sure they do,' said Ralph. 'She didn't have to see me.'

'American, you is?'

'Yup.'

'Cocky lot, the Yanks. Fink they own the bleedin' world. Worse 'n the Ruskies, my Billy sez you are. Global mad.'

Ralph chose to smile. Through his grin he said: 'Miss March has asked for some tea. D'you want to make it, or shall I?'

'Tea?'

'Yup.'

'She don't normally 'ave tea.'

'Well. She wants some today, she's feeling –'

'You don't need to tell me wot she's feeling. There's not a thing about that old lady I don't know. And what would she do if it wasn't for me? She be put in an old people's dying dump.'

'You'll get the tea, then?'

Mrs Burford stood up and wrung out her floor cloth. Her arms, up to the elbows, were red with the hot water.

'Tirin' 'er out, I wouldn't wonder, with all your American chat.'

'Jesus . . .' Ralph began, but he didn't go on. He walked slowly back into the sitting-room where, with the lamp turned on, he found Erica sound asleep. She snored like an old witch, loudly and angrily.

That evening, Ralph started to read *The Hospital Ship*. He had read it twice before.

As he opened it and glanced along the familiar first line, he thought, she hasn't told me yet how she began to write – and why. Then he forgot her as the story began to unfold:

'When the evacuation came, there were one hundred and five who boarded the ship. The ship had arrived in the night, flying a flag no one recognized, and at dawn, when they noticed it, the one hundred and five lying huddled in the bay began to wail and point.

General Almarlyes started to crawl around with his tattered bottom in the air, searching in the grey sand where the merchant crabs had their holes, for his lost fieldglasses. The merchant crabs bit his ankles and ran over his hands, but the fieldglasses were lost and General Almarlyes began to weep for the hundred and fifth time since he had lost not only his fieldglasses, but the war.

The sea was calm. The dawn that morning was kind, and nothing moved, only the merchant crabs and General Almarlyes' ragged arse. And the wailing that went out to the ship could have been song, because it carried hope on that morning of extraordinary stillness, the last hope of the hundred and four and General Almarlyes who were all that remained after the earthquake had come and gone. Above the bay, in the gentle, yellow light, there was no sign of the birds who had circled there for days, waiting patient as death, for their first feast. Eyes stared up, fancying they saw them as usual, eyes blinking. Staring into the sunrise and then voices marvelling in whispers: "the sky is clean!"

Slowly, she clambered down from the ship and came wading in. General Almarlyes sat down on the sand and watched her. He wiped his eyes on his sleeve, blew his nose on his shirttail. He let go an expletive, one pent up in him for days, to reassure himself that he still had a voice and was a man.

Her gown was sacking. She held it in a bundle round her so that only her feet and strong legs were wetted by the green water. She was as old as the ship. A piece of fine canvas, the colour of the ship's sail, was wound round her head and blackly on it, where it wrapped her forehead, was burned the only message she had for the hundred and five: "I am a Daughter of the Lamb."

Where the water slapped the beach, she let her skirts drop. General Almarlyes scratched himself and looked about to see if the hundred and four were afraid. Many of them were retreating slowly, limb by limb, leaving the wounded behind, creeping backwards away from her to where the undergrowth began. They were no longer wailing. Hope had died in them as quickly as it had arrived and fear had returned. So General Almarlyes struggled to his feet. Through one of the rents in his uniform, his sex, grey with sand, gaped vulnerably. It swung, almost imperceptibly, as he spoke now with all that was left of a voice that had once roused a continent to war:

"Bourton-on-the-Water!" he shouted. "Ashton-under-Lyme! And never, never forget it, as you cowards retreat, Stoke-upon-Trent!"

No one laughed. The hundred and four were motionless, transfixed by the words of the madness of General Almarlyes in that motionless morning. So he held wide his arms and walked, as boldly as he could, to the water's edge, and very slowly they followed him. Many could not walk, not as General Almarlyes could walk. Many had to be carried or helped along. Yet they all followed. And now there was a line of them moving slowly, slowly towards the ship. For half an hour the birds returned and hovered no more than thirty feet above the line. But by midday the ship had swallowed the line and pulled in its barnacled anchor and the bay was deserted. The merchant crabs reclaimed the beach and began to burrow in new places.'

Ralph's reading was interrupted by a knock at his door. A polite uniformed boy, the uniform too large for his slight frame, held out a letter and an apologetic smile.

'I'm so sorry, sir. This letter came for you this morning and was put in 261's pigeon-hole by mistake. Reception asked me to bring it up to you.'

Ralph smiled and took the letter, fumbled automatically for some cash in his trouser pocket and then remembered he was wearing pyjamas.

'Hold on,' he said to the boy. The boy waited. Fifteen, sixteen . . . Ralph pondered the boy's age as he searched for money . . . and learning the terrible sleepless hotel trade from the bottom up, all other education forgotten . . . Ralph found thirty pence and had handed it to the boy before he had worked out the relative fairness of the tip in dollars and cents. Then the boy was gone and he was alone with his letter.

Ralph had been moved, as he always was, by the appalling General Almarlyes with his flagging sex and his failing sanity. General Almarlyes was one of his favourite characters in fiction, utterly corrupt, worthy undoubtedly of his extraordinary end, yet redeemed for the reader by his constant search for dignity and by his dreams of being some other man, a man with a thick head of hair and a virgin heart. He began to wonder whether he might come to know one day soon where Erica March had 'found' General Almarlyes.

The letter was postmarked Oxford. Noticing this, Ralph regretted the thirty pence he had given the boy: it seemed miserly. Only one person ever wrote to him from Oxford, with anecdotes about his contented, protected life and offers of rooms if Ralph should ever find himself in England – John Pennington.

John Pennington had done an M.A. in Modern American Literature during Ralph's last year at U.C.L.A. Whenever Ralph thought about that Californian summer – which he seldom did, because his parents belonged to L.A. now and he vowed he'd never go back there – he thought inevitably about John Pennington.

Before leaving New York, Ralph had written to John, really his only friend in England, telling him about his assignment, asking him for some time and giving the address of his hotel. No answer had arrived and the notion that John couldn't be bothered to see him had contributed – unspoken – to Ralph's feelings of dereliction.

The letter was short, characteristic of John's muted style, and in many ways disappointing. But at least it was there:

Worcester College,
Oxford

Sunday evening.
'Dear Ralph,

How nice to get your long letter and to know that you are planning another trip. Indeed of course you are *here* by now, I see from the date, and I must apologize for not replying before you left.

The reason is I am terribly busy, although that isn't the right word – "distracted" I think is more appropriate – writing a book. I believe I mentioned to you in my last letter that I felt dredged by my work on the Metaphysical Poets and I think I must leave them now. I truly thought I would do something on Blake next, but his extraordinary fires don't seem to kindle mine, not *enough,* so I have turned layman and am dementedly writing a novel! Heaven knows if I can succeed.

Yes, you are right I'm sure: Erica March is an important novelist, and has been neglected because she's been silent for so long. *The Hospital Ship* made her famous but my favourite is *In the Blind Man's City.* Good luck with her. She may be too old to say anything important or interesting now.

We must arrange at least an evening before you go back. Would you be free to come and see me here? It's not that I'm afraid of the rail fare but I've promised myself I shall work a little on the novel every day and London would be a ghastly interruption. Don't I sound mean? But I know you'll understand and will journey here to see me, if you can. I can arrange a room.

Yours affectionately,
John'

Ralph read the letter twice, imagining John in a cold room that he had never seen, listening to clocks chime and afternoons pass, writing on and on in his ordered hand, neatly crossing out, rephrasing, leaving off only to eat or sleep, a total absorption. And with this image of John he contrasted his own monkeyish swings and leaps to and from fear: hand never steady unless with the Marlboro pack, sleep becoming elusive, uncanny longing to possess a firearm . . . only with Erica, in her actual presence, Ralph thought, is my mind still.

Ralph got back into bed and picked up *The Hospital Ship* again. He decided to use John Pennington's letter as a bookmark in it, so that he wouldn't lose the letter, and would remember to telephone John as soon as he felt he had made some real progress and could leave London for a day or two. He read until sleep began to touch him. He read how the fifty Daughters of the Lamb came out like ghosts from the depths of the ship and stood with their arms round the hundred and five, whispering to them that the Lamb had sent a wind and the wind had blown the mercy ship to the island and now they would begin the long voyage home. Home to where? some of the limbless and sightless asked. Home to where? But the Daughters of the Lamb couldn't – wouldn't – say, because each of the hundred and five, including General Almarlyes, would travel at his own pace and some would find home before others and some might never find it. And it was then that General Almarlyes noticed his exposed grey penis for the first time since he had sighted the ship and in a very humble voice that no one recognized, asked for it to be covered up.

'I'm so sorry, Ralph,' said Erica, as he went in, 'I was going to tell you so much yesterday and then I just went to sleep. It was dark when I woke up and you'd gone.'

'That's okay,' said Ralph.

The wine was in its place. A black turban with an amethyst brooch stuck into it had replaced the red one. Erica was feeling strong.

'Now, about Chadwick,' she said, 'he never heard from Athelstone again and this was all to the good of course because had he sent postcards, or anything like that, Chadwick's heartbreak would have been unfairly prolonged and as it was he did try, after a fortnight or so of weeping and prostration, to get about again on his poor legs and I could have written to my father and told him I would soon be home, but by then it was too late. For I followed Emily, after that. Not to her death but all the way up to her death and past it. And I don't know to this day what bound me to the movement so utterly. I believe it was the kind of movement to which you were either bound utterly or not at all.

'In Suffolk, on the farm, I hadn't thought much about what Chadwick continued to call the Woman Question. I suppose I didn't even know about the terrible unfair wages and the divorce laws and all the limitations imposed on women so that they were banned from following almost all the professions and had to be content with what they had – and what they had was pitifully little, not even the right to own property if they were married and of course not even the right to vote! But I couldn't see all this, not before I came to London. My world had been so tiny, the world of the rogation and the harvest. I was, as Chadwick said to the Pethick Lawrences, a child of ignorance.

'Emily Davison changed me.

' "The time is now, Erica!" she said, "the struggle is now and if it is not joined now then the movement will be lost and we shall have failed. Let history not write of us that we failed!" Oh she said the most extraordinary things! I felt her words going into my body. They poured into me and I shook. Her favourite motto was "Rebellion against tyrants is obedience to God" and I have often thought of it

38

through my life and let it lead me on, except that I soon had to substitute "humanity" for "God" because I lost my belief in Emily's God, long ago. Or perhaps I never really had it.

'It was June and Emily had been in Holloway since February. During those months she had tried to die twice by throwing herself over the prison balcony and then down some iron stairs, yet she was such an odd companion for death, so touchingly alive. And she hardly spoke of her suffering. She only told me how each one of us who joined the struggle would be "set apart" (apart from what I had no idea but being "set apart" sounded wonderful, *wonderful* and I remembered my father's cows, Primrose and Clover, and I thought, never again will they kick me or shit onto my boots because now I am "set apart"). Little did I know that in two years I'd be back with the cows and Emily would be dead and all the world at war and the women's vote forgotten.

'I had to prove to Emily that I dared to be "set apart." I read that night in the paper she gave me, the *Suffragette,* that "members of the W.S.P.U. are showing a heroism unsurpassed at any time in the world's history" and I determined to join in and defy fortune and face death and so I went to Chadwick and asked him to give me the subscription money for the W.S.P.U., which naturally he did. Yet I was afraid to do anything without Emily. I was afraid to go down to Lincoln's Inn and actually join up. The issues were wide, you see; I didn't really understand about Conciliation Bills or Cat and Mouse Acts – not then, I was rather like an ignorant soldier who leaves his family to go to war and yet he barely knows what he's fighting for. There were many of these, weren't there, in 1914, who joined up with patriotic ecstasy, without ever knowing why, and I was one of them in 1912. All I had was Emily and her words. I suppose she understood this– my terrible ignorance – because she came back a few days later and together we went to Lincoln's Inn where I met Mrs Pankhurst for the first time. The morning I left to go to Lincoln's Inn Chadwick wrote to my father. He said work had been found for me, part time in a reputable tea-shop in Bond Street.

'It was a very beautiful day, I remember, and Emily and I were both dressed in brown which was an odd coincidence and I kept thinking, I wish she was my sister. Why haven't I got a wonderful elder sister like Emily? And on the bus I told her about my mother's death and she put her arm through mine.

'It was my first love affair. Never expressed, of course, nothing sexual. I expressed it in what I did for the movement, in the fires I lit and in my shouting. I don't even know if Emily was aware of it – aware that what I did, I did not for the thousands in the sweat shop, but for her, and then afterwards for her memory. It wasn't difficult to suffer, not once I had begun. I was twenty – almost twenty – and very strong. Even the hunger striking, when we did this in protest at our treatment in Holloway and then again at Strangeways, I could endure it and not be weakened, not very much. Only my dreams, I remember, were extraordinary during the hunger strikes: they were very powerfully sexual and I was ashamed of them and wanted to cry, and I think these dreams weakened me a little.

'We were forcibly fed of course and this was disgusting – an outrage. They'd come in, wardresses and doctors, and the doctors would force terrible steel things into our mouths to hold them open and these steel things tore the gums and bruised our lips and were a terrible invention like all weapons of torture. And then they'd pour some kind of gruel down our throats, the sort of awful stuff Oliver Twist asked for more of and the choking feeling of this gruel going down into your stomach was one of the worst things I can remember. It was impossible to endure it and I always vomited it up over my prison clothes. I dreaded the forced feeding. Strong as I was, I dreaded this and I don't think there were any of us who didn't dread it because I often heard the screams of the others and the retching.

'Asquith was our enemy. I'd never even seen him, but I imagined him, in his wing collar. He was a cunning and clever man. He understood injustice but he balanced injustice against expediency and expediency always won. He was no worse, I suppose, than the politicians of any era, but to us he was the Devil.

'We wanted to truss him up and roast him, and really when you think of it hundreds of politicians should have been trussed up and roasted and instead we've made statues of them in bronze. Power corrupts – always and inevitably. Power within the movement corrupted Mrs Pankhurst, in a way. She was brave, my word, but she wanted all the glory for herself and Christabel. She distrusted even the Pethick Lawrences and threw them out of W.S.P.U. despite all that they'd done and in time she came to distrust Emily. She feared martrys because they steal the limelight, and she knew that Emily was in love with death.

40

'My poor dear Emily! If I believed in God – which I don't at all, Ralph – I suppose I'd be thinking, soon I shall see you, Emily, just as you were that day in Chadwick's rooms, with your smile and your green dress. I'd imagine us going for a walk arm in arm and I could tell her, couldn't I, what they were like – all the years I've lived since then? What rubbish, eh! She's dust under Morpeth.'

Erica straightened her turban and leant back. Ralph now recognized in these little movements her way of saying I've had enough for now, I can't say any more, so he switched off his recorder and leant forward to pour her a glass of wine. Then he felt her hand touch his shoulder and he looked up. She had bent down and was looking at him intently.

'I tried to mention something to you the other day, Ralph. But I wasn't strong enough that day. It's only a little thing, a kind of superstition, and I want to ask you a favour.'

'Please do,' said Ralph.

'I don't know,' said Erica, 'if you'll be the one to carry it out, but I think you may be. I've been waiting for someone like you to come along, you see. A stranger. It had to be a stranger!'

And Erica laughed, 'I'm terribly superstitious now that I'm old. I worry about the positioning of the moon behind a certain building! So stupid!

'And you see . . . I had a kind of dream, a vision almost, quite recently that if I could be sure to organize death in a certain way, in a certain place, then I might be given a little more time, not as me of course and I wouldn't want to be me all over again, but as *something*, Ralph, something that has existence – a beetle or a camel I think, one of these two. And I could live for quite a time as a beetle in a pine forest perhaps and even longer as a camel, and I'd see the desert at last, which I've never seen. But it will only happen if my death is the right one . ... and I'll know the day because they'll be signs . . .'

'I don't really want you to talk about death,' said Ralph and he fingered his tape recorder protectively.

'Whyever not?' snapped Erica.

'I don't want to imagine your death.'

She looked crestfallen. 'I'm very disappointed,' she said, 'I'd convinced myself that you were the right one.'

'For what?'

'For all the organization, dear. For the fight with Camden Council or whoever's responsible for these things. And of course I would have given you power. I'll write it all out. You only have to follow instructions.'

Ralph sighed. 'Please Erica,' he said, 'you haven't finished telling me about Emily. Please can't we go on and not talk about your death?'

She sniffed. 'Certainly we can go on. But we'll have to discuss it one day soon, or you'll be gone, won't you, and my chance to become a camel will be lost.'

That night, in his faded yellow room, Ralph dreamt that he was driving down from New York to Tennessee in a rented car to visit his grandma. The car was an ancient Oldsmobile and he knew, precisely, at which point on the road the car would break down.

He was in the mountains, on the road from Bristol to Knoxville, with miles of mountain roads uncompleted, little hope of a lift, no water and no shelter from the freezing late afternoon except the car. He sat in the car and put his head on the wheel. The wheel became spongy and soft under his forehead and he let himself fall forwards, let the comforting wheel absorb tears of rage and tears of fear. He wanted to hit the wheel and feel its hardness hurt his hand, but it was entirely soft, and soon very soothing to his hand, so he let his hand touch it and begin to stroke it and his fear receded.

He was aware, after a while, that the car was moving again, quite slowly and absolutely silently and when, wearily, he lifted his head from the soft wheel and turned, he saw that someone was pushing the car, straining and pushing the big old car along the mountain road in the dusk. He stared at the figure pushing the car. The figure was running now, trying to keep up with the car as it gathered momentum and finally letting go as it careered on and on down the steep track. Its speed was terrifying. Ralph grabbed the wheel but the wheel was limp and wouldn't steer the car. The car careered towards a curve in the road and Ralph felt it lift it off into the void and saw death, like a bird, begin to gather him in its wide wing.

Ralph woke and he was sweating. He reached out and put on the light. He lay very still, trying to calm the beating of his heart with deep breaths. But the dream wouldn't leave him. It wouldn't leave him because it was unfinished. He wanted – *needed* – to know who had been there on the road, pushing the car. Detail by detail, he tried to recall the shape, size, even the sex of the person running behind and eventually falling back as the car had sped on. But he could remember nothing. Only a grey figure, stooping and then falling, surely? Hadn't the figure fallen down into the dust at the moment when he/she had let go of the car, fallen and lain motionless as the car began to soar above the trees?

For an hour or more, Ralph searched. He imagined the road, exactly as it had been in the dream. He put himself back on the road and started to climb to the point where the car had stopped and then started to move. He recognized the road and the rocks and trees which bordered it. He imagined the exact quality of the light: flat and chill with night coming on. And he knew when he reached the spot where the car had been. He *knew*. But there was no sign of anyone. Nobody was waiting. Nobody lay in the dust. 'Jesus,' whispered Ralph, and sat up. It was half past five.

He ran cold water into his washbasin and splashed it over his face. His hands were shaking. He filled a glass and drank. 'Tell you why we don't like you white 'mericans,' said a laughing black face, 'you give the poor guy his wet dreams!'

Ralph walked to the writing table. He turned down the volume control on his tape recorder and punched the 'play' button: '.. and the burning and destruction of property!' came the artificially muted but still urgent voice. 'Because property – and respect for it – was the bedrock of Liberal England and what Mrs Pankhurst called "the argument of the well-aimed stone" was the one we chose. Because words and pleas had failed by 1912, or so they told me, the ones who knew. All the promises had been broken.

'Emily and I had a speciality we called the "pillar box cocktail". We wrapped petrol-soaked rags in newspaper and hid them in our big handbags. Then we stuffed them into the slit where you posted your letter and pushed them in. We lit them by means of a piece of string, down which the flame travelled, like a fuse. Sometimes it didn't work. The flame went out before it got to the rags, but mostly they went off like a bomb and you had to be out of sight by then.

'We destroyed hundreds – probably thousands – of letters in this way, and the post in London became very erratic. Chadwick wasn't keen on this. He began to say that letters he was expecting didn't arrive because I'd burned them. But I don't suppose I had. I expect

43

the people to whom Chadwick wrote didn't care enough about him to write back.

'He was better by the end of the year. His swellings went down and he visited me in Holloway and brought me a lardy cake made by Mrs Hogan. I had to explain to him that I couldn't eat it because we were all on hunger strike, and he said, "thought you looked terrible my poor child. For God's sake don't die of it, or we'd have to tell your father." But my father never knew. He was courting Eileen by that time and couldn't let his mind travel further than Aldeburgh, where Eileen lived.

'It was strange, I suppose, that he didn't know what I was doing; very sad that I couldn't tell him. I often thought of him, but my lie put a distance between us and we were never close again, not as we had been, as long as he lived. Rumours came to Suffolk, he told me later, that I had joined the Suffragettes. Someone thought they'd seen my face in a picture of a meeting not far from Christabel Pankhurst's. But of course I said nothing in my letters. I said things like "London is very agreeable and I am learning the ways of it."

'It was a kind of apprenticeship for a time that came later. "Agreeable" wasn't at all the right word for it. Not at all. It was a kind of immersion in fire, but I didn't feel the fire, Ralph, didn't know I was in it, till the next summer, and then I felt it.

'You see, I hadn't really believed that Emily would die. She'd often talked about death and done things in prison to make people believe she wanted it. And she often said that what the movement needed was a martyr. But she wasn't a melancholy woman, not at all. She laughed very often. And her eyes were bright like an animal's eyes. And she had promised to be my teacher and help me to grow up. I couldn't believe she would abandon me. There was no meanness in her.

'We spent Christmas 1913 together with Emily's mother at Longhorsley. We were both on bail, I think, awaiting trial for our pillar box cocktails, but it was a wonderfully happy time in spite of this. The weather was clear and clean and we went for long walks in the beautiful beech woods and in the evenings Emily would play and sing. She loved hymns and she sang very well. I think she always believed that God saw and understood her and I suppose, over the months that followed this time, when we were in and out of prison and very weak, she came to believe that God was waiting for her and that nothing, not even the woods at Longhorsley, could be as beautiful as death.

'So she abandoned me and went to try and meet God. For a while it was terrible to know that she preferred God to me. But I hope she did meet Him. She wanted it so badly!

'I was at the Lincoln's Inn office on the morning of Derby Day. I was helping with letters and filing which I often did and I found I was rather good at this kind of meticulous work. I liked the smell of an office. Paper is such a clean thing.

'Emily rushed in to the office, in a great hurry, asking us for flags with the Union colours on them. We found two for her and she ran out. I knew she was excited about something and I wanted to go with her – to share in it. But of course I couldn't share in it. I wasn't ready for death, as Emily well knew. I could never sense God, not even then, as she seemed to sense Him.

'And the rest is known. There is even a photograph of Emily tangled with the horse, and when I look at this I want to rage and weep, because no one is *looking* at her, Ralph! She was dying there and then, yet no one looked. They were all looking at the other horses. And sometimes I feel that this whole episode of my life is captured in that photograph: we were trying to change our world and the world looked the other way.'

3

'You look worried, dear,' said Erica as Ralph sat down.

'Do I?'

'Yes.'

'I'm okay.'

'What are you worried about?'

'Oh, well, I guess I've been thinking a lot about my herbs . . .'

'Your herbs?'

'Yeah. I meant to ask the guy across the hallway to water them while I was away. I meant to give him a key. But I forgot.'

'You grow herbs indoors? I used to do that in the war, to make things taste of something.'

'No. They're on my sill.'

'Then why should they die? It rains in America, doesn't it?'

Ralph smiled. 'Sure, it rains. But the sill is too protected from the weather by the balcony above. The rain doesn't get to them much. Or the sun either. They grow looking north.'

'What kind of herbs are they?'

'Oh, oregano and sage and parsley and tarragon . . .'

'And you cook with them? You like cooking, do you?'

'Yeah. I like cooking.'

Erica took off her glasses and rubbed her eyes. 'Men used to be so frightened of domestic things!' she said. 'Bernard thought his balls would shrivel if he peeled an onion – till I told him otherwise. And then he got quite interested in cooking. But all that old-fashioned thinking is changing. Women have said, "Enough's enough." Yet some of them are like barnacles, still. Clinging to safety and possessions. Now, if I was young, Ralph, I'd say to myself: "Here it *is*! Eve's unimaginable morning!" And I wouldn't let my spirit be

46

shredded by kitchen things. But possessions are our weakness. I really think men care less about them and will therefore always be more free than we are. I've tried to live my life without them, yet, I haven't totally succeeded! You see, I'm very fond of my lamp which cost a lot of money. I talk to it and say: "You are very, very beautiful." So you see? I'm not exempt. And of course the cupboard, which is all that was ever left of my mother, and I will never be parted from it. I suppose I'm entitled to love a few things, now that I'm old. But if I was a girl, I wouldn't waste my time collecting *things.'*

'If you were a girl, what would you be doing?'

'What would I be doing? Oh Lord knows dear. I might be paddling a dugout up the Zambesi River, or I might be sitting on my bum with the Venerable Bede or someone in the Bodleian Library. I don't know! At least I wouldn't be in a Discount Centre. I'd like to burn them all down, those places!'

Ralph laughed and Erica laughed with him. Then Ralph let his laughter subside and asked the question that had been inside him ever since the first day: 'When did you start writing, Erica, and why?'

She was silent. The red turban was on again and she put a hand up and touched it.

'I had to start . . .' she said, after a while. "During the First War I started, when I went back to my father's house and found it so changed and him so changed. I think I wrote to stop myself going mad.'

'Was it the war?'

'No. The war was going on of course, but we were left behind. And what the war left behind was terrible for me. So I began *The Two Wives of the King,* which was a kind of fable about stupidity and waste, and it came out of what I saw and lived through on the farm with my father and Eileen.'

'Why did you go home, Erica?'

'Duty, Ralph. I didn't have much of a sense of duty, but I had a little. And when war was declared, the Women's Movement foundered, you see. Germany robbed us of our enemy. We couldn't fight the government of England when England was at war – though of course I saw later that we should have done. We should have gone on. But we didn't. We folded away our sashes and rolled up our banners and just dispersed like mice. And with the vote still not won! It was so wrong. But patriotism stiffled us. We knew we were finished.

47

'So I sat up all one night with Chadwick. He was very dapper by that time with a new lover called Robin, far too mortal and frail to shoulder a kit bag and therefore safe from the Western Front – or so he and Chadwick thought. And Chadwick said prophetically: "Women will be needed on the land, Erica, because all the young men will go hurtling into the recruiting centres. They'll all go. And how will your father manage if he can't get labour at harvest time?"

'I told Chadwick I didn't want to go. I said I would get a job in a factory in London and start to pay him rent for my room. Because I felt, you see Ralph, that my life had begun the day I came to London and in two years I had lost the part of me that belonged to Suffolk. Even my Suffolk accent had gone, more or less. And my room in Chadwick's flat; I looked at it and thought, I don't want to leave it – it's *mine*.

'I cried that night. I cried for Emily. I cried for the terrible war that was beginning and I cried for myself. I think I knew I would be unhappy when I went home. And Chadwick knew. He kept promising me that I could come to London to see him whenever I wanted to and he would make sure Mrs Hogan made something special. He was trying to be loyal to his brother, though. He knew I had to go.

'I remember that this Robin person arrived very early in the morning and found Chadwick and me sitting at the dining table, exhausted and weeping and he burst out laughing and gave us each a silk handkerchief and Chadwick looked very embarrassed and said to Robin: "Aberration, dear one. Aberration of the heart." But I cried on into the silk handkerchief, on and on until I realized I was alone so I put my head on the table and went to sleep.

'I didn't weigh much. All the strength I'd had from working on the land had gone in prison. I was very thin and white and a bit weak, even though Mrs Hogan had been trying to build me up. Small things frightened me. Things which never would have frightened me before. The journey, for instance. I dreaded that journey home, Ralph. I dreaded it with all my heart. So I did a strange thing. I wrote to Gully. I told him I would be coming home on the train on a certain day and asked him not to tell my father, but to come and meet me and, if he could, let me stay with him and Dot and the little child, Buckwheat, ior a few days, until I felt strong enough to go home. I had often thought of Gully, you see, and hoped he was

48

"getting on" as they say in Suffolk, in his trade. I missed him now and then with his big old head and his hair like a bull's forelock and his laugh. I missed Gully far more than I missed my father because Chadwick had become a father to me and I shared all my secrets with him.

'Gully's reply has stayed in my mind all these years. "This war be some terrible thing Erica," he said, "and you be best out of it." I think Gully thought that part of the war was going on in Bryanston Square! Perhaps he had dreams of the Hun sailing up the Thames in a gunboat! I laughed when I got his note. I knew that he, at least, hadn't changed.

'But why did I go to him? I saw him as a "safe house", I think. I knew I wouldn't have to lie to him, not to Gully. I could just say to him, this is how it's been, Gully, and I don't expect you to understand it, but I know you won't think badly of me and I know you will help me.

'He was at the very far end of the little station. He held his cap in his hands, as if he was at a funeral. He looked very neat and tidy. I think he'd dressed up for me, with a clean shirt. I clambered down with my luggage – all the new clothes dear Chadwick had paid for – and I ran to Gully and threw my arms round him and put my head on his rough jacket and cried. It must have been terribly puzzling for Gully! He'd hardly changed in two years but to him I was a different person: he couldn't recognize me.

'Dot and Buckwheat weren't there. Dot's father had died and she'd taken the little boy to Ipswich to her mother's, to be company for her. So Gully and I were quite alone in his little place above the shop. We were very shy, I remember. The years we'd been together didn't seem to help us. So I started to tell Gully about meeting Emily and joining the Suffragettes and then about going to prison. And he couldn't believe I'd done all this. "I don't know," he kept saying. "I don't know at all . . ."

'We drank his home-made cider and had a little meal – a stew that was mainly vegetables – and when it was time for sleep I asked him if I could come and lie in his bed. I told him I felt very cold, which I did, and I think all I wanted was for him to hold me and let me go to sleep close to him. Of course, I suppose if I'm honest, I'd begun to think of those seventeen times and my evening in the cupboard and somehow, after all that I'd done, to be a virgin still was strange and I was fed up

49

with it. So I expect I was asking for it and never gave a thought, you see, for Gully's loyalty to Dot or anything like that. I never even considered it and I daresay this was very wrong of me. But there it was. He took me and my virginity was gone and I felt a wonderful joy. Gully made love to me three times that night and the weight and size of him was like no other man I've ever met. Then the next day I left, and we've never talked of it again as long as we've lived.'

There was no wine. Only some fresh lemonade which Erica had made herself, and she asked Ralph to pour some out. As he handed her the drink she said: 'They paid me, you know, your magazine, to do all this talking. It's very nice of them. Don't you think?'

'Hers is just one life,' Ralph wrote on page two of his Summary. 'Pointless, perhaps, to imagine that this life, given me second hand and most of it lived in another era, can really help me make sense of mine. Erica's sympathy will not revive my dead herbs.

'Question one, then: "Why have I attached so much importance to this assignment?"

'Question two: "What am I actually hoping for?"

'Because aside from asking questions, I do absolutely nothing. I listen. I get confusing dreams. I remember Grandma a lot, and Joe Beale across my landing, damn it, with his Nina Simone records but no key to my door. Two of my teeth are hurting like hell and celibacy is becoming a pain. Think I must get hold of a) a dentist, and b) a girl.'

Ralph abandoned the Summary. An hour later, he was walking urgently towards South Kensington in search of a taxi. Three hours and forty pounds later he was floating on the red velvet heat of a banquette at *Mr Toad's,* a club where once before he had found a skinny girl twice his height to go reeling home with, skinny English girl with good teeth and thin hair and a body that stayed ramrod straight under his exhausted passion, giving and feeling nothing.

'I came to avenge myself,' he found himself saying, 'to find vengeance on the very very bitter English and unmoving eye . . .' No one seemed to hear him, yet after a moment he was aware of something warm on his mouth and he reached up and it was a hand. He pulled the hand away and saw that it belonged to a well-shaped brown arm. He followed the arm and saw beside him on the red banquette a smiling brown girl.

'Pearl . . .' he mumbled.

The girl smiled and smiled. The shoulder straps of her dress were diamante and blinded him. He leant back and examined the girl, squinting in the light of the shoulder straps.

He wanted to ask her how long she'd been there and whether she was staying or going, staying or going . . . the two words were like a see-saw in his head, unutterable.

'Pearl . . .' he said again.

'Pearl Bailey?' said the girl. 'You that old, honey?'

'No, no, no, no, no, no . . .' said Ralph.

Staying or going, staying or going, staying or going . . .?

'Have some more champagne,' said Pearl.

'Sure.'

The girl poured and Ralph drank. Time was a high wheel, way above existence. He let his hands caress the girl's plump shoulders, the pushed-up tits . . . staying or going, staying or going?

'Oh Pearl . . .' he said and it was a wail.

'C'mon honey. What's so sad?'

'Staying or going?' He said it at last. The see-saw began to slow down, the shoulder straps streamed back into focus. Ralph had a clear and coherent thought: my teeth have stopped hurting.

'Up to you,' said Pearl.

'Up to me?'

'You wanna take me back. Have some treats, eh?'

Yes he did. Yes he did. She was beautiful. The smell of her was an unction. No one could take her from him. He had waited years for her. Pearl.

'I love you Pearl,' he said, 'I'd like to lay my head down . . .'

'C'mon baby. Let's go, eh?'

'Sure.'

'Let's go have some fun.'

'Sure.'

He was falling. Wasn't he? Of course he was falling from the barn roof . . . 'Hey!' The voice was sharp and cross. Someone pushed him and he was upright. But the longing to fall down wouldn't leave him. He had to let go of the ridge and fall and fall . . .

'No!' said the voice.

'Yes,' he said, 'please let me, Pearl. . . please. . .'

'Shit!' said the voice. But the fall was beautiful. The morning sun was warm on his back and the ground drew him gently inwards and covered him.

*

'I'm very worried about Ralph,' said Erica to Mrs Burford. 'He's always here by two and it's ten past three.'

'I wouldn't worry,' said Mrs Burford.

'Well why wouldn't you? It's so unlike him.'

'Could be anyfing, couldn't it?'

'What d'you think it could be?'

'Well. Could be the Ayatollah.'

'The Ayatollah?'

'Well. Yer Americans now. They're targets, 'nt they? For yer Persians, or whatever they calls themselves now. I'd say 'e's been took 'ostage.'

Erica poured herself a glass of wine and sat silently waiting.

At four, just as Mrs Burford was leaving, Ralph appeared at the door. Mrs Burford winked at him as she passed him. 'Thought they'd got you this time an' all!' she said.

He was very white and his hands holding the recorder and notepad shook. He made a gesture of despair as he came into the room.

'I'm sorry, Erica. I've just wasted your time . . .'

'Your *time*. You're the busy one, Ralph. I've got nothing to do.'

'I'm really sorry . . .'

'Mrs Burford thought you'd been kidnapped.'

'Did she? Yes. Well I was in a way. By my own idiocies. I got plastered.'

Erica smiled. 'Do you feel terrible?'

'Yes. More or less.'

'Do you want to go home again?'

'No. I'd like to stay for a bit.'

'Well poor you, Ralph. I wonder why you got drunk?'

Ralph shrugged. 'Lonely, I guess.'

'Were you? Don't you have friends here to see in the evenings?'

'I've got one friend. He's in Oxford.'

'But none here?'

'No. Not really.'

'So you feel lonely, do you?'

'Sometimes. I guess.'

'You miss New York?'

'In a way. I've been lonely there too a bit.'

'Cities, you see. They've become terrible really, don't you think?'

'They're dirty.'

'It's not just that. They've become so empty-hearted.'

'Yup.'

'London more than any. I sometimes think I ought to leave it, but I know I won't. Not now.'

'Where would you go if you did leave it?'

'Where would I go? I don't know Ralph. Perhaps if I was younger, I'd go to Africa.'

Ralph smiled. 'To Africa?'

'Yes. To the desert.'

'It's full of oil wells and petro-chemical waste dumps.'

'It's not, is it? *All* the desert?'

'I guess not all.'

'Well I'd go to a bit that was empty.'

'What about Paris? Didn't you live in Paris for a while?'

'Oh Paris. Yes. I lived there for ten years! But it chokes me, I find. I was too happy there ever to be happy there again.'

'So here you stay. In London.'

'Yes. Here I stay. Do you know I'm fifty-eight years older than the Festival Hall?'

Ralph went to the kitchen and made himself a strong cup of tea. He brought it back to Erica's room and sat silently warming his hands on it.

Erica watched him.

'D'you want to tell me about your drunken evening,' she said after a while, 'or is it best forgotten?'

'It is forgotten. I just can't remember what happened, how I got to bed, anything . . . it's all very vague. I had a kind of fantasy about a girl I once knew called Pearl, but that's all I remember.'

'Pearl? What a beautiful name. Will you tell me about her?'

'Oh no. I don't really want to, Erica. She was years and years ago. I'd rather get on . . .'

'Why don't you talk today and I'll listen?'

'Oh shit no.'

'Why not?'

'I'm too fogged. I couldn't get any thoughts out.'

'Couldn't you try?'

'No I can't. Honestly.'

'What about your herbs, Ralph. Have you found out about them? Did you telephone?'

53

'Oh no. I guess they're dead. Now look, can we get on, Erica? I had a cable this morning – this afternoon or whenever – from Walt who's my boss, and he's threatening to cut my time in London.'

'Is he? What did he say?'

'Oh some bullshit. Something about something cropping up. So I may only have another week or so.'

'Do you want me to go faster? Am I saying everything too slowly?'

'No.'

'I could miss out things.'

'No. I don't want you to miss anything out. Really I don't. Can you tell me about going home today at the beginning of the war and about starting your book ?'

'About beginning my book?'

'Yes. And about Eileen?'

'I didn't begin my book straight away.'

'No?'

'No. It was autumn – the autumn of 1914 – when I went home and I think I began the book that winter, the first winter of the war. It was terribly difficult, you know, to understand the war, from where we were. I used to lie awake and try to imagine it – the noise of the big guns and Englishmen trudging along French roads in straggly lines, with their bully beef and their chilblains. I could imagine them, but I didn't know what they were doing there! I didn't understand alliances.

'As the war went on, more and more changes came – even to Suffolk. There was a lot of "requisitioning" which is a word I hate because it just means taking for very little money and you have no redress. They took the men of course, all the young men of whatever class except Gully who I suppose would have looked untidy in a parade with his head sticking out sideways, and they took our horses in time, hundreds of them. And I tell you one funny thing that happened. A neighbour of ours, "li'l ol' boy Dawson" we called him, he lost all his houses to the requisitioning under the D.O.R.A. and couldn't work his plough. He only had two or three fields to plough, that was all the land he had but even one field – you can't plough it without an animal. So d'you know what he did? He harnessed his two fat sows to the plough. He made a special collar for them and they pulled the plough for him. What a sight – to see those pigs going round and round! But they did it, and Dawson got his harvest in.

And I've often thought, that was exactly how life was then – funny and cruel: pigs pulling the plough and old men following after.

'But now there were two women in our house – Eileen and me. The house was full, *full* of Eileen's belongings, so that when I first went into it, I thought this isn't our house.

'The night I arrived, Eileen cooked trout and we ate our trout with pearl-handled fishknives, and the kitchen table was spread with a white damask tablecloth. There were two framed samplers hanging up by the kitchen range and one said "The Lord Giveth" and the other one said "The Lord Taketh Away". And of course this is exactly what had happened in our house. God had given us this new bric-a-brac and fishknives and, in return, he'd taken away our old ways. There'll be a private war, I thought.

'I ought to describe Eileen. She was a very neat woman who smelled of soap. She was forty-five but well preserved. I expect the soap had preserved her. She didn't like to be touched, not by me, not by the animals, not even by my father – or so it seemed because whenever he did touch her she'd brush him away like a fleck of dust. She hardly ever smiled, but when she did, you saw that she had excellent teeth, as hard and shiny as the handles of the knives. And her heart was hard. It never softened up. I just couldn't understand how my father could have replaced my mother so carelessly. Yet I had to remind myself that he had been on his own without a wife for fifteen years, and of course I should have rejoiced for him and for Eileen too, who had never been married, yet who had collected all these possessions as a kind of dowry. But I couldn't rejoice. I went to my old room and opened the cupboard. I half expected the cupboard to be full of Eileen's hats or boxes of linen but it wasn't; it was just as it had always been with some of my mother's clothes in it and some of mine. So I crawled in among the dust and the soft skirts and rocked myself.

'I hurt inside, from my grand lovemaking with Gully, and I was afraid of what was to come.

'There was work to be done on the farm, I could see that. With the young men beginning to go, we who were left on the land had to care for it. We knew shortages would come and of course they did. We knew we were lucky to own land and animals. I kept wondering what Chadwick would do in London if the shortages became severe. I imagined him saying to Robin: "Now look, dear heart, imports from Russia don't seem to be getting through: no caviar to be seen anywhere!" I missed Chadwick, his little bits of wit and his thirst for what he called "culture", even his search for love. My father had gone so silent you see. He let Eileen give orders, orders, always orders: "The house is my province", she'd say, "I've lived in a town long enough to know how a good house should be kept and far too long to take to farm work. I warned your father when I married him – animals have their place in God's world and so do I and that place isn't the same and never will be."

'I was up at five, milking. I began to pity the cows for their prison shed. A new calf was born in February and I called her Emily. "We heard you were mixed up with her and her like," Eileen said, "and your father agreed with me, there's no sense to any of that vote nonsense. I don't know what women think they're doing, going against God and Nature like that! We put it down to your age and we wouldn't hear a word spoken against you, would we, Geoffrey? But of course we couldn't condone it." My father was silent, always so silent. All he said was, "You're home now and that's the greatest blessing of the war."

'We were "told" (I don't know who by – it could have been Mr Asquith or Lloyd George or Lord Northcliffe or anyone) that the war would be over by Christmas. I can't imagine why they thought that! I suppose they just pictured one mighty cavalry charge and the Germans scuttling back through Belgium as fast as they'd come. I don't believe they ever envisaged trenches. Or if they did, they certainly didn't tell the volunteers, "You'll sit down in France, lads, in the mud and that's what you'll do!"

'The young men who went believed in glory. They got on their trains grinning. My father regretted that he was too old to fight: he said if he was twenty he'd show the Hun a thing or two. And this kind of bravado talk was with us for a while and all the poor young men who hadn't joined up were prodded and pestered – even Gully – and accused of cowardice.

'Gully said to me one morning: "I'm not cowardly like, Erica. Not in myself. But soldiering now, I don't think I could do that." And he never went, thank heavens. He survived all the pestering and carried on. The only thing he had to do was to stop selling anything that sounded German, like Frankfurter sausages. No one in England could sell anything like this any more because of all the whipped-up hatred of Germany. They had to change their names, and relabel them "Best British Viands."

'You wouldn't believe the lengths to which we had to go in our Germany-hating. The *Daily Mail* told us that if we went to a restaurant (not that we ever did) we should refuse to be served by a German or an Austrian waiter, and: "if your waiter says he is Swiss, ask to see his passport." I remember I cut this out and sent it to Chadwick (who went to a lot of restaurants) and he wrote back to me and said 'Arnold Bennett says "one is becoming a militarist", but who is "one" I wonder? Robin and I wouldn't dream of interrupting so delightful an experience as a meal with the display of so mundane a thing as a passport.'

'So Chadwick wasn't joining in the hating. His letter was a rebuke. At the end of it he wrote: "the war you waged in London was worth the fight but this war is despicable and we should not be in it. Tell those who say their prayers, to pray it ends soon."

'I think I was confused. My father and Eileen couldn't utter the word "pacifist" without vomiting. I told them one evening at supper: "Uncle Chadwick's a pacifist, you know," and Eileen spat out a huge chunk of meat onto the table. And then they began a tirade against Chadwick, the two of them, and I saw that even my father despised him, yet he had let Chadwick pay for my keep and buy me clothes and care for me for two years. So I said this. I said: "How could you let Chadwick do this, if you disapprove of him so?" and then of course my father whipped round and came out with my own lie: "we understood you payed Chadwick rent out of your earnings at the tea-shop." And I went mad then: I began to shout at them. I told them I had never worked in any tea-shop, that I had given all my time to the movement and that Chadwick paid for everything, *everything,* even my bus fares. I told them that I had starved for a total of twenty-nine days and that each time Chadwick and Mrs Hogan had looked after me and made me well again and that I hated being home because there was nothing *in* the home, nothing but things!

'I remember that my father went very white and Eileen began to whimper. They both stared at me. So I left the meal and went to my room. I got Ratty May off the bed and took her into the cupboard and I put my head against her flat face and said *"Scheisse"* which I knew meant "shit" in German. I said the word lots of times and after a while I found the word incredibly beautiful. I said it slower and slower: *"Scheisse, Scheisse, Schei-sse . . .* and then I wondered if I was saying it properly, the way a German would say it. I was still saying *Scheisse* when Eileen came up. I held on to the cupboard door so that she couldn't open it but she knew I was in there so she began to talk to me and I tried not to listen. I tried to keep on saying *"Scheisse, "Scheisse, "* to block her voice out. Yet I remember what she said that night. It was the first of her monologues and the one I hated most. She told me that she was a very religious woman, that God often gave her signs of Himself, that He appeared to her in lots of different forms and one of these forms was a lacquered musical box which played *Greensleeves* and it was through the musical box that God had told her to marry my father.

'She said that in marrying my father she wanted to become my "mother" and that God had appeared to her again, this time in a tin of Belgian sardines *(Belgian sardines!)* and told her that I was one of his wayward children and that it was her duty as a daughter of St Paul to help me on to the path again and be my protector. "I have never," she said "done anything in my life that wasn't in answer to a commandment from God." So I was very nasty to her then. "What about the fishknives?" I said, "Did God command you to buy them, and the Chippendale chair and the cushions with tassels on them and the card table and the fire screen and the *Black's Book of a Thousand Knitting Patterns,* and all the gadgets with "patent pending" on them . . ." I went through the list of all her furniture and odds and ends, every single one that I could remember and when I couldn't remember any more I stopped. I thought she would start whimpering again but she didn't. She'd gone.'

Erica stopped talking and looked at Ralph. He had let most of his tea go cold in the mug, yet there was a bit more colour in his face.

'How do you feel, Ralph?' she said.

'I'm okay,' said Ralph. 'Was that it, then, was that the time you began to write?'

'Are you sure you wouldn't like to go home and rest?'

'Yes. I'm sure. It was about then, was it, that you began?'

'Yes.'

'You just . . . began?'

'Yes.'

'And did you feel –'

'No I didn't feel important or anything like that, if that's what you were going to say. I felt confused. I told you. I knew I should try to like Eileen for my father's sake, and I also knew that I couldn't. I felt confused about the war. At that time, we were being asked to love the war, but the war had brought to an end the only thing I believed in and when I heard that Sylvia Pankhurst had gone against Christabel and her mother and was urging working women to oppose the war it seemed to me that she was right, we should oppose it. Chadwick influenced me, of course. I didn't think Chadwick could be wrong. So I started to oppose the war. I was the only one for miles around, I should think, who opposed it, so I had to oppose it in secret and this was very dull and lonely. So it seemed much better to write it all down and I started with my feelings about the war and then, rather by accident, I thought up this allegorical story about the war. It turned out to be more accurate than I could have foreseen, because the country I wrote about was laid waste by invading peoples, all its trees and vegetation destroyed, just like the Western Front. It was also about my father and his marrying Eileen – about stupidity and self-delusion. I called it *The Two Wives of the King.* The King isn't a wicked or a cruel man. He's vain, like the rulers of Europe were vain men, and he lets himself be fooled by a lie: he sticks a kind of suppository – a capsule – up his bum because he's been deceived into believing that it contains untold wisdom and that, with this in his body, he'll become wise and revered, like Solomon. But he doesn't become wise. He loses his first wife and his second wife and then his kingdom.

'I used to write after we'd all gone to bed. I never wrote for much more than an hour because the days on the farm were so long, it was hard to stay awake. I kept thinking the story would founder. I didn't believe I'd get to the end and that later it would be published. I hid each page I wrote at the bottom of the cupboard, and I never told anyone what I was doing, not even Gully. But I began thinking up excuses to go to London to see Chadwick – this was before the first Zeppelin raids – in the hope that Chadwick would be able to tell if my story was worth finishing, or if it was very bad. I trusted Chadwick's judgement and it was only later that I saw I was wrong to do so, and why.'

*

Ralph was on time. He brought the camera again. He had decided to ask Erica if she would go with him in a taxi to Regent's Park and he would photograph her there. 'It's much warmer today,' he would tell her, 'and to get out would be good for you.'

But when he said this, she laughed: '*Good* for me? Heavens no, dear! I don't go out any more, not to open spaces. An open space would terrify me. I'd be blown up into the sky, like a kite, I'm sure I would.'

'So you never go out?'

'Now and again. I go to a shop. They're mostly Indian or Pakistani, the shops around here and they sell things loose in sacks. I like loose things in sacks because they have a smell. Packets of anything don't smell at all. Except detergent. That seems to smell a little, through the packet.'

'We could smell the flowers in the park.'

'What flowers?'

'Crocuses.'

'Are they up?'

'Sure. They're almost over.'

'In winter?'

'It's April.'

'Is it? I can't tell.'

'You didn't know it was April?'

'I expect I did. I expect I forgot.'

She looked down at the two frail hands in her lap. They were bird-claw hands, one bent, one straight. They could be broken off, Ralph thought. And it was difficult to imagine that they had ever been any different, ever filled out with flesh and colour and strength, hands that milked cows.

'I read some of *The Two Wives* this morning,' said Ralph.

'Did you? It's a long time since I've looked at it.'

'I tried to imagine you writing it. I tried to visualize you as you were then.'

'Well, I wasn't pretty. Not at that time. I was too eaten up with hate and resentment. My skin was green.'

Ralph smiled. 'And your father did nothing? He couldn't see you were unhappy?'

'I don't know. I was very sullen as the war went on. I expect he longed for me to go away. But I don't think he ever blamed himself or Eileen for how I was. He blamed my two years in London. He blamed Chadwick.'

'And Eileen?'

Erica sighed. 'I don't know how he could have loved her. But he did. When she let him hold her hand I remember that he held it very, very tightly. And he fussed over her. He had to make sure she was all right amongst her furniture. He let her say grace at mealtimes – a thing we'd never ever done. And he let her be the patriot she was: he bought her red, white and blue wool to knit mufflers for the troops from *Black's Book of a Thousand Knitting Patterns*. She took nineteen mufflers to our local recruiting station and I went with her to help carry them. She was in full sail, with her mufflers. She billowed. But she wasn't given the attention she deserved. The recruiting station was crowded and we had to push our way through. She'd expected to see an officer in charge, not an N.C.O. She'd expected a young lieutenant with a cultured voice and all we got was a sergeant. "Look at this lads!" he said when we gave him the mufflers, "French knickers!" So Eileen blushed scarlet and began to push her way out. "Only a joke lady!" he called, "one has to have a bit of a joke in time o' war. But that's very kind of you, ma'am. Very kind I'm sure." But she didn't knit any more mufflers after that, not for a while. She was active in the White Feather Campaign, though; she wanted them all gone, including Gully. She tried to white-feather Gully, but he wasn't having it. "If you love the war, Eileen girl," he said, "you go on and fight it."

'The Angels of Mons inspired her. I expect you've heard of them, haven't you? They were supposed to have appeared at Mons, which was the place of the first reported victory for the Allies. It wasn't a victory, of course, because really there were no victories. The commanders in the field had dreamed of men dashing in on horseback with pennants flying; they hadn't prepared for a static war with no victories. Eileen stitched a sampler with two angels on it and hung it up between "The Lord Giveth" and "The Lord Taketh Away." "Let us never forget Mons" it said, but of course we did forget Mons! And after the Somme, I doubt whether anyone in England remembered it, except Eileen. The Angel of Mons fell down in about 1917 and I burnt them. I gave them a pillar-box cocktail.

'I wanted to leave the farm. It wasn't my home after Eileen came to it: it was her home. I used to dream of my room in London, and the Thomas Crapper. I dreamed of Emily too. I dreamed I buried her in the garden and planted lily-of-the-valley above her head. I was very lonely.

'And then came the dreadful business of the Tipperary Rooms. This must have started in the summer of 1915. I know a lot of the men had gone to the front by then and our little town, Culham Market, where Gully worked, was very quiet. The older farmers still came in, to deliver or buy and have their ale at the Lamb, but their sons had gone, most of them and they were a poor lot, all tied together with string. I suppose some of them had dead sons already. I can't remember. They'd drink their beer in silence.

'Anyway, it wasn't for them, the Tipperary scheme. They had the pub, even though beer had gone up. No, it was Eileen's idea and it was for the women, a venue for patriotism and knitting! She and her friend, Violet Marshall, formed a kind of club and I think it was called the Tipperary Women's Federation or even the Royal Tipperary Women's Federation, though by what right, I don't know. Eileen went round the town looking for premises. She wanted to invade the Church Hall and take it over but the vicar's wife had just died and the presence of women too near his nostrils brought on his queer turns at that time and so he refused. Eileen and Violet Marshall were terribly angry with the vicar. You see, once they'd thought up the Tipperary Scheme, they believed it was the most important thing anybody had ever thought up, so they pestered us all day and night until it got going. She held collections. Violet Marshall designed a banner which said "Women of Culham Market, what are you doing for the War Effort?" and I wanted to say to her, Eileen of Aldeburgh, what are you doing for my father's farm? Because she hardly let her skirts touch the field. She helped now and then with the butter making, but that was all.

'She got her premises in the end. She got a slaughterhouse! It was an old, high brick building near the station. Mr Haggard had used it to slaughter in at one time and then built his own more modern slaughterhouse and store nearer the shop. It was owned by the railway so Eileen and Violet had to pay a rent for it.

'The rent must have been small because Eileen seemed very content and in a few months a sign was up saying "Tipperary Rooms". It was a terrible place, Ralph! Gully had mended the broken windows for her and Violet Marshall and I whitewashed the walls which were thick with bloodstain. I remember that bits of blood tissue had hardened on the walls so they were never smooth because we didn't scrape the blood off, we just painted over it. I don't know why women came there. I never went near the Tipperary Rooms after I finished the whitewashing, but in no time it was crowded, so Eileen said. Women came with thermos flasks and sat on hard chairs with their knitting. They were middle-class women, like Eileen, with time to spare. They bought a loom and made blankets and rugs. They took it in turns to bring cakes, till sugar ran short. And all through the war, they kept going there. I don't know why.

'The next time I saw that building, where they'd had the Tipperary meetings, was when the farm became mine. I went with Bernard and by then he knew all about Eileen and the pearl-handled fishknives and the "Lord Giveth" samplers and the *Book of a Thousand Knitting Patterns.*

'We went into the building and it felt very chilly. But time had neutralized it. There was no trace of the slaughterhouse and no trace of the Tipperary Rooms. It had become nothing. Just a derelict place where no one ever went.'

The Harrington Hotel,
Harrington Gardens,
London S.W.7.

'Dear John,

Thanks for your letter, and well done about the novel. On no account come near London, which is no place for the very sensitive (you) nor the idiotically depressed (me).

On the other hand, I would like to get to Oxford not later than the 26th–27th. You will note the advanced state of my depression when I say that I am in dire need of friendship. I've become so unskilled with strangers that I've hardly talked to a soul since I got here; only Erica, and she it is who must talk, not I. I'm obsessed with the neglect of my herbs back home. I grew them all from seed and now I've let them die. I could, literally, weep for them.

If I could stay two nights in Oxford, say the 24th and 25th and see you each evening, this would be great. In the daytime I shall conduct myself like a good American and tour the city, and you will write, lucky you, with a piece of work all your own. If I was writing a novel, I don't suppose I'd mind about the oregano.

"And all our vacant space
we fill
with hired things" – J.P. 1964!

Please let me know if these dates are okay (and please say they are).

Ralph'

Ralph considered, only for a moment, going back, cautious and apologetic, to *Mr Toad's,* to seek out the coloured hostess who had arranged his Tennessee fragments into drunken lust, and into whose soft lap he had finally vomited £40-worth of champagne. But the club – and the girl – seemed a long, long way away. Before he left London he would go back – perhaps he might even try to make the girl, if he could recognize her. If he recognized her, he would remember not to call her Pearl.

He lay down on his bed and picked up *The Two Wives of the King.* He read how, some days after the insertion of the capsule into his anus, King Rey, tormented by his lust for his second wife Zabeth who is hiding from him, sends his first wife, Beth, into exile:

'The King commanded that she should journey alone with two camels. The second camel was loaded with all the tapestries Beth had stitched since Zabeth had replaced her in the King's bed and in his heart. The tapestries were wound round the camel like a bandage.

King Rey watched her go. In his dreams of the coming war, Zabeth had appeared to him wearing the Invisible Robe of the King's Primogeniture and told him she would remain hidden forever among the circus people unless Beth was sent from the palace, back to her father's lands. So now he watched her go with all her days and nights of falcon and huntsmen, with all the intricate foliage of her grief. He thought he would forget her.

"Only," said a voice at his side, "when you have forgotten her, shall I come back to you." And the King, seeing Zabeth, reached out to her with a cry. But Zabeth had turned and run. She disappeared inside the palace at the very moment that

Beth's second camel stepped over the horizon. From a high window, a minah bird began to screech: "Men at arms! Men at arms!' and King Rey sat down on the wisdom of generations. His anus was bleeding.

News of the bleeding of the King's anus carried fast. It travelled by elephant and by chimpanzee. Jugglers threw it and caught it in village after village. Doctors struggled into their waistcoats of the Great Emergency they had thought never to wear again and made their way on mules to the palace. The doctors had grown much too fat for their waistcoats of the Great Emergency; they arrived faint on their silly mules and the King refused to see them. He had discovered that the bleeding of his anus lessened the pain in it. The capsule seemed lighter. So he let the blood flow, and concentrated instead on the forgetting of Beth. The doctors undid their waistcoats of the Great Emergency and lolloped back to their villages. Once there, safe in their villages they said: "there is no Great Emergency. The Great Emergency was a lie."

King Rey pleaded for silence in which to count his royal heartbeats. With his bare hands, he strangled fifty-three minah birds. Fat women arrived at his bedside demanding gold for the dead. King Rey closed his eyes.

"Sleep my darling," whispered a gentle, troubled voice and obediently, so weak from the blood that flowed out of him, he slept. Then in his sleep he recognized the voice as Beth's voice and he remembered the camel bandaged with tapestries going over the edge of the world. When the fat women saw the King weep in his sleep, they went away. They buried the minah birds under the stairs.'

In Ralph's (American, 1960) edition of *The Two Wives of the King,* the publisher described the book as 'a powerful satirical novel about love and war by the author of *The Hospital Ship.'*

It wasn't a very long work, the shortest by far of her three novels and deemed to be her least successful. Already, however, Ralph found himself held by the dilemma of King Rey, faintly disturbed by the images that surrounded this extraordinary man. He began to wonder if, at twenty-two, Erica hadn't sewn the first seeds of the incredible General Almarlyes in the character of King Rey. The similarity between the two inventions lay in their humiliation which, in each case, is brought about by their own weakness. Yet almost thirty years separated them and the young woman who wrote, by candlelight, in the first winter of the first war must have been a very different person from the one who, with Bernard for companion, wrote *The Hospital Ship* in late middle age. Ralph closed the book and put it away. He tried to imagine Erica at twenty, Erica at fifty, yet it seemed pointless to do that. Before he slept, an odd phrase crept into his mind: 'she became herself at the age of eighty-seven'.

'There was so much we could measure by,' she said. 'In those days patriotism was a heartbeat, not just a word. For most of my life I was able to join – or not join – movements which bound people, which got them up and doing. Yet today what is there for you, Ralph? I sit here and I wonder: how can the new generation express its humanity? You see, we talk about peacetime don't we? We think we're living in peacetime but we're not. We're at war with our time and our enemies are everywhere, even in ourselves.'

'A lot of us feel washed up,' Ralph said gloomily.

'Yes.'

'I mean I know I have to start with myself. I have to make certain decisions . . . a lot of people I knew at college have just gone for shrinkage.'

'Shrinkage?'

'Yup. I mean they've shrunk down. They've become microscopic in fact.'

'What do you mean, dear?'

'Well, they're not in the world any more. They're not out there. They're just trying to climb inside their own heads. Most of them live out of town and grow things. They're keeping sane, I guess, but only by being isolated.'

'Yes. I've read about people doing that. I often feel I want to warn them that growing things is very hard work and sometimes all that work goes to waste, because the pigeons come and eat the broccoli and the chickens get fowl pest. And then immediately you're back in the world, aren't you? You buy a gun to shoot the pigeons; you disinfect your chicken hut with some chemical made in Switzerland.'

Ralph smiled. 'You didn't ever really like the farm, Erica, did you?'

She sighed and her head went back. 'I liked it when I was a child.

66

My feet loved the grass and my head loved the sunshine. It was all I knew. And there were moments, much later, when I went back there with Bernard, when I felt I belonged to it and I owed it my life.'

'But at the time of Eileen . . .'

'Oh no. At the time of Eileen, all I thought about was going back to London. I'd become very impatient, not only with Eileen but with the slow ways of the Suffolk people. I used to spend some time with Gully and Dot and although I loved Gully very much, I found his company and Dot's rather dull. They talked a lot about meat prices, and the possibility of rationing and of course about Buckwheat whose real name was John, I think, but he was never called John.

'I wrote to Chadwick when I was about half way through my book. It was before conscription came in so Robin was still safe and getting exactly the same kind of silk scarves and first editions of Gide that had been given to Athelstone Amis. Robin was the longest lived of Chadwick's lovers – and the last. I don't suppose he was at all faithful to Chadwick because none of them ever were, but he stayed with him on and off until he was called up, and he was there when I went to stay with Chadwick in the spring of 1916.

'It must have been eighteen months since I had seen Chadwick and I noticed a change in him. He looked very much older – as if the war had aged him – and his hair was thinning. The Hogans were still there but the troubles in Ireland had made them restless and they didn't give Chadwick the care he was used to. Dust and strands of Chadwick's hair were left lying.

'Yet it was wonderful to hear London outside my window. I sat in my room and listened. In part, I listened for the war and I couldn't hear it. You see, no one close to me had died. None of the men I loved – my father, Chadwick, Gully – had gone to war. If they had, then I would have heard it, just like the old farmers who drank in the pub in silence. They heard it.

'The London theatres had been closed when war was declared, but they opened again quite quickly and Chadwick was writing a new play. On the first evening of my visit we dined in a restaurant (without Robin) and Chadwick talked about his play. He told me it was a satire on patriotism and militarism. Its central character was a Belgian refugee who goes through the whole war pretending that his hands had been cut off by the Germans and everyone he meets in England rushes off to the Western Front to avenge the crime and gets killed before they've had time to say "Wipers". It didn't, as you can see, sound at all like Chadwick's other plays. Not a butler in it! And of course he knew no one would put the play on, not while the war lasted. But he believed that when the war was over, the pacifists would come back to popularity, and then everyone would flock to it. It was called *What did you do in the war, Jean-Marc?*

'I let Chadwick talk about the play for a while and then I told him that I had started to write. I suppose I thought he would be glad and offer to help me in any way he could, just as he'd helped me in 1912. Well, he did try to be glad. He pretended he was glad. Yet I knew straight away that he hated me for this.

'It was as if he saw an eclipse: me blotting him out, all his fame and name and money. It was very, very unexpected and strange. Chadwick was such a kind man, so terribly kind. Yet over this one thing, he felt vulnerable and then he could be unkind. He read my book a day or two later, and he said to me "you musn't take any notice of what I say, Erica. You must feel quite free to go on and finish the book, but in my opinion I don't believe this is the best thing for you to be doing – writing. I don't think you're making the best use of your talents, not with fiction."

'It was wounding, wasn't it? You see, Chadwick was really the only person I knew whom I thought would understand the book and be in sympathy with what I was trying to do. I never, never expected him to neglect me.

'It was a miserable stay, after that. I was very silent and Chadwick and Robin ignored me most of the time. They were very affectionate to each other and I was right outside them. I wanted to shout at Chadwick. I wanted to tell him he had betrayed me. I thought of all my countless nights of writing – all gone to waste, destroyed in an instant. It was unbearable, Ralph. It was like a wound.

'So I came back to Suffolk and the war dragged on and shortages came – bread and potatoes and sugar and meat – and we worked harder than ever on the farm, to grow more.

'Eileen's nephew was killed on the Somme and she went to Aldeburgh for a few days to be with her sister. So my father and I were alone. And during all the time that Eileen was away, he talked about my mother. It was as if he'd opened a vein and the blood of his love for her came pouring out. He even talked about the bull and her death in the forget-me-not field and how, after she died, he thought of killing himself and probably would have done if it hadn't been for me. He told me how he had met her and courted her and made love to her beside a pond long before the wedding day and how his desire for her never left him. He talked as if I wasn't there: the most intimate details of his life with her came tumbling out, and then the minute Eileen came back, he was silent and never referred to my mother again. I asked him, at some point during those days, whether he loved Eileen, and he sighed and said: "A man needs a wife, Erica." And I couldn't help smiling. I thought of the children's game played in a circle, and I imagined my father, silent and confused, in the middle with all the children shouting:

> "The Farmer's in his den,
> The Farmer's in his den!
> Ee-ii, tiddly-i,
> The Farmer's in his den!'"

4

'I dreamed of my friend, Claustrophobia. She came to my door and she stared at me in my sleep, without my teeth in. She was dressed all in grey and she was very tall, yet she had her child's face, just as I'd imagined it in the cowshed. Then I woke and looked at her with my mouth hidden behind the bedclothes. She was holding out a basket of strawberries. Offering them to me. And she was smiling.'

Ralph had telephoned for a taxi and the taxi had deposited them at the north entrance to Regent's Park. Erica had been afraid of the outing, but Ralph had wrapped her in a coat and a shawl, guided her safely down the stairs and into the sunshine.

And now they sat on a bench. The horse chestnuts were in pale leaf. Spring was late – later each year, she complained – yet courteous, finally, in its straight clusters of daffodils, apologetic in its sudden warmth.

'It seemed to me,' said Erica, 'that the strawberries were Death. She was bringing me death, in her hands that had never aged, and saying: "taste it".'

Ralph closed his eyes, savouring the sunlight on his face. On their short walk to the bench (she had been afraid that a sudden gust of wind would catch at her and blow her into the sky; she wouldn't be led any further than the bench) he had noticed that he was only a little taller than she was.

'The strawberries may not have been death,' he said. 'They could have been anything. Imagination, for instance.'

'Oh no. My imagination's all dried up. I think they were death.'

Then she looked all around her, as if she'd never seen the park before, the bright grass, the neat paths, the cherry trees . . .

'It's very, very nice here,' she said. 'I'm always rather moved by that bit in *Julius Caesar* when Anthony tells the Roman rabble that they've been given all Caesar's parks – for ever. I think parks are very civilizing, full of order and neatness, yet designed to let nature flower. Very clever.'

'Are you glad you came?'

'Yes. I didn't know it would be so warm. Thank you for taking all the trouble, Ralph, just to get me out.'

'It's okay. Do you like sitting, or shall we walk on? We could go to the canal if you like.'

'Oh no. The canal's very dirty. I don't know how the ducks can live on it and bring up families. If I was a duck, I'd waddle to St James's, which used to be much cleaner.'

Ralph smiled.

'Now we must go back,' she said, 'before we get so used to it that it fades.'

In their returning taxi, Erica's eyes looked red, as if the sunshine had dazzled and hurt them. Tiredness pulled her mouth into a thin line.

'I don't know where I was, dear,' she said suddenly, 'but I don't think I can talk today. I'm so sorry.'

'What have I become,' Ralph wrote in his Summary, 'through reporting the lives of others, doing nothing with mine *except reporting*? Is reporting doing? If the answer is yes, to what extent is reporting doing?

'I *did* something, today. I took the old lady for a walk. I showed her there were flowers and sunshine very near her, and she enjoyed this. I enjoyed this. We were both *doing*.

'Tomorrow, however, I shall go back to reporting – if my toothache can stand it.

'N.B. The last time I *did* anything, I threw up.'

Ralph stared at what he had written for a while. Then he added: 'I've no idea whether what Erica said about "dying in a certain way" and my role in her death was a momentary thought or a conviction truly held. To play some role in her death would be *doing*. Can't imagine what this role could possibly be.'

Ralph closed the book and stared round at his room. In it, he had started to knit time in three colours: the pink of Erica's Tiffany lamp, the grey-gold of John Pennington's Oxford, the brown of Walt's shiny suit.

'The war was beginning. "It will be the Last War," said King Rey to his council, "the only War." And he ordered that the camels be harnessed and made ready.

In her exile, Beth heard rumours of the war. "The circus people and all their lands will be laid waste!" King Rey had boasted. "We shall fight to the last camel, and our camels are the proudest in the world." But Beth had seen the heavy guns. She imagined them moving over the desert now, as silently as they could be moved, and she wept for what was to come. She tried to send messages of warning to King Rey: "All your men and all your camels will be pounded to fragments by the big guns." But the messages she sent were captured by the enemy. They never arrived.

The palace was quiet now. When news of the coming war began to spread, the clowns and the fat women took their elephants and their performing wolves and the bodies of the birds they had buried under the stairs and went away in a procession, leaving only their piles of dung, and a few bales of straw behind.

In the ensuing silence, the King was at last able to sleep. He gave up his search for Zabeth and lay down to dream of a life without her. He slept for four days and nights, and only one dream did he have of her: she came to him and said "If I had been your first wife, I would not have betrayed you. The betrayal, therefore, is yours."

When he woke, his nightgown was stained red from the bleeding hole in him, and the war had begun. The King heard the snorting of his camels outside his window and felt refreshed. He knew that the war was his. He would win it in a day.'

'I slept so well, dear,' she said, 'it was the fresh air and the park. So very kind of you, Ralph . . .'

'Good. We'll do it another day, shall we?'

'Only if I can hold on to you tightly, just like I did. Otherwise, I know I might go off into the sky.'

Ralph laughed. 'I don't know why you imagine that.'

'Don't you? No, I don't think I do either. It's very silly of me, isn't it? I don't suppose old women do get blown up into the air at all. But it just seems so very likely. And I was always afraid of the wind. "The Suffolk Wind", we used to call it and it would sigh round us for days and nights. As the war went on, I used to imagine the same wind, whispering over France, and the soldiers hearing it and thinking, why doesn't it ever stop?

'I was ill in the summer of 1918. I believe I had the 'flu that thousands of us got that winter and died of. I don't think I had ever in my life been ill before – only weak those times after my hunger strikes – so this was a new event for the household and it made Eileen very cross. I couldn't stand up. I crawled to Eileen's room and told her to go for the doctor. She called my father and they lifted me and put me into bed. I remember lying half asleep and wondering if I was dying. I thought terribly self-pitying thoughts: no one will care if I die, not even Chadwick or Gully . . . so much better to have died a martyr like Emily or even a lover's death like my mother's.

'A young doctor came. I saw him so undistinctly, Ralph, it was as if his body was just a patterning on the wall – flat and far away. He switched on a pencil-thin light and looked into my eyes. I tried to see him round the edge of the light, but I couldn't. But when my fever had gone, he came back and smiled at me and all his flatness had disappeared. And I knew from the way that he looked at me that there would be something between us. The war was ending – we knew it by this time – and now this man had come, very handsome, very straight. His name was David. It suited him so well! You could just imagine him naked and upright, with his sling and his little stone. I laughed and laughed from my bed. David indeed! I said.

'Now I was enjoying the comforts of my illness. No early morning milking, no crawling through the strawberry nets on my belly, no bicycling for the vet at all hours.

'Eileen grumbled more than you could imagine. I think in a way she feared the end of the war, because she knew that in peacetime the Tipperary Rooms would make no sense. And women had started going to the pub, you know, and ordering drinks and making noise there: they weren't content to do their talking in Eileen's slaughter-house any more. So she saw it fade and go silent and she sniffed and puffed with hurt.

'But she found a new scheme and this was it: she wanted to marry me off to David! She found out all about him – who his parents were, how much he was paid. She made certain he'd never been married before, wasn't paying out for children in another part of the country. She even discovered that he had an aunt living in Aldeburgh, a Mrs Shuttle, and went to call on her.

'I had no idea she was doing all this, not until she came into my room one night and began brushing my hair – an intimate thing, a thing she *never* did – and as she brushed and brushed she said very kindly: "You're twenty-five, Erica and we must start to plan your life."

'Pour the wine Ralph dear,' said Erica, 'for this David incident is so very funny, so absolutely of its time that I want to cackle whenever I think of it. It worked so *wonderfully,* you see, that Eileen need never have bothered with her visits to Aldeburgh and all her detective work.'

Ralph poured the wine and Erica sat back with her glass, enjoying it. Today, she seemed very strong. Then she looked at Ralph worriedly.

'I hope you won't think I was cruel. I hope you won't write that in my youth I was uncaring and flippety. You see, half of me did love David. I think I loved the bit of him I could see round the edge of the pencil torch and the pencil torch was like a light inside me that he never touched. So a great or a wild love was impossible. Do you understand? He was a very, very gentle young man. Utterly English, like a plain meal and without any of the cruelty of his class. When he called, Eileen would take out her *gros point* and sip his vowel sounds with ecstasy.

'And I went up in her estimation now that I was being courted by someone so polite and correct; she thought the rebel in me was dead.

'We never did very much, David and I. We bicycled to bits of the countryside we liked and sat in silence, listening to the hot days. A fair came once to our town and we went to that and David paid for us to try all the amusements. And one of these was a peep show where you stared into a black box and turned a handle and saw ladies in corsets with their thighs showing, and men with flowers flopping down dead at the sight of these thighs – very puerile! You never saw a bum in those days, let alone anything else and there were many things women weren't meant to know.

'I didn't tell David about my night with Gully. I let him kiss me – on those hot days – and he was full of words of love at that time, yet I don't remember them. They were just part of the summer

74

noises, very pleasant. But I think this exasperated David, that I didn't hear all his swearings of love, because one day he borrowed a little car and drove me to Southwold which was rather fashionable then and full of rich people standing still. He carried me on his back into the sea – the dear, grey old sea of England! – and then he let me fall and I hadn't expected this. I was absolutely drenched and choking, but David swam away from me and laughed and said "Serve you right!" Yet back at our little hut, he said he was sorry for what he had done. He put his arms round me and told me he had finally made up his mind, he would marry me.

'Well, Ralph, goodness *me*! My mind fled to Emily and everything we had been locked up for and persecuted for and I snatched up my clothes and ran. We are cheated and cheated again, I thought. We're like cattle, to be mated or left aside at will. We're the silent swinging udders of the field chewing the cud while the bulls rampage. You *knew*, Emily, I said as I ran, you knew it would never, never change and that's why you chose death!

'But the bull came panting up, with his wet moustache and his blue bathing suit. He seemed ridiculous. I stood still in the road and watched him. I thought of Eileen sitting and doing her tapestry and listening to her voice, and my father watching him come and go, imagining my future safe and secure. I yelled at him. "What makes you think anyone would *want* to marry you? What makes you think I shall ever marry anyone?" I was so cross, I forgot that it had ever been nice to be with him. I despised him.'

Ralph smiled. 'So that was it for David?'

'More or less. Because it was that same day in September, the day we went to Southwold, that the telegram came from Chadwick. "Robin dead at Salonika," it said. "Please come at once."

'So the war spilled back into our lives. Just as it seemed to be ending and everyone was saying – exactly as they had in 1914 – "it will be over by Christmas", there it was again. Senseless. The slaughterhouse war!

'They didn't want me to go, because the harvest was just beginning. And they'd hoped for a harvest wedding. It was to have been a season of bounty. But they knew I would go. They accepted my debt to Chadwick. But they were dreadfully confused: "You won't forget David, Erica, will you dear? Promise us that you'll write to him. He loves you so."

'I did see him again, but that was later, and in my scurrying to London I never thought about him, but only of poor Chadwick. The desertion of Athelstone Amis had been terrible enough, but the loss of Robin was unimaginable. Because I was wrong, I think, to say no one loved Chadwick as he wanted to be loved. From what Chadwick told me, it seems that Robin had loved him quite a lot and not only this, he had hailed him as a genuis, too, which was what Chadwick wanted, perhaps even more than love. And now, there was Chadwick moulting, with no taste of a first night for four years, and Robin killed in the very last months of the war. It was so cruel.

'When I arrived, Chadwick was in bed. He was drunk on port and weeping. A terrible sight, like a sketch by Boz. Mrs Hogan said she could do nothing for him.

' "If his room smells o' piss, Miss," she said, "'tis because we can't move him to change the linen." But when he saw me, he became as obedient as a lamb. He let the tears ripple on and on through his hair (a pool of tears in the hair of Alice!) and I took the port away and helped him to a chair and covered him with a rug while Mr Hogan ran a bath for him.

'I'd never seen Chadwick without any clothes on – only his white legs as I described them to you – but now I did. I saw him almost every day from then on because his broken heart made him cussed and he couldn't bear to be helped or touched by anyone but me. The first shock I had was not the sight of his body, which was just rather large and grey and soft but the sight of his hair which, when it was wet in the bath, began to run, so that the whole bath soon became golden with hair dye. I'd always believed, you see, that Chadwick's extraordinary hair was naturally yellow. All my life it had been yellow and to know that now it was just grey like the rest of him was shocking. I tried to hold his hair out of the water, but it was so long, it kept falling back in. In the end I got a ribbon and tied it back with that. What a sight he was, poor darling! I've never seen anything like him.

'The Hogans were threatening to leave. With Connolly and Pearce dead in Ireland, they felt like traitors taking the wages of the English. Or at least I suppose this was why they wanted to go. I never asked them. I just persuaded them to stay another month. I imagined that in a month I could get Chadwick to stop drinking (in my first week he was either drunk or ill or sleeping) and then I could cope with him on my own. But he was too heavy for me to lift and he often needed lifting. He was like a huge, incontinent child, disgusting and yet lovable. And I knew that he was letting his grief out, not holding it in like the silent men in the pub in Culham Market, and that if he could do this, he might recover.

'Quite a few people called at the flat and they were always shocked by the way Chadwick looked. His agent came several times but always with the same gloomy prognostications: no one would ever *look* at *What did you do in the War, Jean-Marc*. Patriotism had died a little with the tales of useless slaughter but now that many of the soldiers were returning and victory was in sight, it recovered. To have fought in – and survived – the war was to be a hero. Pacifists were out of fashion.

"I know all that," Chadwick would say impatiently, "but when the people really begin to count the cost of the war, then they will see the lies behind it, and the posturing and the waste! This play says it all. It's only a question of choosing the right time to put it on. Robin always said," he used to add, "that *Jean-Marc* was the best thing I've ever done."

'And then, invariably he would cry and his agent would go away looking embarrassed and I would suggest a walk to Bryanston Square where we could sit in the gardens and watch the leaves fall. Oh, it was a sad time! I tried day after day to make Chadwick laugh. I told him about Eileen and the Tipperary Rooms and the Mons sampler which I had burnt by then. I told him about David in his blue bathing suit. And a little grey smile would sometimes appear and he would reach for my hand and say that he was very, very fond of me and perhaps, after all, I might be a writer some day if I stuck to the truth.

'He was recovering. Bit by bit. The afternoons got shorter and each day he was a little stronger to face the evening. We began to go to restaurants again. He went to the barbers and had his hair retinted. It wasn't that he started to forget Robin. He talked about him a great deal and kept writing to Robin's mother in Dorchester saying that her son was the most compassionate and beautiful young man who had ever lived and why on earth didn't she answer his letters so that they could share their grief? But she never did answer. I expect she refused to believe that her son had been queer. I expect she'd had plans for him to marry into a good family.

'Well, as I say, there was no question of Robin being gradually forgotten (as he had gradually forgotten Athelstone Amis after his legs had recovered) but I could see that, physically, Chadwick was getting better. Some of the greyness left him. He bought some new neckties. He took me shopping one afternoon and bought me a blue dress and coat – forget-me-not blue, startling and beautiful and I began to discover at twenty-five that I was considered rather fine, even by Chadwick's sophisticated friends. My hands were rough, of course, from the years of farm work, but the rest of me was coming along quite well. I enjoyed the visits to restaurants and the glances of tne young men. I knew, at about that time that I would fall in love – perhaps quite soon – but I wanted a black stallion for a lover, not a boy with a sling!

'It was October and the Hogans left. Their hearts had sailed home to Ireland long before their bodies so that when their bodies came to go they went easily, longingly and without a backward glance. They said they would send us picture postcards of Ireland to show us the beauty of their country. They had no work to go to, but this didn't seem to worry them. I expect they thought they would live on the Irish air.

'Another couple replaced them. They were called the Warburtons and they were very down-to-earth and strong, very London. They'd never seen any of Chadwick's plays of course but they'd *heard* of him and he was very gratified and said idiotically vain things like: "Well, Mrs Warburton dear, I like to think I have a small reputation, only a *small* one, mind . . ." so I thought to myself, perhaps you don't really need me now, Chadwick, and I had better go back to Suffolk and help with the end of the harvest. I suggested this to Chadwick but he said no, he would die of loneliness. This wasn't true in fact, because more and more of his friends called on him and asked him to dinners now that he was presentable again. For sorrow is sometimes obscene, Ralph, and you need a strong stomach for it. So I stayed and we got used to the Warburtons and they got used to us and then Chadwick died.'

Erica sat very still. She had finished her glass of wine and Ralph got up quietly, took it from her and refilled it. Outside the window a siren passed – an ambulance or a fire engine. Ralph held the full glass and waited for Erica to take it from him.

'I thought,' she said at last, 'that I would be able to describe

Chadwick's death to you. I can remember it very vividly and my life was changed because of it. But I don't think I can describe it; it makes me so sad. I owed Chadwick so much you see – and I don't just mean money, although he had paid for a lot of things. Oh dear, I wanted to build a tepee round his body, like the one he'd made with Gully. I wanted to do a wild wailing dance to make him breathe. I wept for him more than I'd wept for my mother, more than for Emily. I was told afterwards that sixteen million people in India alone died of flu that winter, just as Chadwick died. It was even more senseless than the war.

'I nursed him, but the nursing of him was terrible, because from the start of the illness he *knew* he would die and every day he grew more and more afraid of death and would hold my arm with his burning hands and ask me to save him from these dreams of death which he saw always as a tidal wave, beginning far out at sea and then growing, growing so tall and vast that it blotted out the sun and the sky went dark . . . oh poor soul . . . there was no one but me between him and his fear; no mediator like a priest, no belief in anything but darkness. I *hate* to remember it, Ralph, and yet I so often do.'

'When did he die, Erica?'

'On the last day of November. Nineteen days after the armistice. And we buried him in London.'

'By the twenty-third day of the war, only one of King Rey's camels remained standing: Zabeth's own camel, tethered to a mango tree in the palace gardens, drunk from eating the mangoes which fell and burst at its feet. King Rey knew that he could not send Zabeth's camel to war.

He summoned his Imperial Council and, wearing his Robe of the State Occasion (smelling of monkey's fur, smelling of the dead Minah birds), he ordered them to make a mountain of the dead camel's bones, to dry them in the sun, and then to command that every craftsman in the land cease at once to fashion objects of usefulness and begin forthwith to make necklaces – beautiful, polished necklaces – out of the camel bones.

The King paused and swallowed and said: "We shall put all the necklaces onto our boats, and our boats will travel day and night and never stopping down the longest river in the world, to a point where the river widens into an enormous lake. On the banks of this lake," said the King, "is the City of a Future Time, and the rulers of the City of a Future Time will buy the cargo of camel-bone necklaces and, in return, send us guns made of pig-iron. And our boats will travel day and night and never stopping back up the longest river in the world to our poor suffering land, and then – in a single day with our guns of the Future – we shall win the war."

The war was already lost. The members of the Council knew that the war was already lost. Yet there was no dissent. Not a whisper of it. For the members of the Imperial Council of King Rey were so old that dissent was a word the meaning of which they had long forgotten, just as, long ago, they had forgotten so much else about their lives and about their country, such as the maiden names of their own mothers and what it felt like to be young enough to have a mother and to see in the desert mirages all the wonders of a young man's heart.

The flesh was hacked from the camel corpses, and the desert sun burned the bones dry and white.

King Rey's wounded soldiers, riders with no mounts, began to dig trenches in the sand and to crouch there, waiting their endless wait for the guns that would never arrive, and hearing in their skulls the dry winds of death.'

' "At least the war's over," my father said to me at Chadwick's funeral. He said this as if he was telling me news, as if he thought the ending of the war had escaped my attention. Then he went on to complain: "I heard they danced in the streets – and worse – in London. London's no place to be."

' "There was no dancing in the flat," I wanted to say. The Warburtons went out and made a night of it, but I sat with Chadwick by the gas fire. His fever was just beginning.

'It was very strange to see my father in London. I remember noticing that, standing among the gathering of Chadwick's friends, he looked poor and rough. He looked like a servant. I asked him, when all the guests had been given tea and gone, if he'd like to stay with me at the flat. And he was shocked. "I'm not staying and neither are you, Erica," he said. "The flat doesn't belong to us." And it was as he said this that I knew my life had changed again and my heart did a kind of jump inside my funeral coat. "The flat's mine," I said. "Chadwick left me everything he had."

'This was absolutely true. There were one or two bequests. He'd left my father five hundred pounds and Gully five hundred pounds. And Robin's mother in Dorchester had been left all the odds and ends that Robin had given him, such as a set of ivory brushes for his ripples and some French playing cards with C.M. on them and almost certainly a volume or two of Gide though I don't really remember. The Hogans in County Cork had been left a hundred pounds, but there was nothing for the Warburtons, they were too new. A clause in the will said that I, Erica Harriet March, should be the sole beneficiary of all royalties or payments that might accrue from performances of Chadwick's plays (after the agent's commission had been taken) and that I was free to make my home in the flat or sell it, as I pleased. When all the bequests had been taken care of and the lawyer's fees paid, I was left with a sixty-two year lease on the flat and just a little under ten thousand pounds.

'Now I never dreamed Ralph, that I would ever be rich and as you see, I'm not rich now – it's all gone. But in 1918, ten thousand pounds was riches. If I hadn't been so saddened by Chadwick's death I think I would have danced or run to Covent Garden and bought a tray of gardenias. But all I could say to the memory of dear Chadwick – and I said it softly, with the grief he had caused me still in my throat – was "I think you've set me free." And then I would spend hours in front of a mirror, measuring every line on my face. For the freedom I had was so precious, so unexpected, I knew I mustn't squander it. And so much was changing: the women's vote had been granted that same year and the war was over: there seemed to be no more fighting to be done. So I didn't know where to go, Ralph. I literally did not dare take a step in case it was the wrong one, and there was no one to advise me.

'David turned up one day. He'd dressed very formally – for London! – and you could tell his collar was hurting. He looked as if he had a broken neck! Lots of days must have passed between Chadwick's funeral and David's visit, but I don't remember what I did with them. I believe I just sat and stared at myself. The whole flat smelled of Chadwick's hair elixir; I knew the place was his and could never be mine, but I lingered on there for a while. And when David arrived and saw the flat, he said "My word, how spacious! My word, how grand!" So I said simply: "It was right for Chadwick, but not for me.

'I was very curt to David, very beastly. He wanted a marriage and I wanted a life and the two were far apart. I stood in the drawing room and raged. "You're a doctor," I yelled, "and now you turn up! Why didn't you come sooner and save Chadwick?" You see? Very beastly. It wasn't David's fault that Chadwick had died. But the anger felt so good. I began to come alive through it and feel my blood gush and my brain push. I became delirious with words and it was ecstasy after all my silent days. I said the most extraordinary things! I told David that Chadwick would be reincarnated as a girl and come teasing him along the Suffolk lanes. I told him to marry Eileen and set my father free. And of course he fled. What else could he do, poor thing? He took his stiff neck away and I never saw him again, not until he was an old man, with a wife called Fidelity.

'I moved soon after that. I sold the lease of Chadwick's flat and bought a little cottage house in Hampstead. It was very small and cheap and apart from the cupboard, it was the first thing of substance I ever owned. But the strangeness of my new freedom still made me a bit afraid. I looked at Ratty May and said, "What now?" And Ratty May, who is so wise in her bran body, said, "Write to Gully and Gully will go to the farm in his butcher's van and get the cupboard for you and drive it to London, and once the cupboard is here . . ."

"What then?" I said, but she didn't answer.

'I did send for the cupboard. I wrote to a removal firm and they brought it, and in my little house it looked terribly large. I don't know why I wanted it really. I think I was afraid Eileen would start filling it up with her things and I couldn't bear that. But it arrived just as it had always been, with my mother's dresses still hanging up inside.'

The restaurant Ralph chose was crowded. He sat in a far corner of it, almost under some stairs, and ordered himself a large Italian meal, starting with pasta in a clam sauce which reminded him of home. On the notepad he had brought – weapon against the stares of the other diners – he wrote: 'I have always felt greedy eating expensive food. If I'm alone, I feel even worse, even more greedy, but what the hell. The hotel dining room is getting to me. I could die in there and be buried by a Portuguese waiter.'

The restaurant was warm and softly lit. Ralph felt hidden, on the edge of contentment. At the next table a balding man, neat in his pinstripes yet gross-bellied, held hands with a laughing girl. He refilled and refilled her glass and her laughter had the monotony of a bell. 'Later,' Ralph wrote, 'they will copulate; his heavy body crushing hers. Ejaculation will make him think about his wife, but of course he won't tell Miss Muffet. If he sleeps he'll dream about his kids and if she sleeps she'll dream about being mother to them. It's all dumb.'

For the first time since arriving in London, Ralph felt glad to be alone. The weight of another person, he mused, is often far worse than the weight of solitude. He ordered a second half bottle of wine. The spaghetti came and it was spicy, tasting of fresh parsley and the sea. He marvelled that he could have felt so sorry for himself for so long. 'I'm making good progress with Erica,' he wrote. 'She trusts me more each day and at the end there will be something – a kind of gift of her spirit. Must absolutely refuse to chuck her in till she's offered it all – the whole life – who the fuck else has ever been so generous? Even Ma and Dad lead X-certificate lives, censored lives. So if Walt tries anything, gotta say "out your ass!" '

Ralph giggled. A whole baby chicken arrived, cooked in rosemary and garlic, with a dish of zucchini. As he ate the chicken, he remembered his own herbs, dead no doubt on their sheltered sill, but the thought of their death didn't upset him as it had done recently. 'Other things,' he wrote almost illegibly, 'take shape and grow right here. They take time, that's all.'

His contentment outlasted his meal and his walk back to the hotel. Then, lying in the darkness, trying to sleep, it left him. He felt bloated from the food. His breath was sour. He didn't know where his feeling of optimism had come from – or why. For the day hadn't been particularly good. It had been monotone in its sad repetition of a mourning. And with Chadwick gone, it was as if a lot of bright colour had left the story.

Ralph switched on his bedside light. He took up *The Two Wives of the King* and read till dawn, and the book was finished. Seeing the sun at the window, he thought, there is almost no light in the book.

In her twenties, it seemed, Erica March had said: 'We live in darkness. Day is far off. Day may never come.' Only at the very end of *The Two Wives* was there a flicker of light, long after the cargo ships have returned empty, long after the circus-war has turned King Rey's once beautiful kingdom into a mud waste and the King has journeyed on foot seven hundred miles in his search for Beth. Beth is dead. Her body has been flattened and stretched and painted and turned into a wall map of the Kingdom. Her navel is King Rey's palace. Her breasts are the mountains he has crossed, her mouth the chasm of despair into which he falls. Yet in falling, in letting his despair engulf him, the convulsions of his body are so great that the capsule it has harboured for so long with such exquisite agony is finally expelled.

Only then can King Rey find access to his own wisdom and begin to lead a life that isn't founded on lies and vanity. Very slowly, he makes the seven hundred mile journey home. Nothing is left alive in the palace grounds and the earth is stained yellow with the rotted mango fruit. The King begins scrabbling at the soil on his hands and knees. Deep down in the soil there is life and his tears are the rain that waters it and makes it grow.

Ralph put the book away and slept. He dreamed of a young Erica, wearing her blue dress. 'On the outside,' she announced to him, 'I have discovered my own beauty. In my head, I feel nothing but grief.'

'You've no idea,' she said, 'how difficult it was to get that book published! When I finished it – quite soon after I moved into my house – I went very boldly along to Chadwick's agent who had a smart office in the Aldwych. Did I tell you that he was called Evelyn Borrow, which always struck me as a very idiotic name, so that I found it difficult to say. Of course he couldn't help being called Evelyn Borrow but he did let his friends call him "Eve" (which he could have helped) and when I went to see him with my book, he said "do call me Eve," but I really couldn't! Anyway, I didn't stay long. It turned out he was only interested in plays and looked on books as if they were lavatory paper, so I came humbly out, still with my manuscript and got on a train to St Paul's and I sat on the steps of the cathedral and tried to think up a prayer that would help my book get published. I can't remember if I did think up a prayer or not. If I did, it didn't take effect very fast because I had to wait another two years before anyone would take the book on.

'I found a book agent eventually: a very nice man called Sam Green. There'd been a "berg" on the end of Green but Sam preferred to drop this because it sounded too German. He worked in a small, rather poor office in Hampstead, very near my cottage, so this was very convenient and Sam and I became friends and he talked to me about all the "real" literary people in London, like the Woolfs and Lytton Strachey and Aldous Huxley and this would make me feel very envious and determined to be "real" myself one day, and I began to write a lot of short stories.

'Sam worked very hard for *The Two Wives* and in the end his commission was just a few pounds because a very small new publishing house, Patterson Tree, took the book on and paid me terribly little. But I didn't mind really and nor did Sam. Sam had a theory that, after the war, English people only wanted to read happy things – love stories on trains, that kind of rubbish! – and my book was far too sad for them and serious and they simply weren't up to it. So we'd both become very pessimistic about ever selling it and Sam had begun to say things like "Why don't you start another one, Erica and we might have more luck with that?" But I couldn't start another one. It had taken me so long to do that one, I just couldn't start it all over again. I've always written dreadfully slowly, you see?

'But when Patterson Tree came up with their offer I felt like dancing in the street and to celebrate I began an affair with Sam! We were very alike in many ways, very ambitious for ourselves and not particularly clinging, so this began to make me happy and Sam was happy too.

'I remember that not very long after I began my affair with Sam, I got a letter from Eileen, warning me against the new, shorter skirts that were coming into fashion then. She said: "The women of Suffolk are outraged by these new London garments." But I thought, how can Eileen *know* what the women of Suffolk like or don't like – she only ever meets about twenty or thirty of them. But this was typical of Eileen. If she disapproved of something, she pretended everyone agreed with her. She said: "Your father agrees with me: he hopes you are not wearing them."

'But I stopped answering Eileen's letters about that time. Even my father's letters I didn't answer. I felt as if a green sea lay between us. To swim back to them would take me a lifetime, and my lungs and my heart would burst with the effort.

'Sam and I were very content with each other, but my father wouldn't have understood this. And when I wrote and told him that my first novel was to be published, he was incapable of joy. He couldn't say, "I'm glad you've found a talent in you and used it." He just said: "I'm told there is little money in writing books, and perhaps you might do well to follow your uncle and try a play – if you really believe you have the writer in you."

'So I abandoned them. Years went by after that and I never saw them. I used to imagine them sometimes, eating in silence with the pearl-handled fishknives, or sitting by the "Lord Giveth" samplers, waiting for a cow to calve, or just waiting, always in silence for the darkness.'

5

They merge, the 'twenties and the 'thirties. They were different from each other, yet they merge in my mind. I can't remember the dates of things. I get them muddled. I expect it will be confusing for you, Ralph. I expect you'll keep saying: "When was this?" and "When was that?" and I may not be able to remember, not exactly.

'Because they went so fast, those years! They were the galloping years – before the fences were put up. Sam Green thought I was on the lane to insanity. Because sometimes I would run so fast and then suddenly find I was looking into a black, *black* sea filled with horror. And the things I saw made me so weak that quite often I couldn't stand up and Sam would find me lying down on the floor. And always in these black times, I would "find" my mother. I would see her perfectly, just on the edge of the blackness. And the sad thing was that I knew if I touched her she would vanish, yet I wanted her to hold me. But I started to talk to her and I suppose this is why Sam thought I was going mad, because I talked out loud. I found that the talk comforted me – not at first, but after I'd had a very long conversation that sometimes carried on, on and off, for hours. Then she would go away and I would come out of my black place and Sam would be weeping somewhere very near me, thinking of asylums and restricted visiting.

'But I don't want to talk to you about my black times which I still have, often darker now. I won't talk about them because here was my life beginning, beginning all over again in 1921! I became the writer I had wanted to become for six years. I became a new thing with a new voice. This was the wonder of it, Ralph, finding a voice and knowing that it was my own.

'It was the reviewers' doing. If they'd been dismissive, just swept my book aside with a flick of a duster, then I don't think I would have heard my voice, or if I had heard it, I wouldn't have believed in it. It would have mocked me. But they didn't flick me away. They said my voice was original and brave; they said people should listen.

'Sam and I got drunk at breakfast! We saw success buttering our toast and we whooped like Indians. We celebrated for days, buying things we couldn't afford, food and silly clothes. Patterson Tree sent me flowers; there was talk of an immediate second printing so I suppose they suddenly saw that I might help them grow big, grow into a big tree! It was all very wonderful, like the first taste of a strawberry after a cold spring. I think Sam and I even whispered drunken marriage talk to each other, an eternal literary partnership just like the Woolfs (or the Wolves as I called them) and perhaps we believed it, I can't remember. But it was a time full of colour just like this lamp, just like a sunrise – pink and red. And a time of music, which had never been part of my life till then (only the marching songs composed for us by Ethel Smyth when we were Suffragettes, but no *real* music, Schubert or Brahms or Beethoven). But then we bought a second-hand gramophone with an enormous horn like an arum lily and we began to buy records and Sam, who responded far more ecstatically to music than to literature, began to teach me what was what. It was Beethoven's Pastoral then that I played endlessly, endlessly . . . da-*da*-da, da-*da*-da, da-da, da-da, da-*da* . . . oh I can't sing any more, but it always reminds me of that time even though I don't like it much any more. Only Bach now, his discipline and purity, he's the only one of the whole lot that I like now. When I listen to him, I feel that music going through me, clear as a stream, bright as a knife.

'Sam wanted me to begin another book. It was quite logical of course, quite right. I should have begun another book; got down to work. But I couldn't. I knew that the writing of *The Two Wives* had been painful and I thought it *had* to be just the same with the next one – very painful, a time of anguish – and then it would *be* something, not just a story. I tried to explain this to Sam. I said "I don't think I can Sam, because I don't want to. I don't want to experience that same pain all over again, not now when we're so happy." He said he understood, but inside him I don't think he did. He would question me and question me: "What is it *exactly* that's painful?" And I couldn't explain it, not to his satisfaction. All I could say was that I saw this new time as a time of gathering. You sow beans and then you gather them and in the ones you leave are another kind of "gathering" – the seeds of next year. But you can't plant them straight away. The frosts come and the ground is too cold and hard. "So you just have to wait," I told Sam, "you wait till you can put your back into the digging and the hoeing, till you feel strong enough and then you start . . ."

'Dear Sam! I should describe him. He had the face of the Rabbi, serious and long with a rather short body growing out underneath it. But it was a neat body, quite strong, with a lot more browny-yellow skin tones in it than mine. He was twenty-eight I suppose, just a few years older than me and like me he had no mother, only a father, Louis Greenberg, who was in prison at that time for petty theft. Sam was never ashamed of his father and I loved him for this. We used to have long talks about prisons and what prisons can do to your soul, because I knew about prison first hand and Sam knew about them second hand from his visits to Brixton. I offered to go with Sam to see Louis Greenberg but he wouldn't let me. He said strangers bothered Louis Greenberg. He was a man who liked to be alone. So in the end I never met him because he died in the prison hospital, at fifty, and a terrible thing happened to us then: Sam's mourning coincided with one of my black times so I couldn't help him, not as much as I should have done, and I think he felt very sad and confused.

'But I don't want to talk about that today. Ralph. No sad times. Because for six years, or seven, was it, I was with Sam and we saw London coming alive after the war and even the sandwich men, some with medals from the Crimea, seemed to advertise a new hope.

'We imagined, for a bit, that the angry military men had gone silent for ever and that England was civilizing her heart, being gentler to all her people.

'She was very gentle to me. My stories were finding places in the uppity literary magazines. They didn't pay much, but my name was out, that was the thing. I imagined it flying like a speck over London: Erica March. And hardly anyone saw it, but a few did. Sam thought the speck would get bigger. He thought it might turn into a kite, teasing and turning, "if only you would get down to work . . ." he said.

'I tried. In about 1923 I began a novel called *The Angler* and it was going to be about a man a little bit like Chadwick. He leads a solitary life near a river. He's married to a long-suffering plain thing called Betty but he dreams of boys with bottoms like ripe fruit as he dreams of catching a salmon in his river. But no salmon ever swim into his river so he goes on a journey to find where the salmon begin and makes up complicated plans for redirecting them to his own piece of water. And on the journey, which is a very long one, he meets at last the boy of his dreams and brings him home. But the boy, who is very charming and polite on the outside, is a delinquent inside. He puts poison in the river – to which the salmon have swum – and all the fish die. Betty goes mad and starts jabbering a kind of insane wisdom about man's need to eat up his precious things. And I had an ending for it all but I never got to it, not then. Because Sam said "You can't give them a book about a man like this and with a morality like this." So I stopped. I stopped at the moment the boy poisons the fish.

'Mind you, we were a generation dominated, in London, by Bloomsbury. Part of me hated Bloomsbury and thought it all very high and mighty and a bit idiotic, and part of me longed to join in and have country weekends and be full of wit and light.

'I saw Lytton Strachey outside Hatchard's one day, with his thin body and his beard, and he didn't look at all forbidding, only rather a shuffling kind of man, walking as if he was very ill or weak. I thought of going up to him and saying something like: "I think it's very odd, Lytton, that you've all missed me out." But this seemed too bold, too puffed up. So I just watched him wandering on, and then I ran into Hatchard's and said to one of the young men in there: "I just saw Lytton Strachey outside the shop. Could you tell me please what book he bought?" And it turned out that he'd bought *The Two Wives*! The shock was extraordinary. I wanted to run out and find him again, but I didn't.

'But they haunted me, those Bloomsbury people. I was rather pleased when Lawrence said that they reminded him of black beetles, because part of me wanted to step on them – the jealous part. Then Lawrence came along and stepped on them all! Though of course a lot of things reminded Lawrence of insects: soldiers for instance. And he wanted to trample all the insect people to death. "They're done for," he said.

'People have asked me so many questions about Bloomsbury all my life, and honestly, I've never known how to be fair because I didn't *know* the individuals, not as friends. I think there was a lot of good in what they were trying to do, tempered with some bad, tempered with intellectual sniffery, as if everyone else's work except their own smelled repulsive. I didn't like this about them. It made them appear narrow. And as for Moore's *Principia Ethica,* I've never read such a load of bunkum! It was drawing-room philosophy and no more use to anyone than those pairs of mantlepiece dogs with dead-looking eyes. But then, all the Bloomsbury people had drawing-rooms – just like Lady Winchelsea! – and I expect there were a good many Staffordshire dogs over their fireplaces.

'I had a drawing-room in my cottage. But it was very small, so I called it the sitting-room. In fact it was a study. It had a very small window, so not much sun got in and my bulbs never came to anything. I had Chadwick's huge desk in it, and I worked there, looking out of the little window, out onto the street where hardly anyone passed.

'Except for the farm, it was the quietest house I've ever lived in, very hidden and safe. And I remember the summers in it, sitting at my desk with the window open, smelling the privet hedge which I grew from small plants, and experiencing a state of being that was as sweet and solemn as that smell!'

For some days, Ralph hadn't heard Erica's laugh. Now she threw back her head and her laugh was an odd squawking like a jungle bird battering bright wings on high branches after the rains.

John Pennington's letter was waiting for Ralph when he returned to the hotel. Seeing the Oxford postmark, he at once imagined himself there, in John's quiet room, his mind lively, his pulse normal. They drank wine. John sprawled on big Indian cushions.

Worchester College
Oxford

'Dear Ralph,

Thank you for your letter, which somehow got buried for a day or two under a pile of bills. Refreshing to find you after a demand for £59 from Blackwell's!

But I'm ill. I've got what the doctor calls a "spring cold" but it feels remarkably like the bronchitis I had as a boy. I wheeze and ache and only feel comfortable in bed. I'm taking some yellow pills which are meant to cure me rapidly. But until then, it's pointless for you to visit. I'd just be wasting your time.

I hope your project is advancing. I was reading a book of Lit. Crit. the other day which touched on Erica March but dismissed her rather swiftly. I fear she is out of fashion and you will have to work hard to engender a revival.

I will write again when the yellow pills have mended me.

Yours, apologetically,

John

P.S. If this is what novel writing does to a person, then I don't think much of it!'

Ralph stood in the hotel lobby. He was dismayed by the letter and by his reaction to it. I shouldn't *give* a shit, he thought. Why do I put so much onto seeing John? Yet he wanted to cry. The marine in him was lonely again. His patch was empty of all companionship.

On the way up to his room, he found he was following the girl. She reminded him of the girl he had christened Miss Muffet in the Italian restaurant, the girl with the big-bellied man. He followed her, then passed her and looked back.

'The texture of England grows in my fingernails . . . I play tennis with my eyes . . . my voice is all they taught me, all they expected of me . . .'

Oh, *that* kind of girl, Ralph thought. That's for laughs, who needs it? Yet he found he had stopped, blocked her way, thought up a lie.

'Pardon me,' he said, 'd'you happen to know if this hotel has a dining-room?'

She blushed. She found his American voice rather comic and blushed to hide her laugh.

'Yes it does,' she said, passing him awkwardly. 'But it doesn't look particularly nice.'

'Are you going to eat in there?'

She wore very pale tights, almost white – an odd English fashion – and black shiny shoes. She carried her thin body very straight. Her hair was mousy.

'I'm with my father. He's taking me to see *Evita*.'

Ralph tried to muffle the derision in his voice. '*Evita*?'

'Yes. We were jolly lucky to get tickets.'

'Sure,' said Ralph. But his momentary interest in her had gone.

He let her walk up almost to the landing before he said flatly: 'Hope you enjoy it.'

'Thank you very much,' she said, and smiled. When he didn't return her smile she looked oddly hurt. 'One is very used to being smiled at,' said her face, 'one has grown up to expect it: young men with smiles and large bank accounts, driving BMWs. And if one is treated any differently, well, I mean, you know one feels a bit confused.'

Ralph made a mental note: derision and pity go hand in hand. Where either is present, fucking is impossible.

Then he bounded up after the girl. 'Have you got any idea,' he called after her, 'why Americans are not particularly liked in Europe?'

She stopped and frowned. 'They probably don't understand you in Europe,' she said, 'but of course in England one does!'

'Thanks,' said Ralph and carried his laughter safely to his room where he let it out and out till it began to hurt.

The telephone rang and it was Walt. Ralph estimated that it was about three p.m. New York time. Walt would have just returned from Bianchi's full of seafood salad and Orvieto.

'How's it going, kid?' said the big far-away voice.

'Fine Walt.'

'Got your letter today.'

'Yuh?'

'Talk of movies and all that. Who the hell d'you imagine's gonna back that kind of movie. You know I was joking about United Artists.'

'What kind of movie?'

'Movie 'bout a little old English granny! Who the hell's gonna sponsor that?'

'That's not the way I see it, Walt.'

'What? Not the way, what?'

'It's not the way I see it. This life spans almost a century . . .'

'Almost a what?'

'A century . . .'

'20th Century? You got connections with Zanuck?'

'No Walt. I said – '

'I can't see a movie in it, Ralph.'

'Sure. Well, let's talk about it when you see the kind of material I got.'

'And anyway, things are busy here with the primaries coming up. You'd better cut it short there.'

'I can't do that Walt. I'm very involved.'

'Look, I had to send Willard to Iowa. *Willard*! You should have been covering that.'

'Guess Willard did okay.'

'Okay? He did lousy.'

'I'll be back long before the thing starts getting hot, Walt. Just give me the time to get finished here. This is much more than one article.'

'More than one what?'

'One article . . .'

'It's only worth one article, kid. That's all the space you'll get. 'Less she dies. We could beef it up a bit if she dies quickly.'

'I need at least another two weeks, Walt.'

'No, kid. I want you back here in time for Massachusetts; on the 25th, say the 24th . . .'

'I have to go at her pace, Walt. I can't push, okay? If I push, she'll clam up. And at the rate I'm going, I'll need another fourteen days.'

'Ralph. I am not sending Willard to Massachusetts.'

'Massachusetts isn't imporant, Walt. Kennedy's got it wrapped up.'

'I need the whole team at this time, Ralph. I need a competent team and you're screwing it up.'

'I'm fed up with being a fucking team, Walt!'

'What? What you say?'

'I said I'm fed up with being a fucking team. I'm over here doing something on my own initiative and on my *own,* and I can tell you that it's fucking lonely and fucking cold and I *hate* London but the material I'm getting is good. And no one else is bothering to get it Walt. We have the beginnings of a great book, with a TV spin off perhaps . . .'

'I just don't rate it, kid.'

'You don't rate it because you haven't seen it . . .'

'The 24th Ralph, okay. Not a day later.'

Walt hung up. Ralph felt tired from the shouting. When he was out of step with Walt, he hated the man. And he lived, he realized, with the perpetual fear that Walt's personal greed would become contagious. Even the obesity. He was afraid that would, in the end, be catching.

94

He lay down on his bed and re-read John Pennington's letter. The thought that he might have to leave England without seeing John made him uneasy. It was, he realized, as if he expected John to give him an answer, to tell him why he had come. On his own, he probably wouldn't find the answer, just as he had never found a satisfactory explanation to 'Why are Americans Disliked?' He had got near it and it had eluded him. Now he was getting near to a life that spanned the whole of his century and more. But the movie idea is bluff, he thought, isn't it? So what am I going to do with it all, the hours and hours of tapes? Sometimes I think I know; then it slips away. 'But I can't believe,' he said sadly, 'it's of no value.'

'She was on that settee all night,' said Mrs Burford accusingly. 'She never saw 'er bed all night.'

'Why?' asked Ralph.

'Something you said? Something upset 'er, did it?'

'No. I didn't upset her.'

'Well I put 'er to bed straight away. She was worn out from sitting. So she can't see you today, love.'

Mrs Burford turned away with a sniff and Ralph stood by the door, dejectedly counting the days left to him, knowing there weren't enough. Then he heard Erica call, a frail voice (often her voice was remarkably strong) from the bedroom, which Ralph had never seen.

Mrs Burford took immediate charge. She stumped to the bedroom door, opened it without knocking and advised: "Don't see 'im today, Miss March. He'll only tire you, dear . . .'

But she said she would, she *wanted* to see him if Ralph didn't mind talking to her in bed and without her turban. She looked a sight, she knew, but she had remembered something, something important, and before she forgot it, she wanted to tell him about it so if he wouldn't mind sitting down . . .

'I remembered it last night;' she said, 'when I was going through Gérard's letters. It had nothing to do with Gérard so I don't know why I suddenly thought about it, but I did. It happened during the time, in 1944, when I went to see Eileen, and I told you, didn't I, that this young American airman landed in our greenhouse? I think he'd been doing imaginary bombing raids on Bungay, pretending it was Heidelberg or somewhere in the Ruhr and he crashed his plane and ejected and came down in the greenhouse, so of course he was cut to pieces and blood was flowing from him everywhere. Well, I nursed him while Bernard telephoned for an ambulance and I tried to talk to him very gently because he was in awful pain and thousands of miles from Maryland which is where he came from and the sight of Eileen's tomatoes all round him must have been terribly strange. I tied his wounds up with pieces of sheet, but I couldn't move him because both his legs were broken. He was conscious, though, and just before the ambulance came and took him away he asked me my name and when I said Erica, he managed a wonderful smile and whispered:

"Erica, Erica

Take me to America." and I said – and this is what is so important – I said "No, I can't do that because I shall die there and I don't fancy dying yet." I told him I would die in America! I remember saying that as if it were yesterday. Yet I can't imagine *why* I said it. You see I've never been to America, Ralph, and of course I won't go there now, it's far too late. But I told the airman I was afraid to go because I knew I would die there. And now here you are, Ralph, right at the end. Isn't that strange?'

'I don't really see the connection, Erica.'

She looked very disappointed. 'Don't you, dear?'

'No.'

'No. Well perhaps there isn't one after all. It was just that . . . last night . . . I felt *sure* there was. Perhaps you're right, though. There may be no connection at all.'

She was silent. In the heavy wooden bed she looked small, very very old. Next to the right hand wall of the room stood the cupboard. It took up the entire wall space. It was dark oak with carvings on the panelled doors and along its top. It was much more ornate, much finer than Ralph had imagined it. It might have come out of Hampton Court. He reached out and touched it. Time and Mrs Burford had given it a shine; the wood was pleasing to touch. For the first time – now that he had seen it – Ralph began to understand why she had attached so great an importance to it. It was the only thing in her life that had never changed.

'If you're tired Erica,' Ralph said quietly (she had closed her eyes), 'I won't stay any longer.'

'No I'm not tired,' she said. 'I had a marvellous night! I read all Gérard's letters, every one of them, and they made me laugh with joy

96

because they are *wonderful*, full of wildness and passion and I honestly think, if he were still alive, he'd be like that still, wild and passionate, even though he'd be a hundred by now and blind I expect, too blind to shave, so he'd have a long beard!

'No, you mustn't take any notice of Mrs Burford. She grumbles a lot but she's very kind and protective, a bit like Bernard's labrador. He grumbled! I'd much rather talk to you than sleep. Some days it's all I can do – just let sleep drag me down. On those kind of days, I can't even lift my hand. But I'm all right today.

'I must tell you first what happened to *The Two Wives*. It sold very well after those flattering reviews and it went into a second printing and then a third and Patterson Tree got very excited and started putting out their branches to France, to see if they would publish a translation. I used to go and have long talks with Ranulf Tree who was a very untidy resplendent kind of man, smelling of cheroots, and rather fat. I often thought if Father Christmas were real, he'd look and sound just like Ranulf Tree, and it's a shame he's not, only in C. S. Lewis's head, poor old thing.

'Ranulf Tree had *been* Father Christmas to me. It turned out that he had liked the book and Ian Patterson, Tree's other half, had only been lukewarm. So it was Tree who persuaded Patterson to go ahead and publish it. Without Tree's persuasive powers, Patterson would have sent it back, just as all the others had done. So I had a lot to thank Tree for and now here he was, trying to sell it in France.

'Sam got terribly excited. He said of course, a French publisher would take it because the theme was *mondiale*. He said if that theme wasn't *mondiale*, he didn't know a theme that was.

'So we bought a few more clothes, and more expensive food. We were becoming just like the people Eileen warned us against, wearing short skirts, and white trousers, eating luxuries. And in London it wasn't difficult to do this, to be like this, because all the young people wanted to forget the war and the old men who had started it; they wanted to dance the war into oblivion. I don't think we felt any guilt. Now and again I would feel guilty about not writing and I'd begin something, but Sam was doing well; new writers came to him and we used to laugh over some of the rubbish he got, but quite a lot of it was good. So Sam was growing and Patterson Tree were growing and now here was talk of a publisher in France.

'Tree found a French publishing house. They were called Maison

Cambier and they were small like Tree and Co.; but growing. Just a week before Sam and I left for Paris to begin negotiations with Maison Cambier we got an invitation from the Woolfs – to dinner at Gordon Square! We were going to be away for ten days and we'd have to miss it, and I knew that if we refused, no other invitation would come. It was 1925, the year Virginia published *Mrs Dalloway* and had such a success with it. Everyone in the literary world or on the fringes of it wanted to know her then; they were all dying for invitations to Gordon Square. If my name was a speck, hers was a bright comet with a tail!

'But there it was. We couldn't accept. When I thought about it, I cared more about seeing my book in France (where I had *longed* to go, when Christabel Pankhurst was in Paris) than I did about the wretched Wolves and their intellectual chitter-chat. Sam was very down-hearted, though. I expect he'd thought there'd be a stray writer or two to catch between the soup and the fish course. So I offered to go to Paris on my own, in spite of my not speaking French. Sam and I, you see, always believed we should let the other be free, sometimes just free to be alone. But he said no, he wanted to have the ten days in Paris with me and he thought negotiations couldn't be properly handled without him. I think it broke his heart to refuse the Wolves, so to cheer him up I bought a copy of G. E. Moore's *Principia Ethica* in which they all believed, those Bloomsbury people, and started reading quotes to him over his boiled egg or when he was on the lavatory. There were some terribly ridiculous ones like "the general practice of murder seems certainly to be a hindrance to the attainment of positive goods," and "admirable mental qualities do consist in an emotional contemplation of beautiful objects, and hence the appreciation of them will consist essentially in the contemplation of such contemplation" – and even Sam had to laugh! I think he'd got over his disappointment about Gordon Square. He remembered it later, of course. He remembered a year or two later that he'd given up the Wolves for the trip to Paris, and then, because of what happened to me on my second trip, he felt very angry about missing the Wolves and wrote me a letter saying I had ruined his career. Not that this was true, Ralph. Don't think that, will you? It was hurtful to Sam when I left him for Gérard, but I never "ruined his career". He was successful all his life.

'We stayed in the Hotel Raspail, on the Boulevard Raspail. It was the first time in my life I'd ever been in a lift.

'We had separate rooms because Maison Cambier had booked them. Maison Cambier were in the rue de Grenelle, two minutes' walk away. Sam explained to me that we were on the left bank.

'It was raining and the cobbles were very slippery – worse than London. The first thing I bought was a fishing rod with reel and bait. I kept it in my hotel wardrobe till the weather cleared and I went down to the Seine with it. To fish in the Seine was the *one* thing I wanted to do. Yet the man who sold me the fishing tackle laughed and grinned and shrugged his shoulders. It was as if he couldn't imagine a woman like me fishing.

'Sam wasn't well. He'd been terribly sick on the Channel boat and the hours in a crowded train had exhausted him. In his exhaustion, his ability to speak French deserted him and we mumbled our way around in the rain, paying too much for everything (*far* too much for the fishing rod, Sam said!) and feeling lost.

'I put Sam to bed. I said on no account was anyone to *déranger* him: he was *gravement fatigué*. I got brandy sent up to him which he mixed with tapwater in a tooth glass and he collapsed into a sleep that lasted two days and nights.

'I was very tempted to wake him for our first meeting with Maison Cambier, but he still looked so white and deathly that I didn't dare. I just went on my own and hoped that someone would speak English and that I could explain who I was.

'I expected Maison Cambier to be grand. I somehow expected pillars of marble and polished doors, and all there was was a little tin plaque next to a bread shop, then a dark stairway painted green and on the first floor two rooms, one small, where manuscripts were read and discussed and one very large, where all the design and typesetting and printing went on. It was more like a workshop than a publisher's, and it was run entirely by the two brothers, Jacques and André Cambier. How they had the cheek to call themselves a "Maison" when all they had were two rooms, I don't know. I suppose they knew, in time they would be a proper "Maison" with secretaries and readers and sub-editors and a firm of printers at Auxerre. Just like Patterson Tree, they knew they would grow because now, with the war well and truly passed, everything seemed set to grow again and it wasn't till a few years later that the growing stopped.

'They were very nice to me. Jacques Cambier had learnt a bit of English in the war. He could even sing "It's a long, long way to Tipperary", he said, but I wouldn't let him because it reminded me of Eileen. André was younger and hadn't been in the war and couldn't speak English so all I could say to him were a few formal things I knew like *"Desirez-vous une cigarette"*, and all he could say to me were the patriotic things he knew like "God save the King" and you couldn't call this a conversation! I came to know him a bit better when Sam woke up and deigned to speak a bit of French, but until then I could only talk to Jacques.

'Jacques wanted me to work with the translator for the whole of my stay. Once the contract and the advance had been agreed, by Sam, then this man called Valéry Clément would begin the slow work of the translation. I would dissect the book with him, illuminating anything that needed illuminating (Jacques was very fond of this word, "illuminating") and when I left, Valéry would soldier on until my next visit when he would ask for more illumination. "How many visits do you think this will take, Monsieur Cambier?" I said. And of course he smiled. "As many as you like," he answered.

'I woke Sam on the third day. It was a bit like a resurrection because the sun had come out and was streaming into his room. He refused point blank to believe that he'd slept for two days. He also refused to believe that I could have dared to go to Cambier's on my own. But we went and had a meal in a very nice brasserie I had found and he began to come alive and start to believe things again. I told him all about Cambier's and Valéry who I had met by then. I didn't tell him that Valéry had made my heart race. I didn't say, "Valéry is the most beautiful man I've ever seen". I just said, "I've done as much as I can with Jacques Cambier, Sam. Now it's your turn." So he laughed then. I could tell he was proud of me. Sam loved me best when I was daring.

'I went fishing the next day. Sam went off to see the Cambiers and I sat by the river in the sunshine. I remember thinking, I could be in Suffolk now, slicing winter roots for the cows on the corner of a draughty field. If everything had been different, that's where I'd be. Yet it was almost impossible to believe, sitting there with my fishing rod, in the existence of anything but the sparkling water under my dangling boots and the voices near me, old men and children who had lived their lives never more than a heartbeat from here.

'It's never been difficult for English people to fall in love with Paris. I think they see some spirit at work in its making that they don't have. They love, and they envy and some of them want to stay for ever and be part of it so that they can say, "Paris is mine."

'I think I courted it very, very slowly, one tiny place at a time. I've never been very keen on the grandeur of buildings like the Louvre nor on the incredible vistas like the Champs Elysées: the sheer size of them makes me feel livery! One of my favourite places in the whole of Paris was the bread shop next to Maison Cambier's green stairs.

'They weren't really a success, those ten days. We sorted out the contract with Jacques Cambier and my advance was about fifty pounds. Sam thought it was going to be a honeymoon but it wasn't. I worked all day with Valéry, first in the Maison Cambier office, then in his own room in Montparnasse which was much quieter, and all night, well, I dreamt about Valéry and they were the most shameless erotic dreams.

'So Sam wandered about, sensing what was happening to me, hating all the long hours I was at Montparnasse. I always had dinner with him, but I think he was very depressed. All he kept saying was, he thought it was time to leave.

'I never touched Valéry and he never even looked at *me*. It was an affair of the head which only one of us – me – ached to express in an affair of the body. But I should have known, with someone as beautiful as that, that men were his choice. I don't know why I didn't understand that straight away. Then I would have put him out of my mind and out of my dreams and welcomed Sam in again. But when I did understand – on my last day with Valéry – I wanted to laugh. I wanted to write to Chadwick and say: "I've found paradise for you, darling! But too late."

'We stayed friends though. Valéry Clément translated both my other books. Rather like Chadwick, his lovers would come and go and over the years his remarkable beauty began to sag a bit and he had countless operations to tie his eyes up and stretch his lines away. But I lost touch with him in the 'fifties after he did *The Hospital Ship* and I expect he must be dead by now. I think he was a little older than me.

'It's because of Paris that those years merge. I *think* it was 1925 when I first went with Sam and we met the Cambiers and Valéry Clément. It must have been 1925 because that was the year of *Mrs*

Dalloway and in 1926 my book was published in France. But because I went backwards and forwards so much and my heart was tugged to and fro for a while, I don't remember the months and the dates of things. I know that after the first Paris trip, after we were back in Hampstead, I had a very bad bout of depression and I saw things that were so ugly, Ralph, so obscene and awful! I imagined I had battered Valéry Clément to death and set bits of his body floating on my sea. I kept trying to pick the bits out but the sea was taking me down . . . I so longed for normality, for brightness at the window, for everything in its place . . . and Sam fought a battle for me, bless his heart! He stayed with me right through it, pushing away his nightmares of asylums.

'We were having quite a little success with my stories, so the minute I was well again Sam made me sit down and write. I went back to Chadwick's desk and I thought, the only thing I can write about is change. I feel change. Every second. Our world under the clouds moves in all things as they move, with a restless push and gather and drift. Even my heart. It moves and separates. And the rhythms of my writing are changing, changing and *oh,* all that is quiet and still at my window, it may go. Any second, when the man selling matches passes, shuffling, altering; just the sight of his hands in the torn mittens is enough . . .

'I felt I wanted to have another try at *The Angler.* I hadn't looked at it for two or three years. Now I knew – or I thought I knew – how I could end it. I read it through and thought Sam had been wrong, perhaps. He thought it was all about nothing; lavatory paper for Evelyn Borrow! But I said no, I'm trying to look, I'm to *present* a man with a very wonderful imagination, but that imagination only *works* when it's in search of all that's base in the man – his greed and acquisitiveness, his lust.

'I thought there was only one end for him – as a writer of brutal, pornographic books. And on these, of course he gets rich, restocks his river with the finest salmon, and drowns trying to land one of the fish. I thought it wasn't a bad idea, so I started to go on with it, in spite of Sam's reluctances. He said it was melodramatic, unworthy. But I thought I could handle it so that it wouldn't be either of these things, and I took the manuscript, as far as I had gone, round to Ranulf Tree to let him read it. He rather liked it. He thought I had been very erotic and bold in my description of the delinquent's bottom and he said: "I don't see why you shouldn't end it as you've planned."

'So then I really began to work. Sam was as silent as a mussel! I couldn't prise him open, not a crack, to get him to say anything about it. He was reserving his judgment, that was all he'd tell me, and anyway, he didn't believe I'd ever finish the book. "Why don't you think I'll ever finish it, Sam." I kept saying, but he didn't know. He was just certain, he said, that I wouldn't. But I sat at the desk, and I wrote. The book emerged terribly slowly, a drop at a time, like a strong medicine you administer in tiny doses. Sam watched me. I remember his long face at this time and it was full of sadness and I knew that I had caused him to feel as he felt, yet I couldn't quite say what I had done or what I was going to do. "Everything changes," I kept muttering. "Everything does and this is one of the absolutes in our world – constant, constant change."

She slept then. Sleep came as quickly as it does to a child. Ralph sat and stared at her. He remembered how, at dusk, his Grandma would fall asleep on her front porch, in the middle of a conversation.

6

'This is the exciting bit. This is the time I thought I'd write about one day, when I was old!'

Erica paused, took a sip of wine, and looked at Ralph.

'I never wrote about it because I felt I couldn't *master* it, Ralph. It existed for a time and each moment had its own colour and sparkle. I think those were the most important ten years of my life and for a while afterwards I thought, I will set something down that belongs only and absolutely to that time. But I couldn't, you see. Now in *The Hospital Ship* I made General Almarlyes fall in love and this love of his destroyed itself because it was in his nature never to be satisfied. He needed to *possess* his love. He squeezed all the life out of it and it became brittle and pierced his hand. He thought he was holding it safe in his hand, but he wasn't: he was making a weapon to hurt him. I was trying to tell, in this book, something of what happened to me twenty-five years before. But there was very little of *me* in General Almarlyes. He was a man and a soldier and going mad – and I've never been any of these things. I've made other attempts, in little stories, to describe my time with Gérard, but they failed. Each one failed. They were like collages – bits stuck on, no event or feeling or conversation emerging the way it *was*.

'Just lately – over the last few years – I think I've begun to understand why I failed and failed to capture that part of my life. I think it has something to do with the fact that from the moment I met Gérard, the self – the *me* with all my certainties and ambitions – became secondary. I literally "forgot myself". I lay curled up in Gérard's life like a piece of sand inside a mollusc. The proof is that I wrote nothing for ten years! After my good start with *The Two Wives,* I let ten years pass without setting down more than a few stories and some entries in a diary. I still guarded in myself the idea that I was a writer. I knew, I think, that one day I would write properly again and that writing would be my life. And I felt guilty, of course. Now and then I would take myself off to the Dôme or the Coupole and sit there *pretending* to write, but I wasn't writing, I was living. Every sight and sound in those places was distracting. I wanted to gobble up the essence of each moment so that the external became not merely the internally observed but *became the internal.* I wanted the totality of my world to flow round me in my blood.

'Oh this is difficult to explain, Ralph! What I'm trying to tell you – so that you understand why I achieved so little in these years – is that the self I had valued so highly in its struggles with Emily, in the cold Suffolk winters of the war, on its own or with Sam in London, somehow got lost, no, wanted to lose itself, to experience and be, but not *do,* to lose responsibility.

'I ought to tell you how it came about, yet I don't know if I can. Even now there are so few certainties in this part of my life, just the one certainty that I loved Gérard. For a while they wondered who I was, his friends. Gérard told them I had written an important book and this shut them up. And then gradually they came to see that I didn't exist any longer because of my "important book", I was the girl who loved Gérard – and this was all. I existed in order to love Gérard.

'We met in Cambier's office on my second trip to Paris which I made without Sam whose sense of foreboding made him stay behind. I knew nothing about Gérard. I'd never heard of him or any of the painters and writers who were his friends. Jacques Cambier told me he was doing some drawings for a surrealist work they were publishing. He introduced us and I laughed at his name: Gérard Guerard. He was a very thin man. His features were all pointed, even his eyes which appeared to travel quite far sideways round his face. He wasn't very tall. He looked a little taller than he was because of his hair which stood up very thickly on his head. It was going grey, his hair, quite noticeably whereas there was no hint of grey in mine and we were both the same age – thirty-three.

'I was in Paris to do some final illuminating for Valéry Clément. He had done a very, very good job on the translation and through all the hours I spent with him, I began to talk a little bit of French. I bought a cheap Grammar and learned verb declensions and reflexive pronouns – all the *spaghetti* of the language which is dull on its own and tangled but necessary. I didn't find it very difficult. It was a relief to do that instead of trying to write. And I was hearing it every day, all around me. I gobbled up the language along with everything else.

'I had a week. I was at the Hotel Raspail again and every morning I would walk to Valéry Clément's room in Montparnasse. It was about a seven minute walk. It was April or May of 1926, a beautiful spring. I wore some of the silly clothes I'd bought with Sam in London, even a strawberry coloured soft hat with a flower on it! The clothes were very fashionable, very stupid but underneath them I knew that I was beautiful in a way no one had ever expected. I had been a plain little girl, I was plain, still, when I came to London for the first time and now I was no longer plain. I think I had *become*!

'In the films I had seen – American films – it was always the beautiful women who triumphed. It was fashionable to believe that love and beauty went hand in hand, that plainness limited a woman's ability to love and be loved. Thank heavens your generation doesn't believe that any more; you've grown up in that way. But in the 'twenties beauty was at a premium. I looked very secretly at mine. On my walks to Valéry Clément's room I took a glance at it in a florist's window. I saw myself surrounded by flowers. By the time I got to the Rue Déparcieux I was quite flushed with it, quite hot in the spring morning in my strawberry hat. And on my third or fourth morning, as I turned into the Rue Déparcieux, I saw Gérard waiting outside the street door to Valéry's apartment. At first I thought, he's one of Valéry's friends, just leaving after the night, and then I recognized him as the man I'd met with Jacques Cambier. I think I knew then that he was waiting for me.

'I didn't go to Valéry Clément's that day. I expect he waited for me and was cross when I turned up again, I don't remember. I went with Gérard to La Coupole where he always had breakfast. He ordered croissants and bowls of café crème and hot chocolate for me. He ate as if eating were a rite of utmost seriousness, dipping his croissant in the coffee, bending his head down to bite into it before it dripped. He didn't look at me until the rite was finished. With his mouth full, he talked about himself, now and again searching (in the coffee it seemed!) for an English word he'd forgotten. He told me that he lived rather poorly in small hotels, in rooms with kitchens, that he was experimenting with form and trying to experience new ways of looking at reality. I had never heard anyone talk in these kind of phrases before – only critics who seemed to have a language all their own which they liked to keep secret. Gérard didn't want anything kept secret. He thought the pavement artist was the worthiest of men because the most honest. Deception in art, he said, was as significant as deception in politics – worse even because by ambition politicians are deceivers and artists are seekers after truth. "I'm very far," he said, "from finding the truth, but I can say that I seek for it truthfully."

'I felt very odd. Part of me had flown up to the high ceiling of the Coupole and was staring down at what was left of my hot chocolate, at what was left of me. I thought, I'm so small, so permeable I must fill myself out before I disappear, before I'm bound up by this man and can't breathe. I remember thinking, I've never understood exactly the set of feelings and emotions people are describing when they talk about "falling in love" but now I do understand what it is: it's simply a feeling of breathlessness.

'I tried to save myself by talking. I began to describe how I had written my novel, burning candles in my cold Suffolk room. I explained that it had been begun as a parody of the war, as a way of opposing the war all by myself. As I talked I remember thinking, I must show this person that I'm more substantial than I feel, that the strawberry hat is a deception: underneath it I am struggling to grow wise.

'I've often wondered what kind of account I gave of myself that day. I believe I knew I was about to be swallowed up and before I vanished I had to prove that I had the makings of a life. I remember that Gérard listened very intently, that he seemed rather impressed by what I said and when I finished he smiled with a kind of relief. The smile said, now I can let my feelings go where they will because, despite her idiotic clothes, the woman is something after all, she is worthy of me. So we sat smiling. We'd both said our little pieces and now we could let our eyes creep over each other and be silenced by what we saw.

'Neither of us said anything about our private lives. We both talked about ideas, not about people. So that when I went up the little stairway to Gérard's room I had this momentary conviction that when we got there, I would walk in and find his wife preparing lunch, that I would shake hands with her, have a drink perhaps and then leave by myself. But of course there was no wife – not there that morning in the room – only the room itself with its choking smell of oil paint and some torn curtains at the balcony windows, I went to the window and looked out for a second onto the Rue Chomel. I had never seen a view I liked so much.

'We made love like starved sailors. Time teased us and became afternoon, became sunset and we lay there. I thought, I shall never go from this room. I shall never, never have the strength to leave him. My heart wanted to break. It said, you've found your wild spirit and you will ride it for as long as it carries you and one day it will let you fall. And after that there will be nothing more like it, only replicas.

'We got up at dusk and dressed and went hand in hand back to La Coupole where we had dinner. We were speechless for a while and then the food revived us and we began to talk. I wanted to talk about what we had done because I had to be certain that guilt would play no part. I am quite free, I kept saying to myself. I am free to love in a way I've often imagined and never, until this moment, experienced. I told Gérard, I am quite free to love you. And I suppose he smiled.

'Well, a great love affair is the hardest thing to describe, Ralph. I've tried it, in some of my stories and in *The Hospital Ship* to make my characters experience something of what I had with Gérard. None of these attempts have succeeded because although I have always enjoyed the company of language, it shows a kind of indifference to strong feeling; it says, "there's only my everyday workaday self with which you can explain these things, don't imagine there are any other tools." All I can do, I suppose, is to try to conjure the *essence* of what I experienced, to make you believe that this one great adventure was utterly different from any other that I've had,

'You're the same age, Ralph, almost the same age as I was when I met Gérard. There is no age better than this and yet, you see, I did nothing, only pursue and pursue my own happiness. I let England go. Without a backward glance at it. I kept it, I suppose, somewhere inside me – very tiny – in case I should need it again. When I was alone I sometimes thought of it. I thought of Sam and my leaving of him. I thought of my house which I had sold with all its furniture except the cupboard which I couldn't bear to sell. I gave the cupboard to Sam. I told him that one day I might come back for it, thinking then that probably I never would. I visited Chadwick's grave and said "if only you could come to Paris, darling, then we'd have some times!" But even Chadwick had gone from me then, I couldn't remember him! All I could remember was the gold of his hair that wasn't real and which, once, I had tied with a ribbon.

'I arrived back in Paris with a wad of five pound notes sewn inside my knickers. I brought all the clothes I had and all my notes on *The Angler* which still wasn't finished. I don't know what I thought I was going to do! Move straight in with Gérard and stay silent in a corner while he painted: become his lap dog. When I saw his room again I realized it was so small there was hardly space enough for him and his work. I felt very stupid. So I began to search for a room not too far away, but rooms seemed very hard to find. I knew that until I could speak fluent French at least there was no hope of finding a job in Paris and that the money I'd brought could disappear very quickly on food and rent. I had to find a cheap room. I courted discomfort, too, because I wanted to be like Gérard in all that I did. Comfort separates classes and kinds. Gérard had already hinted at his contempt for the *petit-bourgeois* with their passion for furnishings, their over-heated rooms and I felt tainted by my two years in Bryanston Square.

'The first room I took was a sad kind of place. It was in a small hotel built around a courtyard and it was utterly dark and silent. The concierge, whose husband had been killed on the Somme, had the room next door and she used to sing herself to tears each night and fall asleep weeping. She neglected the place and the courtyard stank of open drains and rubbish. You saw rats there.

'I remember unpacking my bright clothes in this cold place. I tried to scorn my clothes as frippery, to welcome my dirty room as the cradle of my new life. But it was sunless. It bore no resemblance to Gérard's room, with its little fretted balcony and its beautiful light. So I escaped from it as quickly as I could. I bought a map and set about discovering where I was, how long it took me to walk from my room to Gérard's, from Gérard's to La Coupole, from there to the Boulevard St Germain and the Café Flore, from there to the river and so on. I tried to stay out of Gérard's way as much as I could, to let him work.

'But I was often there, uninvited, on his stairway. To keep away was very hard and often his work was neglected. Just like Sam, he began to encourage me to start writing. I mistrusted this. I thought he's tiring of me, he wants me out of his way. But then he would talk to me seriously about his own belief that those who create in one decade, shape the time to come, about the importance of finding new ways of seeing. He began to use what I later thought of as his "public voice", the voice that united him with public events – with a public reality – the voice that I, who had been brave at twenty, now longed to ignore. I'm very ashamed of this, Ralph. It was a kind of sleep, you see, a sleep where there was only one dream, to experience Gérard's love.

'I tried, in my horrible room, to discover the patient, creative part of myself. I worked at *The Angler* but it had no life, I literally couldn't see what I was doing. And I became very depressed. The singing of the concierge was indescribably mournful. And in a dream one night I woke to feel tiny pattering feet on my face; mice had invaded my room. I found their droppings on my clothes. And I knew then that I would go mad in this room.

'So I packed my suitcases and left. I spent three days in Gérard's room with my suitcase unopened on the balcony and I told him I couldn't work, that I found separation from him terrible. He laughed at me. He said I was too pale and needed sunshine. The next day he bought second-hand bicycles and he pulled out an old rucksack from under his bed. He designed a very beautiful decorated message to his friends, to those who might call while we were away, and pinned this to his door. It invited them to write to us, *poste restante* at Aix-en-Provence in the event of a workers' rising or some such long-awaited happening. And then we were gone, taking the overnight train from the Garde de Lyon for Avignon. It was late June. In the middle of our night on the train I remembered that publication date for the French edition of *The Two Wives of the King* was July 10th. Jacques Cambier had promised to organize a little party for me and I would miss it. I would also miss all the reviews. But I don't think I minded. I believed that, away from Paris, Gérard would belong less to ideologies and more to me.

'It is strange how, in my years with Gérard, I was always very moved by the smallest things he did for me. Sam had done a great deal for me and most of this I accepted, without giving it any attention. But when Gérard abandoned his work to take me to Provence, when he cared for me without sleeping once when I was ill – everything he did for *me* – I took as a reaffirmation of his love and I treated it with a sort of solemnity!

'We began to discover each other on our first holiday in Provence.

We gave our bicycles names. Mine was La Reine Victoria and Gérard's was Maréchal Joffre. These names helped us to laugh at punctures which were exasperating and meant hours lost. "He's farted again, the poor bugger!" Gérard would say when a tyre went on Maréchal Joffre, and when mine had a flat I'd groan, "You'll have to wait for Her Majesty. She's fallen down!" We discovered laughter. And somewhere near the point of laughter in Gérard was the scampering urchin who liked to tease and run, take me with him on his back and sleep with me under the stars. At these times, he let his public soul fly away into the black above our heads and a private joy overcome him. To make love with Gérard, then, was no longer a deliberate act, merely the expression of a surfeit of happiness, the reaching out of two dreamers whose only knowledge of morning lies deep in each other's eyes.'

'It is only since she has begun to talk about passion,' Ralph wrote in his Summary, 'that I've begun to see something of what separates me from her, my time from her time. I knew, after the first few days' talking, that there was some fundamental thing, informing what I must call Erica's life but which also goes outward from her and *informs* the times she lived in. I believe this thing is passion, or desire, or call it what you will, a craving of the spirit that's lacking not just in me but whose lack *characterizes this era*. Because if I ask myself – and get this, Walt, with your petty tantrums and all your sound and fury under your necktie – where do I get a whiff of passion or desire in anyone, anyplace? If I ask myself, is there any guy out there showing even the private face of passion, let alone the public thing, I get a NO, underlined. And Jesus, if I go further with this thought, then I have to admit, I've found nothing as scary as this. Because if we all – in the West anyway – have got beyond these feelings we shall simply erode ourselves with boredom – with non-feelings! We've let all the light go out of our heads and we ask ourselves like imbeciles, why isn't there someone around who can see for us? And this is the stupidest thing: we *imbue* people with light – therapists, analysts, so-called prophets – and there's no more light in them than in my ass! They're just a crass part of this lightless, passionless generation. I mean, I don't even know one person, man or woman, not *one* who loves another person, not really loves them in the way that Erica understands and describes love. I guess there was more compassion

– and love – in her for Uncle Chadwick than there is in most women for their husbands, in most husbands for their entire family. Yet she's not old fashioned. She believed in individual freedoms. She didn't pester for marriage and rights and shit. She's like a tall ship. You hear me, Walt? She's sailed a thousand lives.'

Ralph took a sip at the large whisky he had poured himself. He was hungry and began to promise himself another Italian meal. Then he wrote on: 'There is no doubt in my mind, I shall stay on till what I have come to think of as "the end". I don't know when the "end" will arrive. I guess it could arrive any time because she could just decide to stop talking. Heaven knows whether the talking is making her weak. Sometimes she seems to gather great strength from it, but it's hard to say. Perhaps, in her heart, she's finding it a strain. In any event I won't go back on the 24th as commanded by Walt. Who gives a shit about the presidential election anyway: one lying sonofa-bitch outspending another lying sonofabitch. If Walt fires me, I shall make a creative event out of it; I'll start trying to write, and I mean invent, not report. Because we're a generation of reporters. Our favourite pastime is reporting on each other's wars and taking crap photographs of each other's mutilations.'

Ralph didn't go to the Italian restaurant. Still hungry, he bought a glutinous hot-dog from a street vendor and took this with him to a new production of *Hamlet*. To his satisfaction, the Dane was played as a man sidestepping the larva of his own hatred and terror but nearing, always nearing the crater edge, his every breath, in the sulphurous times, bringing his lungs close to bursting. There was not an ounce of the dreamer in this Hamlet, only the sweat and fever of the revolutionary, the rage and solitude of a man who sees corruption steaming at his very feet.

It was apt. Ralph experienced a gentle lifting of his earlier deep gloom. He wanted to shake the actor's hand. Here, at last, had been a *show* of something which passed for passion. The show had happened.

He took Erica the programme the following day and she at once fumbled for her glasses and began to read it. 'I don't know any of these actors any more,' she said 'nor the director or anyone at all. Of course I don't! I haven't been to theatre for years, although I do read the reviews sometimes and hope they'll print a picture so that I can imagine the play.'

'Would you like to go, Erica?' said Ralph.

'To the theatre? Well of course I would in a way. I would love just to be inside a theatre again. But the journey would be awful and if I felt tired, then I'd just go to sleep, so what's the use?'

'I could take you,' said Ralph. 'If I called a cab, then the journey wouldn't be bad.'

She hesitated. 'You're very kind, Ralph. Always very thoughtful, you are.'

'Would you like to go to see *Hamlet*?'

'*Hamlet*? Well I'm not sure. I know how long it is, you see, because I was in it once. I was one of the Players who came to Elsinore. I had no lines and we did a marvellous dancing, rough-and-tumbling kind of entrance which I loved. Matilde was playing Ophelia and she wasn't very good because she was quite wrong for Ophelia. She was a gypsy, Matilde, and she could look wild but she could never look weak.'

Erica paused, handed the programme back to Ralph, asked him to pour her some wine and then she said: 'Matilde was Gérard's wife.'

She took a sip at her wine and waited, as if for Ralph's comment, but he was silent.

'I expect that surprises you, doesn't it. It surprised me at first. I accused Gérard of a terrible betrayal. Because if I thought about it, I had given up everything for him, yet I hadn't come to know about Matilde until our return from Provence in the early autumn. He'd never mentioned her. This was strange in a man who valued the truth so highly. Yet when I came to understand what he had with Matilde – just a friendship that was easy and innocent – I forgave him. He'd married Matilde at twenty. They'd lived together for no more than two years and then gone their separate ways. Only after he had parted from Matilde had Gérard begun what he called his "search for form". The marriage didn't "belong" to him any more and nor did it to Matilde who was in love with Philippe Fernandez, an actor whose father was Spanish. Really, Matilde and Philippe were both gypsies. They looked like brother and sister and among all Gérard's friends whom I came to know, I loved them best.

'I think my jealousy of Matilde lasted for a week or two, perhaps more. I moved out of Gérard's room and into one of my own, with a kitchen attached, not far from Maison Cambier in the Rue de Grenelle. It was a kind of attic, but filled with the wonderful

September light. I could almost see the river from it. On the ground floor was a patisserie with a stand-up counter where you could have coffee and sometimes, as the winter came on, I would treat myself to breakfast in there – two bowls of café crème and two *pains au chocolat* – because the patisserie was always warm and sweet-smelling and my attic was very cold.

'The pigeons used to trample all over my sill. I was watching and listening to the pigeons very early one morning when Gérard knocked on my door and began to shout at me: "I can't work without you! What's this ridiculous sulking and hiding? Are you going to hide up here for ever, or are you going to come down?"

To tease him, I said I had decided to go back to London. I expect I wanted him to beg me to stay but of course he didn't, he shouted all the more. He told me I was petty and childish and then he left, slamming the door behind him.

'I'd been having dreams of our holiday in Provence. We were in the Luberon hills at midday. We found a river of white stones, absolutely dry with lizards scampering everywhere. In my dream we died there. We never got down to the grass road where our bicycles waited. We put our heads between two white stones and they were severed. Our heads went tumbling down where the water should have been. The strange thing was that I *felt* my head falling and I knew that I could bear even this, even death, if my head would only stop tumbling and come to rest on the ground beside Gérard's.

'So I had to decide to forget Matilde after that. I had to stop thinking "Gérard has a wife" and to help myself do this I went to Gérard and apologized and asked him if I could meet Matilde. I think I wanted to be sure that she had a life quite outside him, that she exercised no rights of possession over him, nor he over her.

'So we met for lunch at the Brasserie Lipp – Gérard and I, Matilde and Philippe Fernandez. Matilde was very large and lively and dark. I wondered if she had been called a witch by her father, as I had been. It was rather an enjoyable lunch. I was shy of the bad French I talked and Matilde and Fernandez (we always called him Fernandez and not Philippe, but I don't remember why, unless he chose this himself and liked to be reminded of his ancestors in Madrid) hardly spoke any English and laughed very loudly at Gérard's English when he talked to me, reminding him that he had gone to a posh school where they taught English and fencing. He had also spent six months in

London before the war but he had found it depressing. The only memory of any wonder he retained was being caught in Trafalgar Square one day by a huge crowd who were there to watch a great procession pass. As the carriages neared him the crowd went silent. Then he saw women in their hundreds, dressed in white. He found it very beautiful and mysterious and he had never understood it. I explained to him that it was Emily Davison's funeral.

'To my surprise, Fernandez had read my novel which, I told you, had come out in Paris while we were away. He said it was a most interesting book and that the critics had been right to praise it. He also said that he and Matilde were great friends of Valéry Clément and that he had worked very hard to seek out all my meanings from the text because he believed the book was important, and why were not all writers writing about the sorrows of war so that we would be spared the next one? I remember that Gérard said "The next one? The next one will be a civil war and the working men and women of France will win it." Matilde and Fernandez smiled. They had heard Gérard say this before. They didn't like the self-satisfied bourgeoisie either: they expressed their dislike in the dress, which was colourful and bizarre and in the way they lived – rather like Gérard and myself – in underfurnished rooms with no heating, without possessions.

'As I settled in to my life in Paris, I realized I knew no one who possessed inherited money. I began to feel guilty about Chadwick's thousands, yet on my final trip to England I had discovered that my English bank would be able to make a monthly bank draft to me in Paris. The money would be more than enough to cover rent, meals and new clothes if I wanted them. By the end of the year, as I made plans with Gérard for the little new year party we would have I had decided that until I felt I could begin to write again, I must find a job. Gérard was quite angry. "I don't see how you'll be able to work if you're doing some petty job. And if you don't work, Erica, you're betraying yourself!"

'I tried to explain what I had explained to Sam: that it is difficult to go from one novel to the next, to sustain an idea through all that time. But Gérard couldn't see this.

"I work every day," he said, yet sometimes his day's work consisted of a tiny sketch, sometimes of putting together a mathematical formula or writing down snatches of ideas for his friends to see. His work on canvas was sporadic and it always exhausted him. At those times I kept away until he came shuffling round to my room, very white with a three- or four-day beard and we would drink Pastis and I would make us a meal in my tiny kitchen. His eyes would be very bright in his tired face. Often he got drunk and would make love to me on the floor, shouting obscenities.

'It did trouble me that I couldn't write. I was at last living side by side with writers and painters and from them, with them, I suddenly saw my life quite, quite differently. It had the quality of water. It was everywhere, in the crevices of every building, every face. It sparkled. I began to keep a kind of diary but no *ideas* gathered in it. I observed and noted, I recorded impressions. If you like, dear, I can rummage about and find the diaries. Perhaps you can make more sense of them than of anything I can tell you. I expect they're a lot more intimate and lively and they will certainly convince you that I was very, very happy. I just wasn't able to write a book, that's all; I was too immersed in the colours of each day.

'We had our New Year's party in Gérard's room. We cooked beef with red wine and served it with a dish of noodles. We never bought very expensive food but we cooked well. My patisserie made us a chocolate gâteau. Fernandez was sick out of the window from eating too much of it. Aragon and André Breton were invited. We used to have a café relationship with these people and it was strange to see them in Gérard's room, eating food I had cooked. Aragon arrived very late, very flushed; he said that Matilde and I, who had chosen black dresses, looked like carrion. A lot of actors came, friends of Fernandez and Matilde. They were faces I had seen sometimes at the Coupole or the Dôme or the Flore – young men in sparkling clothes, a Russian girl called Ilyena who wept. The room was lit by candles. When it was too hot to breathe, I opened the balcony windows and the night was very still and freezing. I carried a candle out and stood still listening to all the noises in the street. I tried to imagine that somewhere, beyond all the roofs and river, no more than a few hundred miles away, was England.

'At midnight Matilde came out and we both looked at the street for a moment. It was icy cold and I was shivering. She put an arm round me and said in English "Gérard loves you, so you and I must not be strangers." Then she kissed my mouth. I remember thinking, in many ways she is like a man, with her dark skin and her strength, and I'm glad there is this friendship between us; it's part of all I wonder at.

'It was very difficult to find a job. Unemployment was high. You saw despair in the cafés – the young men who had fought in the war had been promised a better world to come home to and many of them had come home to nothing, to a job here and there, to vagrant lives. The gulf that separated these people from the rich was enormous. But at that time, the rich kept mainly to the other side of the river, the writers and painters were a smelly lot; they didn't often come near us. But if you crossed the Pont de la Concorde you saw them. They began at the Place de la Concorde outside the Crillon Hotel and the Champs Elysées was their bridleway. In spring and summer they paraded there. We used to walk past Fouquet's and hear their clattering; we imagined huge stone bowls of foie gras, sole cooked in champagne, and I'd remember Chadwick's passion for restaurants: "the moment of sheer delight, Erica, when a waiter unfurls your clean linen napkin!" I tried to translate this saying of Chadwick's for Gérard: "*le moment exquise, Erica, lorsqu' un garçon se deroule ta serviette de toile frais!*" and he laughed until he had hiccups. He made me repeat the saying countless times and he would always double up with giggles! Then sometimes he'd say, quite seriously yet with an edge of sadness: "When the revolution comes there will be nothing more like that."

'In the end I found the very job that I was supposed to have had in London: I went to work in a large patisserie on the Boulevard St Germain run by a Corsican called Mr Saladino. Being a kind of immigrant, he wasn't prejudiced against foreigners, in fact he thought it was rather a snappy idea, having an English girl to serve tea in his shop. He put up a sign saying "English Spoken" to attract American and English tourists and quite a few of these came and the English people would tell me how lucky I was to have missed the General Strike and who did coalminers think they were anyway? I *hated* this kind of talk. I asked Mr Saladino to take his "English Spoken" sign down, but he refused. He earned quite a bit from the tourists.

'Now and again Gérard would come to the patisserie and sit in a corner waiting for me until I was free. I gave him brioches and even cakes. I think Mr Saladino knew but the only thing which fascinated Saladino apart from money and confectionery was love. He said lovers were more beautiful than mille feuilles, more complex and wonderful than profiteroles! Whenever he saw Gérard come in, he would run to shake his hand. Yet he never asked his name: he always called him "Monsieur le peintre".

'I worked from half past eight in the morning till six or seven. In the winter I walked to work in the dark and walked home in the dark, but I don't think I minded. To be earning money, not just spending Chadwick's, made me feel my independence with a poignancy I've never forgotten.

'But I ought to try to tell you about Gérard's work. He was on the edge, I suppose of the surrealist movement, yet never part of its inner circle. Breton was interested in him for a while and we used to spend some evenings up in Montmartre at the Café Cyrano. Politically, his heart was with the surrealists: to liberate the irrational in man is to touch man with a new notion of himself and of what is possible in society. He wanted change. His nightmares were almost all of the fat man, the military man, all draped about with medals. The fat man had a tambourine and the little bells on the tambourine made the small tinkling noise of his existence. With the tambourine he announced "I am in command!" And he would bang the stretched skin of the tambourine to remind the world of all the artisans and labourers, all the growers of lavender and the clog-makers and the miners of salt he has pushed before him to the front line – the front line of war and the front line of poverty and ignorance. And Gérard's nightmare of the fat man informed a great deal of his work. Like Breton and his lot, he did believe, to a certain extent, in the omnipotence of dreams and he wanted to shock, not to please; he tried to give his work power, not beauty.

'I think in 1924 he had been closer to Breton than he was when I arrived in 1926. He couldn't, you see, accept the idea of automatism. He thought it was idiotic to let his hand idle about on a canvas because he could always see his paintings and his sculptures as things complete before he started them. To begin a piece of work was to see it already done. It hardly ever changed or *became* in its execution so that the actual execution was sometimes quite tedious; it was in the vision of the work that his excitement happened. So you see he couldn't ride along hand in hand with the believers in automatism. He didn't understand how form can sometimes creep out of apparent chaos, out of sand or a blood splodge or pieces of paper on the floor.

He did a lot of experimenting with textures though. In one of his pictures he cut off his pubic hair and stuck it on the head of his fat man which by that time had become a gargantuan head with the dewlaps of a cow. He painted over the pubic hair with scarlet and let the paint dribble down into the mouth. It looked very frightening – as if the brains of the fat man were bursting out and slithering down his face.

'I expect you've read bits about Gérard in those heavy books they write, those shiny, serious ones, about the art of this or that time. The thing is there's never a sparkle of humour in any of those kind of books. They treat themselves with such reverence! And this reverence was the nub of all that Gérard couldn't stand. Even the reverence of the Mass disgusted him; he could see no light in it. At one time, he did a series of paintings of all the pieces of ourselves we've turned into stone statues so that we can bow down in front of them. He did a very fine sculpture of a person's intestines crammed with bits of strawberry flan and the bones of tiny birds. He believed we'd even turned sex into a ritual; sex and marriage he believed we'd turned to ashes. For one of his pictures he made hundreds of journeys to the Rue Blomet to collect the ashes and clinker from André Masson's stove. Then he invented these two heads, one in a bride veil, one in a large top hat almost covering his eyes. Their bodies are the bodies of innocents yet have the quality of stone. The faces have genitals for nose and mouth, yet the faces are full of agony, terribly sad. And Gérard put the ash everywhere, in their mouths and ears, on the top hat and the veil. So they're trapped in three ways: by their stone bodies, by the suffocating ash, by their inability to communicate except by the tiny movements they can make with their sex. I used to say to Gérard "They're the saddest people in the world." And I think they were so sad because in spite of Gérard's rearrangement of their bodies, they looked pathetically alive. He called the painting: "Monsieur et Madame Dupont" but I always thought of them as "The Smiths" and they're still struggling of course, poor souls, still blackened by the ash from André Masson's stove, but in New York now and you could go and have a look at them one day, Ralph. You could tell them, "Erica sends a petit bonjour."

'I think it was about the time that Gérard made "The Smiths" that I sat down in my attic one evening and finished *The Angler*. It wasn't a novel, nor was it a short story, it was something in between and I called it An Allegory. Gérard read it, but he couldn't understand a lot of the English words so he found it very mysterious and odd. It *was* rather odd. Patterson Tree rejected it. They said they didn't know what to do with it because it was much too short for a book. I thought of sending it to Sam, but I didn't. Sam had written me two very nasty letters saying the devil in him was going to burn my cupboard and that his life had gone brown like a leaf.

'In the end, I showed it to Valéry Clément who was very happy at that time with a friend of Matilde's, a theatre designer called Andreas who came from Barcelona. He liked the story so much that he took it straight round to Maison Cambier, but they wouldn't publish it. They said, "make it twice as long and then we'll take it." But I couldn't do this. To finish it, just as it was, had been a labour. It was as if I'd left the idea behind in England and now it was quite irrelevant; it said nothing at all. So I shut it away. I could have tried to publish it – perhaps in two or three parts – in *Littérature,* but I didn't. I made it my excuse for doing nothing more for three years. I told Gérard that, in discovering happiness, I had simply lost that part of myself which wanted to create books. I thought at that time that it was gone for ever and that my life with Gérard would be my own private work of art.'

She had rummaged about in the cupboard under the clothes and found two thin exercise books. In these were the 'diary' she had kept of her life in the years 1927–1936. They were sporadic jottings. Weeks passed and she was silent, then some event or thought would be described in meticulous detail. The handwriting, often done in pencil, was bold and fluent. Certain pages were smudged, some stuck together. The *cahiers* themselves had life.

Travelling inspired her to write. The first entry, dated July 30th 1927, described her last day at Mr Saladino's patisserie before leaving for Aix with Gérard, Matilde and Fernandez:

'I am voracious for the sight of Provence, waking through its haze. No bicycles this year. We'll go on foot or by bus and Fernandez is bringing a tent the size of a dog kennel. Gérard and I have no tent, but to lie out in the darkness is to have dreams of flying.

Mr Saladino spent the afternoon retouching his new *English Spoken* sign; this in spite of the fact that English will not be spoken in his patisserie for more than two weeks. I reminded him of this and he snapped: "I speak it myself! Tea, sugar, hot water, milk. Excuse me. Thank you very much. Tip not included."

I am amazed to have stayed with Saladino so long. I often wonder how far I walk each day, back and forward from the counter to the tables. I think it's several miles. And hardly a day differs from the next: the same impatience, the same puffs of conversation from the well-dressed women I serve. The money I earn keeps me here and I have grown fond of Saladino who is so like the Fat Man who stalks Gérard's mind that I sometimes think, he is the model, the archetype. Yet he's not idle and his gourmandizing at least has no ceremony round it. Nobody unfurls a linen napkin for Saladino unless, in their short evenings, it's Thérèse, wife and mother he calls her ("Take your fat boy in your thin arms, mother, mother dear and make him wholesome!") when they sit down to their soup and Saladino sighs at the brevity of each night's sleep, at the paucity of each sleep's dreaming. And is it in the night that he beats her – for her refusal of him, his great belly smelling of sugar and flour – or in the morning when he wakes at four to start work and she lies there, worn out by this night of his, his trumpeting release of himself, his snout buried in the pillow in blissful oblivion?

Then the mistress who comes, in her alligator shoes with an eye of the salamander. Orders a cup of tea, unseen by Thérèse, washing linen upstairs, scraping turnips with her head in a bandage. "Celestine!" he wails with joy, "angel of Monday afternoons, angel of every second Thursday! Celestine!" I bring her a japonais cake today and one of the soft paper napkins we offer with the cakes.

Her lipstick is glossy and thick – "the better to kiss you with, my little Saladino, the better to implant the red of my heart on your huge thighs." She is thin, like Thérèse. The fashionable call it slim. They walk without bandages round their heads.

But at six, when I should have been leaving to rush home to make all secure in my attic before departure Mr Saladino puts up his new *English Spoken* sign and says to me in abject misery, "nothing to do with my time off any more. Might as well study English in my time off – excuse me, not today thank you very much, milk, sugar, cakes, Buckingham Palace, would you prefer cream" – might just as well buy an English book and try to study it because Celestine is going to Evian les Bains for two months and you, even you, Erica, are leaving me."

Left at six thirty.'

On August 10th, an entry recorded a day of extraordinary weather, a day of discovery:

'Woke up in a room. After our nights on hard ground, the chewed old mattress swallowed us. We felt a kind of sea-sickness. The curtains kept out the sunlight, however, and we didn't wake till eight. No sooner awake than Gérard tells me he has dreamed yet again of hot chestnuts and cream. I promise him we will go in search of a chestnut tree, but I fear it's too early for the fruit.

We're at Thoziers, a village quite high in the Cevennes. It was raining when we arrived, very worn out, and we were grateful for this room which is above a café painted brown inside and out. Matilde and Fernandez got a barn full of fresh hay. They came to breakfast (in our café) smelling of the hay. They look brown and healthy but Matilde often complains about the cold in the early mornings. I never feel the cold, nor does Gérard or Fernandez. Fernandez now wraps Matilde in a big shapeless cardigan he bought at the market in Aries and we all hope she isn't ill.

We pack up and set off in search of chestnut trees, Gérard and I alone for a few days, while Matilde and Fernandez are taking buses to Nîmes. Our ability to lose ourselves is directly connected to Gérard's longing to stray from the track. We bound like ungainly mountain animals up cols and escarpments. Ravines appear. We jump and slip. We save our lives holding little tufts of brush.

We have lunch on a hillock and beneath us is pine and scrub. The air smells of thyme. No chestnut trees. None discernable. We eat stale rolls and a strong goat cheese, then the watermelon Gérard had carried for us all morning. Then we look for some shade, to sleep. I begin to imagine orchards and soft grass but up here all is white and hard and full of thorns. We climb lower, where the pines are more dense. There is shade and a flat basin of scrub where we lie and listen to the crickets.

Sleep doesn't come. Lust travels from our early morning sea-side bed and we lose ourselves. For a second I see us as two snakes tangling in the heat! Our backs are brightly coloured, our tongues are silver. And then from my snake's body, from my eye near the dry grass I see the two leg bones of a man sticking out from a clump of gorse and I hold my breath. I stare and stare. Gérard's heavy breaths fan my hair. Then he falls on to me and I gently turn his head, very slowly turn it towards these two white bones I can see. I want to shut my eyes and listen to his heartbeat. I imagine his body with no heartbeat in it and I want to wail, "those are not his dead bones, not his!"

Even in the shade, the heat is stifling. We are damp and exhausted, on the skittering edge of fear. We can move only slowly. We stand up naked and walk forward till we are above the gorse bush. Below us is the dead man, not a scrap of flesh on him, bones dried by countless summers and camouflaged on the white rocks. Only his feet are missing. *His feet are missing*!

Yet we're no longer afraid. We pull him out and all his frame is light. When we pull the skull stays behind, half embedded in the shallow soil. Now he has no feet and no head, just a centre. We stare at his hands, the minute bones. Then we lift them and hold them. Gérard strokes his rib-cage, bone by bone, then his pelvis. I go and pick up his skull. It is split from between the eye sockets to the back of the neck.

The sweat dries on us and we are cold. The sun goes and we see big silent clouds bringing rain. Colours go from our high landscape; as we dress I envy Matilde her heavy cardigan, Gérard's mouth is stretched, white. "I want to take him," he says, "I think this is a big discovery of the greatest importance." But I confront the officialdom of death, the town hall at Thoziers? Name? Next of kin? Age? You must not steal bodies, I begin a protest but Gérard is tense, watching the approaching rain, measuring time for our descent. To where? There is no village in sight, and we can see for miles. I scan the trees for a bell tower, an old roof the colour of coral.

"Take him where?" I say.

'It doesn't matter where," comes the answer, "as long as we get him to Paris."

The rain begins as we start our walk. I carry the empty rucksack and Gérard has the bundle of bones in his arms. I imagine our procession into a village, if we should ever find one, old woman in black staring as we go boldly to the one hotel or café: "a room for three, s'il vous plait."

But then Gérard finds an old sack. Earwigs cling to it and he shakes them off. He asks me to hold the sack wide and our white friend is pushed into the sack. We try to tie the neck of the sack with some grasses, but they snap and won't hold, so we bunch the sacking together like that and we go on. We are drenched and tired but something in Gérard is on fire with excitement. "The miraculous", he says several times "is everywhere."

At six we hear a bell chiming and we try to follow its direction. The sound is peaceful and seems to summon a gleam of warm sunlight from among angry clouds. And the clouds take off – west, north, south? I have long ago lost all knowledge of direction: all I know is that the sun's gleam is hesitantly to our right and that the bell is ahead, in front of us. But as the clouds speed on, we can see that we're walking more or less due south. At dusk we reach Thoziers les Colombes.'

Intrigued by the story of the skeleton, Ralph searched in the first volume of the diaries for another entry which would tell him what became of it. But the next two entries were devoted to Erica and Gérard's arrival at Nîmes (still carrying the sack?) where they found Matilde seriously ill with bronchitis. Fernandez literally carried her from their hotel room to the hospital and in bleak silence the three friends wandered about Nîmes, waiting each day to visit her, waiting for her recovery. In his desolation at her illness, Fernandez recounted miserably to Erica and Gérard how many times he had been unfaithful to her.

During their visit to Regent's Park, Erica had described the English spring as 'surly'. It came on with a bad grace; it made you ill-tempered with waiting. But now in London it arrived. The daffodils shone; the chestnuts put on leaf, in the squares you saw almond trees and forsythia and magnolias and the air was warm.

Ralph felt such a relief at the sudden change that all his fear of the city of solitude seemed suddenly to leave him. He found a dentist not far from Erica's flat and persuaded the receptionist to give him an emergency appointment. One more day of pain was all that he would have to suffer. Then without the pain, which was constant and exhausting, he promised himself he would make progress on his Summary. He would also write to Walt, unafraid. He would simply inform Walt that he wouldn't be back in New York until May 1st.

He found Erica sitting by an open window. She had sent Mrs Burford out to buy mimosa – she *longed*, she said, to smell that incredible smell of Southern France. But there was no mimosa in Camden Town. Mrs Burford had returned with tulips and narcissi and stuck them at random into a glass vase.

'It's something,' said Erica to Ralph, 'but it conjures nothing.'

And then she apologized.

'I've talked too much about Paris, haven't I? You want to hear about my work, Ralph, don't you, and of course in the Paris years I did none, hardly anything worth mentioning, and it wasn't until I went back to England that I began *In the Blind Man's City*. So I can go straight on to that, if you like. I can miss out quite a bit of time.'

'Please don't,' said Ralph. 'I want to hear more about Gérard. There must be so much more, isn't there?'

'Did you look at the diaries?'

'Yes, I dipped into them. The bits I read were about Mr Saladino and then –'

'Saladino! He was indestructible, Saladino! He kept going all through the war, all through the occupation, bribing people to sell him flour and sugar I suppose. And chocolate! How on earth did he get chocolate, when the shops had hardly anything in them but lentils and swedes? But he kept on. He was there when I went back, just that once with Bernard, after the war. He was so pleased to see me that he cried. He told me that his mistress, Celestine, had been bombed in her bed. "But they found two bodies, Erica. Some other *salaud* died with her! With my Celestine!"

'I often thought of leaving Saladino's patisserie, but in the end I worked there for nine years. Nothing changed in it. The *English Spoken* sign came and went to be repainted, and Saladino's English

125

never got any better. My wages went up. He wasn't stingy with money, not to me, because he saw me as an "asset"; he loved to show me off to Americans – a real English girl serving what he advertised as Best English Tea. I often explained to him that all the tea in England came from India or Ceylon or China, that there was no such thing as "English Tea". He seemed genuinely surprised. Perhaps he'd imagined tea plantations on the slopes of the Pennines, I don't know! But he went on advertising Best English Tea and his customers kept drinking it, so everyone was happy. And I was happy to be there, in a way. Sometimes I imagined the things I could be doing, the useful things. But I had no qualifications to do anything really useful. And in the winters it was marvellous to work in a place that was so warm. And often Gérard came in and our friends came from time to time and Saladino got to know them all and teased them about their lives: "painters, actors, riff-raff!"

'He used to bully Thérèse. This was the basest aspect of Saladino, this sadistic bullying of his wife. She was from Calvi, she told me once. She could remember fishing for crabs off a high wall in the old port and she longed to go back there, to Corsica and the sea. Paris was a grey tomb to Thérèse.

'I tried to stay out of Saladino's rows. They didn't concern me. I don't know to this day why he used to beat Thérèse or why she didn't leave him and drag herself onto a boat back to Calvi. Perhaps her family in Calvi were all dead and she had no one and nothing, only Saladino and the patisserie. I often wanted to say to him, *why* do you hurt poor Thérèse who works for you day and night? Why d'you *do* it? But I never said it. When I told Gérard he said simply, "All married men beat their wives. It's part of the ritual."'

Erica stared at the flowers Mrs Burford had bought. 'They used to sell mimosa in London, you know,' she said. 'I think it's my favourite flower on the earth. When I die, Ralph, I'd like you to pack my head round with it and put it over my eyes and then who knows if I might not be reborn as a butterfly, in the Marché aux Fleurs in Nice?'

'You're not going to die while I'm here, Erica. You may have years and –'

'Oh yes I am! I couldn't tell you which day because I have to wait for certain signs . . .'

'I don't believe that, Erica.'

'You must *start* believing it, Ralph.'

'Why?'

'Then you'll be ready, dear, and do everything properly.'

'Do what?'

'Help me.'

'Help you with what?'

'Help me to die. Because I'm so ready for it, Ralph. I want to run to death like a lover and yet I'm afraid to do it yet because nothing yet has shown itself to me on the other side of death. No hint of anything but eternity and silence. But something will show itself – it *must.*'

She was silent, staring at the flowers. Ralph heard Mrs Burford close the kitchen door and quietly leave. There was no wine today. She had forgotten it. Ralph felt thirsty and got up to get himself some water. When he came back with the drink, she had turned away from the flowers and was watching the sunlight on her arm.

'Tell me about the skeleton,' said Ralph. And she looked up sharply.

'What skeleton?'

'The one you found in the Cevennes in 1927, the one you put in a sack.'

Her face creased into a smile. Smiling she looked older, even, than she was.

'Oh that!' she said, 'we lugged it all the way home. Gérard was full of ideas for putting it to good use. He planned a series of big canvases looking at man's aims and pathetic aspirations in the light of his brittle mortality. We brought the skeleton right to my door in a taxi, but we'd both fallen asleep on the way from the Gare de Lyon and we got out of the taxi without it. Gérard was demented by its loss. He walked around Paris for a night and a day, taking taxis in the hope of finding it. But he didn't. And while he was away, the police came. They thought we were murderers. We spent hours at the Gendarmerie explaining ourselves away. But I don't know where they buried it. Perhaps they sent it back to Thoziers les Colombes by post.

'Gérard began his series without it. He manufactured bones with plaster of paris. He studied his old anatomy books. Bones absorbed him for three years. He lost weight so that he could feel his own bones more closely with his hands. He wanted, literally, to put his own bones into his pictures, to give them his own life. He became very morbid. He began to hate the confines of his studio, so he started looking for a very large room that he could lease or rent. He was fed up with hotels.

'He found a room in the Rue Pierre Nicole. It was opposite a bicycle factory and had once been used for storage. It had nothing in it, so we spent days at the flea markets, buying cheap utensils and chairs, and a brass bed that had been painted white. By the time we'd fixed it up – with a kerosene stove, too – for the winter mornings – Gérard had begun work.

'Until this time I'd never seen him go into a piece of work with such a fury. He destroyed everything he'd done with the plaster of paris bones in the Rue Chomel and started again, He'd work sometimes for twenty hours without food or sleep. He stopped coming to Saladino's. He gave up spending nights in my room. He became like a stranger. I knew he would come back – in his own time. It was during his exile that I got the tiny part in *Hamlet* and Matilde did her Ophelia. I spent a lot of time with Matilde and Fernandez, even a night in their bed, and we smoked hashish. But I felt very cold, without Gérard's love, terribly terribly cold. I asked Saladino for a month's holiday, which he gave me. I let my room go and I came to England.'

7

'I suppose it was the winter of 1927. There was a storm in the Channel and almost as soon as our boat had set out from Calais it had to turn back. I've never seen such a sky. It was like the sky that comes round me, when I feel I'm losing hold . . .

'I found a hotel room for a few francs and I lay in it listening to the storm. I thought, if storms came every day there would be no travelling to England, only in a little plane and even the plane would be swallowed up in the black. Then I slept, with all the shutters banging and I dreamed of Gérard struggling to make sense of his bones.

'We crossed over the next day and it was snowing in Dover. I think I cried in the train. There was desolation in England. And the trouble was, Ralph, I didn't know why I was there! It seemed idiotic to be there when all I wanted was to be with Gérard. And I began to have such fears. I thought, he'll become so thin, he'll waste away to nothing. I thought, his eyes will sink back into his skull.

'As soon as I got into London, I wrote to him. I tried to describe my love, which was as black as the sky over Calais and as bright as the midday heat at Thoziers les Colombes. Separation from him was like a wound and I wondered if he felt it, too, a kind of bleeding in him. I think it's very terrible, to feel the weight of another person on your heart. I began to remember my father and to wonder if, when my mother died, he felt it, the silent weight of her, and had to carry her around year after year, till he met Eileen and the weight unravelled itself in the *Book of a Thousand Knitting Patterns*.

'I expect I told myself that I should go and see my father, but I knew I wouldn't. I imagined him growing old and I was afraid of this. I remember thinking, Gully will take care of everything.

'I stayed in a hotel in Bayswater. It was a very drab kind of place, much worse in its way than my room in the Rue de Grenelle, because it was full of old women and ugly furniture and there was an air of piety about it, piety in whispers, piety in the fabric which smelled of hassock seeds. There was a coal fire in my room, though, and this was kept in most of the time. I sat by it and wrote letters and waited for letters to arrive. The snow fell almost every day.

'After a week, I plucked up courage and went to see Ranulf Tree. He was wearing an overcoat because of the cold and he looked very, very large. He stared at me in astonishment and told me that I had become very beautiful! He bought me lunch in a warm restaurant and asked me, where is it then, the new novel? And when I said I'd done nothing, only *The Angler,* which neither he nor Patterson had liked much, he gave me a lecture on idleness and waste. I tried to explain to him that writing had become very irksome to me. I told him I would write another book – one day – but he would just have to be patient. And of course he was very pessimistic; he said *The Two Wives* would soon be forgotten and my name with it. You simply must follow it up soon, he said. So I knew he hadn't understood. I wanted to get cross with him but the food was too good, and I expect I was glad to be talking to somebody at last, instead of writing my letters and waiting by the coal fire.

'After ten days there was a scribble from Gérard. The pages were all stuck together with something sticky and purple which could have been blackcurrant jam so it quite difficult to read. He told me that the loss of the skeleton was still driving him mad, that he'd been up to the Père Lachaise cemetery, to see if anyone could be dug up "in the interests of contemporary art and man's understanding of his eternal dilemmas." But of course they wouldn't let him dig anyone up, not even someone very ancient whose grave no one visited. They thought he was insane and sent him away like a dog. So he began all over again with the plaster of paris bones, but the longing to use real bone never left him. He told me, very openly, that he'd slept with a whore in the Passage de l'Opéra but that she'd smelt of rubber and he didn't know now if she'd been real or if he had imagined her. He said he didn't understand what on earth I was doing in England and he described the joyous part of himself I had stolen from him by leaving. And after that first letter, he wrote almost every day. He became obsessed by the girl in the Passage de l'Opéra. She must have lost her smell of rubber, I suppose, because he went to her quite often, sometimes at four in the morning when he couldn't sleep. He always called her Erica and imagined she was me – or so he said – but when I later asked him her real name, he said without hesitating that it was Claudette. I don't suppose he called her Erica at all!

'When I left Paris, I promised myself I wouldn't go back before a month was over. When the snow melted, I walked around a great deal in London and took trams to places I'd never been like Kew Gardens. Since then, I've always rather liked Kew. It's very easy to imagine botanists with little moustaches and white legs like Chadwick's, struggling down the Congo in dugouts searching for rarities and then bringing them all the way back to London to grow in that artificial heat. And Queen Victoria going round and saying, "Pray tell me what this is, and this with its thorns and were the native bearers unmannerly!" The very idea of a tropical garden in London is utterly strange to me, and yet there's something very wonderful about it.

'Sam found me one day. He'd heard from Ranulf Tree that I was in London and Ranulf Tree must have told him where I was. He was the last person I was expecting and to find him in my hotel made me feel seasick. I believe Sam had promised himself that he wouldn't be angry with me, because what was the point of it? But when he saw me he couldn't *but* be angry. He'd been harbouring very jealous feelings and now they came out in a rush and the pious hotel was stunned. He told me I had spoiled his life and that if I was unhappy with Gérard, I was well punished. He said if it hadn't been for him, I would be no one and my book would have stayed shut up in the cupboard forever, turning yellow.

'He was probably right about the book, but this hurt and fury was dreadful nevertheless. I told him to be quiet, or I would be thrown out of the hotel and I dragged him out into the Bayswater Road. We walked down it and into Kensington Gardens which were very dead, with all the trees dripping, and Sam stopped on one of the paths and put his arms round me and rested his head on my shoulder. I felt very sorry for Sam. I wanted to hug him like a brother. But I couldn't feel any desire for him, none at all. It was hard to believe I had shared my life with him for so long. What I'd felt for Sam in those years was utterly unlike what I felt for Gérard. Utterly.

'Like Ranulf Tree, Sam was appalled to hear that I'd done no writing. He refused to believe that I worked in a patisserie. He said I was wasting my life. And I thought, oh lord, if only I could tell you, Sam, that far from wasting my life I am living it, almost for the first time since the days of 1912. And if I work in the patisserie till Saladino is a hundred years old, too frail to beat Thérèse, too weak to climb the stairs to Celestine's bed, I don't mind! Of course it's a haunted life, with Gérard's bone pile staring out at its edge and the girl in the Passage de l'Opéra staring in, but love is by its nature followed everywhere by ghosts, no more no less than life itself is led side by side with death. Isn't that true, Ralph? Isn't it true?'

In the dentist's waiting room, Ralph opened the first of Erica's diaries at an entry dated February 26th 1927:

'I am back with Gérard. London was an interlude, like a watch stopping for a while.

His room is white with plaster dust, like a sculptor's place. The first bone collage is finished. The bones are "anchored" to wood by very old nails and the thing is called simply *Crucifixion*. He has used stones also and painted anguished eyes on them. And there are tattered bits of red and black rag and feather. He says they're vultures.

We lie in bed and stare at this thing and we sleep exhausted, tangled up, bone on bone. Then a day goes by and we don't get up. We make love like spring toads, clambering about. Fernandez comes round with the news that Matilde is pregnant. He says the room smells like a brothel. We make coffee. I would like years to pass in this way.

Then I am back at Saladino's. Nothing had changed. Thérèse creeps down the stairs with the washing the customers never see. She hangs up sheets and shirts and overalls and aprons in the tiny courtyard behind the shop. Saladino makes a birthday cake for Celestine. He hides it on the "special orders" shelf. Oh yes, there is a new assistant, Joseph, in the kitchen. He is quite inexperienced – therefore paid very little. I'm surprised at Saladino who is very patient with him and helps him all the time. No attempt made yet to find a room. I am at Saladino's all day and Gérard's compulsion to work at night has (temporarily) left him. So we eat suppers at the

Coupole for which I pay and our life is ordered, but we both mistrust this. Gérard even comes to Saladino's and sits in his usual corner. Saladino teases him: "She left you, Monsieur le peintre! Eh? She left you for a month!"

I had a dream of Emily last night. She came and offered Gérard her bones – on the one condition that I move out of his studio and rediscover that part of myself which doesn't belong to him. Yet I'm still there today. I can't find the strength to go.'

'Will you go in, Mr Pears?'

The clean, smiling receptionist, the black leather chair, the light on a mechanical arm, the washing of the dentist's hands, the instruments laid out – all was formal, ritualistic. Ralph let the ritual begin with the clipping of a little towel round his neck and the tilting of the chair under him. He longed to sleep, to wake up on another day when the ritual was over. As the probing of the pain began, he remembered Walt saying once: "I have never understood, Ralph, with your education and your intelligence, why there is so much of the coward in you." With considerable effort, he resisted an urge to weep.

'So pain has receded, almost to nothing,' noted Ralph in his Summary. 'Begun to feel a) wholesome again and b) relieved that my teeth will stay with me for some years yet. English dentists are less pessimistic and less expensive than American ones.'

'To celebrate, I got laid. Realized, no, remembered how much I crave coloured girls and probably always have done. Katherine, hostess at *Mr Toad's,* no exception. In the dark, the whites of her eyes looked aquamarine. And she forgave me the night of vomit. Was all sweetness. Paid her a fortune to stay the night and bored the hell out of her talking about the white master in the white man. Told her all the zap's gone out of his look. Cracks his whip (frayed old whip) and strikes himself!

'Guess in my (what passes for a) heart there's a coloured maid struggling to get out with her tray of tea and muffins. Seduce, subdue, they're in there somewhere, these words. And Grandma nods, out there on her porch, nods and says nothing.

She remembers Pearl. "No darn good, that Pearl!" she spits at last, "she'd have herself these nigger boys, night after night. They'd ride in from the town on *bicycles*!" Oh hell! When I get home, a lot's gonna be different. We live in the era of the Intimate Deodorant and Gary Gilmore. The roll-on shrink locks us away from life – for life.'

'In the spring Gérard's old room in the Rue Chomel became vacant and I moved into it. It had been partly refurnished, with a little desk put near the balcony window, and all through that year I made attempts at sitting at it and trying to write. I think I finished two stories – two or three perhaps – but no one published them. They stayed in the room like litter.

'Fernandez went off to Spain in that year because his father was dying. He was in Madrid when Matilde's baby was born and his father died the same day. They christened the baby Julio, after Fernandez' father. But it was born early and it was a sickly baby, very small and pale and not at all like Matilde and Fernandez who were brown and strong like Indians. Matilde started to go grey with worry over that little Julio and Fernandez seemed to be drifting, half in sorrow at his father's death, half in dread of his responsibility towards Matilde and the baby. He began sleeping with a very young girl, hardly out of the Lycée, called Xavière. Xavière followed him like a spaniel and begged him to leave Matilde and the child.

'Sometimes Matilde would wheel the baby to Saladino's and bring it in, bundled up in ragged woollen things. It would cry and cry and Saladino told me Matilde would have to stop coming in because the baby upset the Americans drinking their Best English Tea. Matilde said she came to Saladino's because it was warm and the two rooms she had weren't heated and besides she was dying of loneliness and liked to be with me. Fernandez would go out early and she'd be left alone with this poor little Julio thinking of her years as an actress all gone to waste.

'I explained all this to Saladino, and Thérèse crept down the stairs and heard every word. Thérèse said she would take the baby upstairs if it disturbed anyone. She said she would sing to it while she did her work. Saladino liked Matilde, who reminded him of a Corsican girl, so he agreed to this. He let Thérèse take the baby and Thérèse knitted it some new shawls to replace those rags. She grew very fond of little Julio and sometimes Matilde would come into the patisserie, go straight up the stairs to Thérèse, dump the baby with her and go out again. I think she went off in search of Fernandez. She found out where Xavière lived. She told me she would kill herself if Fernandez left her for Xavière.

'But the baby died. Fernandez and Matilde came together again and were closer than they had ever been and Xavière was forgotten. Neither of them grieved. It was as if they *knew* what would happen and only, after it was all over, could they begin to love each other again. They went to Alsace, to the mountains, to forget death. They sent us cards full of rapture about the spring flowers and log hearths. They said they walked for miles every day and often slept very high up in the mountains, in rest huts, and that from these heights they could see new visions of the world.

'I was glad they were together and not scarred by everything that had happened to them. But at Saladino's it was a bad time. Thérèse was heartbroken by the death of Julio and she neglected her work. For days no overalls were washed and the stairs gathered dust and Saladino's evening meal – the most important event of his day – was forgotten! Nobody sympathized with Thérèse. Matilde had just forgotten her and Saladino kept shouting at her "The baby wasn't yours! Save your tears for the thing's mother!"

'It was a dreadful state of affairs. From the kitchen you could hear Thérèse weeping in her bedroom and Saladino would shrug his enormous shoulders and say, "It's a kind of madness. We'll have to see about it." And if you went up there, to comfort Thérèse, she would tell you that she could have made the baby well, that if only it had been hers, it wouldn't have died. She said she'd fed it secretly, that it cried because the mother couldn't give it enough milk. She said Matilde was a murderer.

'When I looked at Thérèse's life and at mine, I saw a void between them and more than ever I remembered Emily and everything we'd tried to do to haul women out of their bondage. But we'd never imagined little dark-haired girls fishing for crabs off stone walls in Calvi; I expect we thought all the wrongs were in England with its mildewed old Empire and the barking of Mr Asquith. Paris was always a sanctuary for Christabel and I used to picture her reading in a garden. I think I believed that in France women were free – to be scholars, politicians, anything they chose. Yet of course they weren't and Thérèse's life was as bleak as any woman's in the Bow Road in 1912. It was a life of abject servitude. The only things she treasured in it were her memories of Corsica and her love for her patron saint, Théresa. Pointless, though, to accuse Saladino. He believed in his "rights": he thought his rights were *in* him like his saliva and his blood. No one could have persuaded him otherwise and until her desolation over Julio, Thérèse colluded with Saladino's feudalism; she led a creeping life, she tried day and night to please him.

'It was during the incident with Thérèse and Matilde's baby that I decided never to marry and never to have children. Gérard was divorced from Matilde during that year, but we never talked about marriage until I said to him one day: "Promise *never* to marry me! Even if I forget my resolve and begin wanting to be your wife, you must promise to refuse me!" We celebrated our non-marriage with an extravagant dinner with champagne. And we walked all night along the quais. We sat down and waited for dawn at the very spot near the Pont Neuf where I'd gone fishing on my first visit to Paris with Sam. I think it was a summer dawn because I don't remember once feeling cold. And Gérard was never happier than at this time. His work was at last "unfolding" as he called it. He had begun to see where he was going.

'But of course as the 'thirties went on, it became very difficult to hold any kind of private optimism in the face of a public misery that just gathered, silently, on street corners and then suddenly, like something unexpected in darkness, lashed out. It was as if our poor earth had taken poison and vomited up confusion everywhere.

The owner of the bicycle factory opposite Gérard's studio went bankrupt. It was only a small factory and I suppose it employed about a hundred men, that was all. But when I remember the confusions of the early 'thirties I always remember the faces of those men, arriving for work on the bicycles they had helped to build, so early it was hardly light, but I had spent the night in Gérard's studio and I was up making coffee, getting myself ready for the long walk to Saladino's. They arrived and they found the doors of the shed closed and a notice nailed to the doors. They waited in groups. They rolled cigarettes and slapped themselves against the cold and waited for something to happen. They didn't believe the notice of closure. They wanted the owners to come and tell them they could go in, that the notice was a mistake and their jobs were safe. But no one came. And as it got light and the working day began, they banged with their fists on the metal doors and kicked them and shouted obscenities. I was afraid to go out because they filled the street. They called the owners the filthiest names they could think up and a man with ginger hair kicked his bicycle over and began to weep. And then, gradually, they left, one by one. But their rage and despair lingered. They had written it on the dented doors and it filled the Rue Pierre Nicole for months and months to come. And in those months we saw everything change. I suppose the rich still drank at the Ritz Bar and ate at the Tour d'Argent and dreamed the dreams of the unassailable in the Crillon and the Georges V. But the poor and the unemployed were arming themselves, not with knives but with ideologies. Demonstration and counter-demonstration. March and counter-march. Left, Right, Left, Right: everybody in step somewhere, forming alliances, prodding the air with fists and with slogans. And hunger marched with them: they shouted from their stomachs.

'Gérard described himself at this time as a *somnambuliste*. He saw himself walking with the Left, marching with them hand in hand. When Laval came to power he began to believe that what he called the "old order" would go and we would rebuild our world. But he *did* nothing. He couldn't make the bridge from "sleepwalking" in his studio to marching in the street. He wanted to make it and yet he couldn't. He was very restless and exhausted by his own indecision. He began to believe that he'd lost touch with his heart and that he was growing old. He said "old men sit down with their pipes on their doorsteps, but the marchers in the street are all young and on fire – and where is the fire in me?" It wasn't that he didn't feel afraid, you see. He hated what was happening in Italy and Germany. He saw France being surrounded by Fascists and he hated them, with all his being. He would talk for hours, usually with Fernandez and often with Valéry Clément who was a little in love with Gérard at that time and who was suffering from a terrible fear of being alone. He had nightmares of thugs coming to arrest him.

'I tried to understand the dilemma in Gérard and I think I got near to it. It was the struggle between the militant in him and what I could call the mystic – the creative part of him – which was also making pathways to change, but they were different paths. The two grew in him side by side. They grew in the same soil, breathed the same air and most of the time they were never in conflict because the militant nurtured itself on words and let the mystic act. And now the militant began to feel guilty. It devalued the achievements of the mystic. What good is art? it said. I should be burning pictures to warm the people? Yet the artist still wanted to be left in peace, to be *apart* from the people so that it too, in the quiet of a room, could discover new answers and then, only then, give those answers to the people. And for a long time, the artist had its way.

'But of course I see now that all of this was a prelude, the first shivers and shudders of the convulsions to come. The conflict in Gérard went on inside him for several years, as the public events slowly shaped themselves. But when I think about it all now, I can remember days and days that were ordinary, when the conflict was buried among the ordinariness of simple things – a walk in the Luxembourg Gardens, the completion of a collage after a whole night's work, breakfast at La Coupole. I remember also thinking, there will be an end to all this – perhaps. Our favourite waiter at La Coupole was called Etiènne and he had an epileptic fit one morning on the floor beside our banquette. It was a Sunday and we were drinking pastis. We had the train fare for an afternoon trip to Fontainebleau. But after we'd seen Etiènne's epileptic fit, we couldn't make the trip. We felt afraid, full of horror. And this was exactly how our lives were led – keeping hold on what was familiar, knowing that from one minute to the next it could go, and when we looked up again, something else would have replaced it, something we couldn't bear to see.

'The bicycle factory stayed shut. People came and stuck up advertisements for concerts and plays on the doors. One advertisement was for a string quartet playing Mozart and we found this very strange, the contrast between a string quartet in their tail coats in a room with chandeliers and the red-haired man crying and kicking his bicycle. And it must have been then that Gérard began work on his enormous painting called "Mozart and the Bicycle Factory". I expect you've seen it in books, haven't you? When he began it, Gérard talked a lot about precision – the precision of Mozart and the precision of the bicycle wheel. But then the idea of the bicycle factory workers represented as crochets and quavers came to him. He saw similarities, because the people could be scratched out or set moving along certain lines, according to the composition of the society at the time, exactly as in the composition of a piece of music. And after this painting all Gérard's people looked terribly thin, like crochets and quavers. They were stick men with little twigs of limbs that could snap.

'The painting was exhibited at the Galerie Bonjean and the critics didn't understand it, just as they didn't understand Miro or Picabia. They said a baby could have painted the crochet men. But Gérard was pleased with the picture and he didn't mind. He felt he had made progress since the struggles with the plaster of paris bones. To be free of the bones felt rather wonderful, I think. He started coming back to Saladino's and eating brioches.

'Matilde went back to acting. She was finding it more difficult to get parts in the 'thirties because her gypsy beauty seemed to vanish after the birth and death of Julio and her eyes looked puffy. She couldn't play Ophelia or anything like that; she had to play people's mothers and this made her feel old. She began to mourn for what she'd been. She was jealous of Fernandez who didn't seem to age at all, and some of her jealousy spilled over onto me because I was two years younger than she was and I never thought about ageing, only about keeping my love alive.

'She began to keep company with some of the younger poets and writers. She took a lover called Jan who was Russian. He was terribly white and nervous, just like I imagine Raskolnikov in *Crime and Punishment.* But he intrigued us all with his pronouncements. He said that the French xenophobia which grew as the unemployment got worse was as repulsive as Fascism. "France deserves Fascism," he'd say. And he talked a lot about going back to Tblisi, which is where he came from, just as Fernandez began to talk about going back to Spain.

'Gérard hated this talking about going back to Spain. He persuaded Fernandez to come with us to Chamonix in the summer of 1935 and we left Matilde behind in Paris. We stayed at a tiny place called La Bucherie. The only other guests in our hotel were an English couple called the Sloanes. We spent our days walking and listening to Gérard. "Look at us!" he'd say, "we've walked in step for years, so how can you think of leaving us, Fernandez?"

'The first days of our holiday were fine. We saw some beauty in everything, every colour, every sound. And it was a year for wild strawberries; we found hundreds and quenched our thirst with them. When we thought of Paris, it felt black and noisy. We wondered if we could go back.

'But then it rained. It was a grey gentle drizzle and the peaks of the mountains vanished in it. I think the Sloanes, who came from Taunton, felt terribly cheated: it was an identical drizzle to the one which fell on all their Devon springs. They sat and played two-handed bridge and drank *fine à l'eau* and talked of going south to Monaco. And of course the more it rained, the more Fernandez began to imagine sunlight in Spain and the brass bands of the *corrida* and pimento bushes. He told us that he and Matilde were "lost". He was tired of Paris and the theatre. He said, "It's all finished for our generation in France." We argued with him. We said, "France will never let Fascism in," and Gérard promised him that his time of somnambulism was over. But the weather defeated us. I believe we travelled back to Paris in absolute silence.'

With Ralph's key, the hotel receptionist handed him a telegram. It said simply: 'Please confirm your return April 24th. Walt.'

Ralph took it up to his room, crumpled it and let it fall into the metal waste paper basket.

Exhaustion from his long night with Katherine had crept around his body all day. He had struggled with a desire to lie down and sleep, and images of his night kept coming back to him, interrupting Erica's voice so that it became almost inaudible – something whispered and gone. Thank God for the tape recorder.

To atone for his inattention, Ralph got into bed with the two volumes of the diary. He noticed that the pages of the first volume smelled faintly of olive oil. In the second book, the pages were dry and brittle. Before Ralph slept he decided she wanted to preserve the first and let the second turn to dust.

But in an hour he was awake. There was dusk – dawn? – at the window. The curtains hadn't been drawn and the telephone was ringing.

'Ralph? You got my cable?'

'Walt?'

'Yeh. Is it night time over there or what. You sound kinda muffled.'

'Yup, it's night time.'

'You got my cable, Ralph?'

'No.'

'What? You didn't get it?'

'I don't think I got it.'

'Shit. Well look, kid. I just want you to confirm you have an April 24th flight. We need you back in the office on April 25th.'

Ralph was silent. Walt said, 'You hear me, Ralph?'

'Sure.'

'Can you confirm this date to me, Ralph?'

Ralph tried to think fast: lie now, lie later? Try to wade right on through without lying?

'I can't confirm that date, Walt,' he said flatly.

'What? What 'you say, kid?'

'I just can't confirm the April 24th date.'

'Now see here . . .' Walt began.

'You said when I joined *Bulletin Worldwide,*' Ralph interrupted, 'that the judgment of what you called "the man on the job" is always superior to that of the office. You said, sure, the office *dictates* the policy but at *Bulletin Worldwide* we trust our men in the field to decide exactly what importance – and therefore time – should be given to the issues they're facing. Now you said precisely that to me, Walt. You talked about "free hands" and "on-the-spot sensitivity" and all that crap, so just don't go back on it! I need the full month for this job and I'm gonna take it.'

'I'm sorry kid . . .'

'I'm just gonna *take* it, Walt!'

'Now I don't want you to think that my attitude to the man on the job has changed at all, Ralph. It's a principle of successful journalism and I learned that when I was seventeen.'

'You're bullshitting, Walt.'

'But there are exceptions . . .'

'You're bullshitting.'

'And we have an exception situation here, Ralph. Not only do we have the run-up to the presidential election; we have a Russian presence in Afghanistan and no movement at all on the hostage question in Iran.'

'I know all this, Walt.'

'Sure you do. But I just don't think you've got the full impact on board, kid. There is simply no time available, and I repeat, *no time available,* for investigations into minor lives.' Walt then shouted, 'April 24th, okay?' and hung up.

Sonofabitch, Ralph thought. So used to getting his own way. Like a drill sergeant. Everyone clicking their heels for him. Five years ago, Ralph had admired him: Walter B. Beresford, hot from his desk at *Time-Life*, hard as hell inside his soft body. Under Walt's editorship, the circulation of *Bulletin Worldwide Inc.* had trebled. It was now published in England, in West Germany and in Japan. The company now owned an entire building on East 53rd Street. They played canned music to you in the elevators; the plants in the over-heated foyer were spotlit, the offices had carpets. But to work on Walt's corridor was to become aware of the man's growing megalomania. Orders were barked; memos were curt; and his footfall, it was an apparently deliberate flapping, as if his shoes were five sizes too large for his feet. Ralph had nicknamed him 'The Frog'.

And to be away from Walt was a profound relief. Ralph likened it to a pain in his gut that had gone away. Freed of this, freed of his toothache, he felt he could now begin to look squarely at himself. He was glad to find that his decision not to return on the 24th, to disobey Walt for perhaps the first time in almost six years left him absolutely unafraid. For a moment longer, he pictured Walt, pouring coffee from his Cona machine, swallowing restaurant food flat out, talking as he swallowed, taking laxatives as he gave dictation, voice lowered a little for his secretary who made him horny – with the world of world events all within his reach, every share price fluctuation, every global pronouncement, every un-American death.

Then he put Walt out of his head, deciding only to move hotels as soon as he could so that the man wouldn't be able to find him.

It was half-past eight. Ralph dressed and went down to eat. Soup 'of the day' and some slices of gammon in a sweetish sauce passed, almost unnoticed, into his stomach as he read hungrily from Erica's diaries:

September 15th, 1935
'Paris is full of movement. At Chamonix we seemed to be set apart from all *happening*. The damp silence now seems astonishing. There were times when the quality of the green made me think of England. I wondered if I should write a letter to Suffolk to ask, what are the English thinking? Have they noticed the rise of Hitler and Mussolini? Will England and France be allies in the event of another war? But of course I didn't write. I don't expect I ever will.

Fernandez is definitely leaving. He is applying for teaching posts in Madrid. He is offering the idea of doing some kind of drama work with the children, but no schools have responded and he's getting downhearted. He says he feels old. Gérard has stopped trying to persuade him to stay. He knows this is useless now. But he also believes that Fernandez is his greatest friend and that when he goes, he will feel like a mourner. We laugh about the fact that he now has a little money to compensate for the loss of Fernandez; a young American collector has bought "Mozart and the Bicycle Factory" and two other paintings (in the Fat Man series) and we have some dollars to flaunt!

The socialist newspapers say there are almost two million people without a job in France. I wonder about the red-haired man. His family? His bicycle? You see men and women scavenging in dustbins outside restaurants. Sometimes, I expect to see him, yet always hope I won't.'

October 5th, 1935

The price of books goes up and up. Someone told me this has something to do with the price of trees from Finland. But it's difficult to believe that France imports trees when there are so many already here.

I mention this because of two occurrences: D. H. Lawrence's *Sons and Lovers* from my friend on the Quai St Michel is marked at 2/6d in the English edition but he's asking five hundred francs. I tell him off, but he refuses to bargain. I buy it anyway.

Secondly, Maison Cambier have at last moved into a Maison, or rather they now have two floors of quite a large building in the Place Saint Sulpice instead of one floor in a tiny building in the Rue de Grenelle. Jacques is looking prosperous and overweight. I suppose, in difficult times, a lot of people shut themselves up in cold rooms or sit in warm cafés and write. And Jacques Cambier says to me sadly, "Why are you not doing this? After such a beginning . . ." But I don't have a satisfactory answer, except my private answer which is cowardly and very womanly in all the bad ways: if I lost myself in a book, I am afraid to look up and find Gérard gone.

October 19th, 1935

Fernandez is gone. I went to the station to see him off, but

Gérard wouldn't come with us. He said he was going to walk up to Montmartre and get drunk, but he didn't do this; he worked all day.

One of the schools Fernandez wrote to has asked to interview him. He believes they will take him and he was full of smiles as he left. He has invited us to come to Spain as soon as he's "settled" – if indeed anyone can be settled in these ravenous times. I cried to see him go, for all the days and nights of talk, for the journeys in Provence, even for Chamonix which has taken on the substance of a dream. To share something and then lose the sharer, is to lose the thing.

I don't think he said any goodbye to Matilde, who is drunk a lot of the time these days. She paws her Russian and talks about the world being full of traitors. Gérard, I know, believes Fernandez is one of these. Yet already he's worrying. "Do you think Fernandez will write to us? Can we save up and – next summer – spend a holiday in Spain?"

December 1st, 1935

The sudden cold weather seems more terrible to endure than any winter I can remember. Walking back from Saladino's, I go into cafés or stores that are open late just to get warm.

With the American dollars (most of them) Gérard has bought a new stove that burns wood and coal. A special flue and chimney had to be put in. If we can continue to afford the wood (from Finland is it all, it's so expensive?) and a few lumps of coal, then the room stays wonderfully warm. Mine is desolate in comparison, but Gérard seems to want me with him all the time, so I'm hardly ever at the Rue Chomel. Our loving of each other is the only thing (apart from the new stove) that has any warmth and comfort in it.

In bed we make elaborate plans for our visit to Spain, which neither of us has ever seen. We try to imagine that all is laughter there, and dance and hot paellas. We've even begun to scour Paris for Spanish restaurants – all of this in memory of Fernandez, the Judas of our hearts! He has written us only one letter since he left Paris, telling us he failed to get the school post and is working "on the roads". We don't know if this means cleaning them or making them.

At Saladino's, the Americans still come to tea. Secretly,

Saladino is making designs for a *bûche de Nöel* for Celestine and I don't want to ask him: "Who will she eat it with, Saladino, while you sit face to face with Thérèse and hear her dreams of Calvi?"

'Of course we had other friends than Fernandez and Matilde. Gérard "flirted" with Breton and his crowd and they "flirted" with him. But there was never a complete involvement with them. We stalked different beats. We became very close to Valéry Clément and there were perhaps five or six other people we saw quite often. One of these was an English writer called Roger Walters. He was an imitator of Hemingway, who we occasionally saw in the Closerie des Lilas. We knew he (Hemingway) had a passion for horse racing and we couldn't understand this. And we found him rather prickly.

'We saw more of our other friends after Fernandez had gone. I think they were all writers or actors or painters. The Englishness of Roger Walters amused Gérard. It was the Englishness of Harrow and Cambridge – the firm bridge of the nose, the loud voice. Gérard did an extraordinary painting of Roger Walters, which is why I remember him. The face is almost the face of a horse, toothy and proud, but the body gapes open onto an enormous heart, very moist and dark but clamped to the limbs of the body, held in place if you like, by wrenches and pulleys and pieces of steel. Roger hated the painting but Gérard was very pleased with it. He believed it captured, with a maximum of visual shock, the essence of Roger Walters.

'So there he is, framed somewhere, and bought for a fortune no doubt and I will never, never forget him. Yet some of the other people we knew have just vanished from me. I believe they've gone only recently. I think I remembered them for years – how they painted, what they wrote, what we were to them and they to us – and then I just forgot them.'

Erica bent forward to pick up her glass of wine, and dropped it. After Ralph had scurried for a cloth, wiped the table and the carpet, refilled Erica's glass, he looked up and saw that she was trembling.

'I'm in trouble again, Ralph,' she said. 'When it comes to anything very awful – like Chadwick's death, you remember – I can't bear to talk about it, not long enough to make sense of it for you, dear.'

'Don't fret about it, Erica,' said Ralph, 'just pass on to wherever you want. I know that Gérard was killed in Spain. You don't need to say anything about it.'

She paused, then with her eyes closed and her head low on her chest, she began talking again.

'You know,' she said slowly, 'that no help was sent from France, no guns, nothing, when the Spanish Civil War began? I simply don't know why. With help from France, Franco could have keen defeated but the Blum government just stood aside and watched. And the defenders of the republic of Spain couldn't believe it. Of course they couldn't! They couldn't believe that France would let Fascism into Spain – especially when we had a left-wing government – they couldn't believe it.

'Gérard and I had planned our holiday in Spain for August. But after July, it was impossible. We started going on the "arms for Spain" marches. We were at last on the street and all the years of somnabulism were past and gone.

'Then there were the letters from Fernandez. He called the French *salauds, cochons* – all the abusive words. He said the working people of Spain would fight to the last stone. All through the year the letters came. They said nothing about the road cleaning or the road mending – whichever it was – they simply mocked and chafed us for our betrayal. And Gérard saw everything, *everything* differently after that. He said his art was wasteful self-indulgence, absolutely without meaning.

'So I suppose I knew he would go to Spain. I knew he would go and fight. I don't remember ever talking about it, but there it was – a certainty.'

She looked up at Ralph and her eyes were wet. She put a frail hand up to them and said quietly, 'I'm sorry, dear. I can't go on.'

8

A letter from John Pennington arrived the same day, Ralph's last day at the hotel in Harrington Gardens:

Worcester College
Oxford

Dear Ralph,

The yellow pills have helped me over the illness. I can breathe again, thank heavens.

The weather is glorious in Oxford now, and I wouldn't like to think of you going back without seeing the sun on our famous stones. They are transformed by it, and one feels idiotically privileged to be here.

As I am well, so is my novel sickly. I'm trying to invent the kind of love affair I've never had, I know that what I'm writing isn't felt, and therefore doesn't work. Yet the love relationship is central to the book. When I started, I really thought I could succeed, but now I don't know. Perhaps, after all, I can't create anything – only analyse and criticize, safe behind my exquisite window!

So please come up and stay and perhaps you can tell me if I should go on with this fiction, or creep back into my don's camouflage; the stick insect who thought he could become a humming bird: I suggest May 2nd or 3rd – or both if you can bear the sofa for two nights. It's very difficult to get anyone a decent (cheap) room in term time these days.

Yours ever,
John

Ralph was glad to have the letter, not only because he now knew that he would spend some time with John before going back to face Walt's anger, but also because after a brief and sad afternoon with Erica he knew that he had a lot he wanted to write down. It was more comforting to write it in a letter to John than to make it part of his Summary:

Dear John,

Yes, I will come and see you on May 2nd. To stay two nights will depend on state of work here and London and on flights home.

Well, ol' pal, I want to say, the whole BIG question of love – not just the fictional kind – has to come under close scrutiny and quick, before we all die right off in our totally unpeopled hearts. I'm thirty-five and I've never sniffed at love. Lust follows me obediently. Fucking isn't at issue. But love? Blame my foul-mouthed mother if you like, but that's too easy. Blame me? Well, nearer. I've never had a go at nurturing so much as a goldfish, not to mention my total un-nurturing of people – women, men, I wouldn't care which, if I could *feel* the thing – no, not to mention my total inexperience of absence of anything I could define as love.

Kinda weird, your letter arriving today. The old lady (E.M.) has been remembering Paris and her celebrated affair with the painter, Gérard Guérard. 'Affair' is a dumb word; 'passionate involvement' is better. At the end, she was so broke up, she couldn't tell me how he died or when. Yet she knew him *fifty years ago.* Her whole life is held together – kept intact, a life truly *lived* – by her extraordinary ability to love. Not just Gérard, though I guess she's never been able to feel with anyone else what she felt for him, but *everything,* people, things, ugly, broken, surprising, miraculous. It's as if love was a state of being or at any rate the kind of "outer skin" of a state of being; other feelings could exist in her (she found Hemingway "prickly", she abhorred Fascism, she was afraid of Gérard's black moods), but her life was informed by open, positive *loving* feelings. Love sharpened her vision, of everything she saw, just as I think it always had done before because she had deeply loved other people: her mother, her uncle, Emily Davison.

Well, shit, I don't know why I feel so depressed, John. And yet I do. The only thing Erica March simply couldn't do during the Paris time was work; when I look at my life and all around me, all I can see is people working their asses off. Greedy fuckers – like me – putting work way up there in front and never feeling one goddamn thing from November to November. We've really gassed ourselves, John boy. We're down there in the slime at Ypres – minus patriotism even, to blow our noses on – and, from where I'm standing I just can't see us getting up again: it's the wasteland from now on in. Well, go on, set the spires dreaming for me. If we can't feel things, perhaps we can dream them?

Ralph

P.S. Sure you'll never be a humming bird. Name one humming bird!

Mrs Burford opened the door to Ralph.

'Finders keepers,' she said to him.

'What's that?'

'Well, left your tape recorder, didn't yer?'

'Yes. I guess I did.'

'Finders keepers!' And she grinned. But then she stalked off to the kitchen, turning only to ask, 'You nearly finished with 'er?'

'I don't know,' said Ralph.

'You didn't ought to be doing it, you know.'

'Doing what?'

'Gobblin' up 'er life.' And the kitchen door slammed.

Ralph hesitated. There was no sound in the flat and he wondered if Erica was asleep. He remembered the day of her 'rain sickness'.

He moved to the sitting-room door. Erica was sitting, as she always sat, near her Tiffany lamp. Facing her, in an armchair, was a stranger, a man of perhaps fifty-five or sixty, deliberately smart in a faded suit, the woollen tie clumsily knotted. Erica was smiling at him. In silence, the stranger, too, was smiling.

Ralph knocked on the door and they both looked at him. The remains of a cold lunch was on the table between them, the pink wine, usually offered to Ralph, had been drunk. Erica looked flushed.

'Come in, Ralph dear,' she said, 'come and meet Huntley who

149

has travelled all the way down from Suffolk to see me. Huntley is a wonderful modern farmer.'

The man stood up and shook Ralph's hand briskly. He was a heavy person, pink from his outdoor life. His hands were strong.

'I'm just on my way,' he said.

'Oh no . . .' Ralph mumbled, 'look, please don't go . . . if you've come down from Suffolk . . .'

'Oh he never stays,' said Erica, 'do you, Huntley? You just tell me all about the marvellous milking parlours and all of that. That's what you come to tell me, isn't it? And then off you go back to the farm. Huntley detests London, don't you?'

But she didn't let him reply. She turned to Ralph and said, 'Huntley is Bernard's nephew and when Bernard died, we gave Huntley the farm, which was what Huntley always, always wanted, a farm of his own. And now, he's turned it into something modern.'

'I wish you would come down and see it, Erica,' said Huntley.

'I know you do, dear, but you see I often tell Ralph, I'm afraid of open spaces now. They're the only things I'm afraid of. I'm afraid of the wind.'

'There's not a lot of wind at this time of year, and we've planted a cyprus hedge –'

'In Suffolk? Of *course* there's always a wind. It just blows in from the sea and it hardly ever leaves you alone.'

There was a moment's silence and then Huntley said cheerfully: 'Well, better be getting the tube back to Liverpool Street. Splendid lunch, Erica.'

'Only cold meat, dear. I can't cook anymore. Except spinach. Sometimes I cook that.'

'Jolly good lunch.'

'I expect I imagine spinach will give me strength, like that Popeye person. But it doesn't. I've got no strength at all, have I, Ralph?'

'We went to the park . . .'

'Yes. Wasn't that nice? Ralph took me to the park – in a taxi.'

'Good for you, Ralph,' said Huntley, 'dare say you're one of what we used to call the Yanks, aren't you?'

' Yup. I was born in Tennessee, but I live in New York now.'

'New York, eh? Well, must be casting off, Erica.'

'Yes.' Then she whispered to Huntley, 'I'm terribly near the end, Hunt. I can feel it, you know . . .'

'Oh tommyrot, Miss March! Wouldn't surprise me, if you lived another hundred years. Eh, Ralph?'

When Huntley had gone, Erica looked down, disappointed, at her hands.

'He's a very silly man, you know,' she said, 'dreadfully kind but very silly. Bernard and I used to be rather fond of him. He was the only bit of either family who was going to continue. And it was quite right that he had the farm. But I should think the cows *hate* his milking machines and the soil hates the things he throws on it. But he's made it pay, you see, so he's all cockahoop about it. But I don't think I'd want to go and see it. I never have gone. I've made a point of not going.'

Erica shut her eyes. Ralph wondered if, with this gesture, she was dismissing him too. Huntley's visit had seemed to elate her, remind her perhaps of places she had long forgotten. Then, suddenly she was tired of him. She remembered he was a silly man.

Ralph was on the point of getting up and quietly leaving when Erica said: 'I wanted to tell you today, dear, that as soon as Paris was over, I did begin to write again. I expect you've been thinking how undisciplined I was during all those years with Gérard and it's true, really. Yet I couldn't write – nothing important – at that time. I simply didn't have anything to say.

'But I was very ill after Gérard died. I believe it was a kind of shock illness, because I couldn't get warm, even though it was summer, and I cried all the time, just like Thérèse crying over that little Julio.

'One day I began to believe that I would die like that, just freeze to death in my room. I had hallucinations of death. Then I saw Saladino standing in my doorway. I don't believe anyone else had visited me until that time, but Matilde might have come, I can't remember, or Valéry Clément. I don't know. I wasn't aware of anyone else, but on the day Saladino came I could see him very clearly. Thérèse was with him and they had brought me some soup. They had a very loud argument about whether to take me to hospital. I tried to tell them that I didn't want to go to the hospital, but I couldn't speak. I swallowed the soup and then almost at once vomited it up. So as they cleaned the mess, they began their argument again.

'I think this was one of the very few arguments that Thérèse won because Saladino wanted to put me in the hospital but Thérèse said no, she would look after me and when I woke up again I was in a strange room.

'I think a doctor was called because Thérèse would bring me pills in the early mornings and again at night. And she wrapped me in the same kind of coloured shawls she had knitted for Julio. When I saw myself, I looked like an old woman.

'And it was this sight of me, Ralph, so white, with dirty hair, swaddled up in these shawls that made me want to come out of the death I was in. I began to have dreams of England. Without Gérard, Paris had become terrible – a place to die in. So I struggled to get well. I let Thérèse bath me and wash my hair. I ate her soups and they stayed in my stomach. But then one afternoon I crept down to the patisserie, I stared at the banquette where Gérard used to sit and I thought I saw him there. I started to shout out to Saladino and he picked me up in his arms and carried me upstairs. But I knew, after this, I had to get to England somehow. I asked Saladino if he would call Valéry Clément and persuade him to help me get to England, if he would come with me. Saladino said I was too weak to travel and for days – even weeks, I don't know – he refused to go to see Valéry.

'I left sometime in the autumn of 'thirty-seven. It was turning cold again. Very cold on the boat, yet we sat on deck and I thought of Athelstone Amis sailing off to Venezuela.

Thérèse and Saladino both cried when I left and they hugged and kissed me and told me that Corsicans had never held Waterloo against the English! I didn't know how to thank them for what they'd done. They probably saved my life – I don't know. I wrote to them during the occupation. I told them all the Americans who had drunk Best English Tea would take off their mackintoshes and their houndstooth jackets and put on uniforms. I said the Americans and the English will save France for you – if only in return for my life!

'I don't remember the journey to England. Only sitting on the deck of the boat. That I remember. But when we got into Victoria Station, Valéry asked me where I wanted to go. And of course I had no idea. I didn't want to go anywhere or think anything out. I longed for someone to take charge. So we sat in the station buffet at Victoria and I tried to piece England together. And it got dark and bright lights came on in the buffet and all I wanted was to sleep.

'Valéry got us into a hotel somewhere. There was only one room available, so we shared it. Before I went to sleep Valéry said to me, "Now you must work, Erica. There's nothing else for you to do." And it wasn't very long after this that I began again, Ralph. I began to write.

'I slept all through my first day back in England. When I woke up, it was dark again and Valéry had gone out. I lay very very still and listened to London. I remembered my first night in Chadwick's flat, hearing the bell-chimes. Now there were no bells, only lorries and trams and sudden shouts. I didn't know what street I was in. Even when I looked out of the window, I couldn't recognize it. It just looked very black and drab.

'So I thought, I don't think I can make sense of London, not now, not for a while yet. I began to think, if I go to Suffolk, they will let me have my old room for a while and let me sleep, and at least there will be silence.

'Strange how, only a few months before, when I still had Gérard, I never would have dreamed of going to Suffolk. I thought then that Suffolk and my father and Eileen were gone for ever. I wanted them gone! But now, all I could think of was resting and being away from London, which I didn't understand.

'Valéry and I had dinner in the hotel dining-room. There was an orchestra playing and some people got up to dance. The grandeur of it all was most peculiar. I said to Valéry, "I don't know why you chose this grand place." Yet I admit it was oddly comforting, the formality of it; everything keeping its distance. Even the couples who danced. Very straight, they were, like skittles face to face.

'The meal wasn't good, but Valéry ordered some wine and I felt like a spectator at a show, in a comfortable seat. I told Valéry I would send a telegram to my father the next morning and wait in London only until I had an answer.'

'It was like that other arrival in 1914. Seeing no one at the station at first, then Gully, years older but still in the same attitude, holding his flat cap. There was only one difference. This time, he looked afraid. When I put my arms round him, I felt him stiffen and pull away. I wanted to say I was sorry for my neglect of him. I wanted to explain that there was a world of silence now between his life and mine and I hadn't been able to cross it. But he wouldn't let me speak.

"Just don't yew talk, girl, till I've said it," he snapped. "Just don't yew say nothin'!"

So I looked at him and I thought, heavens everything in the world had changed, as I once saw it changing in the clouds above my window. I am ill with change. Only the little station was unaltered. I could see leaves on the oak trees.

'I was staring at these last leaves when I heard Gully say: "Went down that ol' field, see? Night-time last winter, he did. An' he took his ol' gun and shot himself."

"Who?" I wanted to ask, but of course I knew.

"Your father," he said, "and mine."

'But there was no weeping left inside me, Ralph. None. From that day to this, I don't believe I've cried at all. Gérard took all my tears, all that were left in me after my mother went and Emily and Chadwick, and I've never shed any more, not for a soul. In dreams of course, I hear myself crying sometimes, but it's a very distant sound, like an echo.

'Questions crossed my mind: why did no one try to find me and tell me? Which field had he died in? The forget-me-not field? Why had he done it last year instead of years and years before? But I didn't ask them. I stared all around me and then up at the sky. I could see a bird, circling. It had been raining in London, but here it was a bright morning. I can't remember what I said to Gully. Perhaps I said nothing at all and we drove to the house in silence.'

Erica stopped talking. She leant back and closed her eyes. After a moment or two of silence she mumbled: "I'm so sorry, Ralph dear. That silly old Huntley tired me out with all his farming talk. If I just lay down, would you read to me for a while? Would you mind? I love it when people read aloud. It's very peaceful.'

'Sure,' said Ralph.

'I'll try not to go to sleep. Then we can talk a bit more, afterwards.'

'Sure.'

'Would you fetch the eiderdown from my bed, dear? Then I can just lie here.'

'Would you rather go to bed?'

'Oh no. Never in daylight. Not if I can help it. It seems so wasteful.'

Ralph cleared away the remains of the lunch and took it to the kitchen. Mrs Burford had gone.

Then he went into Erica's bedroom, turned back the torn

candlewick bedspread and pulled out the eiderdown. He noticed the softness of the eiderdown, real eider feathers in it, surely, not bits of rubber, but the fabric which covered it was faded, and torn in places.

Erica lay down with her head on a cushion and Ralph covered her. The sun, at her window, was bright.

'I try to read,' Erica said, 'at night but the print seems to have got very small and it tires me. Yesterday, you see, after you'd gone, I wanted to have a look at *In the Blind Man's City*. If I read it, I knew I would remember for you how and why I had written it. But I couldn't read it. The words just danced about in front of me. They wouldn't stay on their lines. Perhaps you could read me a little of it, Ralph dear, would you mind? It's years since I looked at it. I can't even remember the story.'

Ralph searched along her shelves till he found it. It was stuffy in the room. He sat down in his chair and began:

'The missionary told the boy that the boy was black. In the thick shade of the baobab tree where he had been put, the boy touched the skin of his knees. He tried to feel what black was. The missionary had told his mother that white doctors would cure his black blindness one day.

Yet his blindness served.

Now that the white man had arrived, there was money in it. His mother Ngumbi wouldn't send him to the mission school. She sat him on his little mat with his wood bowl in the shade of the baobab tree at the edge of the market place, and the white men threw money into it – francs and pennies. Sometimes the coins missed the bowl and hit his feet.

The year the white men came, he was no older than seven. At midday, his grandmother, Matarina, would bring him a little hot maize-meal in a bowl and some brownish water in a gourd. He had been taught to feed himself and wipe spilt food from his face and body. His arms were strong from working in the fields with Ngumbi and he could tip up the heavy gourd with ease.

While he ate, his grandmother squatted by him in the dust, her skirts hitched above her knees. Nobody knew how old Matarina was – only the witchdoctor's father who had been buried with ceremony in the forest. Monkeys now chattered above the old witch doctor's tomb, but the witch doctor was silent on the question of Matarina's age.

Unknown to the boy, Matarina had offered koki-beans to the mission teachers to teach her a word or two of their language, and she had painted a sign which she brought out to the boy one day with his maize-meal and his water. With a charred stick she had written on it in English and in French: BLIND CHILD, ENFANT AVEUGLE, and propped the sign against an upturned bowl quite near to the boy's mat. The boy knew nothing about the sign.

The horseflies shared the shade of the baobab tree. They stung the boy's neck and his thighs. He swore at the horseflies, just as he had heard Ngumbi swear in the fields in the days when she had taken him to work with her.

It had been very hot in the fields, but the boy knew that the world of the fields was a world of women, safe and wide. And they had given him small jobs to do – stripping the maize husks into huge baskets, fetching water from the stream, in wooden buckets, tethering Ngumbi's goat to its pole in the little basin near the river where the grass was still ereen. And the talk of the women had shaped the day for him. It was slow, weary talk in the quiet early mornings; it brightened with the sun. At midday when he was given nuts, fruit, sometimes a little cheese wrapped in a cloth, the woman-talk was like a clustering of birds and their squawking laughter rang out across the fields. Then there was a period of quiet; the women felt sleepy: they remembered the old men or the village who lay down in the cool of the huts. But as the evening came on, they would begin to talk happily of food: there would be antelope meat for supper with a good sauce, Matarina was making *foo-foo* balls . . . And the boy was content to be near them. Their warm, strong legs were the anchors of his life.

He didn't understand why he now sat by himself all day under the baobab tree in the dust of the market square. Ngumbi had told him that the coins dropped into his wooden bowl were very precious. With these coins the family would soon be able to buy tin plates and paraffin lamps from the Indian traders. Yet he still didn't understand, either the need for these odd-sounding things or the new pattern of his new life, in which no one spoke to him – only Matarina, in the dust of midday – and the babble of the market, its smells and flies made his head ache. Some of the traders came to urinate under the baobab tree and the sour urine would splash the boy's shoulders. All day he would wait for the feel of the cooler evening air on his face and for the sound of Ngumbi, singing as she came home from the fields.

There were days when no coins where thrown into his bowl. Ngumbi would complain and shout. She said the boys from the mission school had crept up and stolen the money. She told the boy to hold the bowl in his lap, to spit if he heard a child's footstep near him. And he would hear her complain to the whole village, "the boy got nothing again today. He doesn't know how to beg." And he would think, I don't recognize your voice my Ngumbi, my mother. One day, I shall come to hate you.'

Ralph paused. Erica opened her eyes and smiled. 'Africa!' she said. 'It was terribly important to set this story in Africa, yet of course I knew nothing about it. I knew, you see, that I couldn't possibly write about Suffolk or London or Paris: there was far too much to crowd my mind in these places. But Africa! I knew that there, my story would begin to work. And with all my writing the same pattern had appeared: to make sense of what was on my doorstep, I had to take the story far away – to somewhere like Africa, or to a made-up place. The settings for *The Two Wives of the King* and *The Hospital Ship* were both made up. People have tried to liken these places to actual countries, but that's very stupid. They exist in my mind, that's all.'

'How did you come to know Africa?'

'Well. I went there once with Bernard, to Kenya – but that was much later. When I wrote the book, I just invented Africa. All I'd read was something called *Diary of a Missionary* which I found in my father's bookshelf. It was written by a woman called Alice Morahan who was in the Congo for six years. I suppose she must have been a nun, but I can't remember. She gave me some very good descriptions of the mud houses of the villages and all the vermin in them – cockroaches and mice. She also seemed to be rather moved by Africa and say extraordinary things like "the blood of Christ our Saviour flows in the red lilies of the Congo basin." Anyway, she helped me. She was all I needed.'

'To begin?'

'Yes. Though I didn't begin with Africa. That came later.'

'But you began something straight away?'

'No. I began *wanting* to write straight away, because that was all there was left at that time in my life – the writing. But it took me a while to get used to England and used to discipline. I suppose it was the following winter that I began.'

'Gully was very, very upset about my father. Dot told me that at the burial, which was a grudging, brief kind of thing, reserved for suicides, his poor old sideways face had been awash. I expect he thought I had grown hard and unfeeling, because I didn't cry. Certainly he was very formal with me, as if he hated to remember that long-ago night we'd spent together. And even our childhood. He didn't seem to want to remember any games we'd played or the peculiar sums we'd done about Spanish noblemen with twenty-five castles, or even the day when he pissed on Sonny Aldous and John Tomkins in the playground. The only thing we still had in common was our dislike of Eileen. Gully had his own home and family (he had another child by then, a little girl called Ellen Jane) and he never went to see Eileen or help with anything up at the farm. Most of the land had been let to Haggard's son and he kept it very well, with good deep ditches and all the hedges trimmed.

'But the house – that was Eileen's. There was very little left of my father in it, just a photograph or two and his pipe, which she kept in a blue jar. She'd replaced him, almost straight away, so Gully said, with Miss Pinney. Miss Pinney was someone she'd known at Aldeburgh. She became Eileen's "companion".

'She was younger than Eileen who must have been sixty by then. She had a little flat face and eyes that watered a lot. She spoke very softly and started to tremble if anyone on the wireless was rude. Her favourite pastime was making pictures out of shells and dried flowers. She told me this was the ancient craft of her ancestors who came from New Zealand – shell pictures! She let Eileen carry on just as she'd carried on before, doing her ceaseless rounds of spit and polish and fold and tidy and dust and flick. It was Eileen who decided what they ate and with which sets of mats and plates. It was Eileen who took them endlessly to church. It was Eileen who hired a Suffolk girl to do the dirty work of the house and then bullied her. Miss Pinney never talked to the girl. She thought conversation beneath her. And the girl left in tears. Before she went, Eileen made her kneel down in front of her latest sampler, "Blessed are the pure in heart", and ask God to send her some manners.

'When I arrived at the house, there was dismay. Gully drove me there and left. Miss Pinney opened the door, and when she saw me she called out to Eileen in a terrified voice. And Eileen came and they both stared at me. Eileen told Miss Pinney to go to her room, which was my old room. Then she looked at my suitcase and said "I'm sorry Erica. Miss Pinney has your room now. There can be no staying." But I pushed past her and into the sitting-room, where there were new curtains and new covers on the chairs and a large brown wireless on one of the tables. Eileen followed me and waited in the doorway. I turned round and said to her very quietly: "Please tell me how my father died." But she looked away. She looked past me at the new furnishings and said "I've told Miss Pinney and I told Gully, I shall not have that man's death spoken of. Not as long as I'm alive!" And she went away.

'I suppose she thought I would get up and leave. I went outside and down to the cowsheds where I had first seen Claustrophobia and then beyond them, along a track we used to call Hobman's Lane to the forget-me-not field. Haggard's cows were out grazing. There was no sign of a forget-me-not. It was much too late in the year. I sat on the gate and watched the cows and there was absolute contentment there. It was a place quite without ghosts. It was sunny and quiet and at peace, and I felt no sadness at all. I remember saying to myself, they're born again somewhere – perhaps: they're swallows now flying down to Africa! And I suppose this was when the idea that a person might be born again first entered my mind, when I felt that stillness of the forget-me-not field. I'd never been able to imagine this for anyone else, Emily or Chadwick or even for Gérard whom I would love to have seen on my window sill – a pigeon from the Luxembourg Gardens. But I've often thought, while I've gone on with this life my mother has had ten or twenty and in each one she has been careful to keep my father by her, strong and proud as he used to be – not the silent, impotent man that he became.

'I went back and told Eileen I was staying. I suppose I knew she couldn't really turn me out. She gave me Gully's old room in the attic and it was full of hatboxes. Some of them had hats inside and they were all very old-fashioned, wide hats like dinner plates with dinners on them made out of net and feathers, the kind of thing Mrs Pankhurst used to wear. There must have been twenty of them in that room! I remember thinking, I expect at dawn they'll all wake up and start jabbering through their boxes about all the weddings they'd seen and all the drinking of tea in bone china, I expect I shall have to silence them, I thought. They'll be too noisy for me.

'After my walk to the forget-me-not field, after Eileen had given me Gully's room, I lay down in it and went to sleep. The hats were very quiet. I slept for hours and a wind got up and began to slip into my dreams. I thought I was in a trench in France and my helmet was made of bone. The wind got stronger and stronger and I was afraid my bone helmet would blow away and go rolling off towards the German line. I crouched down lower and lower in the mud, waiting for the command, but no command came because there was no one to give it. I was the only soldier left alive.

'It was quite dark when I woke up and there was no candle in this room, so I made my way downstairs where I found Eileen and Miss Pinney sitting in a blaze of light. Electricity had come to the farm! It was most extraordinary. It changed the colours and the size of the room.

'We ate supper under a pink lampshade. Our hands became the colour of salmon. It was a kind of stew we ate, very thick and English and full of carrot. Eileen and Miss Pinney behaved like deaf mutes, making little signs to each other, but not saying a word. I wanted to laugh at them – and at myself. I didn't know what I was doing there. I tried, as we ate, to make some plan for going somewhere else, but I knew that I was dreadfully tired and not strong at all. I believe I was afraid that if I was left completely alone, I might forget to eat and drink and my black sea would wash me away. But as it was, my hatred of Eileen was like a raft. Can you understand this? I thought that, with the raft, I could gather some strength – and then I would go away for ever and never think of her again nor of her needlework and her knitting and her Belgian sardines. Never, never! But I have thought of her, of course. She's one of those people I haven't been able to forget.

'When I went to bed, I took up a candle. I didn't want to turn an electric light on the hatboxes. There was a little table, in the room where Gully used to do his homework, and I sat at this and thought,

I could write here. When I'm well again, this is what I must do – sit at Gully's table and write. Then I put a coat on and went out. I walked very silently to the village which still had its pond and its tiny church and its one signpost pointing three ways and all its little cottages (none with electric light) where the farm workers lived. It hadn't changed at all, not since the days when Chadwick used to wander about in it, looking for members of the Garrick at midnight. I sat on the bench by the pond and I thought of the evening I'd been locked in the cupboard for teasing Gully. I suppose I was letting my memories of Suffolk come back.'

The hotel Ralph had found was in Chalk Farm Road. It was a cheaper, smellier kind of place than Harrington Gardens; the rooms were old and the curtains thin. There was no dining-room. But it was no more than five minutes' walk from Erica's flat, and this tawdry piece of London seemed to possess a kind of disordered life which suited Ralph's mood. South Kensington was too smug behind its railings. Burglar alarms told of family silver in every house, Staffordshire cottages on mantlepieces. Here, the wind seemed to blow people about like litter. The traffic roared through blind. There was nothing to admire.

Ralph's room looked out over a concrete courtyard, two sides of which were owned by a garage. On a large sliding door a red and white sign said 'Spares. Accessories.' 'That's you babe,' said Ralph to himself. 'Time you became the whole thing – body and engine. Time you fitted the words to the life.' Then he took the Summary from his hastily packed suitcase and wrote: 'She cheats me of every death. Doesn't she know we're all My Lai men in our generation? We want to see the bodies.

'How – precisely how – I want to ask, was Gérard killed. Like who by and where? And then, how did the news get back to Paris? Did it come from Fernandez? But she won't tell me. I can look up the date of the death in an art book and the rest I would have to invent.

'My only brush with death is Grandma: funeral packed with black people come to make sure this time she's really gone. "Oh my," they wail, "she was one stubborn old lady, your Gran," and then with relief, "there ain't no more like her left. She all was the last one, man!"

'Remember my mother sat in the rocking chair and smoked. Chiffon dress. Tanned legs. Smoked and smiled. She was always fond of endings.

'Dad and I gave out cakes and drinks, but not many whites had travelled so far. One old guy was a rose grower. He had an acre of glass, he said. His roses bloomed in February through November.

'Dad said "I'm selling the ranch, son. Lock stock and barrel. Your mother and I don't see ourselves living here. We're far too used to civilization."

'And that was it. No sequel. Nothing kept or treasured. Not even the rocking chair. Dad and Ma got a plane out. But I stayed there a night to keep her absence company: the dead burying the dead! Tired old nigger shuffles in at sunrise. "Told me she'd leave me something, sir. Some kinda something." "No!" I yell from an upstairs window, "my folks got it all."

'But they left it all and strangers bought it. They took the money and ride it like surf. Their lives are lived on the big breakers.'

It was seldom that Ralph allowed himself to think about his parents. It amused him to notice that by jotting down a few scattered thoughts about death he had let them in: his mother with her fine legs and the scarlet smile of a star, his father in his beach shirt, dying a slow death from barbecue smoke and saturated fats. He imagined their deaths all right: ground to fragments, both of them, in a barrel organ and passers-by would stop to listen to the exquisite music of their dying. In the distance, the sea would explode onto the beach.

'I started writing again in the winter of 'thirty-seven. I'd recovered a bit by then – I made myself walk quite far each day to try and get some strength back into my legs. And then the hatboxes got me going. They were the voices I used and the novel was going to be called *Old Hats*. I told you, didn't I, that it was about Eileen. The only characters in it were hats and some of them were ancient and full of moth, but they could all talk, these hats and little by little they unfold the life story of the women – Eileen – who used to wear them.

'It was rather an extraordinary idea and I think Ranulf Tree thought I'd gone mad when I sent him the first chapter. But after being with Gérard for so long I think my mind was somehow hitched up to the "extra-ordinary" and it was satisfying to be writing something rather bold.

'I watched Eileen very carefully. I saw a lot about her I'd never noticed. She took to blowing her nose a lot, for instance, as if she wanted people to think she was crying. And she was getting fat. Her clothes were always tidy and spotless, but now she bulged out of them. Miss Pinney's idea of companionship with Eileen seemed to be all mixed in with cakes and sweet puddings because these were all Miss Pinney ever made, and Eileen kept eating them. One of the hats gives a running commentary on all the food she's eaten at coffee mornings and sewing guilds and meetings of the W.I.

'None of the hats – because their lives are all in the past – give any warning of what may come. They paint a picture of a woman who has always tried to conform and be useful in a useless, niggling way. She's very fond of rules and hierarchies and has begun to wonder, even, if England wouldn't be better run by the Germans with their sense of order, when a jackboot walks into the room where the hats are chatting and blows them all to shreds. Bits of them – feathers and net and petals of artificial flowers – float around for a while and then come slowly drifting down. The jackboot then gorges itself on all the pieces and becomes very stiff and erect like a phallus. By the end, the room is empty except for this thing, this dismembered member.

'Well, it was rather odd, but the work I did on it was precious because I became alive through it. Just like *The Angler* it was too short for a novel, too long for a story, but Ranulf Tree liked it in the end and for a while, there was talk of putting these two stories in a volume together and publishing them. But Patterson wasn't keen. They hung on to the manuscript for months wondering what to do with it, and meanwhile I began other stories – much shorter ones – and all of these too had Eileen at their centre. She had pushed her way into my mind, just like she had pushed her way into the recruiting centre with her mufflers. And I suppose I wanted to be the sergeant, mocking her and making jokes about French knickers. Yet the more I wrote about her, the more I came to see that she was one of these women whose own ways make them rather miserable, and you feel tempted to ask, "I wonder why you never got over this habit of obedience to *little* things and let life froth up a bit in you like beer?" You see, she didn't seem to get any pleasure from anything she did except perhaps when she spoke to God in her musical box and He spoke back. She baffled me, really. She'd become a miserable thing with her *gros point* and her silence. Miss Pinney would stare at her anxiously with those watering eyes of hers and sometimes tears came out of them, but you couldn't tell what they were, those tears, sorrow for Eileen or just the natural overspill of her eyes. And I never asked because neither Eileen nor Miss Pinney liked talking to me. They were very glad I shut myself away and wrote. They didn't want to hear about Paris and I didn't want to tell them. The only thing we ever seemed to talk about was the war – the war that came. Neither of them believed there would be a war. They thought England should try to go on being friends with Hitler no matter what he was doing in Austria or Czechoslovakia. As long as everything here stays the same, they thought, we don't care what happens in Europe. And when I said Fascism must be fought, just as it's being fought in Spain, they'd look up from their needlework and say: "Spain needs a man like Franco."

'I knew I'd have to go away. In the spring I began to make plans, but I can't remember what the plans were; they changed each week. I think I was well again by then, but I didn't seem to have any roots anywhere except there, in Suffolk. Sometimes I'd make a plan for dying. I'd remember Gérard and the memory was terrible, like a blade going in me and then I'd imagine how an actual blade would feel and think this preferable. One thing distressed me terribly. After my illness at Saladino's and my haste to get away from France, I'd brought back nothing of Gérard's, nothing at all. And sometimes I'd even make a plan for going to Paris for a few days and bringing back some of his pictures at least. I knew I couldn't bear anything that had actually belonged to him, but the pictures were part of him and yet separate and I had no idea what had been done with them all. Sometimes I imagined them hanging up in Matilde's room and I'd feel jealous.

'I didn't go to Paris. In fact I didn't do anything except exist – side by side with Eileen and Miss Pinney but not *with* them. I'd go for walks and sometimes see Haggard and talk to him about Hitler. "I reckon them Fassists 'now gitting more'n their fair share of the rabbit," he'd say and I'd agree. And I saw Gully now and then and he'd say to me sometimes, "You're terribly changed."

'I had a feeling at this time that I upset Gully so I'd never stay long. He was the one person I might have talked to but I think he dreaded this; he didn't want me to talk. So I'd cone back to the farmhouse and go on and on with my writing and it was in the winter of 1938 that I discovered I was going blind.

'And my black dreams began. I'd kept them at bay for ten years, so that I remember thinking, when we were at Chamonix with Fernandez, they'll never come back, not as long as I love Gérard. But now they came. They were uglier than they'd ever been because I was so afraid of blindness, Ralph. They were dreams of burial, of unbearable weight on me, the weight of black earth and creeping ants pushing into my eyes and sealing up my throat, *oh,* they were terrible! I tried to hide what was happening from Eileen. I thought she'd get me taken away to the mental hospital. But one night, when I felt the weight begin on me, I stumbled into my old room. I think I was trying to find the cupboard and shut myself in and I'd just forgotten that it wasn't there any more. I tripped over the wire to Miss Pinney's electric fire and fell down. The electric fire went over too and the rug in front of it started to smoulder and I could see all this and I could hear Miss Pinney screaming from her bed. And then I remember Eileen's voice telling me to get up, and I thought, Sam used to lift me very gently when this happened, why doesn't she lift me and put me down in the cupboard where I shall be able to breathe? But of course she didn't know I couldn't get up. She kept shouting "What are you doing? What are you doing?" But I couldn't answer.

'I suppose Eileen and Miss Pinney dragged me into the attic room because I woke up there, in my bed, and there was a blinding light in my eye. I remember thinking, they've moved my room to Africa and this is the extraordinary African sun that I've never seen. I felt someone lift my wrist and I was told afterwards that it was the middle of the night and no doctor was near enough to fetch but Eileen had gone for the vet! The light I had seen wasn't the African sun at all but the odd little torch a vet used to look down a cow's anus.

'I've often thought how funny that was, Ralph. It was the same old vet I'd gone running for when I was a girl. He was a Quaker called Cyrus Webley and very old by that time, not too old, I suppose, to diagnose fowl pest or pull a calf out of its mother on a cold morning, just too old to see blindness!

The next day, they sent for Gully. He came over in the evening, after his long day's work at Haggard's shop. I remember it was bitterly cold and I'd spent the day huddled up in bed, hardly moving.

Eileen had looked in on me twice, with a grave stare. The stare said: "You'll be the death of me, Erica March."

'And I stared back. I was very hungry but I didn't want to ask her for anything and no food came. I think Cyrus Webley had told her I had a fever and should be starved. They were all utterly confused, you see. It had never occurred to them that I might be mad, but now it did.

'When Gully arrived, he came straight up. I expect Eileen wanted to speak to him privately; I expect she had some old rubbish about the God in the jar of Marmite who had revealed my insanity to her while she made sandwiches for elevenses. But Gully never listened to Eileen. He never had and he never did as long as she lived. I think her voice gave him a suffocated feeling.

'I don't know why, but I didn't want to tell Gully about my eyes. Probably I thought, if I tell Gully, then this question of my blindness will be kept in Suffolk and all I will see when everything begins to wobble and fade will be Eileen's furniture, and outside, all the empty winter fields. I knew I had to get away while there was still time.

'So we talked about Gully's family. I asked him what it was like to be a parent and to see your own children growing up, but I can't remember what he said. In the town you heard gossip about Dot being moody and sometimes rude to people in the shop, but I think on the whole they were happy, Dot and Gully. Loyalty was very strong in him. But he told me that evening he felt I didn't belong in Suffolk any more. He said he thought it was the place that had made me ill and that it would be best if I went away. For a moment, I wondered if Eileen had made him say this, but I don't think she had – Gully wouldn't have let her. No, I just think that Gully had his safe world which he treasured and there was something in me he mistrusted now – something foreign and dangerous.

'He looked at the room and the hatboxes. When I told him there was a hat inside each of them, he shook his head and said: "I reckon the way some women carry on makes 'em the laughing stock o' the world." And we laughed. And then with Gully's help, I began to make plans for leaving. We'd just go back to the station where he'd met me, and I'd get back on the train for London. He thought I had friends in London who would meet me and places to stay. I think there was only one thing he wanted to add, but he didn't say it. He wanted to ask me never to come back.'

166

Outside Erica's window, it had begun to rain and it was cold in the room – England's false spring. 'I don't believe,' she said turning to look at the drizzle, 'that I have ever written anything successful about England. I think we've tolerated each other, England and I, sort of grudging friends. But you know, it is quite depressing to write about bad weather.' Ralph pondered this for a moment, and then said: 'When you chose Africa for *In the Blind Man's* City, were you blind already?'

She closed her eyes, took off the heavy glasses and touched the skin of the eyelids with her left hand.

'No. Or at least, I don't know exactly how blind I was. It was very difficult to see the words I was writing. At first only my right eye was going; so I used to cover this and keep on just with my left eye. But the day war was declared, I know that both eyes were very very bad. I remember squinting at the newspaper and thinking, I've left it too late. All the hospitals will be full of the wounded back from France now, so I shall wait years for the operation.'

'You knew there could be an operation?'

'Oh yes. I knew what I had. I went to the British Museum Library and looked up all the causes and effects of blindness, and I diagnosed correctly. They call it a cataract, when the lens deteriorates and becomes stiff. It's more common in people whose bodies are all stiff and deteriorated, yet mine wasn't. I was thin and still quite strong. Only the black dreams brought a dreadful weakness. And I wasn't old. I was forty-four when the first signs came and two years later, when the second war began, I was forty-six. I remember thinking, I shall hear the war, touch it even, but I won't *see* it.

'But there! I was fortunate in a way. I thought of the red-haired man in the Rue Pierre Nicole and it was the sight of him that had haunted me. Now I imagined him putting on his uniform, polishing his boots and his rifle – until France fell, and then I tried not to think of him any more or even of Saladino or anyone I knew. I stayed in my imaginary Africa and had a war there.'

'Matarina ran from the forest. She and the other older women of the village had been visiting the tomb of the dead witch doctor, bringing spices in wooden jars, when the vultures began to circle the tomb. Never, in all the years they had lived between them, had the old women seen vultures above the tomb of a witch doctor, so they knew that the vultures had Meaning. On limping thin legs they ran from the Meaning.

The boy in the dirt under the baobab tree heard the scuffling of the old women's feet and their gabble which was full of terror. He picked up his bowl and fingered the two coins that had been dropped into it. He thought, if there is some terror in the forest, hiding, it may creep out of the forest and encircle the villages. But the villagers have no weapons against terror and the missionaries have no weapons against terror, none except their white suffering Jesus who is a Jesus of peace, so says Sister Catherine and even Father Lemanteloupe who is not a peaceful man but an excitable one with his strange vowels and his love of children. Even he, Father Lemanteloupe whose body may one day float down the river with the river flowers, even he talks of a Jesus peace and presses his wooden cross on his thin lips and kisses it with a sound only I can hear, an inaudible sound which is loud to me – the sound of a man sucking on his evening soup.

The chatter of the market faded. Old men and young men began to cluster round Matarina. A dog wandered to the baobab tree, sniffed the boy's feet. He kicked the dog away and it cringed sideways out of the shade, into the flat, bright heat of the market square, to join the listening group, squatting on its haunches as some of them were squatting, listening to Matarina and the old women with their eyes aghast from the sight of the vultures circling over their precious place, the ancient witch doctor's eternity. And thinking, of course, what the boy thought: what weapons do we have against a terror of this kind, which is not the terror of the armed enemy, but the terror of the invisible, a terror that rides astride dreams, making no sound, but which pushes up and on into the deltas of capillaries, surges faster and stronger into the silent streaming of the blood and only leaves and lets you be when everything has been altered, when the villages are cinders, when the friend sits on his rump in the burning ash and remembers the friend who was sold for a sliver of monkey meat. When Father Lemanteloupe floats headless to the sea, when the chatter of the forest is silent because the forest has been torn down.

The boy could not see them, but he knew that many of

them were looking all about them, trying to see in the peaceful scene they had laid out the exact place from which the terror would come. They wanted to believe they could recognize it, that they had interpreted the Meaning of the vultures as best they could and that, being strong men, they would defeat the terror before it crept inside them, long before it had created in them the storms and terrible yearnings that would begin to destroy them.

Away in the fields, Ngumbi worked on. No hint of any terror could reach her there as yet. She swung her arms and made her bundles of cane and her dress that day and her turban were as yellow as maize.

The boy longed for distance to separate him from the village. He longed, for an instant, to be deaf, dumb, insensitive to touch – kept in ignorance of what was happening and what was to come. And he wanted to be with Ngumbi, to put his head on her waist and his arms round her legs and protect her with the little rhymes that had come floating out of the mission-school windows on all the countless afternoons when he had sat still under his tree, head tilted, waiting for footsteps, waiting for francs and pennies to buy Ngumbi a paraffin lamp:

> "Gentle Jesus, we thee pray
> Help us understand thy way.
> Gentle Jesus, we are sinners,
> Please remember we're beginners."

He tried to think up more of these rhymes – protection for Ngumbi's soul which would surely be one of the very first to be taken by the terror – but he was soon distracted from his chanting by his awareness of new deliberate movement not far from where he sat. It came from Sarm's stall. Sarm was the oldest Indian trader to come to the village. Over the years his goods had become more and more inviting to the African – kohl for his woman's eyes, breast unction to endow her, boxes of cotton pads for her menstrual bleeding, aphrodisiac powders to stimulate her in caskets made of mother-of-pearl.

Yes, they valued Sarm. They knew he bought cheap in the cities, sold dear in the villages, yet he sold them magic. No price was too high to pay for magic of this kind.

The boy lifted his face. Not a breath of wind touched it. Sarm was near to him now. He must have put all the goods into his handcart as quickly as he could and now, barefooted, his body between the shafts, he was wheeling his handcart away. By dusk he would be on the steamboat with his wares, heaving back towards the city. "Sarm . . ." the boy called, lifting his face higher. But the old man didn't answer. And a moment later his name began to ring out among the men gathered round Matarina "Sarm . . . Sarm . . ." they said the name with venom. Because it was plain to most of them now: here was the place the terror lurked – in the magic and sly profit of Sarm and his kind. Of course it was here. Why hadn't they seen it the very moment Matarina had come back from the forest? How stupid they were to torment themselves with other fears, when here lay the enemy, tangible, visible, cunning as a snake and now trying to creep away back into the forest, trying to scramble onto the steamer with his money and his useless potions, "Sarm! . . . Sarm!"

Pointless to think he could escape them. It was his magic that had brought the vultures – the breast unction and the kohl and the powders that smelt of no flower that grew in Africa. "Sarm! . . . *Sarm!* . . ."

The door of the mission school opened and the boy heard the cries of Father Lemanteloupe as he came running out, but at the same time he knew that the crowd gathered around Matarina were coming nearer. He heard Sarm cry out as the first stone hit him and now the whole of the market place was alive with anger and shouting. The second stone missed Sarm and came bouncing over the hard ground to graze the boy's leg. With his head still up and listening, he crawled round to the far side of the baobab tree. The ground underneath him was moist from urine; the smell of it held a kind of burning.'

9

'I'm going to date this Summary from now on,' Ralph wrote.

'Today is the 23rd and of course I should, by Walt's understanding, be back in New York tomorrow – the 24th.

In fact, by my own scheduling, I've got eight more days with Erica. Then I go to Oxford to see John, on May 2nd. Guess I must book a flight home for May 4th or definitely LOSE MY JOB.

I'm beginning to feel a sense of urgency on two counts: hell knows if I can gather fifty more years of a life in eight days. Because this feels like a package tour – that marvellous cheap deal which I guess we invented – where you pick over externals and leave, not with a sense of loss, but with a sense of nothing begun. My friend Al, who travels a lot in a Dormobile, is as mean as hardcore shit on travel packages. I love to hear him talk!

Second sense of urgency/unease: E.M. has a game of Cluedo going with this death of hers. (To my shame, I hear Walt's voice: "I guess we can beef it up a bit if the old lady dies"). Doesn't say what she means. Doesn't know what she means? Somehow, she's got it tied in to that airman who landed in Eileen's cucumbers.

If I'm honest, I want no part in it. "Get in, get your story, get out" – Walt again. Yet I have never met, never will again meet anyone like her. She's a sparrow to see, but the songs in her . . .

Guess I'm hoping J.P. will know what to do. In all that ancestral silence, he should surely be able to work out a matter of life and death. Yet perhaps even there, *especially* there, he can't. He has humming bird fantasies, damn it! No wonder education's creaking!

Found a quiet and good Italian restaurant a few blocks away from here. They seemed rather to court than to shun my solitude. So I told them I'd be in most nights. We discussed sea-food salads, which Americans go crazy on ever since they heard Frank Sinatra pronounce "Calla-marees". We had a laugh – at the expense of America's gullibility.

One odd thing: I've begun to like London. Time seems to blow people around up here in Chalk Farm. They appear to say "What the hell, why not try a smile before the next gust arrives?" The Marine's gotten himself a spot of company.'

It had rained all night, was still raining at two, when Ralph arrived at Erica's flat.

He had spent most of the morning at the Fawcett Library, choosing suffragette pictures to take home with him. For the war material, he had been told he should go to the Imperial War Museum in Lambeth; 'They got all the wars there mate,' a clerk at the Fawcett Library had remarked.

He had found the picture of Emily Davison's death which Erica had described. He remembered that during her account of her activities with Emily, she had been visited by what she called her "rain sickness". And now, when time seemed so precious, it was raining again. The sickness could arrive unannounced like her moods of black depression, a kind of death. And there was no recovery from it, she had told him, until the rain had gone.

But she was well, she said. She wanted to begin straight away. The wine and biscuits were there on the tray. It was as if some of Ralph's urgency had communicated itself to her, as if the act of telling the life had become as important as the act of recording it, as if she had once known, the voice and the machine, will one day meet and then . . . She mistrusted people who wrote their memoirs, she said. They tried to puff themselves out to be important pigeons. And memoirs was such a pretentious word: it belonged in Chadwick's stage drawing-rooms! Yet it was surprising how it gave her pleasure, not just to remember her life, but to reconstruct it for Ralph, event by event, leaving unsaid only what it became physically impossible to say. She realized, she told Ralph as he poured the wine, that she had been very lonely since the death of Bernard. She had never before minded solitude, but in the winters now she had begun to mind it, and to talk to Ralph each day for a few hours was rather pleasing. Those hours were just enough. The rest of the time she needed to be alone.

'When Huntley came,' she said, 'I was very pleased to see him at first. I thought, dear old Hunt, he's cruising on in his world, obtuse as a battleship but rather dear, like an old relic. But then I remembered how silly he is and greedy about money and I just wanted him gone. He's always saying I should go and see him – he's said it for fifteen years – but I never do.

'Oh well, never mind Huntley. He's not important at all. Now let's get on and I must tell you what happened when I left Suffolk again and came to London.

'I came back to nothing, you see. The cupboard was there in Sam's flat. I had that – and a little money, enough to buy somewhere. And I came back to the war which began in the spring when Hitler invaded Poland.

'I've never really understood alliances which are made and knocked down like sandcastles because the tides change. I don't think I even knew that we had an alliance or a pact or anything with Poland which was terribly far away, so it seemed very extraordinary to be going to war for a country we couldn't save. Especially when neither we nor France had done anything about Spain, which we might have saved, just by sending arms.

'I held a very dim view of Mr Chamberlain but when Churchill stepped in, he seemed all wrong to me, too fat. I thought we needed someone more measured than him, but I think I was wrong. I believe he rather loved the war and got very excited about everything in it. I don't suppose you remember him, but for the British during those years he was everywhere: it was as if the great bulk of him was divided up hundreds of thousands of times and pushed into people's wirelesses. And his voice; when he went in 1945, I thought, he was just like Falstaff, a man for a certain season, replaced when a new wind blows in! But for the war years, his voice had the chimes of eternity in it; it seemed to come from the bottom of an ocean.

'I was in London a few months before war was declared. I think at that time, after Munich, most people thought they'd been spared: Hitler would go goose-stepping on somewhere else but England would be left alone. And then when war did come, there were no bands like in 1914, there was just a lot of muddle and waiting. You saw children playing games with their Mickey Mouse gas masks.

'I went back to Hampstead and stared at my old house. Someone had planted geraniums in a window box and these had died with the frosts and never been taken out. And I thought they're a bit like me, frost over my right eye, frost in my heart: I should be taken away and hidden from view, not left to go grey in London. I felt vulnerable. I kept saying to myself, there should be someone to take charge.

'I lay out on Hampstead Heath and it was ridiculously cold. I tried to count the stars. I thought, if I can see a hundred stars perfectly, then the actual day of blindness is months off, years even. I went to sleep trying to count the stars and I woke up and it was snowing. And I began to laugh at it all, at my pathetic attempt to count stars, at the snow which was like glue on my eyelashes, at all the strength or illusions of strength I had had in Paris years now utterly gone, and there I was, being obliterated.

'The trees became very beautiful in the dawn, grey-white and still. I thought, how extraordinary if people were rooted to the ground like them. And thinking about the trees must have put Ranulf Tree into my mind, because I remember that he came next, after my imaginings about rooted people, he came into my mind wearing his overcoat and I think only because his overcoat seemed so warm did I sit up and decide to go and see him.

'I walked to Hampstead High Street. A café that served hot chocolate opened at eight. I drank three mugs of hot chocolate and my wet coat made a puddle on the floor. It was difficult to get warm, even in the warm café and I felt very confused about how to get to Ranulf Tree's office. I knew he'd moved – he and Patterson – to Bedford Square, to the land of the Wolves! But I'd forgotten London. Just forgotten my way around.

'A cab took me. As we drove, the cabbie told me his wife was German. He said if war came, he'd be ostracized in the pub. He said his pub mates would be kicking dachshunds in the street if war came, just like in 1914. And he'd had no answer from his Member of Parliament. He'd written to him to ask him what would happen to enemy aliens in the event of war, but no reply had come. He said none of it was fair.

'Ranulf Tree didn't seem to want to talk either about the war or the lack of it, and I was glad. He showed me round his new offices which were nice, in good proportioned rooms smelling of beeswax polish and books. I gave him the stories I'd written in Suffolk and he asked his eternal question: when will there be a novel? As an answer I wanted to say, Ranulf, I'm going blind. I wanted, at last, to share my knowledge of the blindness with someone else and let them help me. But I didn't. I started to talk about the very beginnings of my idea for *In The Blind Man's City*. I explained to him that I wanted to write about fear and the way, because of fear, people commit crimes that are unimaginable. The blind child in my story, who becomes the blind man, is the barometer of a society infected by fear, because he can smell, touch, breathe all the currents of feeling around him. He remains in touch with the progression of things; he remembers the beginning and what came next. It's as if *all* that happens, happens *in* him: yet it doesn't contaminate him; he commits no crimes; he remains sane. And when the destruction of his world is complete, he's chosen to be the one to rebuild it. But then of course there's the ending which I wrote just as I planned it and lots of people have criticized it: when the blind man is elected leader, white doctors and surgeons come to him – as the missionaries promised years ago when he sat begging under his tree – and they cure his blindness. But what he can now *see* is a world of unutterable horror. He hides in the mutilated forest and stabs himself. The last things he sees with his new eyes are the vultures circling over his own body.

'Talking to Ranulf Tree, I think I realized that I had the whole book – even the ending, which a lot of the critics didn't like – in my head and I was desperate, then, to begin it. I wanted to start straight away – that very morning, but I had nowhere to stay. I told Ranulf that I thought I had the strength for writing now, but for nothing else. My night on the heath had been very stupid because it had made me weak. All I could keep thinking again and again was, someone must take charge.

'Patterson came in and nodded at me. He'd never liked me, Patterson. I was too odd for his taste. He nodded at me as if I was nothing – a decorator of lavatory paper. Ranulf started to tell him that I had a new book planned out, but he wasn't interested; he just remarked that I looked very tired. Much later, he confided to me that he'd noticed something odd about my eyes that day, but that was bunkum! No ordinary person can detect a cataract, not at that very early stage. Later there's a kind of greying of the pupil, but even that, you don't notice it. Even the vet with his torch had seen nothing.

'Patterson and Tree began a conversation about a man who wrote about butterflies. I went to sleep on a leather chesterfield near a gas fire and I had a dream of Gérard's bones buried under a Spanish road. Tanks and guns and trucks came down the road and his carcass underneath it was broken to pieces.

'When I woke up, I was boiling hot and Ranulf was talking very quietly to a stranger in a tweed coat. It was Bernard.'

She handed Ralph the photograph. Faded and brown, it showed a man past his best. He was smiling into the sun. He seemed large in a cumbersome way, overweight, inside his baggy trousers. He held a butterfly net.

'That's him.'

Slightly at a loss, Ralph said: 'He looks very British.'

'British. Oh yes, he was. He could have come from no other culture, not Bernard. He had the flag folded round his heart.'

'And when was this taken, this picture?'

'Oh I don't remember. In nineteen fifty-something. He's standing on what Chadwick used to call the lawn.'

Erica took the photograph from Ralph and looked at it.

'I'd forgotten he had his net with him. It looks like a hot day, doesn't it?'

Then she put it aside, face down on the sofa.

'He didn't look very much like that when I met him. He was thinner and not so grey. Yet in fact there was a part of Bernard that never, never changed. His quiet ways, he never lost them, nor his patience. And his smile for that matter. That hardly altered.'

'So he was the one then,' said Ralph, 'the one who took charge?'

Erica looked surprised. Then she nodded.

'Yes. I suppose he was. It's very strange isn't it, how we become entangled in someone's life, just because they're *there,* waiting for a bus or doing a survey of animal lovers – doing the most ordinary or extraordinary things, and they just happen to glance up . . .

'He was a teacher then, the day I had my sleep on Ranulf Tree's chesterfield. He taught classics. He'd been teaching classics ever since the first war and yet his love of the classics had dwindled quite early and been replaced by his love of butterflies. He still enjoyed the precision of Latin, its sparingness and lack of ambiguity, so he said, and he used to read me bits of Catullus sometimes, though I can't remember a word of him except a very stupid line in the vocative case which went "O, Lesbia, Lesbia, Lesbia, Lesbia!"

'He taught in Surrey. It was a small public school, called Crowbourne, a regimented and ambitious place. It had a high quota of Jews – rejects from Eton and the other snob places – and Bernard always said its academic standards were very high because of all its gifted boys. I never got on with it very well, not with Crowbourne. I remembered my own education – the vicar scattering nuts in the hall at Christmas – and I've found it difficult to accept the public schools. I know this is very two-faced, as Bernard often pointed out: I accepted Chadwick's money – none of which I'd earned – and this of course was privilege, yet I couldn't accept private education. I think if I'd had a son, I wouldn't have sent him to Crowbourne or anywhere like it. Somehow I imagined all the parents of these boys having holidays in Paris and waiting, just like Chadwick of course, for waiters to unfurl their napkins at Fouquet's. I don't know, Ralph. I think the revolutionary part of me – the Emily part, the Gérard part – had gone a bit silent by the time I met Bernard. And I'd begun to see the world through a kind of grey soup. Sometimes I wondered if all of me – mind and heart and everything – wasn't slowly going blind. There were so many confusions.

'I suppose the greatest confusion was the war, which couldn't seem to get going and then when it did, our part of it was inept. They tried to pretend Dunkirk was a victory, but the victory only disguised the enormous failure behind it. We left hundreds of French soldiers behind, too. Did you know this? We just left them on the beach at Dunkirk, for the Germans to intern. It's never talked about, that, but it's often haunted me. I wondered if any of our old friends were among the ones they left.

'At the time, Bernard helped me to forget about France, about my years there. Even Saladino began to grow thin in my memory! I found a flat in Haverstock Hill and for the second time in my life, I sent a removal van to get the cupboard. From that day in 1939 it's stayed with me. I've never lent it to anyone or even left it for long, only to go into hospital and to go abroad.

'The flat had one very nice light room which I furnished before the years of utility things, and it was a place to begin. That was how I felt about it: "Begin again," I said when I sat there and watched the afternoon come on, "try to begin something." So I began the novel and Bernard went back to Surrey and perhaps I would have forgotten about him except that he kept sending flowers. And with the flowers there were sometimes long letters telling me about himself. He told me that he'd fought in the first war and tried to write poetry in the trenches. But poetry just hadn't come out of him – only feelings, which he couldn't express. Ever since then he'd envied writers and wished he could be one, and then he'd discovered butterflies and now he'd written a book about them. Only after that book was published did I find out that Bernard had done all the careful, beautiful drawings for it himself. He never mentioned the meticulous draughtsman in him, only the failed trench poet and the brother killed at Vimy Ridge and then the marriage to his cousin June who had left him in one year for an Olympic swimmer.

'They were very curious interruptions to my world of invented Africa, those letters from Bernard. I was trying to imagine swamp and damp and forest shrieks and children with dusty feet, and in they'd come, these quiet pulsebeats of an Englishman. I don't think I really wanted them and yet I knew they were important. "The more I let them in, the more sane I shall become," that's what I thought. And there was no one else. Only the voices on the wireless telling of this new regulation and that. And the darkness. That's what I remember: "If the enemy can't see you, he can't hurt you." Yet enemies are made in the mind. In my book, the choice of the enemy is arbitrary.

'Confusions then. More confusions. Bernard wrote to tell me that as a Local Defence Volunteer he'd been given a weapon. The weapon was a piece of lead pipe with a bayonet welded onto it. He said "It's very hard to present arms with this contraption and no one seems to know exactly what to do with it." No wonder! We were all utterly confused – the whole country – all in darkness. I think when the first bomb fell in 1940 it threw some light on things. I think we *saw* war after that, instead of just imagining it. We put in our Anderson shelters and planted vegetables where there had been flowers. These were things you could see!'

Erica reached for the photograph again, turned it over and stared at it.

'He had a little car,' she said, 'and while you could still get petrol, he used to come and visit me. I can't remember what we did. I expect we walked on the heath and listened to the wireless and Bernard talked about Catullus. We never touched. I think a year went by before we did. Or perhaps we held hands when we walked, I don't know. But then the letters from Crowbourne become more and more frequent. I think at one time, there was a letter every day and gradually the trench poet was burrowing up in them, trying to say something yet never alluding to it, when we met, as if, until it had finally been found words on paper, it had to be held in.'

She smiled. 'It was so silly of him, wasn't it? Why did he think that love had to be written down?'

The girl at the travel agent's desk flashed Ralph a weary smile.

Pan Am flight, 201. Arrive New York 10 p.m. local time. May 4th. Okay?'

'Okay.'

Ralph paid with a credit card and left. In the bright early evening light, he went with his camera in search of the two places in Hampstead where Erica had lived. Neither was hard to find. The Haverstock Hill flat, the second floor of an untended Edwardian house, was now part of a hotel, the Britannia. Partitions blocked off sections of windows; Ralph imagined cardboard walls, easily shaken by the traffic that roared up and down the wide road. It seemed cheap and inhospitable; blossom fell on the tarmac garden. London's tourist boom had reached it and claimed it, seemingly for ever. No one would ever again live here.

The village cottage was as undisturbed as it had been in 1921. Huddled in its narrow paved-over street, the sun had already left it. Ralph photographed only the front door, now painted brown. In contrast to the Britannia Hotel, the house was expensively cared for; the solid brass doorknocker announced the quietly privileged life within.

'You an estate agent or what?'

An upstairs window had shot up. A middle-aged man in shirtsleeves was leaning out.

'Pardon me?'

'Why are you taking snaps?'

'Oh . . .' Ralph touched his camera apologetically. 'Only of the door . . .'

'The door? Taking a snap of the door?'

'Yup.'

'What on earth for and who on earth gave you the right?'

Suddenly tired, tired from the day, tired from all the days he had now spent in London, Ralph stared at the man in antagonistic silence.

'Did you hear me?' said the man. 'Who on earth gave you permission to take a photograph of my front door?'

'It's not a punishable offence,' Ralph said wearily.

'Spy are you, or what? or just an infringer of other people's property?'

'Neither,' said Ralph, beginning to wander off. 'Just one of those commodities you used to call Yanks.'

The man was still shouting, but Ralph was out of the street, walking fast. 'Jesus Christ . . .' he murmured as he turned into the sunshine, 'the English can be pains in the ass!'

For the first time for a week or more he experienced a sudden longing to join hands with his own life again. Even Walt's blustering seemed, for a moment, acceptable, because it was all in its place, in the familiar, in a world where you owned things and were somebody, not just a stranger with a camera. The eight days remaining felt like a penance, yet at the same time Ralph knew that they weren't enough. I've fucked it, he thought.

Back at the Chalk Farm Hotel, he lay down on his bed and started to read through the pages of his Summary. They seemed hopeless – a lot of vain scribbling.

'Yet what else would you expect,' he began to write, 'of me now in our starving generation ? Generations of sleepwalkers.

'If I'm on the road to Knoxville in my dreams in a mutilated car, then of course I'm in the driver's seat, powerless, waiting for someone to push me in the right direction. But I'M ALSO THE GUY BEHIND, PUSHING! Sure, I am. And the guy behind says: "Use all of you, not just the terrified flabby part on the flabby wheel. *Find* a direction – not over the hilltop road and into darkness – get out of the damn car and start to walk!"

'And then what? Exhilaration and cold of the walk. Mourning for company by sun-up – the car radio with its pulp talk and its time checks. By nine or ten I'm exhausted. Grandma's house is still miles off, and what's her place, anyway, but the one exquisite memory of the past?'

'I'm facing the wrong way.'

The dreams came, under the all-night throb of traffic: voices spitting from the barbecued meat – his mother's, moist and ticklish, his father's, hard under its Southern skin – talking of a future in a blaze of white and coral, the midday of their lives lived out beside a swimming pool where a neighbour's child once drowned. And their laughter, their everyday accompaniment to the passing of time, unbearable laughter, noisy as breaking ice. But slowing, quietening into an early evening of accusation, bewilderment: "It's so hard to get any picture of your life, Ralph, when you don't come to visit. We heard you were covering the primaries, but politics is a dirty word with you, isn't it, dear? But do tell us . . ."

Arrivals. Interruptions. A man called Tom she kisses on the mouth. His father prods the four oozing steaks, asks her if she's made relishes, or what?

But there's no answer. To the question of relish – no, she can't be bothered, only takes Tom's hand and smooths it out and puts it, smoothed enough she decides, against her cheek.

The steaks are carefully turned. Momentarily, flames leap from the charcoal and lick them. "Doing the primaries, then, son? We're Reagan people. You knew that? Actor, see? That's what this country needs. Know what? Man who knows how and when to act."

His arms in the coral shirt sag. Wouldn't have said the barbecue tongs were heavy. But the evening presses on them perhaps – bowls empty of relishes, Tom's body, well preserved in pale blue, but carefully placing his napkin where she begins to arouse him. And the meat – awful to chew the meat by itself undisguised, a hunk of flesh. So he empties today of its humiliations. With a sigh, he turns again to his son and begins to talk of tomorrow. "If you have it in mind to stay over for once, we could go surfing . . ."

'Supposing *you* talked today, Ralph?'

'No, Erica.'

'Why not? I've talked and talked.'

'I booked my flight home yesterday. I have to go to Oxford on May 2nd and then home on the fourth. So I'd like you to tell me all you can . . . till I have to go.'

She looked hard at Ralph, then away from him. When she spoke, it was almost a whisper.

'When you come back from your friend in Oxford, you'll drop in to say goodbye?'

'Sure.'

'You won't forget?'

'Forget?'

'Yes. You might forget.'

'No. I won't.'

She looked relieved, and smiled at him. Then she sat back.

'Bernard spent most of the war trying to get divorced. His cousin and the Olympic swimmer had moved and it became very hard to divorce a person you couldn't find. He fretted a lot about it. After we began to sleep together, marriage was always on his mind. I think this was because he was rather a Christian man. He told me that lepidoptery had converted him from Sunday hymn singer to believer in divine creation. His god was the god of butterflies, of all things bright and beautiful – a child's god. And he, of course, was the loving obedient child. He made love very gravely – as if this was a grown-up thing hallowed by grown-up rules – but afterwards he'd turn onto his back and sleep like a little boy. Happiness and fresh air turned his cheeks pink; the merest sad thing could make him weep. When I told him about my blindness, he put his face near to mine and let his tears run into my eyes.

'I grew terribly fond of him. I don't know if my fondness was ever mixed with any love; I don't believe it was. But all through the war, when I was often alone and he was safe in Surrey with Virgil and Catullus's wretched Lesbia, I'd find myself thinking of him. I'd finish my day's writing and pin up the blackout curtains and eat a little meal that was all vegetables and then wait for the air raid warnings, and start thinking about Bernard. There was about a year, from the middle of 1940 onwards when bombs were dropped every night. Patterson and Tree's new offices were bombed early in 'forty-one, and Patterson had a kind of breakdown with all the symptoms of shell-shock, even though he'd been safe in his Anderson shelter at the time. I think he was put into hospital for a while – though heaven knows where, when there were so many wounded in London – and Ranulf Tree went on without him, just working from his own flat and trying to make inventories of everything he'd lost.

'I would go down to Crowbourne sometimes. It wasn't far from Epsom race-course, but I never went there: I imagined I would see something, some purple or white tatter, left behind from all those years ago.

'The school had a lovely park. In it, you couldn't imagine the war. The boys played cricket and gardeners went round cutting the grass, and Bernard would talk about our wedding. The boys used to titter when they saw us walking together: lovers! I minded the tittering very much. I wanted to say to those sheltered boys: "No, you haven't understood. This is friendship, companionship which now and again expresses itself in an oddly muted version of the sexual act. This is not love. We are not lovers."

'But I suppose Bernard had told them we would be getting married – one day, when he had divorced his cousin, when something had been done about my eyes. One day.

'Yet I never pretended to Bernard that I would marry him. I never lied and said I would. He was just certain that, in the end, I'd change my mind. I expect he thought of marriage as a kind of reward for everything he'd done for me; he thought he'd *earned* it. But the marriage talk became very tedious. For a while I left him. I said I couldn't go on with our friendship. I said I wanted to be left alone to write.

'So he was very sensible. He left me alone and sent no letters and I stopped going down to Surrey to see him. But I found I often thought of him, in his room with its hundreds of books and its two microscopes and his little boxes of water colour paint and his narrow bed where I had occasionally slept. I didn't want to think about him, and yet I did. He was in me somewhere and I had a sense of all the years to come and I thought, if I don't spend them with him, I shall probably spend them quite by myself.

'I finished *In The Blind Man's City.* It had taken me almost two years and by the end of it I knew that my left eye which had done the work of two for a long time was very bad. I remember it was at the start of this new blindness – of the left eye – that I wrote to Saladino and told him the Americans would come in and there would be a joint Allied landing and France would be saved. But I never had any reply and I wondered if Saladino was safe.

'Ranulf liked the book. He took me out to one of his famous lunches to celebrate and we had potted shrimps which were a great luxury in the war. He told me that paper was terribly scarce. We might have to wait at least a year to publish the book, and this depressed me. I thought, I won't see it, then. It was years since I'd seen my name on a book and I wanted this now. I wanted the book to be praised.

'But the potted shrimp lunch was the end of it – for a long while. It finally came out in 1945 and by then I had almost forgotten it: so much else had happened.

'I was paid a small advance and I went to see an eye specialist in Wimpole Street. I think the eye specialist took all the advance money. He told me I would have to have two operations, the first on my right eye to remove the lens, and a later similar one on my left eye. He explained to me that the period between the two operations would be one of distorted vision. Special glasses would be made with an artificial lens for my right eye, but to co-ordinate the vision of the two eyes would be difficult, almost impossible.

'I wrote to Bernard. I didn't think I could go through these operations on my own. There were too many questions I hadn't asked and I suppose I thought Bernard would know the answers. All those hours he spent with the microscope – I thought they might give him the special answers. But of course they didn't! He knew all about the ommatidia of butterflies but nothing about the human eye. I don't know why I ever imagined that he did.

'But we became friends again. Bernard had been mourning me, and he was glad to be out of his black armband. He wanted me to leave my flat and take some cottage or something to be near him in Surrey. But I couldn't do that – not then. I had three months to wait for the operation which would be in Guy's Hospital, unless the air raids began again and it was blown to pieces. I couldn't plan anything until at least the first operation was over. And then, after this there would be this second time of waiting, and I didn't know what to expect. I wondered if I would begin to see the world upside down.'

'There was hardly any pain. But perhaps there was shock in my body, I don't know. I know that the war filled my mind. Under the bandages, my eye, without its seeing part, became global. There were dreams at first of the red-haired man in Paris, then the certainty that my eye was marching, rolling along with the stamping crowd: "Arms for Spain! Arms for Spain!" But my eye knew that these things were preliminaries. There had been light on these times and now there was none. The Jackboot – the gorged Jackboot of my story about the hats – was hung up above my bed. It was hung on a thread of saliva and the thread would soon snap. We knew by that time about the camps. The bursting of the saliva thread would signal death.

'The specialist from Wimpole Street came, but I saw him as a camp *Kommandant*. I tried to say: "My father used to tease me about my black hair. He used to say I was a witch, but I'm not Jewish, not that I know. But then of course I did lie with Sam Green for more than a thousand nights and Sam had a father called Louis Greenberg, in prison for petty larceny, but preferring that to the world, preferring to be left alone . . ."

'So the camp *Kommandant* went away, and only in my dreams did he come back and hold my eye in the palm of his hand, my round, moist eye, toss it from one palm to the other and say: "This is how the world moves, you see. Not round and round as you expected, but in a series of leaps or jumps, expertly controlled so that it never falls and breaks up, not quite, though of course this threat is always present, and will become greater as time goes on . . ."

'Nurses came and said I was disturbing the other wards with my screams. I remember their soft arms holding me. I was given injections to make me sleep, but the pain of one injection seemed to last all through that one sleep till the next. The needles were like Bernard's welded bayonet, making colossal wounds. I shouted to Bernard to throw his weapon away for ever.

'One of the worst dreams – illusions, whatever they were – was believing I was a cow trying to graze off a little bare patch of scrub, dying of hunger for fresh clean grass but knowing that every time I put my head down to nibble the scrub, my eye would fall out, yet still be attached to me by the kind of ropes and pulleys that held together Roger Walters' heart. It would roll around on the ground in front of my mouth and because I couldn't see it, I was always in danger of eating it up. Then the ropes that held it would be snapped and it would be gone for ever! It would become manure and Eric Haggard would spread it on his land – my eye that could see the whole of the world, not only the oak trees and the skies of Suffolk, my eye that *was* the whole world!

'Well, I haven't remembered it for a long time, that time. Sometimes I remember that it only lasted a few days – so Bernard said, yet it seemed like months, years even. But then it was over and I was calm and I saw that Bernard had brought me roses, I thought, perhaps the end of the war will be like this, a wonderful gentle calm and white roses in a jar.

'I could see light when the bandages came off. With the spectacles they gave me I could see everything clearly but it was terribly difficult to judge distance or size. I often bumped into things.

'The *Kommandant* (I always thought of that eye specialist as the *Kommandant*!) told me that only after the second operation would they be able to match exactly the two artificial lenses and then, with the spectacles, my sight should be quite good. But the thought of the second operation was frightening. I told Bernard I didn't think I could go through with it.

'It was in the spring of 1943 that I had the first operation. I came out of hospital at Easter and Bernard was on holiday from Crowbourne. He stayed with me in London and he told me that he had located his cousin in Aberdeen. Her swimmer had been sent to North Africa and she was tired of the war, tired of his terrible absence. She agreed to the divorce: it gave her something to think about – and papers were being signed. But Bernard was careful at that time not to nag at me with his hopes of a marriage. I was fifty that year, anyway, far too old to think of marriage which I've always thought is something you do at twenty or not at all. And of course my beauty had quite gone. Almost suddenly, it went, because when I first met Bernard some shreds of it were there. But now I was very grey and the glasses made me ugly. So vain to be depressed by this, but I was. I think, secretly, I'd always been very proud of my black hair. I used to say to Bernard: "I wish you could have seen it. I wish you could have seen me at thirty-five." But of course he didn't mind, the dear Bernard! He used to say longingly, "One day I shall have you and I shall have the butterflies – in some country place after the war – and then I shall be happy." '

Erica stopped talking. Ralph turned the recorder off and poured her some wine.

'Caviar on my last day!'

But she shut her eyes.

'Never mind about all the rich things,' she said quietly, 'just let me explain to you, Ralph, that I can't trust anyone to take charge, dear. Only you.'

Take charge?'

'Yes. Huntley would do it all wrong, you see because Huntley is someone utterly bound by rules. That's the way he likes to live – all strait-jacketed up, but you Ralph . . .'

'I'll do it, Erica. Whatever it is. Just tell me what to do.'

She took a sip of her wine. Ralph waited. He noticed that his heart had begun to beat fast. For some days now he had tried to put away from himself the possibility that she would ask him to kill her.

'Mrs Burford wouldn't do it either,' said Erica, 'authority is very cruel to her and she's afraid of it. It's not unusual for someone like her to be afraid of it.'

'No,' said Ralph.

'And the neighbours in the building, I don't know them. Sometimes we say good morning. Sometimes I hear the man upstairs practising the 'cello, but I don't even know his name.'

'No. It's always like that in big cities.'

'D'you know his name?'

'Who?'

'The man who plays the 'cello.'

'No. I've never seen him.'

'Well, you see, there's no one. Plenty of people in fiction who'd do it, but what good are they? Raskolnikov would be all right, but where is he? And Hamlet. He'd dither, but he'd do it in the end. But I don't know where he is, do I?'

'No.'

'Well. So there it is. It's terribly simple, Ralph. You'll find me in the cupboard, dear, that's all. I'll make certain I'm there and I'll put a scarf around my face so you won't even have to shut my eyes, which is a thing I hate doing. And all you have to do is to go out and see if you can find, even from some expensive shop, some mimosa to put round me. And then lock the cupboard with me inside, and make sure that I'm buried in it, not in a coffin which they knock up, these days, from any old bit of wood. And the silk inside isn't silk, but poly-something or other. Just tell the council or the undertakers or whoever it is, that I am not to be moved out of the cupboard and that this is my last wish. I know it's very large and I suppose someone will have to dig a wider hole than normal. But I've left plenty of money in the bank to pay for this. It's all very simple.'

'But Erica – '

'What, dear?'

'Supposing I'm gone before – ?'

'On no, I've thought of that. You won't be gone. And anyway, Ralph, I'd like you to have the Tiffany lamp. Huntley wouldn't appreciate that, and I know you like it.'

10

Ralph sent the cable:

"Erica March is dying. Must delay return to May 4th. Ralph."

He gave no address nor telephone number. He imagined Walt trying to call him at the Harrington Hotel and getting the bald information: "Oh no, I'm so sorry, Sir. Mr Pears has left us."

I'm very near the edge, Ralph thought. There may be no job to go home to.

Sitting alone in the Italian restaurant, he drank. The waiters hung about, waiting. They regretted their friendliness of some other evening when he hadn't lingered to keep them up. 'I cannot,' he wrote on a wine-stained notepad, 'let her die before I have asked all the right questions.' He knew what they were: practical questions, ethical questions, questions to satisfy, if not everyone who could come to know of her death, at least himself, the whole self, not just the reporter in him who had gone round a continent with a single lament, 'Why are Americans not loved . . .?'

But the questions hung just out of reach. One question seemed to obscure another. The waiters hovered near him, yawning.

'I can't remember when the war turned. I think by the end of 'forty-three, when our admiration for the Russians was so great, and the Americans had come in, I think we knew then that we had a chance.

'The bombings on London began again in 'forty-four, and Crowbourne was bombed.

'I suppose the Germans thought they were over London and they weren't. Because why would they want to drop bombs on Surrey,

189

unless – but this is unthinkable – they knew the school was full of Jewish boys, sleeping? I don't think they could have known, could they? Not about the boys in their dormitories – it's too macabre. But they almost all died. Bernard told me how he had helped the firemen to dig them out, hoping, just hoping that some had miraculously survived – but there were very few.

'The nightmare of the bombing of Crowbourne stayed with Bernard for years. He couldn't accept that those children had died. It was terrible. But of course they weren't the only ones. Sixty thousand people died in the Blitz and a lot of these must have been children asleep. And we committed the same horrors. We burned Dresden . . .

'All my books have been allegories of war – some kind of war. When I write about a character, I know at once what he's capable of – the self-delusions, the crimes; I know the war in him. You see, General Almarlyes is the embodiment of war. Even when he's making love, he hears the soldier in him talking. And I think, Ralph, this is why people have praised *The Hospital Ship,* because they recognized their own dreams in it and their own visions of hell. It was right to make Almarlyes flawed and tattered, capable of love even, because then people could identify with him; he stopped them saying: "I'm not like that. I don't recognize humanity in him." They couldn't say that because Almarlyes is human: he's the insurance salesman, he's the boy with the penny whistle. And his insanity, well, so many of us are mad, aren't we? Even Bernard, he was "crazed" as they say in Suffolk, after Crowbourne was hit, and the next year Miss Pinny went mad. She went mad the day the American airman landed in the greenhouse and she never recovered.

'I'd had my second operation by then – with the artificial lenses of course – my sight has lasted me out. Without the glasses, all I can see is patches of light and sometimes, you know, this is rather comforting – to take out the shape of things. I've seén so much that I would prefer not to have seen.

'The second operation didn't seem to be as frightening as the first. I wasn't afraid of the hospital any more, or of the bandages. I didn't have any nightmares of the camp *Kommandant* (though he came to see me, this same specialist) but only this one dream, and all my life I've never been sure if it was a dream or if it happened. I asked Bernard hundreds of times "Did it happen, the thing I dreamed?"

but he would never say yes and he would never say no. He'd smile. He'd say, "Imagine what you like." But time has confused it further.

'All I remember is that two nurses came and took the bandages off my eyes and the *Kommandant* came and stared at them and put the glasses on me and I could see everything in the ward, but it all looked very far away and tiny. I saw Bernard and he was holding some white flowers and I think he came close to me and put the flowers into my hands because I could smell them. I think it was lilac I smelled and it was beautiful. And after this a man came in, wearing robes and a sash round his neck and holding something which could have been a prayer book. And they started to talk, the man with the book and Bernard and the *Kommandant* and one of the nurses who had stayed behind holding the white bandages. And then of course I knew what it was: it was my wedding! I let it go on. I didn't try to sit up or say anything to stop it. I knew that after talk had gone on for a while, the man with the book would ask me a question and that Bernard would tell me what to say. "I do." "I will." I said the words and all the people began to smile and then I could feel something wet on my hand and I knew these were Bernard's tears. There was no ring; only the ring I had worn since my father's death, my mother's wedding ring. But it would have served. The nurse could have slipped it off my hand when she unwound the bandage and Bernard could have slipped it on again while I held the flowers. I know that I heard my name, Erica Harriet March. I *knew* I heard it. Yet I don't remember hearing Bernard's name, only mine. And this, more than anything, has convinced me over the years that it was all a dream, this absence of Bernard's name. Bernard Edgar Williamson. I never heard that: Bernard Edgar Williamson. So I've concluded – yet without any certainty – that none of it happened, only the flowers which were put into a vase for me and Bernard's tears perhaps, because he cried often.

'How strange and idiotic – not to know if I was married or not! I could have gone to Somerset House, couldn't I, and found out? Yet I preferred not to. I thought, in my heart I will never be married yet in Bernard's heart he is. And that's what's important in our two lives, our different ways of relating to each other which do the other one no harm and yet enable us both to keep our balance – and our love, such as it is, and in this way, not knowing about the marriage, I allowed a little love into me and it got stronger with time.'

'Bernard had no job after the bombing of Crowbourne. What was left of the school was closed down for the duration of the war. The cottage that Bernard had shared with two other of the Crowbourne masters hadn't been touched, but apart from this, all that was left was the gym and the chemistry lab and the sports pavilion.

'So he came to stay in my flat and volunteered as a fire-watcher. His fire-watching post was near Kenwood. In the summer he saw butterflies there in the early evenings.

'We became very used to each other in the war. We never thought of leaving London – not until the farm was left to me. I think after my two operations and after Crowbourne, we needed to stay put. All the monotonous "dos" and "don'ts" of the war we found rather comforting. Even rationing: we became quite inventive with carrots and swedes and powdered egg. It was astonishing you know, how much people talked about food in the war. The less they had, the more they talked about it, always remembering some fantastic lunch or dinner they'd eaten years ago. And sometimes even I, when I was very hungry and I knew all we had left of the rations was a tin of spam, I'd remember the profiteroles at Saladino's and the hot croissants and the mille feuilles . . . and Saladino's stomach of course! I didn't know how large that could be any more. I didn't know what the war had done to that!

'Miss Pinney wrote to me in the summer of 'forty-four. She told me Eileen was very ill and I'd better come down and look at her. "Well," I said, "I honestly don't want to go and look at her, Bernard! I didn't enjoy looking at her when she was well and I've seen enough ill people in my life." But Bernard was very excited about the butterflies he might find in Suffolk. He said a Swallowtail had once been sighted near Framlingham. So I wrote back to Miss Pinney saying I would come to see Eileen with my friend, Mr Williamson. I told her we would walk from the station because I didn't want her to send Gully. I thought, we'll just slip into Suffolk like ghosts – ghosts with butterfly nets! – and no one would know that I've come back, unless of course Eileen dies and the whole farm becomes mine. But I couldn't imagine Eileen dying; with her upright bosom and her fleshy face, she radiated a kind of permanence.

'But she was dying. David (you remember David, who had once taken me to Southwold?) was her doctor now and he had told Miss

Pinney that Eileen had cancer of the bowel. She'd lost all her flesh, even the bosoms had shrivelled, and she lay in her room – my mother and father's room – like a plague victim waiting to hear the handcart and the bell. We tiptoed round her and brought her soft soups of the kind Thérèse had made for me. Bernard showed her his book of butterflies and it mesmerized her, this. She would prop it up in front of her and stare at one drawing for hours. I expect she was thinking, if I wasn't dying, I could copy one of these pictures onto a sampler and spend the autumn making a cushion cover for Miss Pinney's dressing table stool.

'She didn't talk very much, not to me. She told me I had gone grey – as if it was something I hadn't noticed – and that when she looked at my eyes through my spectacles it was like looking into a deep well. And I expect I'd just turn away, but I knew that in the well there was nothing for Eileen, only spite. I walked round and round the old house staring at the rooms stuffed full of her things. Even the *Book of the Thousand Knitting Patterns* was there on a shelf and the fishknives cleaned and put away in a kitcher drawer. I imagined an enormous bonfire and we'd throw everything onto it, all the bibles and the chintz chairs and the samplers which had doubled in number since the beginning of the war, and the hats in the hatboxes and the tins of paint ancient with rust that we had slapped on the Tipperary Rooms. We'd get rid of every trace of her.

'It must have been on our second or third day at the farm that the American airman crash-landed. I was sitting in the garden with Bernard and we saw him float down. As he swung nearer and nearer, I had this extraordinary notion that he was arriving with a message for us, and that he would do his landing roll right at our feet and stand up and salute us as if we were General Patton's field command! I never expected him to land in the greenhouse. We weren't prepared for this kind of emergency. But Miss Pinney saw it all from Eileen's window – the splintering glass making wounds, and the tomato plants all falling over – and her scream was as loud as the actual crash. So we ran then and we found the airman with both his legs broken and blood pouring from his head and neither of us dared move him, so that when the stretcher finally took him away there were squashed tomatoes and bits of leaf all over his uniform. Poor boy, he was terribly young, but I should think he survived. Perhaps they sent him back to Maryland for a while with his legs still in plaster, and then let him go again – to fight the Japanese. He may have died in the Philippines.

'For us, it was a most extraordinary day. Eileen was sick over Bernard's butterfly book and Miss Pinney started to go mad! She decided to become a cat. She started to lick her body and when things were spilt in the kitchen she wanted to lick them up and we had to hold her back. When she sat with Eileen, she would often pick up Eileen's arm and lick that, going all along the little hairs, very gently. She taught herself to purr. It didn't seem to take her long. It was the strangest noise, very very low and monotonous.

'I remember how glad I was to have Bernard there. He was lively and happy, day after day, in spite of all that he had to do – for Eileen and for Miss Pinney. I think he was discovering for himself that slow tempo of Suffolk, not in the house of course, but on his early morning walks, with his net. He often said to me that he'd never experienced a summer as beautiful as this one. It was as if he could separate out the beauty of his walks from everything else – from the terrible crammed house and the death going on in it and the pathetic lappings of Miss Pinney the cat. Yet he wasn't afraid of the chores we had to do, or disgusted by them. He'd get up in the night when he heard one of them cry out. He said it wasn't fair for me to do all the work. And I can't think, Ralph, what I would have done without him. I believe I might have burnt the house down.

'We saw quite a lot of David and once he brought over his wife, Fidelity. He was greyer than me; very thin. I think he looked older than he was. Yet he'd led such a quiet life, never leaving this one village practice, marrying the vicar's daughter. I wondered what on earth had made him look so old? He was very polite and correct and of course no allusion was ever made to my rides in his car or the silly marriage proposal. I told Bernard all about it and he laughed. He said I would have gobbled David up.

'He came over one evening and went up to Eileen and Bernard and I were sitting on the exact spot where Gully and Chadwick had made their tepee with the *Illustrated London News*. I remember it had been a very hot day and the scent of the flowers that grew near the house – the roses and the irises and scattered bits of catmint – was wonderful. I looked at Bernard and I saw that his skin was quite brown. I was glad to be near him and I reached out my hand to touch him, but before my hand got to him, we heard David come out of the house and say: "Eileen's dead," and my heart began to beat so fast, I thought I might topple over in my deck-chair. Bernard got up and touched my shoulder and then he and David went back into the house and I was left outside, on that beautiful evening, with the knowledge of Eileen's death. And all I could whisper was: "At last." "At last, she's gone."

'We buried her and not many people came. Not Gully, holding his hat, nor any of his family. There were two or three women I recognized from the Tipperary days, but that was all. Only Miss Pinney who shivered and purred and licked her own tears off her prayer book, she was the only one who mourned.

'We drove Miss Pinney with her few belongings to an address – a sister or a cousin, I can't remember – in Aldeburgh and left her and we thought we'd seen the last of her then, but we hadn't.

'We took my father's will, which had left the house to Eileen for her lifetime, to a solicitor in Norwich. He confirmed that the house and farm were now mine. So we went back and stared at it and Bernard made little circles round and round it, as if he couldn't believe it could be owned. He took it for granted that we would leave Haverstock Hill and come and live there, and his trays of butterflies would be piled up higher and higher as the summers went on. But me? I don't know. I didn't really want to own it. I reminded myself that during the happiest years of my life I had owned nothing at all, only my paypackets at the end of the week and Saladino's smile on a Friday afternoon.'

'It was Cotton Eye Joe (damned nigger! Never learnt to reverence the name of Stratford-upon-Avon!) who held the tiller. He wouldn't let it go, not even to sleep, but steered on and on, on and on while the Daughters of the Lamb crept about with bandages in the bowels of the ship, crept about with tincture of iodine and a blood coagulent discovered in South China, and General Almarlyes fell in love.

Six of the hundred and five had died during the second day and six more during the third day which was a day of storms. The Daughters of the Lamb had laid out the twelve on the tilting deck and let them roll and tip until they nudged the ship's rail. Cotton Eye Joe looked down from the bridge and asked his slave soul to wander in their sacking death bags, repeating formless questions about freedom to the eyes he found wide open. One of the corpses was black, but salt and

195

slime sucked out the channels of his voice; there were no songs in him and no answers. And at dawn, when Cotton Eye Joe woke from a sleep that had lasted no more than five minutes, all the bodies were gone and the empty deck, washed over and over by the storms, glimmered in hazy sunlight.

General Almarlyes came slowly up to bathe his body in the gentle day. He had forgotten about the twelve who had died (his men) and awaited burial with full military honours; he didn't notice that, in the darkness, the twelve had plopped untrumpeted into the water and were gone for ever, but only stared like a baby at the heat gathering soundlessly on the colossal beating of his pulse.

Lazily at his wheel, Cotton Eye Joe began to sing:

> "Let me tell you what the wise men say,
> Say we' gonna have a judgement day
> But I don't believe in judgement
> Don't believe in prayer
> Don't believe God's gonna leave
> My share."

General Almarlyes looked up and wanted to ask, "Where are we sailing, Cotton Eye? Will I walk out one evening and smell the cool familiar air of Lyme Regis? Who decides where the ship goes? Who decrees the precise and ecstatic moment when fear flies away like gorged carrion – to go and torment the merchant crabs on the beach where we waited for death – and love comes, in a random tide, to flush out the cruelty in me that has been in me ever since I was a boy and held a cane in my hand . . ."

But he said nothing and walked to the rail where the twelve had slipped away. The ship was travelling fast and he knew that the man he was, lonely in his trifling wars, homesick and full of holes till the earthquake camel and the ship took him, had begun to change. Imagination's eye wound his heart with protective threads; his heart was a pupa left on a white leaf, left to unravel its own extraordinary metamorphosis on the breast of a virgin.

His uniform had been mended and washed. The colours of

the ribbon medals had run and faded. Touching them, he said aloud: "All remembrance of acts of outstanding bravery has made way for silence. Only when there is absolute silence on the subject of acts of outstanding bravery, killing and mutilation . . . only when this is absolute . . . will the girl consent to part company with her God . . . to keep company with me." And above General Almarlyes walking the early morning ship, the nigger sang on:

> "Let me tell you what the black men shout
> Shout about the wise men falling out,
> 'Cos he don't believe in wise men
> And he don't believe in dreams
> Yet he's sown a dream of freedom
> In his seams."

It was the fourth day out from the island and at midday Cotton Eye called to the Daughters of the Lamb to come up into the sunlight. He had seen land.'

There was a flat, grey dawn at Ralph's window. For most of the night he had been wide awake, watching General Almarlyes watching the girl moving silently about in her robes, seeing – at last, in this girl – the peace for which he had fought and won so many wars, the peace which had never arrived.

Ralph hadn't intended to read till morning, but sleep had eluded him. Worries about money, about the rights and wrongs of his decision to stay on in London had trundled round a brain that was beginning to feel tired, from the hours of solitude, from all the hours of talking to itself. Only the book could push the worries to one side. For Ralph, *The Hospital Ship* held an extraordinary compulsion. It was one of the few books – of the many he owned – that he would read again and again throughout his life. And it was, in effect, the book that had brought him to England. If Erica had stopped writing in 1940, he wouldn't have made the trip.

At the Imperial War Museum he searched through volume after volume of pictures of life in Britain between 1939 and 1945. Near the end of the fifth or sixth volume he found a faded print captioned "Bomb Damage at Crowbourne School, June 1944". Two men in tweed suits stood helplessly contemplating the rubble. In the distance, beyond the fallen joists and bricks, was a small flint house which might have been Bernard's cottage. Ralph ordered the picture along with others of Blitz damage and was told they would be sent to him within six weeks. Prudently, he gave his home address in New York. When asked if the pictures were for publication, he snapped: 'I don't know yet,' and left, allowing himself the luxury of a taxi from Lambeth to Camden Town, in which he slept.

When he arrived at Erica's flat he found her pacing the sitting-room. 'Sometimes,' she said, 'I get letters from strangers asking for money. From young writers. And I always try to send something because I know they think I'm rich, and if I was, I'd help them more. But I'm not. I never learned how to keep money and make it grow or whatever it is you're meant to do with it. I spent all mine or gave it away. I gave all Bernard's money to the Bertrand Russell Foundation. But this morning I had a horrible letter from Gully's daughter, Ellen Jane. She didn't grow up at all like Gully with his dear old gentle head, but dreadfully loud and discontented and fond of yellow cars and that sort of thing – terribly greedy for possessions. So what shall I do? I don't want to send her money for steam irons or meat slicers. I really don't. But she knows how fond I've always been of Gully; she knows I'll send it. It's a very dirty trick!'

'She sounds like my mother,' said Ralph wearily.

'Your mother? Oh dear, is she like that, Ralph, so loud – ?'

'Greedy.'

'For yellow cars?'

He smiled. 'I guess. Though we don't have too many yellow cars in the States, probably because the cabs are yellow. She's greedy for everything – food, men . . .'

'And you never talk about her?'

'Well, I do, sometimes . . .'

'Not to me. You never mention her.'

'I don't love her.'

Erica stopped pacing and was silent for a moment. She looked at Ralph. 'I wonder,' she said after a while, 'if that isn't sad for you. You see I find it very difficult to imagine *not* loving my mother. But then of course all I've ever loved is a memory – and a smell. And I know this is very widespread, the hatred of parents, and perhaps if my mother had lived on, I would have found nothing in her to love, adult to adult, who can say? Do you think when you were little you loved this mother of yours, Ralph?'

'Oh no. Not much. They used to send me off to Grandma in the vacations. I was a drag for them.'

'And your Grandma? What about her.'

'Oh hell, I dunno! She was the old breed, you know. Fierce and proud and rude to everyone, especially her servants. I don't think she was lovable, much. But she used to sing really good. Even when she was old, she'd have a go at singing and I liked that when I was a kid. No one ever sang at home.'

'She's dead, I suppose?'

' Yup. She died in 1970 and her house was sold.'

'How old was she?'

'When she died?'

'Yes.'

'I dunno. About eighty. She looked eighty.'

'So you think I ought to send something then?'

'What, Erica?'

'To Ellen Jane?'

'Oh that. Well no, I wouldn't, if you hate to do it.'

'I expect I will send something – just for the sake of Gully. But I think I'll have to ask her not to ask me again.'

'Yes.'

So the matter was settled in Erica's mind; now she could sit down, and begin. Begin where? She couldn't remember where she had left her life the previous afternoon. She needed a reminder.

'Eileen's death.'

She made no attempt to disguise the smile. 'Well the war seemed to hurry to its end after that. When V.E. Day came we were in London and we let ourselves dance with the crowds; it seemed right to be part of all that emotion, we just let it bathe our wounds. I've never been a good patriot: there is so much that is stiff and cruel about Englishness but I think a little patriotism ran in every vein with the ending of the war, even in mine, and then with the Atlee government of course we had high hopes for the years to come. We knew now there would be changes.

'But there was part of me then, when the new government turfed out Churchill and my second book was published, which wanted to be travelling again. I couldn't bear the thought of the farm and

Bernard – not for ever and ever, not when I'd seen so little of the world. So I got on a train one day at Victoria, and told Bernard I was going to Africa, which he didn't believe. All I had with me was a small suitcase and of course I never did get to Africa – to see the place I'd invented – until years later when Bernard and I did a kind of butterfly safari. But I got as far as Nice, where I'd never been, and no spring in France has ever been as glorious as the spring of 1946 – I'm sure it hasn't.

'I wanted to get on the old white steamer to Corsica and see Calvi and Thérèse's wall and then go on to Sardinia and across to Italy to see what war had done and how the people were living. But I ran out of money and I ran out of clothes! On my last night, I slept on the beach and it was dreadfully cold. I realized then how threadbare I was – so thin on the powdered egg and all my things with darns in them! I must have looked strange to those people on the Riviera. "Poor England," I expect they said, "she's a rag-and bone country now."

'And to my surprise, I'd begun to miss Bernard. I had dreams of him and Emily doing a sad waltz at Epsom – a waltz for all the dead. So I sent him a postcard saying "Decided against Africa" and I got on a train which stopped in Paris in the middle of the night and I woke up and I knew at once where I was and part of me wanted to leave the train and go running out into the empty streets. But I didn't. I stayed on the train and the next day I was in London.

'Patterson and Tree were very proud of me that year. *In the Blind Man's City* went into a second printing after good reviews and there were little celebrations, private ones with Bernard and one most lavish public one in the Connaught Hotel where we drank champagne and even Patterson began to smile.

'Valéry Clément was invited to this and he arrived with his new friend, both dressed in white and looking like actors. I was so glad to see him. I wanted him to tell me how Paris had survived the Germans, but he wouldn't talk about it. He said those had been the years of *honte,* the years of *enfer.* And they had aged him. I suppose he was in his fifties by then and it was soon after this that he began to have operations for his face, to tighten it up. Neither of us mentioned Gérard, out of tact for Bernard I suppose, or because we knew we couldn't – we knew we'd spoil the occasion with out sorrow. We talked mainly about the novel. Cambiers would publish it in 'forty-seven and of course Valéry would do the translation. I told him that, this time, I didn't think I could come to Paris to do any "illuminating" for him (though I'm sure there was a lot that needed illumination in my pretend Africa!) and he agreed to bring the work to London.

'Walking home after this celebration, through Hyde Park and then up past Paddington and Little Venice and St John's Wood (a lovely walk) I persuaded Bernard to let us stay on in London till the translation of *The Blind Man's City* was done. Then we'd go to Suffolk. I suppose he knew and I knew that I was putting it off. I think honestly I wanted to sell the farm, or just give it away, which is what we did in the end and stay on in Hampstead, because there was no *permanence* in our flat, no garden to reproach us and no memories except our own. If there was a ghost, I daresay it was the ghost of Crowbourne but Bernard had a weapon to frighten it away – not the piece of lead with the welded bayonet, oh no! He had the trays of butterflies.

'Bernard went ahead of me to Suffolk. He promised me he would give all Eileen's things away even though he didn't know who to give them to because no one could find her will. No will was ever found, and this was very odd, wasn't it? Because there was so much to leave – all those things so carefully collected – and in the end Bernard just held a sale in the sitting-room and women came crowding in from all the villages round about and the pearl-handled fishknives were sold for seventeen and ninepence. He gave all the proceeds to the church, and with them new hassocks were bought. They were tapestry-covered hassocks – perfectly right for Eileen – so we never felt any guilt about selling her belongings, until Miss Pinney arrived one day and told us that Eileen had promised them all to her.

'She came back more than two years after Eileen's death. She walked in one morning not long after I arrived and the house was still very bare because almost all the furniture, except the few things that remained of my father's time, had gone into the sale and Bernard told me that one woman had ridden off with a chintz armchair tied onto a butcher's bicycle! I suppose we intended to buy chairs and new curtains but we hadn't; we'd begun to work at the vegetable patch instead, reclaiming it from the horseradish and the brambles, and all we'd done to the house was to clean it from top to bottom and paint the outside which was very dingy with verdigris and moss gathering on the walls, and in Gully's room we made what we called a lepidoptarium for Bernard.

'So Miss Pinney came into this bare place with hardly anything in it except my books and Bernard's books and a few glass cases of rare moths. I suppose she expected to find the old comforting rugs and the tea trolley and the lace mats and the samplers. I think in some corner of her mind she expected to find Eileen, because she went straight to her room – which was our room now – and looked all round it, even in the cupboard. She was trembling and her skin was yellow. She looked like someone who had been kept in darkness for years on end. We sat her down in the kitchen by the Rayburn, and Bernard made tea while I tried to talk to her. I asked her how she was and whether she was still living at Aldeburgh, but she didn't answer. Her trembling never stopped. She drank the tea and stared at us and I tried again with some more questions. She seemed very frightened of us and almost as soon as she'd drunk the tea she wet herself and a pool of urine dribbled off her chair.

'She had no coat on and it was late autumn and it was Bernard who understood that she was in care now, in one of those mental places. "How did you get out?" he asked suddenly, and his voice, which was always a bit booming and loud, seemed to terrify her because she got up and walked out of the kitchen and then we heard her in the sitting-room and she was calling for Eileen.

'I went upstairs and got a big cardigan and I put this round her. She was terribly thin and I honestly don't know if they fed her well enough at the mental hospital or if they just neglected her because often and often since then I've read of cases of cruelty and neglect.

'We didn't know what on earth to do with her. We knew there was a hospital near Blythburgh but we couldn't remember the name of it and Miss Pinney wouldn't tell us. She'd stopped being a cat anyway. She was a person again – on that day – and this was a relief. But she wouldn't talk, only to point to all the spaces in the room and say "mine". So Bernard told her very patiently that no will of Eileen's had been found and that her things had been sold (even the hats, which children bought for a few farthings, to dress up in) and that now the church had new hassocks and the vicar had sent a letter of appreciation. But she kept on and on saying "mine" – just like babies I've seen with their plastic toys – until a very large woman arrived, driving a Wolseley, and took her away. She was driven off still wearing my cardigan, so she'd claimed something after all, even if it wasn't Eileen's. And over the years, when we used to go and visit her in her hospital, she was always wearing it. It wore out at the elbows and no one mended it. One day, I offered to take it home and darn it for her, but she wouldn't be parted from it.'

Ralph left Erica early and slept. The glare of the bright afternoon behind the thin curtains continued to cast an extraordinary light on his unconsciousness. Sleep and moments of waking merged in and out of each other so that the sleep was almost without refreshment. He woke tired in the late afternoon, stained by his dreams.

There were four more days. Time, in her tall ship, was almost at the horizon's edge. And then what? Ralph was certain now that he could make no coherent explanation to Walt of the week stolen; he had a beginning, that was all, which went 'Can you understand, Walt, that I'm half way through my life . . .?' No doubt Walt could. He would wait for the meaning behind the statement, one that would satisfy the waste of company time, the extra funds . . . But Ralph would offer nothing. Perhaps there was, in the end, nothing profound to explain, merely his professional concern to see an assignment through. And Walt would have to be satisfied with this or "let him go" as the euphemistic jargon for sacking now ran, pitch him back into the ramshackle life from which *Bulletin Worldwide* had rescued him. And you saw them, the ones who believed imagination could buy bread and mortgages, in the Village bars you saw them, talking always of the screenplay, the mythical mirage of the screenplay that would put recognition on their pallor like paint. Drink and time had replaced work; the writer had stopped writing.

'Bernard started going to sales to buy furniture for the house. You could buy oak in those days because it wasn't fashionable: it looked too workaday, I suppose, like a cowman's hands.

'So the rooms filled up a bit and I bought an old sewing machine with a treadle and made new curtains.

'I suppose I must have noticed middle age. Bernard began to go grey after Crowbourne and, as I told you, I was grey already and all the black shine had gone out of me. But I never thought, we're getting old here. We worked very, very hard on our vegetable growing and although the Haggard family still rented most of the land, I often got

up early and went to help young John Haggard with the milking –
just to feel the cold of a Suffolk dawn again, you see, to remember that
part of me belonged there. He was a very silent boy, John Haggard,
so there was no chatting and swearing over the milking like years
before with Gully, only this silence and cold and the warm body of
the cow and a saliva strand of memory going back and back.

'I often thought of Gully. He knew I was at the house and he
came once or twice to see us and brought his children and Dot who
had grown warts on her hands. But I don't know what it was with
Gully after my father's suicide: he was never the same gentle, teasing
man, not with me. I saw him be patient and sometimes full of
laughter with his family, but never with me. He looked at me like a
trespasser. I think he wished I'd followed the instructions he hadn't
dared to give and left Suffolk to its own people, people like him who
had never travelled away but all his life stayed near the clay pond,
where once I imagined his birth. I expect I thought, I've as much
right to be here as you, Gully March, orphan boy found one day by
accident stealing our chicken scraps. And in front of him and
Bernard I once told the story of his pissing in the playground on the
first day of school. But he shook his old bull's head. He didn't like
me telling the story. He didn't like to remember

'One night I said to Bernard, I believe Gully blames me for my
father dying. And we had a conversation about this sitting up side by
side in bed, in the dark and I was so struck, suddenly, by the oddness
of this way of constructing a conversation that I began to laugh and
laugh and I can't remember really what Bernard said about Gully
blaming me or not blaming me. I expect he said something like "I
wouldn't wonder" or "It wouldn't surprise me" because he was full of
little phrases like this that seem to be rather without meaning and when
I hear one I always imagine Bernard saying it and yet thinking something entirely different and irrelevant like: "In the hills of Umbria and
Tuscany, seven or eight strains of Marbled Whites have been noted,"

'He spent hours and hours in his lepidoptarium – Gully's old
room, that still had the desk where Gully had worked out his difficult
sums. He had begun research into the fungal diseases butterflies get
but I think the research was beyond him because we never saw the
end of it, nothing written down with footnotes. He just went back
to his wonderful, precise drawings and he did a book for young
beginners in the butterfly world with instructions on how to kill

them and how to stretch them out and how to recognize a dead leaf from a pupa.

'I remember very beautiful summers, though perhaps they weren't. The sun came up opposite the cowshed door and I'd be hungry by that time. Bernard had a frayed beige dressing gown and he'd wander about in this when I got dressed for the milking. And I often – even now – imagine him by the Rayburn in this old dressing gown, cooking mushrooms for our breakfast and making tea. I think we were happiest in the early mornings and by nightfall we were silent. Perhaps it was then we thought about our middle age.'

The next day was wasted. Mrs Burford sent Ralph away and called the doctor.

'Why?'

'Burned 'erself.'

'Only the light of the lamp, dear,' she told him later, 'I went to sleep with my face right under it and you can see, it's burned me. I thought I was in Africa. I had a dream of Bernard and me in a Masai village in the terrible old Landrover we hired. We were admiring things. This is what tourists do in those villages. They admire the children and the dung houses and the blood pot and the flies are everywhere, even on the eyes of the children they're admiring. I dreamt Bernard gave all the Masai children butterfly nets, but there are no butterflies on that dry scrub and the nets just filled up with the black flies. We put all the flies into a sack and the sack weighed us down so we crawled along, slower and slower, with this weight of flies till the sun woke me and it was the Tiffany lamp.'

Ralph smiled at her gently.

'Erica,' he said, 'I've only got one more day – after today – and then I go to Oxford.'

With her claws of hands she tried to straighten her body in the chair.

'Yes,' she said quietly, 'I thought that was it.' Then she leaned nearer to Ralph and whispered, 'I lie awake now in the night and I can hear a little movement in there . . .'

'Where?'

'In the cupboard.'

Ralph was silent, staring at her. She looked away from him towards the window. The sun was bright.

'I expect it will get louder – something I can identify – tonight or tomorrow night, and then I shall know . . .'

Ralph let the unfinished sentence go. A phrase, very familiar now, formed itself in his mind, asked to be uttered: 'I'm half way through my life.'

'What, dear?'

But he didn't know if he had said it or not.

'I'm afraid for you, Erica.'

'Afraid? Oh no, you mustn't be afraid, Ralph. The only thing you must do is to follow my instructions. I haven't made them very difficult.' Then she sighed, 'I suppose you think it's all rather gothic and silly.'

'No. But I don't understand. You're not ill or anything . . .'

'Yes I am, Ralph. To be very old like me is to lose all that part of yourself that was capable of *doing*. I don't *do* any more and this is a dreadful disease, this not doing. I dream of course and in my dreams I run and travel about but where's my body? Here or in my bed. I sit or I sleep, sometimes I cook, very feebly, and I can still get down the stairs to those Indian shops, but that's all. I've been ill in this way for quite a long time. Long enough. But I knew, I suppose, all along that someone would come and I've been very patient waiting.'

'I'm afraid of death.'

'Yes. Well you would be. I was at your age. I was afraid to be cheated by it, just as Gérard was cheated. Heaven knows the wonders he might have made . . . but I won't make anything more now, or say anything, and I'm tired of my little pitter-patter, my silly pitter-patter, oh heavens I'm tired of it.'

Ralph took out his Marlboro pack and stared at it.

'I feel . . .' he began.

'What, dear?'

'Well . . .'

'What?'

'I feel . . . you're wrong.'

'Oh no Ralph. Please don't say that. I must not be wrong, because, if I am, then there will be nothing for me, dear. And for years I've had a certainty that there will be something, and then I shall have to get busy, being whatever it is I am.'

'There is nothing, Erica.'

'I won't listen to you, Ralph! I've never listened to any of your generation because almost all of you are content to be crochet-men, *minim*-men, set moving along your pathetic lines. And the symphonies you make? I haven't heard them. So why should I believe that any of you have wisdom or knowledge? Why should I? You make no sound at all. Sometimes I want to cry for you because I can find so little *in* you!'

Ralph fingered the Marlboro pack, took out a cigarette and put it quickly into his mouth.

He thought, now . . . perhaps . . . I can't hold them back any more . . . tears not for the ugly spoiled city, tears not even for Erica's death, but tears for the half of my life that's gone, year threaded to year, question to question, years unrecorded, questions unanswered . . . Why are . . .? Why is . . .? Why am I crying now in a stranger's room, unembarrassed as a kid, if I was ever a kid, clinging to Gran no doubt while Pa threatens some beating with his willow branch and Ma curls her lip . . . irrelevant now of course, buried in time, irrelevant absolutely to what I am, to what I must become . . .

'I'm so sorry, Ralph dear. I'm very, very sorry. I didn't mean to say anything wounding. I'm sure, you see, that the fault's in me. Of course it is. I don't understand your generation of people because I don't belong. Everything I belonged to has gone, you see?'

Ralph fumbled for his lighter and lit the Marlboro. His tears were falling onto his hands and onto the Marlboro pack. He thought, the room is dilapidated with tears, yet my fingernails shine . . .

'Oh Ralph, I'm so very sorry, dear.'

He was making no sound, none that he could hear, yet he wondered if some sound wasn't there, far off, yet belonging deep inside him.

'Bernard used to cry in his sleep, Ralph, and wake me up, but I never knew how to comfort him. I think it was his nightmares of Crowbourne that made him do this, but I simply don't know why you're crying, dear, so what on earth can I say that will be any good, except apologize for what I did say . . .?'

It will never stop, he thought. It's a kind of flooding of the whole mind and body, my nose filling and dripping now and running into my mouth, this salt flood which has been gathering ever since I left my herbs and got on the plane . . . and only she will have seen it and been amazed to see it flow on and on in her room. For no reason.

II

'In his cabin, lined from wall to wall with the medical and evangelical writings of the Daughters of the Lamb, General Almarlyes waited to be told, the land is safe General, Sir, the land is at peace and untouched by the earthquake, unvisited by carrion and blessed with the gentle air that breathes on Lyme Regis. And the message came, from the advanced guard of ten he picked from those who remained of the hundred and five, the land is empty of people, General, but we have seen streets of white houses and avenues of trees taller than palms bearing camellia flowers, and all may now be ready for us to leave the ship and even the sick and the dying will be carried ashore in their bandages smelling of iodine and laid out in the cool of the white houses.

So General Almarlyes went up on deck and stared at the land and the wind that sighed through his body was calmed in the expectation of a time when Acts of Outstanding Bravery would no longer be necessary and that part of his mind that had slipped away from him in his wars and lay hidden in his dreams of Bourton-on-the-Water would return, and he would be at peace.

It was a turquoise sea that lapped the ship. The bay, General, is full of oysters, the forests hung with fruit, said the advanced party of ten. The dried figs and the salt sacks of nuts of the hospital ship can be emptied into the sea and we can fill our bodies with fresh food, and there are no merchant crabs on the beaches, Sir, none that we can see.

So General Almarlyes gave the order 'Women and wounded first!' Cotton Eye Joe came down from the bridge and washed himself in the clear water and the Daughters of the Lamb with their burden of wounded lowered their eyes on his black nakedness. The scent of the camellia trees fermented in the heart of General Almarlyes unfamiliar longings not entirely unconnected with his boyhood at Lyme Regis and the scent of fuchsias at his mother's window, but which he couldn't express, only in his eyes which searched, as the Daughters of the Lamb came out of the ship for the one he had chosen to be the angel of his forgetting, mother of his children who would never suffer as he had suffered, no never as I, General Almarlyes, have suffered in my wars, body and mind for more years than I can remember.

The sun was high above the ship as the last of the wounded were brought out and General Almarlyes could hear, far off, the shouting of his men as they saw for the first time the streets of white houses shaded by the trees and believed they had found paradise. He was alone on the ship in his mended uniform. His mother called to him out of the forgotten ages of her apricot-coloured negligee to be first not last, to be first, son, in all that you do, and then you will win prizes and cups and badges of merit and we shall be proud of you, so proud! And he knew that he was last: left behind on the ship, and that when he came to the white streets described to him by the advanced party of ten, there would be no house left for him, no silent room – confessional of his love – in which to be healed of his madness and renew himself on the breast of his chosen virgin.

"But I am full of resolve," he said aloud. "I am General Almarlyes, and to the General must be allotted the greatest share of this new silence. If necessary this shall be taken by force, with the revolver I have kept hidden on my right thigh even through the days of the earth tremors and the time spent with the merchant crabs waiting to die. Yet there will be no bravery in it. I shall not violate my order that all Acts of Outstanding Bravery cease for ever and for always, only shoot my man from behind, roll his body in a death bag and say to the Daughters of the Lamb, "This man was a usurper and a thief, an undeserving subject of this new gift of peace."

General Almarlyes climbed down into the water and only

then as he turned on his back and let the tide float his body ashore did he find that his gun was gone.'

Ralph stopped reading and slept almost at once. He dreamed he went to Oxford and met, not John Pennington at the top of some musty stairway, but Walt, smelling of sticky cologne and the body odour of airline travel. He tried to push past the man but he was prevented: Walt held out an enormous box to bar his way and shouted to him that box was full of wooden bobbins for lacemaking, bought in Brittany. There were hundreds of them, the little shiny bones. Ralph stared at them and knew that if he only had the skill (possessed by so very few, surely?) to use them rightly with the minute pins and the cushion to manufacture lace, then Walt would hand him the box and let him go by him and he would never see Walt again as long as he lived.

'I can *learn* to make lace,' he yelled back at Walt, but Walt only smiled and rattled the bobbin box.

'It will take you the rest of your life,' he said.

To escape from Walt, Ralph woke himself up. He lay in the dark which, behind the thin curtains, was the dark of one or two o'clock. Only the occasional car passed, yet at five the lorries would begin.

He lay and examined the dream. The exact shape and feel of the bobbins was very clear to him; he could hear them clack. Then he tried to put Walt out of his mind. He remembered his weeping and wondered why there had been so much pent up misery inside him. He knew the answer was there (even in the dream of lace-making – yet just fractionally out of reach. He remembered Erica's kindness to him – she had given him an extraordinary frayed silk handkerchief, once smart bright green; she had made him drink some wine – and knew that it was the child in him who had wept. Yet he didn't feel ashamed.

As the dawn crept to his window and the traffic began its ceaseless rattling through Chalk Farm he thought, this is the beginning of the last day. Fear of what it might bring kept him awake till sunrise. Then he slept for a few hours.

'Well,' she said brightly, 'I sent Mrs Burford out for vodka and caviar but of course you can't buy caviar any more – only in Fortnum's or Harrods, I suppose – so we've got a little pot of what they call lumpfish and the Indian shopkeepers say this is very good. I hope you aren't disappointed, Ralph.'

'I'd forgotten,' said Ralph.

'Well I knew you would, dear, after all that sobbing yesterday. I felt very stupid you know, very inadequate, like one of Bernard's butterflies just perching there by your waterfall.'

She was suddenly downhearted. 'And there's very bad news about the cupboard,' she said, 'I opened the door, just a crack, yesterday evening because I could hear a strange little noise in there and I was longing to see what it was, I was certain it was something I could make sense of. But it's mice.'

'Ah, shit!' said Ralph.

'Well quite. It's not as if I've ever even liked mice. I told you that in that room I first had in Paris – the one with the singing concierge – I used to feel them crawling over my face, and I hated this. So I had to shoo them out. I got a broom and I tried to push them out onto the stairs. I told them to go and find the 'cellist, but they bolted under my bed. They go like bullets, you know, so fast.'

'D'you want me to get them out, Erica?'

'On no, I got them into the kitchen in the end. They'll be all right in there because there's a lot of old packets of things that I never eat. They can have a feast. Just as long as they don't go into the cupboard. But let's not think about them, Ralph. Mrs Burford is going to put the lumpfish on some toast for us, and I told her to buy a lemon and then we can talk and have little sips of vodka which was one of Chadwick's favourite drinks. Not that he approved of Russia, of course, even though we were allies at the beginning of the war. I think he imagined all those grand drawing-rooms being ransacked by the mob and that made him feel frightened, yet although he was a snob, he wasn't a cruel man and he didn't like repression at all, so I've never been able to see quite why he wasn't on better terms with Lenin. It was very odd of him.'

Ralph smiled.

'Are you feeling happier today, dear?'

'I guess.'

'You go to see your friend tomorrow, don't you? I shall think about you in Oxford, which is very beautiful in parts. Saladino had a picture of Oxford, you know, on his landing, though I can't imagine why. It was an engraving. It said underneath "Oxford au

Dix-septième Siècle" and of course it looked very small and quiet and rather black and dirty which it isn't now. They've cleaned it up. I used to stare at that engraving when I was ill. I think it came from the Quai St Michel.'

'Tell me about Saladino. You said he survived the war and you and Bernard went to see him.'

'Oh we did, yes. It must have been in 1954 when *The Hospital Ship* came out and there was such a fuss about it. I had to go to Paris to see Jacques Cambier who was very old and ill by that time – too ill to come to England – but he wanted to publish the book very quickly, before he died.

'I didn't want to go to Paris. Bernard and I were happy then, in our quiet life with the farm and the butterflies. We hardly ever went to London or did anything. Only our trip to Kenya. He loved Suffolk – more than I ever did. He was having the life he'd always wanted and even his dreams of Crowbourne were lessening. And I wanted us to stay put, so that nothing would threaten us. I thought if we stayed put and I had Bernard's wonderful love and caring, I would become a proper writer, someone who wrote every day and for a time I was determined to be this. When I wrote *The Hospital Ship* I wrote for six or seven hours each day and it was finished in six months. It was thrilling.

'But then the Paris question came up and Jacques Cambier started sending cables. So I went. I wanted to leave Bernard behind so that I wouldn't have to talk to anyone. I decided that if I had to see Paris again, I just wanted to see it silently and pretend I was invisible. I knew I'd have to talk to Jacques Cambier and Valéry Clément who was still in the same flat in Montparnasse, but otherwise I didn't want to have to *be*. But I couldn't explain this properly to Bernard; I couldn't find the moment to say "Please don't come with me". And he was full of excitement about the trip. He promised to give me lunch at Fouquet's.

'When we arrived, I felt very ill. I found the whole place suffocating. Bernard went for walks along the river and I stayed in bed and listened to the cars on the cobbles. The cars had changed of course and they swooshed more. I think I wanted to be in one of them, going away. But I had to get up and go to see Jacques Cambier. He was very drugged because of the pain he was in. He kept stroking my hand and whispering: *"Étonnant. . . étonnant . . ."*

I can't imagine how he'd been able to read the book, but he had and Valéry had begun work on the translation. But I couldn't bear to see him full of morphine and dying and I got away as quickly as I could and, without really guiding myself, I found I was in the Boulevard St Germain, just a few hundred yards from Saladino's patisserie. I thought of turning back but I didn't. I went on. I don't think I believed it would still be there – not after twenty years – but it was. I stared at all the cakes, the mille feuilles and the japonais and the tartes aux pommes and then I noticed that the "English Spoken" sign had gone, so I thought, it doesn't belong to Saladino any more. Someone else has taken it over. And I was about to walk on when I caught sight of him. He was at the back of the shop, as usual, by the coffee machine and he looked up and saw me staring in.

'He'd hardly changed. His hair was grey and he was very bald and red in the face and fatter than ever, but I would have recognized him anywhere! And when he saw me he came darting out and took me into his arms and kissed me all over my face and there were tears in his eyes and he said "You were right about the Americans – they came! And we all fought for France, all of us here." And then he begun calling for Thérèse – in front of everyone eating their brioches and their florentines – and Thérèse came hurrying down the stairs, just as she'd always done when Saladino called and when she saw me she ran to hug me too and I noticed a wonderful change in her! She was much older, of course, but there was colour in her face and her straggly hair was all tidy in a bun and she smiled and laughed and wiped her eyes on her apron and Saladino put his fat arm round her shoulders.

'So you see, time had mended Thérèse and Saladino. I suppose he was too old to go running after smart women any more – too old and too fat! So he stopped beating Thérèse and decided to be kind to her and she told me how every year now, he took her to Calvi in September.

'They made me sit down – on the same old banquettes but re-covered now in red leather, and Saladino made me a cup of tea. We laughed at the tea and I asked him, "What about the sign, Saladino? What about the English Spoken?" And he said he'd tried to learn but he'd never got much further than "tip not included", so he'd had to take the sign down. So we laughed and laughed and only when Thérèse had slipped out with some cups and saucers to wash did he whisper to me about the death of Celestine. "Two bodies in the bed, Erica," he said. "Two bodies! So who in life can a man trust?"

'I didn't mind talking to him, being with him. I was so glad he had patched up his life with Thérèse and of course we hardly spoke about the past because it was much too sad. He told me the patisserie was doing very well. People had money again, he said, after all the bad years. And he'd hung on, mainly through his connections with the black market. He'd kept going in a meagre sort of way, even making strudel for the Germans and spitting behind their backs. And me? What about me? he kept asking. So I told him I'd never married but that I had found someone to be with and we had a quiet life and all I wanted now was to be quiet and do my writing. But he made me promise to bring Bernard to the shop the next day. I tried to refuse. I suddenly imagined Bernard sitting on Gérard's banquette and not knowing that it was 'his' and talking on in his schoolteacher French and I thought, I don't want him here because this isn't what we share, this is another of my lives and he's got no business in it. But Saladino said he would make us a special gateau and Thérèse would put on her Sunday dress. He said he'd be honoured to meet Bernard. I kept saying no. I tried and tried to explain that I didn't want to come back; it was enough to know that he and Thérèse were well. But he didn't understand and looked very hurt. So in the end I agreed.

'We went at four or five the next afternoon and there was a magnificent cake layered with chestnut cream. We didn't sit anywhere near Gérard's banquette, thank heavens, but it was still dreadful. We were all very serious and embarrassed and Bernard in his tweed jacket seemed very, very far away from me and I found myself thinking, I wish he was a stranger and in a moment, when the tea is over, we'll part. I felt all my love for him slipping away. I wanted to resurrect the past and have it there again, every incredible moment of it. It was so foolish, Ralph. I'd been content with my life for years. There was no one in the world who had ever been kinder to me than Bernard. But in Saladino's teashop I just let him go. I did, Ralph. And this was precisely what I'd been afraid of when I'd tried to stop him coming to Paris with me. I didn't want to let him go and yet I knew I would. It's impossible, you see, to replace one person with another: they must be separate and live in different worlds.

214

'Saladino and Thérèse were very confused by Bernard. After seeing me with Gérard, he wasn't what they'd expected. I know they'd prepared the cake for someone quite different, someone they just imagined. So they wanted the meeting to be over quickly too and we didn't stay long or eat much of the chestnut gâteau and when we said goodbye, it was a very formal thing, even though I knew I'd never see them again. I remember thinking of all the questions I wanted to ask them and never would and all my life I've thought of those questions I never asked. But they're dead now. They must be, or they'd be a hundred. And I expect the patisserie's gone.'

Mrs Burford opened the door with a sniff. She carried a laden tray very carefully to the table and set it down. She gave Ralph a gleeful smile.

'Last day, eh?'

Ralph nodded.

'Ralph's going to Oxford,' said Erica.

'Oh yeh. Nice there, is it?'

'Yes. I think so,' said Ralph.

But Mrs Burford had gone, closing the door behind her. She'll creep away, Ralph thought, when her work's done and I won't see her again, never get the chance to say: "Why are Americans . . . Why d'you hate me so when we're on the same side? You help Erica in your way, and by her own admission, she's found something useful, even valuable, in me." Absent-mindedly, Ralph poured the vodka.

'It's odd,' he said.

'What is?'

'To be drinking this in the afternoon.'

Ralph noticed that, in Erica's room, he'd become afraid of silences. It was as if, when the room was quiet, he expected a dismissal. And she was silent now, taking up her little glass of vodka but not drinking it, her eyes behind the thick lenses staring beyond him at some object on the wall.

'I don't know,' he said quietly, 'if it was painful for you to tell me about the trip to Paris and Saladino. If it was, we won't go on. But I'd like to know if things did change for you and Bernard after that, or whether –'

She focused on him and her mouth was a hard line.

'Yes, they changed.'

Ralph took a sip of his vodka and waited.

'I went to see Valéry Clément that same evening. I think I'd planned to go the next day, but I left Bernard at the hotel and went straight to Montparnasse in a taxi. Climbing his stairway was awful, and the smell of his room, it hadn't changed. But he was an old man by that time, Valéry Clément, with all his good looks stretched into tiny lines and very curious dyed hair which looked navy blue. I got very drunk on his red wine and tried to tell him what a terrible folly it is to mix up lives like cocktails. I was very, very unhappy, because I just couldn't see how I could ever love Bernard again, not as I'd been loving him in a contented way. I told Valéry I would rather be by myself till the end of my life than try to love someone I couldn't love any more. And he said love was unimportant. He said, it's unimportant because its base is a fundamental absurdity – the absurdity of our notions of time. He told me to spend my life preoccupied entirely with human folly and human cruelty, exposing these in all their manifestations and to forget love absolutely, as if I had never felt it.

'I don't remember what else he said, because I was too drunk. I think he would only talk about the book after that. He told me its only weakness was General Almarlyes' belief that love could save him. "I despise those who believe they love," he said and I knew that inside all his white suits, for years, and years, he had been feeling bitter and betrayed. But we were a silly pair. We just wanted to be young again and we weren't!

'So I came stumbling out at about midnight and I was sick in the hotel bathroom and Bernard ordered coffee and a hot water bottle because I was shaking. It was all disgraceful and sad. I'd let my head fill up with memories and they made me unkind. Yet even the next morning when I woke up and looked at Bernard I couldn't find all my old feelings for him. I just couldn't remember how content I'd been. I couldn't.

'I think we went back to England the next day or the day after and I've never felt so miserable. It wasn't as if I could say well, that portion of my life is over – the portion with Bernard – and pack my things and start somewhere else. I was sixty, not a thing of twenty-five in a strawberry hat! I kept saying to myself it will all evaporate like a dream, the Paris feeling, and then I shall get back to work and Bernard and I will be just as we've always been and he will

216

understand that what I feel now is something temporary, a kind of illness.

'But the illness dragged on, Ralph. Saladino, Thérèse, Valéry Clément . . . I was haunted by those people and by the smell of the streets and the stairways. They followed me around like the porpoise treading on the whiting's tail or whatever it is. I'd get up very early, but not to milk. I'd go for long walks, further and further each day. I suppose I thought, if I can walk far enough away from Bernard, then when I meet him again, I will feel differently. You see, he was becoming very morose and defeated and his nightmares began again. I was damaging him terribly and I didn't want to do this. There was no spite in me or hate for him: just indifference. I'd stopped caring about him.

'But I was becoming a bit of a celebrity that year. They put pictures of me in the newspapers and I went on the wireless. So I had to go to London quite a lot and it occurred to me that perhaps if I stayed in London for a while – on my own – I might recover and then I could go back to Bernard and we'd be all right. I remember we discussed all this in the kitchen. I don't think Bernard wanted me to go away, but we both knew anything was better than living as we were now in this unfair way. So I went. I rented a little flat from a radio producer in Ladbroke Grove and I began to go on very silly panel games like "Twenty Questions" and try to be witty and clever. And I gave talks. I think I only had one talk but I gave it to a lot of different literary societies and even at lunches and of course I began to meet all the writers of the day which was very nice.

'I suppose this was the only "literary" period of my life. I'd done a very long apprenticeship for it – about forty years! – and now *The Hospital Ship* had let me qualify. And I won't pretend I didn't enjoy it. I liked being in a city again, especially London which I've always loved from the moment I first came to it. And it was still very nice in the 'fifties, quite proud of itself and quiet. I walked around it a lot and I thought about Chadwick and about Emily and I found I was perfectly happy to be on my own.

'Bernard often wrote to me – very cheerful letters all about the garden and the farm, telling me how well the sweet peas had done and the marrows . . . I can't remember if I wrote back. I don't think I did because I had nothing to say so I suppose, as a year went on, he must have worried about me and thought I was never going back.

I often imagined him of course, with the house far too big for him, cooking mushrooms for himself in his beige dressing gown and spending all day in Gully's old room with his butterflies. I remember dreaming once that I went back to Suffolk and there he was, in his same old clothes but aged beyond recollection, all stooped and white and with overgrown eyebrows and grey hairs sticking out of his nose. I expect I had lots of dreams about him because he was often on my mind, but I can't remember any others, only that one of him getting old.'

Erica took a sip of her vodka and smiled. 'It's very warming, isn't it? That's why the Russians can't do without it – that and those flaps to cover their ears. I wonder if they have this lumpfish now in Moscow? I think we'd better try it, hadn't we? They say it's Swedish, so it's probably very good for you.'

Ralph passed her the plate. He didn't feel like eating and chose the smallest piece of toast. He thought, it's meant to be a celebration and yet neither of us know what's going to happen. We celebrate the momentous solemnly, in expectation. We only know that our time together's run out. Unless of course she knows it all, exactly as it will be yet keeps it to herself . . .

'Do you like it, dear? Isn't it rather salty?'

'It's okay.'

'I think it's salty, but I suppose it goes rather well with the vodka.'

'Sure.'

She smiled again. She seemed alert and happy, perhaps more so than on any other day.

'I'm so glad they sent you, Ralph. It's very odd that they should have sent you now when I don't suppose anyone remembers my name.'

'I sent myself.'

'Did you? But it hasn't been easy for you, has it? All the days when I couldn't talk to you . . .'

'It's been fine. I don't like London too much, but I feel okay here, especially when your lamp's on!'

'And have you got all you want? I don't think there's much more I can tell you.'

'Yes, there is, Erica. I'd like to know what happened . . . to you and Bernard.'

She stared into her drink and sighed. 'Well,' she said, 'I often

218

think my life might have stopped there, in 1955. I never imagined living so long. I don't know why I have. I suppose I was very strong when I was a Suffolk girl and that strength has lasted me out. I must have been born with bones as hard as cow horn, mustn't I? Because they still let me walk – without a stick – and none of them are bent, only my hand. But although my body's gone on and on, I've never done another book. I never became the real writer I wanted to be and a lot of people have asked me why. But I don't think I've ever known the answer. It could be that all my books, even *The Hospital Ship* which was very popular for a while, have failed in their intention which was to make people confront the repulsiveness of aggression. But England in the 'fifties was still imperialist and greedy and when Suez came – with all the greed and conspiracy surfacing again – I wanted to burn poor old Eden and his government just like I burned Almarlyes. Oh I hated that Suez business! I became very ill with a black, black depression when I heard we were sending an army. I just sank down into my dark sea and the horrors I saw in it – none have ever been as terrible. Terrible, terrible! They're gone now. I don't remember them. But I remember lying by my flat door in Ladbroke Grove trying to hold something back with my body. I don't know what I was trying to hold back: all the men and planes perhaps, but I knew I had to stay there. But after a few days – I don't know how many – my neighbours broke down the door and found me and I was put into a hospital. I was so weak I couldn't move a finger and I had to have a drip in my arm. And then I saw Bernard.

'I can't remember how he found out where I was. Perhaps the producer from the BBC wrote to him and said I was dying. He looked just the same of course, not aged as he'd been in my dream, and when I was stronger, he told me that he'd been in Switzerland in the Bernese Oberland and had found some wonderful butterflies there. He looked very brown and healthy, and I thought, only with him will I ever come out of this darkness. I can't do it on my own and I don't want to lose myself like Virginia Woolf and go walking into the River Ouse.

'So I asked him to take me back home to Suffolk, and try to forgive me. I didn't know how it would be: there was a lot of confusion in me then. But I suppose I knew if we had a chance to be together again it was now.

'We got on a train and I saw London slipping by me again, all the ends of walls and a few bomb sites still, with willow herb sprouting out of them. It was strange how, all my life, I watched myself leaving London again and again going back to the Suffolk house, never certain somehow of what I'd find there or how I'd feel, but letting myself be taken there, seeing the fields begin and the sky come down to them, but knowing that I didn't belong anywhere – only parts of me to certain places – and that I would never ever feel it, this sense of belonging.

'I kept on the flat in Ladbroke Grove and in two years or so I was back there again. I'd met Bertrand Russell in 1955 when the CND movement began and he wrote to me and asked me to speak at a meeting. I knew what it would all mean: banners again and marches in the rain, but I had to do it of course. But Bernard wouldn't let me go alone. Perhaps he thought I'd fall down in a puddle and be trampled to death on the way to Aldermaston, or perhaps, when he remembered the fire at Crowbourne, he thought it was his turn to do something.

'By the time we joined Russell we'd recovered some balance at home. We could let ourselves get back on the train and see Suffolk disappearing. It was harvest time, very hot in London. I thought about out own vegetable harvest going to waste. And John Haggard's wedding – we'd miss that.

'I was glad Bernard came to London that time. He stopped me falling in love with Russell which would have been very idiotic and painful. And he worked harder than I did – pamphlets, speech writing, petitions, scuffles with the police – all the paraphernalia of something small but growing and with a bursting heart. We didn't think we could lose. We believed that armies can be stopped by the old woman who lies down in the street, but it's not true: the army marches on with a wumping chant of "progress" and the old woman is crushed to powder like a moth.

'We went back to Suffolk from time to time, to rest. We'd sleep for two days and nights sometimes, but now Bernard slept in Gully's room and I was alone in the big bed of my parents. I don't think passion was ever in our lives, even at the beginning. We used to like to put our arms round each other and feel the lifebeat of the other one and we often did this. But after 1955 I preferred to sleep alone. Sometimes I'd lie there and think how wrong this was. It's a fallacy to believe that passionate feelings conveniently leave you when you get old and your hair loses its weight. I tried to imagine how my life might have shaped itself if I hadn't met Bernard in Patterson Tree's office the day I fell asleep on the chesterfield. But I dare say it wouldn't have been very different. If I hadn't found Bernard, I would have found someone very like him, because no love affair could have matched what I had with Gérard: I needed to love without loving. Do you see?

'I suppose we put the passionate sides of ourselves into the movement for several years. Bernard was sent to prison in Glasgow for two months and a lot of the younger people were in prison on and off all the time. So I'd go and visit them and take them bits of food I couldn't really afford and try to make an hour or two bearable for them by saying: "At least you won't be force-fed with gruel like we were in 1912, all strapped up to the chair." But there was a rail-strike in 1958, the year Bernard got sent down, so I couldn't get to him in Glasgow and I found that I worried about him all the time.

'His family – Huntley in particular – wrote me very nasty letters saying they "didn't approve" of Bernard being sent to prison. They said the family would suffer. They were all very ignorant and conservative so I threw their silly letters away. And it was only ten years later, when Bernard was very ill, that Huntley came grovelling round offering to pay for private specialists and private this and that.

'I don't know what they did to Bernard in Glasgow. He came out looking very thin and terribly afraid of crowds and loud noises. So back we got on the Suffolk train and he seemed quite bewildered by everything he saw. He said he had been cold all the time in his cell, too cold to sleep and then, in the warm train, he slept and when we got to Culham Market, I had to get two men to help me carry him off the train because he couldn't wake up properly, just as if he'd been drugged.

'I nursed him for a month but even after that he had no energy or strength. He wouldn't go out into the garden but shuffled around all day in his dressing gown or sat by the Rayburn warming himself. I tried to keep a life going between London and the farm but I felt defeated. We knew our hopes for disarmament had failed. We tried to keep them alive and believe there could be a change of policy but it was difficult to feel any optimism and I couldn't bear to think of all the wasted suffering. So we fell out of the movement. It went on without us and the bomb still hung above our heads. I used to imagine it on a saliva strand above the forget-me-not field.

'We went back to Switzerland in the summer of 1959, to try to make Bernard strong again. We went to Wengen at a time when the gentian flowers were out and I thought it was extraordinary, that untouched Switzerland with its sense of safety and neatness in the midst of those mountains. It was a very glorious summer there – none of that drizzle which fell on us at Chamonix – and we'd climb up into the grass slopes, a bit higher each day (I made Bernard walk and walk). The hotel packed up picnic lunches for us in pink paper bags and very high up we found a flat meadow used by a saw-mill as a kind of first base for the pine trunks. It was surrounded entirely by trees and no one ever came there except some children one day who sang for us in German. So we used to eat our lunches there and sometimes go to sleep in the warm grass. I suppose we looked like two very old people to those Swiss children, like the Sloanes playing their two-handed bridge and dreaming of Monte Carlo.

'But it was wonderful for Bernard. By the second week, we were taking all the butterfly paraphernalia with us – the nets and the chloroform jars, and our whole collection, by the end of our stay, was blue. A thousand blues! Some were as dark as the gentian flowers, some pale purple. They were very beautiful. They helped Bernard get well and forget his fear of cold and his fear of noise. Yet on the sleeper coming back through France, he remembered it again and started shivering. I had to lie with him on the narrow bunk to try and keep him warm.'

Erica sat back on the sofa and finished her glass of vodka. Ralph was about to switch off his machine, but Erica sighed again and began:

'I think this being afraid of things was with us always – on and off – after that; so I knew we had to stay in Suffolk. London frightened Bernard and he refused to go there. We gave up the flat in Ladbroke Grove and turned back towards the house and the garden. For the last ten years of Bernard's life the house and the garden were what mattered to him; he'd lost the spirit for everything outside them.

'I expect he knew he would die there. He got pneumonia in the winter of 1967 and I suppose he should have gone into hospital as Huntley suggested but he didn't want to. I moved him back into our big bed and slept on a mattress beside him. I'd lie and listen to his breathing which was all wrong. He made extraordinary noises like jungle cries. And then one night they stopped. The jungle was silent.

'I got up and went to turn on the light, but there were January storms and there'd been a power failure. So I groped my way to the larder and got a candle. And seeing his death in the candlelight was extraordinary. I could never forget it. I didn't close his eyes, but sat on the bed with him holding my candle and holding his hand. The winds outside were very fierce, but I didn't feel at all afraid; either of them or of Bernard's death. I'd known all along that I would outlast him.

'But I've outlasted everything, that's the trouble, Ralph. I've outlasted my own usefulness and every single person I've ever been close to – all except Gully.'

'He's still alive, Gully?'

'Yes. Though I haven't seen him for years, not since Bernard's funeral. But Huntley notices him from time to time. He tells me he goes to the pub and sits there, with his old bull's head nodding. I expect he's batty by now. I expect he's still trying to puzzle it out – how to throw a girdle of barleycorns round the world.'

'Yet his kids write to you.'

'Oh yes. They think, because I was a name once, that I'm rich, and they ask me for things. But I'm not rich because I gave everything away when Bernard died.'

'Everything?'

'I was wooding – we used to call it that, going into the woods and getting kindling and small branches for the fire – very early on a winter morning and I thought, this is one of my first memories, being sent out for wood on cold mornings and now here I am again, getting old, still stooping down and feeling for dry sticks. And it's like a circle – a beginning (here) and then a life, and then an ending (here). But I didn't want this. I didn't want to end as I'd begun – oh my God, no! So I called Huntley over and said he could have it all, the house, the land, everything. I said I would take the cupboard and one or two other things that I didn't want to part with, but in the end there wasn't much else. And in return for all this he pays my rent on this flat. It was very cheap when I got it, but now it's thirty pounds a week.'

'D'you ever regret it, Erica – the house?'

'Oh no. Imagine me living there on my own. I couldn't manage. I'd have to pay someone to nanny me and I couldn't bear that. And Huntley has made it all fine, you see. He's put central heating into the house and thick carpets, and he's built silos and milking parlours and pulled down the old dairy and the cowshed where I met Claustrophobia. He's changed it all and made it very clean and efficient which it never was, not in my parents' day and not in my day when Bernard and I struggled with our vegetables. It's in beautiful countryside of course and I do sometimes wish, if I had an arm to lean on, I could walk to the forget-me-not field and then beyond it into the woods. But that's only on summer days, when I remember the oak trees.'

They heard a door slam as Mrs Burford left. Ralph refilled the two glasses with vodka.

'She always goes off like that,' whispered Erica. 'She could put her head in to say goodbye, but she never does, not when you're here. She just slips away.'

'I think she's resented me.'

'Has she? I don't know why. I told her how very considerate you are.'

'She thinks I tire you.'

'Tire me? Well, you do! Talking about my life is very tiring, Ralph. But it's been awfully helpful, dear. I've often thought, my life needs tidying out like sometimes I tidy the cupboard and find things in it I never knew I had. And if you hadn't arrived, I never would have done this, because I've grown lazy. I wake up in the morning and I think, I can't bear to do anything today; I can't bear to *be*. So I lie there. I hear the man upstairs playing his 'cello and I wish I could do that – play an instrument. But I don't do anything. I just let my body stay alive.'

'And you never, never wrote again, after *The Hospital Ship*?'

'No I didn't, Ralph. I think I lost my zeal. I've never been one of those writers who just think up plots and then put them down; I've always had to feel that something was wrong and that I was going to change it – even a little – with my writing. I don't suppose I've actually changed anything at all, just as nothing changed in spite of all our efforts for C.N.D. When you think of it, it's heartbreaking, and when you're sixty, as I was, you see so clearly that for all your self-importance and going on panel games, your piece of work is something so pitiful and tiny and the world goes rollicking on and you lose touch with the young people, and your hunger for words, which used to be so strong in me, leaves you. I suppose it's a bit like hunger for a person: when it leaves you, you never get it back.

'So I thought it was better to be quiet. There was no one left alive to bully me into writing and I suppose I knew that in *The Hospital Ship* I'd said the best of what I have to say.'

'The day General Almarlyes started to paint the house, it began to rain. Rivulets of whitewash ran down the walls and made puddles at his feet. His uniform was sodden and flecked with white, and all along the street he could hear the laughter of his men – Fine day to choose, General! Didn't you know the rains were coming, General, Sir?

But he had to cover it up, the stain of his year's tenancy in the house – from the first stain of the first occupant's blood, to the last stain of the dead camellia flowers blown into his gutter by the autumn winds and now, with the rain, oozing a brownish-pink excrement down his walls.

Because she would not come to him. Not until his house was white again and fresh and smelling of the winter jasmine he would gather for her in great armfuls. Not until he had whitewashed every wall and every doorway, even the walls of his own room and the doorway of his own room and even the hinges on the doors that creaked where the summer heat had warped them. Only then – to this perfectly white miracle of a house would his future bride come silently, when the men slept, drunk, on their thresholds and the Daughters of the Lamb slept, chaste, on their hard mattresses, and Cotton Eye Joe had wandered back to the sea-shore to sing his freedom songs to the hidden coral of the bay. Only then.

For so she had promised him countless times. In answer to a pleading that had taken on the words and the cadences, even the unbearable beauty of a prayer that lapped the silent grey of her virgin head with longings buried, deep, deep inside her and which caused her, at her sunset devotions, to turn her face from her sisters and whisper: Mother, Mother of us all who sees my blush and feels my pulse, cast me out into your blue eternity for so I should be cast and damned for ever for my thoughts of love and a bridal bed in the arms of Almarlyes, soldier born in sin and grown to terrible manhood in his numberless wars.

"But the day is not far off," said General Almarlyes to the scampering lizards and the crested birds which had left the trees and come to shelter under his roof, "the day is coming, in a winter we have never experienced, when I shall part company with each and every remembrance of madness and together with my bride, I shall put down roots into the soil."

The rains blew from the south. They were the warm, sour rains that brought sickness and lethargy, not the pure rains of heaven, so said the Daughters of the Lamb, but the rains of another continent, harbouring death. So as General Almarlyes worked and the whitewash covered his hair and dribbled into his eyes, the sixty-three remnants of the hundred and five stopped their laughter and closed their doors warped by the summer sun and lay in the darkness of their houses and dreamed of women and wars.

And it was then, with the beginning of the rains that some of the men noticed for the first time that they were no longer free. It was then that they understood why the previous inhabitants of the town had come and gone leaving the white houses empty and shining in the sun yet inside smeared with bloodstains and filled in every room with coiled and tangled fibres like the bodies of pale snakes. The ends of the fibrous growths were brown with dried blood where they had been hacked away and to touch them was to touch a soft mass, like the limbs of babies. But General Almarlyes had ordered that a pit should be dug, at the very end of the avenue of camellia trees, and armfuls of the horrible fibres were thrown into it and buried and the Daughters of the Lamb said a prayer standing in a wide circle round the pit in case they had buried part of a life.

They were almost invisible at first, the new thin roots that grew out of the limbs of the men and hung like cobwebs down to the ground. Yet they had begun to burrow and push through the dry rushes and leaves into the bare, baked earth of the floors, and while a man slept on his hammock, with his hand dangling to the floor, that hand would be anchored to the ground and when he woke and tried to move it, the pain of wrenching and tearing at the roots that were part of him was a pain he had never imagined and never thought to endure, even in death.

So once more the Daughters of the Lamb came and bound up the bleeding limbs of the men with fresh bandages, painted each finger, each toe with the last of the blood coagulant saved from the hospital ship and stifled their screams with their cool hands and at dusk while the rains fell, they enquired of their Gentle God: "Who has sent this new tribulation Lord, and when will it end?"

Almarlyes worked on till darkness. In the night he heard the screams of his men and lit a fragile candle. He was afraid.'

Ralph put down the book and lay still. He lay and looked at John Pennington's room and at the black beyond the window. Ducks which had slept in the shade of huge willows all afternoon began to fidget with sound, but their squawking seemed only to add to the weight of silence, not to disturb it. Ralph imagined that it had a liquid quality, this silence of an Oxford garden. He drank it gratefully, and was satisfied. It was more refreshing than sleep.

And after London . . . after the eternal push of traffic on Chalk Farm Road and a sky that was never completely behind the thin curtains, here, suddenly, was a night blacker than Tennessee, moonless but full of stars. Outside the window, wisteria in bud gently tapped the glass. The room smelled of paper and pencil shavings. Next door John Pennington slept on a narrow bed, but Ralph, on an ancient sofa, slightly ludicrous in a purple sleeping bag, was content to keep company with the night, to store its peace in his body. Dawn, he knew, would begin, not at this window which had seen the sunset, but far behind him, behind countless courtyards and roofs and belfries that he might or might not have seen on his afternoon's walk round the city. Here it would show only palely, the ducks and the lily leaves would be motionless in its early mist. There would be dew on the grass where, during the afternoon, students had arranged metal and canvas chairs in a semi-circle, dew on the stone benches with their solemn carvings, dew on the window and on the iron balcony beyond it. Then, perhaps,

Ralph would sleep. John would get up and put on the dressing gown he'd worn since his last term at school, look in and see Ralph still curled up in his sleeping bag. He would make toast and coffee and bring it in. The last day would begin.

Ralph couldn't think beyond breakfast, couldn't imagine this last day that would end in his flight home and all the sleepless hours to follow . . . Walt snapping like a general, dead plants on his window sill . . . America! He wanted to stop time here, so that night and silence were endless, eternal. And in it he would unfathom all the mysteries that remained. *'For myself,'* he whispered, 'because in the end no one comes up with any answers – none that I can use!' Not even John, in his other culture, lifelong friend and stranger, so why had Ralph counted so much on seeing him, on having time to talk? They'd talked – yet not for long enough, or perhaps, once again, Ralph had simply asked the wrong questions. They had sat by John's window, open on the quiet sunset, with a bottle of cheap Italian wine between them and Ralph had tried to explain what he could only express as a sense of commitment to his assignment on Erica March. He knew it had a place in his life – in a life that found room for so little and so few. He knew it counted. Yet he couldn't say why (the two basins of corn were the nearest he'd ever got to saying why) and hoped that John, who always seemed so wise, even in his silences, would explain the truth of it to him, would tell him in fact why he had come to England and what he had done. But John had only smiled, sipped the wine, looked out lazily at the darkening trees and said 'I don't know. I don't see why it's important to know, but if it is, it will come to you, one day.'

'But Erica saw that it was important. She believed it was important for her, too.'

'I expect she was flattered. She's been left alone for years now.'

'No. She saw some significance in it – beyond any immediate feelings such as flattery. She alluded to it very often.'

'To what?'

'To my being there. She often said: "I knew someone would come, one day," and she believed it was me, the someone.'

'To bury her in her cupboard?'

'That's her riddle. She gave me instructions but I couldn't believe in them – not completely. I think it was a kind of dream of hers, just one of many. I don't think she'll die.

'But you can't be sure?'

'No.'

'You've taken the risk?'

'Coming here?'

'Yes, and leaving her.'

'I couldn't have stayed with her all night, John.'

'No.'

John paused, made some comment on the cheapness of the wine relative to its palatability and then said half-seriously: 'What do you think about the novel? Dying, dead or buried?'

Ralph parried the question: 'Your novel?'

'Oh no, not mine. Mine's a weak fledgling, still in the nest. I mean The Novel.'

'They ask that one on chat shows now. I can't give it my attention.'

'So you don't know? Don't care?'

'Sure, I care.'

'Well, then?'

'Well, it's kept alive. Just by a few good surgeons . . .'

'I won't be one of them.'

'How d'you know?'

'Like you said, the metamorphosis is too traumatic. I can't find a voice. Not only that, nothing *breathes,* there. Certainly not love, which is what I'm after.'

'Why love?'

'It's what I want to record.'

'So why can't you?'

John had made a rich meat stew. Said he'd scrounged tarragon from the Provost's garden. Ralph remembered that John had always liked cooking and served meals very carefully – butter and parsley on the vegetables, hot bread in linen napkins – and they sat at a tiny table, neatly laid in one corner of the room, eating by candlelight. It was all much as Ralph had imagined it, the feel of the very ancient in the stone corridors, but then the room – well proportioned with its one exquisite window – was full of John's patient work, papers and pamphlets piling up where shelves no longer had room for them, more books than Ralph possessed in his lifetime, an oak floor smelling of beeswax, the inevitable old sofa. I suppose, Ralph thought, as the meal went on, he's found that he belongs. I doubt that he'll ever leave these rooms but grow old and dry and a bit crazy in his colourless clothes, and be seen walking round the Pump Quadrangle with a stick, still remembering the novel he never finished, the novel about love. He laughed at the image of John as a very old man.

'When you're old and a celebrity here, John, some second-rate journal will send a young American to do a profile of you!'

'As long as it's only a "profile"; I've always thought I looked very odd face to face!'

'And you'll scare the shit out of the guy with some notion about suicide.'

They laughed.

'Well, if I look at my work, Ralph, perhaps I ought to end it all far sooner than that. I mean long before the young American arrives. You see, I'm not even on speaking terms with the Metaphysicals any more. New ideas have come out about them and they seem to like the new ones far more than mine. Yet I used to think I was an authority.'

They laughed again. Ralph noticed that in John's pale face his nose was becoming red, as if the wine he had drunk had lodged itself there.

'No,' John went on, 'it's my novel now, or nothing. I'm set on it and yet it doesn't work. And I've told far too many people about it which is idiotic of me. Even the manager of Blackwell's said: "I hear you've completed a novel, Dr Pennington." Completed! It's a farce: I don't know where to put myself.'

It had grown dark very suddenly. Only the corner of the room was lit by the candles, the rest disappeared in shadow. Ralph remembered Erica and knew that by now her Tiffany lamp would be on. Wondering suddenly whether he would ever come to possess it – the lamp that had shed its pleasing light on all the yards and yards of conversation – he imagined for a moment that her room was in darkness and next door in the bedroom she had bundled her body away, to wait for death in her cupboard. The door of the cupboard was open and the moon glimmered on her face. Her mouth still moved: she talked on and on until unconsciousness rolled in and she was silent.

'I think,' he said hurriedly, 'that *The Hospital Ship* is an extraordinary novel – perhaps rather great.'

'I don't know,' said John, 'I couldn't ever really get on with the Almarlyes character, although I know he's meant to be something "universal": he always seemed too much of a fool. I don't think she was rigorous enough with him; she just let him happen.'

'Oh no, John . . .'

'And this writing about pretend places. I find it all oddly irrelevant.'

'To what? Irrelevant to what?'

'To anything one's experienced or has knowledge of.'

'She told me it was primarily about England after the second war. Soldiers coming home and trying to find themselves – to find something important, something that was worthy of all the sacrifice. And then stopping their search, letting themselves become the Rooters . . .'

'And Almarlyes?'

'I don't know. I think –'

'Exactly! You don't know.'

'No, I think . . .'

'What?'

'He's the only one who keeps on searching. The Daughters of the Lamb tell the men that some of them will find "home" quite soon and some will never find it. Almarlyes knows, in spite of his virgin bride and the wonderful trees, that the first island isn't home. He has the courage to tear away from the roots and get back on the ship.'

'He's a killer.'

'Yes. But no more than any of us . . .'

'Much more.'

'Only because he has *dared* to see more than we can bear to see. Untold horrors . . .'

'But how can one sympathize with that?'

'Why not? I think there's a sense in which we can – and are meant to – admire him. He's very bad at expressing what he feels, yet he believes . . . he knows what the human spirit could be capable of – all the incredible possibilities – he senses their infinity. And he knows that the women from the ship have reached a higher plane of awareness, which is why he has to start living with one of them. He's too afraid because of his wars and the crimes committed in those wars to believe in Gentle Jesus, but he has to experience the virgin – to rediscover the virgin in himself so that he can begin –'

'The rapist in himself.'

'Both. The two poles – the mutilator and the mutilated. And his eyes are opened on the Possible.'

'It fails to convince.'

'No, John. Read it again. In the fire at the end –'

'I don't think I ever got as far as the end.'

'In the fire – '

'Don't tell me. I might read it. One day.'

'Sure. Well, it's worth reading.'

'And you, Ralph? You're going home to resurrect her, are you?'

'Resurrect Erica?'

That's your tryst to yourself?'

'I don't know, John. I was hoping you'd tell me what I was doing.'

'Me?'

'Yup.'

'I tell no one anything any more. Even the students: I've stopped *telling*. I'm struggling to learn!'

Ralph heard a clock strike two. Sleep was still far off. He imagined John snoring, unaware that Ralph had come hoping for so much and been given so little. It's not his fault, he thought. He's doing life in this college. Very little outside it seems important. Only the place itself, in its privileged peace, had put a bandage on Ralph's uncertainties. And in the moments before he slept he discovered in himself an infinite contentment.

When he dreamed, it was all of Oxford. He was in the college gardens with John. In the centre of the lake, out beyond the willows, the sun was dazzling on the water. A group of French tourists, all younger than they were, passed them, chattering happily. Ralph was aware of a kind of agility in them – both verbal and bodily – which he lacked. And to compensate, to show them all, anyone who passed, that he was still young enough, audacious enough, to be daring, he began to walk to the lake where a cluster of lily pads was green and dense and to let his body glide onto them like a skater. He was barefooted and the feel of the leaves was like thick satin. John began calling to him from the bank. The young French tourists stopped and stared, the ducks, woken by this extraordinary feat, waddled away. He glided on. The leaves now covered the entire surface of the lake, and the faster he went the better they seemed to hold him up. The sun was on his head and on the lily leaves and on his bare feet.

He reached the far corner of the lake and saw the students, in their semi-circle, turn and stare at him. He let go a sound from his throat which was pure pleasure. Then he saw that the lake, which had been no more than a large pond, had become enormous and that John, standing on the other side of it and calling had lost all his size and bulk. He was a black note, dancing. He was a crochet-man, far far away, making silent music. The lake had become Ralph's world and he was buoyant in it, unafraid. There was an ecstatic murmuring in his head, and to this his body kept perfect time.

He woke and it was still dark. He pondered the dream for a while, remembering vividly its quality of joy, then slept and dreamed again and woke. And now he saw, just as he had imagined it, a misty dawn at the window. He felt cold.

Turning, she thought. My body turns. So many countless thousands of turnings, to face this, now that, now this, now that . . . and now this. It has grown old, just like the world, in all its turnings and, like the world, it waits for silence.

Death is easy. Death is the throat, swallowing. Ten swallows. A Swallowtail in Bernard's net. The swallows of all summer – so *easy* with their knowledge of the seasons and temperate zones, to sit in a line on a telegraph wire when I wore pinafores, grubbing for sticks by the thinned hawthorn and blackthorn and my mother says, 'Count them. Count the birds. Tell your father what we saw. Swallows on a line, with us till autumn.' But I couldn't count. Too small to know that a rich man has twenty-five castles and in each of these twenty-five rooms; waist-high I was, or less, holding sticks in my pinny, taking her hand, but "mind how we go because wood's scarce this year, scarce because he won't touch them, not the oak trees outlasting kings and dynasties, says it's wrong to burn in an hour a thing that will outlast us, outlast even you, tiny child with so little knowledge of how much and how many and *why*, why they could outlast you, with your whole life to come and a farthing a week pocket-money, in your brown boots 'hand made by Alfred Taylor and Son, Norwich', – why indeed, yet we must get wood like scavengers, like the poacher with his gun swinging a rabbit home to the pot, pleased as pie, dreaming of a full belly and the warmth of it by his own fire with his own pipe in a blue jar on the mantle, just like your father's – jar and pipe and an ounce or two of Riley's Virginian

– just like him! oh, who knows the sum of things and even the spiked ways of noblemen, going from castle to castle, even that and a lot more besides when we sit hand in hand at nightfall and you sleep upstairs with a bran doll tucked under your chin, doll made of rags by your Gran the day you were born . . ."

She is full of words trying to make up for almost eighty years of silence and empty dresses that wore out in time, yet she won't come out into the lane where the early morning sun is blinking through, but hides in the shadow and doesn't turn to me so that I see her face and won't let me run to her – 'my black witch running to her mother, indeed, and she'll be five this summer!' – though I wish she would turn, only the one time, or let me run to her and let her stroke my hair which hangs in plaits and hear me say . . . I never knew you woman to woman, friend to friend and only when the heavy flowers were thrown on you did I understand the finality of you and whisper to the doll 'she is quite dead, not dead like some plants in winter but quite, quite dead, Ratty May, more dead than you whose body holds its shape and who takes on very often the warmth of my own body. And after your death, there was no finding you – only in my dark dreaming, yes only in the dark and standing always to one side, out of reach – just as I can't find you now yet I know I'm with you in the lane, and my feet are small.'

'Death is quite easy, Vicar, isn't it? No harder than dreaming, which comes from nowhere. Is it? No harder than a sum which tires you out in your head and then you want to lie down and sleep. Is it? No harder than these?' But I am sent away, still not certain if suffering is necessary. I am a child, he says. And he drowned in a well the following winter. A very difficult death for keeping his lambs in ignorance of what he did not know. I want to laugh at the vicar's death. But the sound I make isn't laughter. I think it's only my breath pressed awkwardly out of me by the weight of the cart carrying some cavalcade up the ruts of my spine . . .

But I am no longer in the lane, nor by the well where the vicar drowned and heaven knows how they got his icy body out before it rotted and poisoned the water . . . I am nowhere that I recognize, but I hear two separate breaths, three, counting mine. So I am not alone as I imagined and I wait to see – unless vision is going now as it did once before right in front of the *Kommandant*'s eyes and for months the death camp was dark – I wait to see who pushes out these

comforting breaths to reassure me, no we are not alone when we die!
We die hand in hand with the miraculous.

All night they talked, until an hour or two before dawn when the
wind got up and now they sleep, side by side, oblivious of the wind,
yet I am sent to warn them, the winds getting up, Chadwick. Gully,
the wind's blowing from the north-east and squalls of rain are
coming on the wind. Sleep and sleep. The tepee rocks. Two breaths.
And mine outside; the one sent to wake them. The wind's coming,
Chadwick! North-easter you can tell by the shaking and trembling
of the leaves. Wake up Gully. *Chadwick*! And I long to run to the
comfort of my room, where the wind is kept out and the darkness
hidden by a candle. Oh god, the wind's coming fast, Chadwick, and
blow you both up into the sky, it will . . . so at last they hear me and
I know that Gully is coming out. Don't look at me, he says, I'm not
covered up, because this is my habit, now that I'm too old to feel
shame and my body is like yours, used up and white as a maggot,
even my ole Long John you liked to watch swinging and thinking of
it hard in you . . . and if you heard two breaths, two sleepers in the
tepee, then one of them was the wind, and they say lies are blown
into our heads through holes so small in us, we can't detect them
and that they swarm on a north-easterly like a cloud of locusts and
are dispersed in us.

He has crawled out now and sits hunched on the grass. His bull's
head lolls and his eyes in it are tired. His body is thinner than it has
ever been and wrinkled and all the hair on it is grey and sparse and
of uneven length. Gully. And behind him the tepee begins to break
up, its sewn-together skin torn and flying away over the roof of the
house. 'So come in, Gully. There's a candle in my room – if the
draught hasn't caught it yet and blown it out – and I can go down
and make two mugs of cocoa and I promise you, I'll never speak of
it, the other breath I heard side by side with yours, though I swear it
was Chadwick sleeping – long before he knew Athelstone or Robin
or his hair ran into the bath in golden rivers . . . I swear all this on
my mother's soul, if I knew where that was, if I could ever learn
where it hides, in what part of my mind you see, in what part of me,
Gully . . . of course I would swear if it makes you happy. Yet what
could it possibly matter now, old man, when all that waits for you
at the pub is an ending of some kind . . . the handcart on your bull's
back . . . oh, Gully, I don't know why, at the end of so many

journeys, you were always there, holding your cap with a look of such solemnity and why – oh Lord! – you ever took me to bed in the bed of your wife. I suppose you paid your price for me to her in kisses on her hands and you couldn't have known that wherever your lips touched her palms and her fingers, warts would come up, and though you burned them out for her, they kept growing and growing till no one could bear to look at her hands and she hid them in mittens.

The skin of the tepee is almost gone . . . Chadwick. You went away and left Gully to the winds, left us all in the end, unable to speak of you without tears. You hear me? Chadwick? Sulking in some expensive restaurant. Where's your sleeping breath that was comforting? I can't hear it any more, and I feel such a terrible weakness, dear thing, I know if I tried to move my feet, even wrapped up as they are, I couldn't do this, yet I know my body still turns – from this to that, from that to this – it flows and moves, without any pain I can locate, yet is unable to hold things in place. Dying is to become fluid then? A spilling of the self until features and shape are gone just as yours – did they? – ebbed into your eiderdown, grey as damp clay, and all we buried was the little moisture the bed had not absorbed? Yet you didn't want to die, Chadwick! You were a seasonal man and you thought spring would come back and start trilling in your throat. You kept on and on with your mumblings . . . 'buying a horse to ride in the park with the chestnut flowers coming on, because riding's the only thing, Erica, so somebody said, to keep a man healthy and full of vigour, and it isn't as if with my money I couldn't afford . . .'

There are horses, I suppose, pulling the cart that weighs me down. They patiently plough me till I am turned, dark side up, to a September morning and the seagulls fly in to pick me over. There are countless straight lines of me, all the earth of eighty-seven years, laid out under the sky. Death is a turning over. Huntley picks up a clod of soil in his hands and feels its texture, not knowing it's part of me that he crumbles and scatters, but then he has, all his life, been a slow silly man wearing his old ideas as foolishly as suspenders and killing all the butterflies with a suffocating spray. So that if you went there now, Bernard, on this early September morning and walked all the hedgerows of my field, you'd find nothing, dear. They're all gone. And the cowshed and dairy are gone, did I tell you? I knew they'd come down as soon as I moved out. Even before. I knew when I sat with you – with your body still wrapped in your beige dressing gown – and held your hand and held my candle, I knew it would be all changed, because change is what *is* Bernard. Change is our one certainty. Yet the change from life to death . . . I thought it would be quicker. I feel death immobilize me, as the horses go patiently, round and round. Movement, all except some involuntary flickering of the eye and my breath which can still keep time with the two sleepers I found out there in the dark, yes all movement is over. I couldn't say to the young man who came at the end, "Let me pour you a glass of wine Ralph dear." The young American, short for an American, but courteous with my life, custodian of the turned earth which is all that's left of me . . . surely he will grow new herbs in me and under them I shall have some creeping existence which understands neither time nor grief and is not haunted by the terrible cruelty of man and his manufactured fire, his plaything . . . beginning now as a speck in the sky and the girl, no longer a virgin but heavy with the child of General Almarlyes picks up her fustian skirts and runs screaming into the sea to push out a little boat and calls and calls to the hut where the General sleeps wearing only his boots, 'Almarlyes! For the love of God!' Oh for the love of God! but the sky is black with machinery and the flame is brighter than any noon-day, wrapping the shore from end to end. And no one comes to ferret in the ash. The land on which the thousand pieces of the body of Almarlyes still lie is dead land, dead for all eternity, 'Like your souls, little children, at this Christmas-tide if they cannot let Jesus enter in at the door! When your bodies die, as die they must, if you let go this world without the love of Our Lord, then you will find nothing on the other side. So even as I scatter these offerings for you, this precious food, go home and tell your Mother and your Father that the Church is good . . .' Yet he drowned in an icy well, his pockets full of nuts, our vicar. No one ever went to the well to say a prayer. And in his after-life he was a coconut, so I dreamed once. An African child poured the milk of his existence into her starving belly.

I have begun to count. I can't tell what I am counting or even if I am saying numbers, yet I feel some beat or pulse near the surface of me, keeping time. Perhaps I am counting in years, yet I have forgotten the total. I don't know when I should stop. Or are we marching . . . heaven knows where or when, yet if I am marching then surely it is with you, *Gérard. Gérard! Gérard!* Oh I can feel the two syllables of you, of course, yes, feel them deeper than my womb, but so many worlds lie between our two deaths, I never imagined I could start to cross back, across this open and plough-turned sum of years, years I can't count, not to you, oh not to you! Yet here we go, in step, invisible surely because I can't *see* you yet I feel your shoulder against mine and if I could move, if *only* I could move, I might reach out a hand. Are your feet marching? And mine? I can hear no crowd, no shouting, no songs. Only us. Oh, are we moving, Gérard? Us two along a road? Gérard?

I think the road is white. Melon plants straggle it. It's no more than a track. And heat shimmers, the heat of midday. Where is it and where are you? I keep swallowing your name . . . Gérard, Gérard . . . but you are nowhere, only inside me, gentle, gentle companion of my death, navigating all the channels of my blood. It was you I drank, pill by pill, sip by sip, the forty-two years of your existence one by one releasing the slow breaths of an ending. Here. On a dry road in Spain. And what better death could ever have awaited me? What more miraculous? Yet the white road is endless. There is no horizon, just an eternity of road, dry and warped. So how can I dare whisper an ending while I still have consciousness and breath, and the road goes on and on? I am not ended. The ending is still to come. But let it be here. Before the clouds gather, as they did so suddenly in France, on the day we found the dead man, so terribly, suddenly and frighteningly that it became . . . No! My mother with your seven lives, your eight lives, save me from the darkness that Chadwick saw . . . like a tidal wave, obliterating all. Save me from the clouds that gather far away but nearing, like the clouds we saw the day we found the dead man, the terrible clouds we saw the day we found the dead man . . . black clouds, so vast and heavy . . . on the day we found the dead –

*

Ralph couldn't remember ever having felt so tired.

In Walt's over-heated office he was handed strong coffee in a paper cup by Walt's secretary who left immediately, unsmilingly, closing the door quietly behind her.

Ralph looked at all the familiar things in the office: the array of telephones; the photo of Walt's wife, Nancy, taken twenty years before; his single golfing trophy on a stand; his maps and graphs and random news cuttings pinned to wallboards; the cocktail cabinet made of maple wood; the bottle of Biofeed for his plants . . . all stubbornly unchanged – day to day proof that the man existed and that he existed to work.

'You know you've left me no choice?' Walt's voice knocked like a mallet on Ralph's exhausted skull. 'You know you've blown it, kid?'

Ralph looked down at the black coffee and began to sip it, thinking, whatever happens, I musn't doze off because this moment is probably one of the most important moments of my life. Sentence is being passed: years are being decided.

He cleared his throat and looked up. 'She died, Walt.'

Here was his plea of mitigation. Pale plea. But no lawyer could have stated it more succinctly.

'I *know* she died. The whole world knows she died by now – anyone who gives a damn. But you know as well as I do, Ralph, that *Bulletin Worldwide* has a policy of minimalization on deaths on this kind of category.'

'What the hell d'you mean, Walt?'

'We are not, kid, and never have been, concerned with minor lives. I thought I made this clear at the outset –'

'This was not a "minor life", Walt!' And shouting now: 'I've got it all in my apartment – nine tapes . . .'

'I'm sorry, kid.'

'What d'ya mean, you're sorry?'

'Company rules simply have to be followed, especially when any member of my team is away on an assignment.'

'Walt –'

'You broke company rules. You checked out of one address without informing this office where you could be contacted . . .'

'You were hounding me, man! I just couldn't make you see that, if it was going to be worth anything at all, I had to go all the way with this job.'

'And you are thirteen days – thirteen days! – overdue on your return date!'

I wish I had a goddamned attorney, thought Ralph. Then he could say it all, everything I'm too tired to say, and it could go on like a play in front of me, and I could close my eyes . . .

'So you see, kid. What choice do I have?'

'Oh, I dunno, Walt.'

'Dunno? What the hell kind of answer is that meant to be? I honestly don't think you're getting the seriousness of this . . .'

'I told you. I had no choice either.'

'Sure you had a choice: to obey or disobey. You disobeyed.'

'This isn't high school, Walt. I had my own instructions and I had to carry them through.'

'What instructions?'

Oh for the lawyer again, to summarize and simplify to make the eccentric sound like the ordinary . . .

'When I got back from Oxford –'

'Oxford? You went to Oxford?'

'Yup.'

'Why?'

'To get advice.'

'On what?'

'On everything that was happening to me.'

'You're not making sense Ralph and I have a meeting at ten-thirty.'

'Oh for Chrissakes, Walt. You're not giving me time.'

'Time! You've had a month and a half!'

'Time to *explain*.'

'I'm not sure I'm interested in explanations. You've let me down and you've let the team down and I don't figure I have any choice at all but to let you go. But you go right ahead if you want to. You explain.'

How could I have briefed the attorney anyway, Ralph thought. He wouldn't have understood. He would have wanted straight answers: "This is so because . . ." "I did this because . . ." And I have what Walt would call a deficiency here: I can never answer "because".

'I'm waiting, kid . . .'

'When I got back from Oxford, Walt, I went to say goodbye as I'd promised, and it was then that I found her, and the note to me. You see the note was specifically addressed to me: "Dear Ralph . . ." It was impossible to ignore it, so I sent you a cable.'

'Never mind the cable.'

'The note reminded me to make sure of the burial in a certain way, with the mimosa blossoms and a grave big enough –'

'Why you?'

'Why me?'

'Why did she pick on you?'

'It's complicated, Walt. She had a notion that –'

'She musta known you had a deadline.'

Ralph smiled. In spite of his editor's title, Walt sometimes betrayed an extraordinary clumsiness with words. It was as if he lost control of them. Because he uses them as weapons, Ralph decided. Attack, attack! They are always hard and stinging. They make your skin smart, like a whipping.

Walt noticed Ralph's smile with profound irritation. He stood up.

'Look, Ralph, I'm not sure I'm interested in any of this gothic stuff . . .'

'I can only assume,' Ralph interrupted quickly, 'that there was no one else – or she felt this – no one else to take charge and do what she wanted done. But burials are slow, Walt. There's a lot of formality . . .'

Days of waiting, he wanted to add, with only the search for the mimosa to occupy him while they took her body away to the mortuary. Then the inevitable meetings, with Mrs Burford, with Huntley who had to be summoned (and who refused Ralph permission to take the Tiffany lamp because nothing had been written down about this), with the press who turned up. Yet already they seemed far off, these peculiar days, part of a Time Before, when there was no Familiar, no Ordinary, only day following day in unexpected shape, lit by the lamp, monitored now and then by the Summary, days that were *his*. Only when he had gathered strength would he let them back into his life and examine their importance in it. Staring at Walt's plants, he had a momentary recollection of his dreams of the lily leaves at Worcester and the incredible gliding of his body. He was aware that his heart was beating very fast.

'So you see, Walt . . .'

Walt picked up the Biofeed bottle and held it in his hand, as if trying to guess its weight. Then he sighed.

'I've always trusted you, Ralph. You had some quirky ideas, okay. But I thought you were a guy to trust. I can tell you that this is very, very disappointing for me when I see you go right against me and against *Bulletin Worldwide*. Very disappointing indeed. And when I ask myself if I have a choice . . .'

'It's very hard to explain it all, Walt. You've got a meeting and I've had no sleep trying to make sense of it all. But I've got good material, Walt. And I mean really good. Stuff that no one else has ever bothered with – enough for four – maybe six – in-depth articles . . .'

'No, Ralph.'

'What d'ya mean, "no"?'

'There isn't the market for it, kid. Go copy it all out for some small-circulation literary rag, if they'll take it. We're not interested.'

'Sure you're interested, you punk! It's one helluva life!'

'The obit's been done, Ralph.'

'What d'you mean, it's been done. Who did it?'

'Just don't quarrel, kid. It's been done.'

'Who by?'

'I don't recall.'

'Let me see it. How long was it?'

'Sure you can see it.'

'How fucking long was it, Walt?'

'Six or seven. I don't remember.'

'Six or seven what?'

'Lines.'

Ralph put down his paper cup on Walt's desk. He stared at his hands empty in his lap. Suddenly the coffee tasted sour in his throat and his head ached. He felt a wave of nausea. He twisted his fingers together, hating the inactivity of his hands. He knew that Walt was watching him and thought, I hate him. It's as straightforward as that. I despise him. He didn't look up. Another wave of nausea had come and gone, he heard Walt slap the Biofeed bottle down on his blotter.

'I'm sorry, kid.'

Still Ralph couldn't bear to look at him.

'Sorry about what?'

'I had great hopes for you at *Bulletin* and I know we were good buddies . . .'

'Out your ass!'

'Have it your own way. You always did, I guess. But it's no birthday party firing a friend.'

Outside the *Bulletin Worldwide* building, Ralph stood and stared at the traffic. It was a bright morning, the sky above East 53rd Street a deep blue. Slowly, he set off in the direction of his apartment, but walking in the warm sunshine was no pleasure. His stomach was still nauseous and his legs felt unaccountably weak. He climbed gratefully into the first cab that stopped and rode home in exhausted silence.

Climbing his stairs, he held grimly to the polished rail. It's as if, he thought, my sense of balance has gone: too much has happened; I'm ill with events. Yet the loss of his job came as no surprise. He'd known for some time – known but not admitted? – that he was pushing Walt too far. Walt was Walt, unchanging and unchanged in his enormous body. The body would push back, and that would be that. An ending. The canned music would go on and on in the elevators, the telephonists would simper their repetitious greeting: 'Bulletin Worldwide, can I help you?' Walt would swallow his daily laxative with his first cup of coffee, go round with the Biofeed bottle before the serious work of the day began . . . already it was meaningless, a world too contained in itself to contain him. And now that he was free of it . . .

His telephone was ringing.

'Ralph? Walt here.'

He was breathless after the climb to his door. He carried the telephone to the bed and lay down.

'Ralph? You there.'

'Thought you had a meeting, Walt.'

'Yes. I'm in a meeting. That's why I'm calling. I've been reminded that you're in possession of Bulletin property.'

'What the hell are you talking about?'

'The tapes. You said you had nine tapes.'

Ralph was silent. I can't stand his voice, he thought. I hate it.

'You there, Ralph?'

'Sure.'

'Okay. Well I've made a promise on your behalf that the Erica March tapes will be back in this office by tomorrow afternoon. Otherwise legal action will be forthcoming.'

'Forthcoming?' What an idiotic word to use, Ralph thought.

'Watcha gonna do with 'em, Walt? Have them for breakfast?'

'Tomorrow four o'clock. Okay?'

'Put yoghurt and sugar on them?'

'Cut the garbage, Ralph. Just bring the tapes back.'

Walt hung up. Ralph rubbed his eyes then put his arms behind his head and stared at the ceiling.

'Sonofabitch,' he whispered.

*

When he woke, there was a strawberry sky at his window. Across the hallway his neighbour, Joe Beale, was playing a track from Nina Simone's *Baltimore*. He must have played that track a thousand times, Ralph thought, playing and playing that darn song, when he could have been watering my herbs, if only I'd remembered to give him a key. 'Hi Joe!' Ralph called. 'I'm home and jobless!' But Joe Beale didn't hear and the song went on:

> There is so little
> left alive
> you can be sure of.
> Rain comes from the clouds,
> sunlight from the sky,
> humming birds do fly . . .'

Ralph got up and walked stiffly to the open window. It was hot in the room and already the cold of London seemed very far away. He leaned out and touched his plants. The soil was dry, yet all the herbs except the parsley had survived his absence and were in full leaf.

ROSE TREMAIN

The Way I Found Her

'Quite simply magnificent . . . *The Way I found Her* is a
magical invention of page-turning suspense, of sadness, grief
and passion, whose sure and delicate exposure of a sensibility
flowering one hot Parisian summer teaches
us the price of experience. Do not miss it'
Elizabeth Buchan, *The Times*

'A scary, funny and ultimately very affecting novel . . .
Tremain lets us glimpse the adult-in-waiting; reminds us that
life – tinged with joy, sex, pain – takes its whole shape from
such moments'
Mail on Sunday

'This novel has the sparkle of sunlight on water . . . Such is
Rose Tremain's skill that she simply bewitches you into
believing . . . You too are in Paris, on holiday, caught up in the
heat and the enchantment . . . once more Rose Tremain
beguiles you into suspending disbelief'
Independent on Sunday

'Surely one of the top 10 novels of the year, with Tremain more
original, funny and captivating than ever'
Elle

VINTAGE BOOKS
London

ROSE TREMAIN

Evangelista's Fan

& Other Stories

'A master-class in the art of storytelling'
Observer

'Rose Tremain is a writer of immense talent, one who is prepared to take risks, a daring walker on the high wire. In this superb collection of short stories she displays a dazzling versatility, taking us from Regency London to a hospital room in Hampshire to the battlefield of Agincourt in 1415 . . . Rose Tremain's writing has a rare subtlety, and her imagination is extraordinary'
Harpers & Queen

'Goes on resonating in your memory after you have shut the book'
Independent

'Tremain is elegant, cool and teasing . . . she is an extremely accomplished writer, ingenious and acute, compassionate and always in control'
Daily Telegraph

'A perfect demonstration of Rose Tremain's beguilingly original and quirky mind, and her ability to set words on paper in the most spellbinding way'
Daily Mail

VINTAGE BOOKS
London

Also available from Vintage

ROSE TREMAIN

The Colonel's Daughter

& Other Stories

'Demonstrates a wry talent and considerable fertility of invention'
Guardian

'A true writer of fiction . . . A writer whose every book has been
a pleasure'
Scotsman

At the moment that Colonel Browne is standing in the shallow
end of the swimming pool of the Hotel Alpenrose, preparing
for his late afternoon dip, his daughter Charlotte, carrying a
suitcase, is getting out of her car back in England, preparing to
rob the ancestral home. It is not just another day: it is the
culmination of hundreds of days, hundreds of disappointments
and misunderstandings, and thousands of very small lies . . .

'Rose Tremain goes from strength to strength. *The Colonel's
Daughter* is a winner . . . a riveting and satisfying read'
New Statesman

VINTAGE BOOKS
London

Also available from Vintage

ROSE TREMAIN

Letter to Sister Benedicta

'Funny, sad and intensely moving, it is a joy to read from beginning to end . . . Miss Tremain does something to restore my confidence in the vitality of the English novel . . . *Letter to Sister Benedicta* should be seen as a triumph of the human spirit over the afflictions which beset us'

Auberon Waugh

Fat and fifty, educated only to be a wife and mother, Ruby Constad has reached a point of crisis. Her husband, Leon, lies in a nursing home after a stroke that has left him paralysed; her grown-up children are gone. In her anguish Ruby appeals for help to a half-remembered figure from her colonial Indian girlhood – Sister Benedicta. Gradually, the events leading up to Leon's stroke are revealed and a woman emerges whose capacity to love, hope and understand are far greater than she realises.

'An original talent clears the hurdle of a second novel with pathos and humour'

Guardian

VINTAGE BOOKS
London

www.vintage-books.co.uk